Damian Garcia: PHD DRUG SMUGGLER

OPIUM & HASHISH

CHRIS MOSQUERA

abbott press®

A DIVISION OF WRITER'S DIGEST

Abbott Press books may be ordered through booksellers or by contacting:

Abbott Press
1663 Liberty Drive
Bloomington, IN 47403
www.abbottpress.com
Phone: 1-866-697-5310

Because of the dynamic nature of the Internet, any web addresses or links contained in this book may have changed since publication and may no longer be valid. The views expressed in this work are solely those of the author and do not necessarily reflect the views of the publisher, and the publisher hereby disclaims any responsibility for them.

Any people depicted in stock imagery provided by Thinkstock are models, and such images are being used for illustrative purposes only. Certain stock imagery © Thinkstock.

ISBN: 978-1-4582-1313-6 (sc)
ISBN: 978-1-4582-1314-3 (hc)
ISBN: 978-1-4582-1312-9 (e)

Library of Congress Control Number: 2013921940

Printed in the United States of America.

Abbott Press rev. date: 12/23/2013

PREFACE

THIS is the story of Damian Garcia and the international drug trade in opium and hashish by PhD graduate students in New York City, circa 1972. It is a story of friendship, family, loyalty, and an exceedingly discreet and extremely profitable drug smuggling business plan. The business plan was a new combination of opium and hashish product, which the family branded as *O/H*. The targeted demographics for O/H were graduate students at major university campuses, and nurses and doctors, attorneys, and accountants worldwide.

O/H became the professionals' drug of choice.

The mood of the country was fading from the glory of the Woodstock nation of 1969 to the realities of the Vietnam War of 1972. The music was changing, and free love was fading into free infections. America was turning from a nation of peace and love into a nation of hate, violence, and hard drugs.

Graduate students were intellectually curious, politically liberal, and anti most things establishment, and definitely anti-police. They were the perfect consumers for marketing the business model for opium and hashish. The financial returns vastly exceeded their wildest imaginations, with significant monies going towards social services helping those in need, professional development, and legitimate business investments worldwide.

The combination of both opium and hashish into a high-profit, higher quality product was a true marketing genius for the time. It took the combined brains of graduate students in international business, banking, and law to practice what they studied in school.

If only their professors knew how talented their students truly were! O/H became an international enterprise unknown to all but a few. Those who knew would never tell; that was the family code.

The story is through the eyes of Damian Garcia, looking back in another day, when life was more trusting, the social and political climates were more interpersonal, and relationships truly mattered.

This is their story . . .

** *The characters, names, locations, and descriptions are fictional. Any resemblance to reality is purely coincidental, and completely unintended.* **

CHAPTER ONE

Damian Garcia and the O/H Family

WHEN we first met Damian Garcia, he was a street-wise man from New York City, both in spirit and attitude. Damian wore his hair long with sideburns and a mustache. He always carried a pocket watch like the railroad conductors favored, wore wire-rimmed glasses, and his clothing was mostly jeans or dark pants, a shirt, and a sports coat. His body was built lean and hungry, and he walked briskly like a man on a mission.

Damian's draft number was 69, which meant he was front line Vietnam War fodder. Damian was a peace-loving vegetarian, and dropping napalm bombs on innocent people in a foreign land that just happened to produce the finest marijuana was not on his agenda.

Passport ready, Damian Garcia was ready to move to Vancouver, Canada, for the rest of his life, if the alternative was going to war. Graduate school was the only deferment available, and given the circumstances, it was an excellent career choice.

Damian was a fast learner and survived by instincts. Hard experience taught him to read the streets and be alert for signs of trouble. He could sense by the hairs on the back of his neck if he was being cased for a hit.

Once when Damian was walking home alone in the dark, four punks, two on each side, blocked his path. Damian kept his eyeglass case on a clip on the left side of his belt, partially hidden under his sports coat. As the punks approached, Damian casually reached his right hand across his belt, towards the left side, and put his hand on the eyeglass case.

Damian observed one punk on his right side had a six-inch, double-sided switchblade knife in his right hand. One blade had a serrated edge, and the other blade was sharp as a razor.

The punk on Damian's left side was holding a .38-caliber revolver police special in his left hand, blued in color so it would not reflect light. This was the issued weapon that detectives and patrol officers for the New York City Police Department carried.

Damian thought to himself, *Why is this south paw, left-handed punk carrying a NYPD gun? Is he a cop killer?*

Damian processed this information in a microsecond, and he acted.

As Damian passed by the four punks, two who were visibly armed, he tipped his hat with his left hand, while resting his right hand across his belt on the left side.

Damian said in a tone of authority, "Good evening, gentlemen."

He borrowed this demeanor from a popular television police show. Obviously, the four punks were not smart enough to separate fact from fiction.

The punks stopped, thought about it for a second or two, and allowed Damian to pass. Damian kept his normal pace and slightly nodded to the four punks. He had a look on his face that said, *You do not want to piss me off tonight, punk!*

The left-handed dude could have shot Damian in the back as he passed the punks. The right-handed switchblade punk could have stabbed Damian in the chest or back of the neck.

Damian was lucky this time.

The lessons learned were that the outside world sees only what you show them. Damian showed the four punks that he was either a wise guy or an undercover cop, and it was in their best interests to leave him alone.

With training, Damian reasoned, you could become anybody you wish the world to see you as. Your inner soul may stay the same, but you can determine your own external image. Public image can translate to strong passive security, in that who would suspect a graduate student of being an international drug importer and money launderer?

By flying below the radar, one avoids observation.

That was powerful information, and the basis for survival and success, which Damian later incorporated into the business plans and operational procedures for O/H Incorporated. This was required learning for all O/H investor-franchisees and their distributors.

He lived his life in the shadows and always below the radar.

It was safer that way.

George Carlin Dog met **Damian Ogden Garcia** one cold morning in January 1972, when Damian was on a breakfast mission, and late to class as usual. Damian stopped to watch a very personable and friendly-looking dog, of many uncertain breeds, peeing on the yellow line in the middle of a major New York City street. Taxis and busses were passing by, and this dog was quietly doing his thing, oblivious to the hustle and bustle of the world whizzing around him.

They made eye contact. The dog slowly strolled over to Damian with his tail wagging and a happy smile on his face. Damian and Mr. Dog sat on the front steps of the apartment building he was sharing with other graduate students. Damian started petting and talking to Mr. Dog, and he responded with licks and a happy tail. They spent the next hour communicating on the steps as the human race went by.

Damian looked at the railroad conductor pocket watch he always had with him, and realized he missed that class.

Life does have its priorities, and meeting a new canine friend took precedence over a boring lecture. *I will get the notes from some chick in class anyway,* Damian reasoned in his head.

Damian brought Mr. Dog upstairs, gave him a warm, sudsy shampoo bath, and dried him off with a bath towel.

Damian exclaimed, "Mr. Dog, you look so much cleaner and you smell better too. Let me give you a good brushing, my canine friend."

Mr. Dog enjoyed the affection and attention as much as Damian was enjoying his new friend. That was the start of a beautiful relationship. They became inseparable soul mates.

Damian made two peanut butter and jelly sandwiches, one for Mr. Dog and one for himself, and placed a bowl of fresh water on the floor. They munched their meals happily, communicating in silence.

Apartment 3A's door opened, and the graduate student housemates walked in. They had been doing laundry and food shopping. In this neighborhood, it was safer to shop as a group than individually. The concept of safety in numbers was well understood in the animal kingdom, and they were living in the human version of the animal kingdom.

When everyone sat down, Damian said, "Ladies and gentlemen, I would like to present my new friend and our new housemate, Mr. Dog."

Vash, Roger, Howard, and Marguerite all bent down and took turns introducing themselves.

Marguerite said to Damian, "I like our new housemate. I am a dog woman, and he has a big personality. We could use a dog for security. This is not a safe neighborhood, especially for a woman, you know."

Howard added, "I will second that."

"Likewise," Roger nodded in agreement.

So it was decided that Mr. Dog would be Director of Security and provide escort services whenever someone left the apartment alone.

Mr. Dog bonded with Damian and the housemates, as the group was bonding with each other. The addition of a cool dog for friendship and security was a positive influence.

A few evenings passed and the group was sitting in the living room, smoking hashish, drinking wine, and watching TV. George Carlin, the comedian, was doing his politically incorrect comedy routines.

"That is a perfect name," Damian announced to everyone, exhaling hashish smoke during a commercial. He declared, "Mr. George Carlin Dog will be your name!"

Roger added, "I like that name."

The group agreed.

George responded with a tilt of his head, as if to say, *I like that name also. This may turn out to be a nice place to live.*

Damian said to George, "Welcome to the family, George Carlin Dog. Your adventures, my friend, have just begun."

As Director of Security, George was in charge of all things human. He proved to be a brilliant studying partner for the small circle of over-stressed brains, reminding them when it was time to take a break from studying, and a walk in the park was required.

George would say, *Grey matter requires rest to rejuvenate; otherwise it collapses into useless mush. Therefore, humans, I require a long walk in the park. In other words, get off your sorry asses and open the damn door, please and thank you.*

The humans obeyed his command, because George knew best.

George had no clue what a leash was. He never wore one, and he never needed one. George responded purely to quiet voice and subtle hand commands. He would wait at intersections, following Damian very closely, hugging one leg, as they crossed the street together.

George would sit quietly in front of a bodega or ethnic grocery store while Damian shopped for groceries. When Damian walked out of the store, George would follow closely. George would agree to casual petting and attention from strangers, but he would not allow anyone to get too close.

George Carlin Dog was as human as a dog could be, and Damian considered the concept of "dog food" disrespectful. When the humans ate, George always enjoyed the human meals. The group was mostly vegetarian, by economics, choice, or culture, and George by default was a veggie. If given the opportunity, he would gladly chew on a steak bone.

Damian Garcia, Lori Wilson, Vash Gupta, Roger Rajiv, Marguerite Nguyen, and Howard Pavel, all between 27 and 30 years old, started as graduate student housemates of Apartment 3A. They were placed together, along with George Carlin Dog, by fate, providence, or pure luck—either bad luck or good luck, depending on your perspective.

Over time, they grew to become a lifelong family and the brain trusts of the international O/H drug trade. The quiet O/H family of highly educated graduate students living in Apartment 3A included diverse, brilliant, analytical, and devious masterminds of the international drug and money-laundering trades. They also believed in the concepts of giving back to the community and helping those in need, and over time, large sums were invested in non-profit humanitarian foundations.

On a blustery Sunday, the group decided they should nestle in for the evening and connect. Schoolwork was up to date, and it was time to relax, bond, and talk. Food was a priority, and the group was very adept at making small quantities of different stuff, merged to become large wonderful meals. A jug of wine was placed on the table to be enjoyed, as was a bong crammed with hashish.

They enjoyed life on a shoestring. The group shared wonderful meals, family, and friendships together, and Vash happily provided the family with excellent opium and hashish for all to enjoy. They were poor, happy, highly educated, and high.

Damian asked Vash, "Vash, my friend, I love the products you always have available. How do you get this stuff? I have been around

New York City for a long time, I know people, and I cannot get this stuff."

Vash said, "Funny you should ask, as you Yankees like to say. I will tell you about my family, and then you will understand completely.

"I come from a very large extended family in northern India, where various family members collectively own thousands acres of fertile farmland."

Damian smiled broadly in recognition. "Exactly what are the crops you grow, and how fertile are we talking about?"

Vash smiled shyly. "The land is very fertile, and we grow only high-value crops, using a farming cooperative method, and we share in the success and failures equally. The family farms produce the finest opium, hashish, and marijuana the world has ever known. And that, my housemates and friends, is how we are smoking the finest hashish and opium unavailable anywhere except Apartment 3A."

The group smiled in complete appreciation.

Vash Gupta was tall, skinny, and very friendly, with a happy smile on his face, a wicked sense of humor, and seriously smart. Vash was studying for his PhD in Economics. His expertise was statistical analysis and all things math, which were not Damian's friends.

Vash said to Damian as they shared food and wine, "Thanks for the cooperative effort writing the parts of each other's assignments that are our personal weaknesses."

Damian replied, "And likewise, my friend. We complement each other to help each other. That is what friends do to help each other succeed."

The bowl of hashish was lit and passed around the table. George made himself available as each person exhaled into his mouth and nose. George became exceedingly stoned, rolled over on his back, and watched his humans upside down. The group laughed.

Vash said, "You know, I had a choice of places to get my PhD, but I chose Cardiff University because it offered an excellent economics program and because I wanted to live and work in New York."

Marguerite said, "The centers for international business, finance, engineering, and law are in New York and London. That is why I am here also, as I am sure is Roger."

Vash said, "I must admit, back in India and London, I lived in nicer neighborhoods than we live in New York. I feel like we are living in the slums and ghettos."

Damian said sarcastically, "Yes, we are, my friends. Welcome to New York City! As bad as this area is, I grew up in rougher places. From my perspective, Vash, I am moving uptown, and up the social ladder. It is nicer than the neighborhoods I left."

Roger said, "And from our perspectives, we have moved way down the food chain."

Marguerite noted, "This is a drug-infested, crime-infested, dirty and dangerous place to live, especially if you happen to be female."

Damian added, "Life is all about perspectives, and objectives."

Howard said, "It is also about attitudes and philosophies of living. Like Roger," he continued, "I come from a very comfortable and highly educated background. My parents are prominent doctors in India, as are my brothers, sisters, and other family members. The Pavel family is inter-connected with the medical industry in one form or another."

Vash added, "And living in this neighborhood in New York in these turbulent times is a rude awakening. How do you say it? A reality check."

Howard quipped with a big smile, "The reality of life in this city is not exactly what the travel agencies portrayed in those pretty brochures."

Smart and ambitious people adjust quickly, and Howard was both.

Howard Pavel was studying for his PhD in International Finance, and he was not a man to be underestimated. He was more devious than he was brilliant, and he was truly brilliant. Howard would make a huge impact on the financial community and influence future economic events.

Howard's character was more conservative than liberal. He wore his hair closely cropped, favored dry martinis, stirred not shaken. Howard preferred white shirts, dark ties, and dark business suits during the day, and he wore matching pressed pajamas to bed at night. He was fastidious.

Howard would iron and starch his clothing on Sunday evening so his wardrobe would be ready for the week ahead. The man was so punctual you could set your watch to his habits. This was good, because somebody had to keep the unruly housemates in line, and Howard de facto volunteered.

As our resident consultant on international banking and money laundering, Howard understood the finer points of moving mountains of cash worldwide. He provided strategic expertise in business processes, operational procedures, funding mechanisms, money laundering, and credit instruments, including the Swiss banking system; all needed to keep the wheels flowing as the enterprises prospered into the future.

Howard said, "I wrote a paper last week, outlining various business models and operation plans. Obviously I changed the names and enterprises, as usual, but I am sure you can put it to good use."

Marguerite said, "Of course, it is flawless and on point, because Howard has the innate ability to visualize into the future."

Howard added with a smile, "If I can give you the road map to follow and prosper, then my job will be done, and I will be a happy man. I like to plan and organize and make things happen. That is what I do best. Soon, I will make my mark on the world, creating really big, complicated financial deals."

Without question, Howard Pavel was destined to control the future.

Howard advised, "It is important to anticipate business interruptions, and to build layers of liability insulation to protect the inner organizational core from potential problems. The U.S. dollar is the strongest currency in India and has extraordinary buying power in the black market economies. Buying goods in U.S. dollars yields far better returns than buying the same goods in rupees. The dollar is like gold. It is king."

Howard was also the driving force for better grades. He would tell the group that discipline and concentration were important, saying, "School first, family second, career third, and social life is last."

He would lecture, "Through disciplined study habits, you get the best grades. The best grades equal the best jobs, and therefore the best employment opportunities. I am very ambitious. Ultimate success is my ultimate goal. Work harder than everyone else and you will succeed. For me, it is a very simple formula."

Marguerite smiled. "How does one argue with rational logic?"

Vash said, "I am going to add some opium to the hashish, and I would like your feedback on this combination, please." He smiled. "Ladies first. I would like Lori and Marguerite's opinions on the combination. Then we will reload a bowl for the men. George will be our test canine."

The group agreed the opium and hash combination was exceptional.

Roger Rajiv was earning his PhD in Chemical Engineering. He possessed a highly analytical mind, with the ability to process vast amounts of data at warp speeds. He usually wore a white lab coat with pocket protectors.

Roger was always trying, mostly unsuccessfully, to get as much sex as he could. Occasionally he would get lucky, and he would be chipper like a songbird for days.

As a chemical engineering doctorate student, Roger had access to the university's labs. He utilized the labs during the overnights and weekends when he had the privacy to perform experiments. He would bring donuts and coffee for the security and janitorial staff, who thought he was working late.

During the day, Roger would go to classes and write esoteric papers. At night, he would lock himself in the university lab, wearing his white lab coat with pocket protectors, like a mad scientist, and refine the O/H experiments until they were beyond perfect. Roger preferred to wear his white lab coat around Apartment 3A also. It was his signature.

How Roger stumbled upon the method of using steam infusion was one of those rare eureka moments. One Sunday while Howard was ironing his dress shirts, Roger observed that after steam ironing, the shirts were not puffy on the ironing board. Perhaps, he reasoned, opiate-hash could be steamed, making it pliable, bendable, moldable, and compressible.

Roger went to work in the lab, and a week later developed the technology to steam O/H into various shapes and sizes and to compress the volume. When you are dealing in kilos of product, compressing the volume into smaller sizes is very beneficial. Steaming the product greatly improves the freshness and quality by preventing the products from becoming dry and brittle when exposed to air. The steam infusion process increases the shelf life and chemical potency. A moist opium/hashish product smoked cooler and cleaner, with a smooth high.

The finished products were shrink-wrapped to seal in all the delicious qualities. An odorless product was vital because border crossings in Europe and the U.S. used drug-sniffing dogs.

Dogs never detected Roger's packages.

Marguerite Nguyen was Apartment 3A's legal scholar. She provided the legal framework needed to develop and implement the O/H business models and operational procedures. Marguerite advised on methods to maximize profits, minimize exposure, increase assets, and keep the family prosperous, socially conscious, and out of prison.

Marguerite was a brilliant researcher, with an extremely well-reasoned and analytical mind, resting on an exquisite frame. Marguerite's father was British, her mother was Vietnamese, and she was multilingual and educated in Vietnam and London. She wore a size six; her hair was long and silky.

Marguerite was gorgeous, and she knew it.

She was fond of saying, "If you've got it, flaunt it." She had it, and made sure others noticed. They did.

Marguerite would find the worst-case scenarios, and the group built the business plans and operational procedures based on her legal opinions. The research she provided was part of her legal course work.

Marguerite said, "I chose Cardiff University, and New York City, because the combined Jurist Doctorate International Law program is world-renowned, and New York is the place to be."

Marguerite would always be the controlling queen of her world. Nothing would stop her sweet-smiling ambition from acquiring whatever she chose, whenever she wanted, and whomever she sought.

Marguerite said, "I have been thinking how our relationships living together are developing. Friends are family you choose. We are family."

She added, "I will be straight up with the family. I have high expectations for myself, and I will always make my own destiny in life. I will never screw over anyone, without justifiable reasons, and I will never allow anyone to shaft me. That I promise you."

There was not a shred of doubt in anyone's mind about Marguerite's capabilities, tenacity, intellect, and beauty. This woman had it all.

Eye candy is a wonderful thing.

Marguerite had the sweetness that kept the group happy and smiling, and the intellect that kept the family out of prison. Her brilliant legal talent created the framework that would make O/H an extremely profitable, low-key enterprise, known only to a handful of people who would never tell.

The men favored Marguerite, and she quietly returned the favor. Howard and Roger were her personal favorites.

Lori Wilson was a feisty and fiery redhead, and an emergency room nurse. Lori had piercing blue eyes and a determined personality. She was highly intelligent, highly gorgeous, very high maintenance, and usually high on pharmaceutical drugs. She could be adorable, warm, kind, and funny, or a complete bitch.

The sex was always delicious, and Damian was captivated. Damian's main weakness in life was that he was attracted to strong women, much as a moth is drawn to a bright flame.

One evening when the housemates were relaxing in Apartment 3A, Damian said, "Let me tell you a true story of life in the urban jungle, and how Lori and I met. They are part of the same story.

"I was walking down the street early one evening, and the first thing I feel is the crack of a baseball bat on my head. The four dudes beat me to a bloody pulp for what must have been a good ten minutes. I remember a crowd gathering to watch. Survival adrenaline kicked in, and I started swinging at everything. Apparently, I must have connected with the punks, because after a while they stopped. I fell to the ground. The crowd applauded. The beating was the show. I was the show. No one helped, and no one called the police or ambulance. No one cared."

Damian said, "That is the message. The attack was street theatre and the crowd applauded."

Lori said, "In New York no one cares."

Damian continued. "When it was over, I was barely conscious, and no one came over to help or take me to the hospital. My body hurt. I remember lying on the pavement, unable to move. People were stepping over and around me, and no one stopped to help. That was the sad reality."

George put his head on Damian's lap in sympathy.

Damian continued. "I found the willpower to help myself, knowing in my beaten brain and body, I had to find a hospital or die on the streets. All I remember, I was a bloody mess, staggering across major avenues. No cab would pick me up. The cab drivers probably did not want to clean up the blood on the seats. Nobody wanted to get involved with a crime scene, and no one wanted the police asking questions. I stumbled into the hospital and fell unconscious on the waiting room floor."

"I remember that," Lori said sweetly. "I was on duty. You were a bloody mess and in very bad pain," she said sympathetically.

Lori picked up the story. "When Damian regained some form of semiconsciousness, the doctors were removing pieces of wood from his head and stapling his wounds."

Damian joined in. "My left eye was swollen, I had deep cuts on my face, and my right knee was twisted. I hurt."

Lori said sweetly, "Morphine solved your pain, Damian."

Lori said to George, "The nice part, George. I took Damian home." She paused and said, "To my home!"

Damian replied with a smirk, "Sweet!"

Lori added with a smile, "And that is how Damian and I first met."

Damian said, "And we shall see what the future might hold for us. Seriously though, I want to make a point here. I was lucky. I lived, and survived, and it has taught me to be cautious and continuously read the streets."

Lori said philosophically, "Life does have an interesting way of turning seemingly random acts of violence into lifelong journeys."

The family lived in a decaying brownstone next to Mario's Garage, an auto repair shop. When you walked into the building, the front door was broken, one light bulb was hanging from the ceiling by a wire, there were broken mirrors on the walls, mice and roaches scurrying around, and the stairs were creaky and dark. The building smelled of old piss, rotten garbage, and mixtures of ethnic cooking.

Apartment 3A was a combination of all the apartments on the third floor, and it was large and funky. It had two living rooms and a large dining room, two semi-functional kitchens, six bedrooms, three funky bathrooms, and extra alcoves used as studies and workspaces. It easily accommodated the group's needs. Security consisted of gates on the windows, cross bars on the doors, and multiple locks. George provided additional security. It was big, cheap, and within walking distance to school. It was home.

To survive in New York City during this time, one needs to understand urban living in the lesser neighborhoods. Heroin, cocaine, and meth were major street problems, causing crime waves of legendary proportions. The city and state budgets had been cut; the various city unions were angry and on strike on a regular basis. The police stayed away from our neighborhood. It was a hostile urban environment. New York was suffering from a decaying infrastructure, corrupt government, corrupt cops, corrupt unions, and corrupt politicians. It was business as usual.

Life on a daily basis for the group consisted of school, work, and normal domestic chores, like food shopping. Daylight and early evening were relatively safe, if you were cautious.

The graffiti on the walls marked each gang's territory, usually divided by the streets or avenues, and being caught in a crossfire could be costly. Gang gunfights and bodies were common, and violence against the police was up. Snipers would shoot police cruisers from rooftops. It was the urban Wild West. During the day, they watch you. At night, they catch you.

You could buy anything you wanted on the streets of New York. In 1972, vendors selling clothing, stereo systems, and all things electronic sprang up everywhere. "Name-brand labels for less." This business model did not escape Damian's attention, which was to sell nice stuff for cash, stay mobile, and stay low key. Cash businesses are harder to trace.

The house decided they needed to buy a dynamite sound system, with a mega amp controlling four big speakers, and a balanced turntable. They found a system that met their needs at a pawnshop. Apartment 3A had a super sound system and a great collection of albums stored in milk crates.

The Rolling Stones sounded so good when they were stoned.

The Beatles sounded excellent when they were tripping.

Food in New York was everywhere. Pizza, hot dogs, and knishes were the staples of poor graduate students' diets. It was fast food, before the real fast-food market exploded. For a few dollars, one could buy two slices of pizza, or two knishes, chips, and a can of soda. It may not have been the healthiest diet, but it was cheap and filling. Graduate students were notoriously broke and always hungry.

The group house was in need of all types of furniture, and shopping at a furniture store was not in the budget. The first major item deemed vital was a large table for eating and gathering. The group required something big, comfortable, and familiar.

A picnic from the park was the clear choice. The motley crew consisted of four stoned men, one woman stoned on hash, one woman drugged on pharmaceuticals, and one stoned-out dog. Late one evening, the group liberated the special picnic table from the park. It was large, solid, heavy, and easily could seat ten people.

The seven amigos borrowed two four-wheeled dollies and moved the picnic table half a dozen blocks back to the apartment building. There were extensive discussions about angles and best methods to maneuver up the three flights of stairs and into the dining room of Apartment 3A.

The special table expedition and acquisition became an evening-until-the-next-morning event. The new picnic table needed extensive cleaning, followed by sanding and painting. With the aid of superb hashish and good friends, a vital piece of furniture looked better than new by morning.

A few days later, the group sat down to eat and talk about life.

Marguerite interrupted the flow of conversation, saying, "We need to have a blackboard and a whiteboard to cover the gray peeling wall. We can use the picnic table as a conference table, and convert the dining room into a board of director's suite."

Queen Marguerite was getting ready to rule the legal world.

Howard announced, "I know where there are a bunch of blackboards and whiteboards that are on wheels, in the basement of the business library. Apparently, the school is painting some rooms, and they are storing stuff in the basement. I am sure we can liberate as needed, Marguerite."

Problem solved.

A few evenings later, George took Damian for a walk in the neighborhood, and Damian found two large red beanbag chairs. George sniffed the beanbag chairs in approval.

"Another person's trash is our treasure," Damian said to George.

George guarded the remaining chair while Damian carried the first chair home. At the apartment, George surveyed the two red beanbag chairs and informed the group that the larger chair nearest the kitchen was his.

George asked, *Are there any questions?*

Over time, George and Damian became tired of living in poverty. The house was broke. Damian needed to find a job. It had to be flexible, to work around school, studying, and sex. Damian's answer was to become a New York City taxi driver. He passed the tests, received a hack license, and started driving a yellow cab. The cab garage was six blocks from home.

New York City has thousands of cabs prowling the streets 24 hours a day. The yellow cabs were medallion or licensed cabs, mostly owned by large taxi companies. The drivers preferred to cruise the streets in safer, more populated areas. The other type, called car services or gypsy cabs were private cars, and worked the parts of the city yellow cabs refused to go.

The way the taxi system worked, the driver and the cab company split the meter fare, and tips belonged to the driver. The money could be decent, about $75 per shift on a good night. Each fare was a challenge. Speed was more important than safety. It was like driving in a sea of yellow bumper cars racing around the city looking for fares.

Most fares were normal pick up and drop off. Damian picked up this one fare in front of a very nice hotel. The fare jumped in the cab and straightforwardly asked Damian, "Would you do a couple of complicated runs with me, on the meter, and I will give you a tip of $200 above the meter?"

Damian understood he would be driving a drug dealer around town as the fare was making his rounds. "No problem," he said. "Where are we going?"

The man replied politely, "I will tell you as we get there."

What impressed Damian was he did not look like a drug dealer. He was clean cut, spoke quietly, carried a briefcase, and dressed nicely.

After a few runs, he asked Damian to stop at an abandoned building with burned-out cars on the streets.

He told Damian, "Keep the engine running, with the back door open, and be ready for a fast escape. If I am not back in six minutes, or if there is too much activity on the streets, leave before the shooting starts."

The man was serious.

Damian looked at his pocket watch and set the stopwatch feature. Four minutes and four seconds later, Damian heard two shots in the building as the dude raced out, dove into the backseat. Damian sped out of the area.

When they were safely away, and sure they were not being followed, the fare leaned over the seat, reading the hack license posted, and said, "Thank you very much, Mr. Damian Garcia. That was some good driving."

Damian replied, "My pleasure. Are you all right?"

"Yes, I am," he replied. "Thank you for asking."

After a few minutes, Damian asked, "Where are we going next?"

"Next stop, Staten Island."

At dawn, the passenger handed Damian a $500 tip, plus the meter fare and a nice bag of clean cocaine. The dealer said, "Thank you for a job well done." He stepped out of the cab and into the crowd.

The house enjoyed the weekend. Damian now had money to pay the rent, buy food, pay for books, and live for a few weeks.

The graduate student poverty lifestyle could not go on forever. Apartment 3A was living hand to mouth and sometimes missing both. School was primary, and income was secondary. The family needed solid employment of some sort that was flexible, creative, and paid well.

Vash always had a nice supply of opium and hashish, which the group enjoyed. He had a business concept for a niche product of marketing opium and hashish as a combination product to sell to graduate students.

The following Sunday, the group was seated around the conference table as Vash began his presentation. He walked to the blackboard.

"I suggest we create a unique product and therefore a profitable business model. It must be a product not currently or easily available, therefore eliminating competitive pressures, and it must be a product where we create the demand, and we control the supply."

Vash paused to allow the group to process the information.

"It must be a product where we have direct control of the supply chain from start to finish. There must be adequate profit for all parties concerned to justify the risks, expense, and exposures. And, this is most important, we do not get caught. No gangster stuff and no prison time, EVER."

Vash clanged his wineglass and said ceremoniously, "Ladies and gentlemen, I have the product solution to our poverty dilemma."

The group listened attentively.

"We have all enjoyed the opium and the hash separately. It is even better when you combine the two in the correct mixture. Therefore, I propose we combine the two into one product. We shall call it O/H, which is descriptive of the product's active ingredients, opium and hashish."

Vash had the group's complete attention.

"We will create a new product, unavailable on the open market. The high is exceptional. We are smoking it now."

Damian added, "Reality cannot be denied. The high is exceptional, and we have enjoyed this for a while."

Vash continued. "Since we control the product, we can control the quality and type of high. Here is the cool part; we sell our product exclusively to graduate student types on major college campuses. We can also wholesale it to suppliers, and they can handle distribution on other campuses. The details can be worked out."

The group was speechless.

George was asleep on his red beanbag chair. It was time to refill the bong, refill their stomachs, and process this data. The group went into deep thinking and analyzing modes.

Marguerite suggested, "We sell the product in a very discreet fashion and fly below the radar, so to speak. I would also like to make the product cost effective so that students can eat, do the laundry, and get high. If we are nice to our graduate students, they will be nice to us."

Roger said, "Marguerite, you are a lawyer for the people."

Howard added, "Our product would cost less than dinner and a movie, and two could enjoy a wonderful evening of sexual bliss."

Marguerite said, "O/H is a special high. It gives me a clear-thinking look at the world. I write my best papers after a few solid tokes." She smiled. "And the sex is superb."

Roger and Howard smiled slyly in complete agreement.

Damian said, "Marguerite is correct. The high is special. The sex is special. It is a clear-thinking high, which gives the user physical and mental energy, deep analytical thinking, and an understanding of everything."

Howard interjected, "The product will sell itself. Companies want happy customers, and we will keep our customers happy. That is how we will succeed."

"As word gets out, and the benefits understood, we will control the graduate student and university market," Roger advised.

Howard said thoughtfully, "The problems I can foresee are how to control expansion, supply chain issues, and how do we invest the profits. If O/H becomes an international success, we will have volumes of cash to move around and invest in legitimate businesses. Money laundering is the backend of the drug business."

Vash said, "Transactions involving many countries, continents, and cultures must be considered in this business. The financial transactions must look legitimate, yet not excessive. The objective is not to attract the attention of law enforcement or government agencies."

Lori suggested, "The operating principles are to sell a product at prices consistent with quality; to ensure repeat and loyal customers; know your customers well; develop trust relationships; live life in the shadows and below the radar; and the most important, be very discreet."

The house agreed by unanimous consent.

Howard advised, "It is important to follow a business plan. We must all be on the same page."

"Marguerite," Howard added, "what have we decided our mission statement should be?"

Marguerite read from her legal note pad, "The Mission Statement: To sell a high-quality opium and hashish product, called O/H, primarily to graduate students at major universities; with the objective of keeping the prices affordable so students can eat, do the laundry, and get high."

Lori stated, "As a boutique product, business should be conducted by invitation only. Exclusivity creates demand, making it easier to control the product and protect our people."

Vash added with a smile, "O/H plays on so many levels. It is a combination of the two products, opium and hashish, and O/H sounds like a one-word expression when said, 'Oh,' and it describes the high you get when you smoke our product."

Lori added with a big grin, "Take a toke, and I feel oh so good!"

Howard said, "Welcome to Marketing 101 in the real world."

Marguerite continued. "We must develop the legal framework for the O/H business plan. Without laws and regulations governing how we do business, we potentially could risk anarchy within our ranks. Every business has bylaws that govern their actions."

Damian said, "I agree."

Lori added with a smirk, "However, I cannot help but think what an oxymoron that really is. We want to develop a legal framework for what is essentially an illegal business."

Damian added, "I find that rather amusing, would you not agree?"

Lori said, "Thinking about this more, I am in total agreement with Marguerite. We must run our small enterprise as one would run any other business, legal or otherwise. Every business does need operating rules."

Vash interjected, "It is interesting you brought this up, Marguerite. The India drug trade does have binding rules and regulations. If the rules are not followed, the offending party rarely sees court. Justice in India in these matters is handled quickly and often very harshly . . . if you get my meaning."

The group looked at each other knowingly.

Howard said, "In my humble opinion, I think it is best to develop prototypes so we can learn from our mistakes. Sometimes what looks good on paper does not work that well in the real world."

The group decided that was excellent advice; develop a campus prototype, study the results, and using that data, adjust the business plan.

Vash explained, "The black drug market trade has been going on for centuries, and with bribes, products move with a fair amount of security and relatively freely. My older brother owns Livingston Books, a small reputable book shop near London. We could use his store address as a shipping point. He does a nice trade sending special-order books worldwide. It is completely legal. I am sure he would be happy to join."

The group smiled collectively, realizing they were onto something.

Howard said, "As far as moving currency to pay for materials, we have options. The money movement must look like a legitimate business transaction, from business to business, or business to consumer. Providing invoices for products sold, especially when it passes through a legitimate business, should not attract attention, especially in smaller amounts. It all must look legal and normal."

Lori added, "Discretion is paramount."

Marguerite said, "We can all agree on that!"

Vash said, "What we have said tonight is all true. Let me explain the ancient art of the courier system. The couriers are actors playing a part. When a courier is transporting large amounts in U.S. currency, for example, our family likes to use a man and a woman with kids. They look and act like a family. This appears normal."

Lori asked the obvious question that was on all their minds. "What happens if they are caught? What happens to the money and the family?"

Vash finally replied, "If they are caught with cash, the excuse is the family is planning a major purchase such as a house, car, boat, or whatever is appropriate. If they have established collateral coverage, and can back up the reasons why the family is carrying hundreds of thousands of U.S. dollars, then the scenario usually works."

He continued. "The couriers know the risks. It is part of their trade. If the couriers are caught, they do not inform on their own. For their loyalty, their real families back home are protected and their needs are assured."

Damian had concerns about repayment responsibilities if the monies or products were compromised. "Who pays for the loss? I do not want to get whacked by your Indian-Mafia friends. I do not do gangster stuff. Not my style."

The group nodded in agreement.

Vash said, "If it is through no direct fault, no one is held responsible. It is the cost of doing business. This stuff happens. Investors do not like losses. It is bad for business."

The following Sunday afternoon, the group sat down at the conference table for another meeting. Pastries, coffee, and teas were on the table for all to enjoy. George chose his pastries wisely, as did Damian.

Lori packed the large water pipe with Vash's combination opium and hashish product, for all to enjoy. George was happy and stoned, and watched his people on his back, upside down.

Vash opened the conversation, saying, "Here is the dilemma: How to move product and money both ways, openly and legitimately, without going to prison for life?" He opened the question to the floor. "Are there any ideas?"

Lori said thoughtfully, "In this age with increased drug security, one cannot just walk across the border carrying pounds of this stuff in a duffle bag without expecting to be caught."

"I know. I found that out the hard way," Vash replied. "I had arranged with a 'friend' in customs to check my bags and pass me through. I paid this friend in advance. The supposed friend kept the money and called in sick for his shift. I was caught. It was most likely a setup.

"Every cloud has a silver lining," he added philosophically. "I found a great attorney in Detroit, who is trying to work out a plea deal. We will see what the final outcomes are. This attorney, his name is Gershwin A. Grain, specializes in drug and immigration cases, and I hear he has a good reputation for success. Another drug dealer dude I met in jail referred him. He was moving kilos of coke from Vietnam, and got busted by Customs at the dock.

"Customs, Border Patrol, various local and state police, and international police agencies are excellent at detecting drug smuggling and money laundering, and they are very aggressive. The drug dogs are good at their jobs, and the Feds use x-ray machines that see through packages and outline objects. They compare actual package weights to the invoice weight to detect drugs. This means we must do serious and extensive research."

Damian said, "We must find vulnerabilities in the government law enforcement systems, and develop our business plan to take advantage of those vulnerabilities."

Marguerite said quietly, "Research is what I do best. Let me analyze the scenarios and work on the various options for moving the drugs and moving the money."

A few days later, Vash, Howard, Roger, and Damian were sitting around the special table, talking, eating leftovers, and drinking espresso coffee.

Lori was working another 36-hour crazy shift at the hospital.

George was curled up asleep in his big red beanbag chair.

Marguerite came home and dropped a large pile of heavy books on the table. "I spent $200 bucks on these law books. They must weigh over twenty pounds each. They should sell books by the pound. How the hell am I going to carry all this stuff to class?"

"Use textbooks as a method of moving the product to the U.S. and sending money to London," Damian mumbled quietly.

Marguerite stopped and said, "Damian, say that again."

"Use textbooks as a method of moving products and money between London and New York," Damian repeated in a stronger voice.

George rolled over and went back to sleep.

Roger said thoughtfully, "If we could compress the products into the covers, reseal the covers, and send them to college students . . . it might just work."

An epiphany had hit Apartment 3A.

This concept made perfect sense on many levels.

Howard said, "If we could use books as a transportation method, using a bookstore address, complete with invoices and purchase orders, we could logically ship books worldwide and send payments to London, without attracting attention."

Howard declared, "It is perfect."

Vash said, "My brother's bookstore would make the perfect address, and a legitimate distribution point."

Roger added, "Excellent idea to use the inside of book covers."

"Brilliant," said Marguerite, "we now have our delivery method."

Howard stated, "The devil is always in the details."

Roger said, "The books must weigh precisely the same, and not a gram difference. The cardboard contents of the front and back hard cover must be weighed. The contents must be substituted with the exact weight of opium or hashish product. The product must be compressed, and odorless."

Roger's mind was processing the technical details at warp speed. He said, "This is important, because Customs is trained to look for discrepancies. The product must be compressed and shrink-wrapped, with all trace of fingerprints and fibers removed. The covers must be carefully re-glued. The finished books must look original, and feel and weigh the same. The density must be the same, so it is not visible when x-rayed."

Damian said, "We obviously need another bong hit, or two, or maybe three. Collectively we just solved a major dilemma."

George wanted to go for a walk in the park and informed the group.

Damian loaded a few travel pipes of opium and hash for the walk. Smoking with the family in the park was a great way to clear their heads and keep thinking through the logistics.

Damian said, "We need to do a detailed risk-benefit analysis to determine our strengths and weaknesses. We must plan for the unexpected and prepare for as many possibilities as possible. We must be flexible and adaptable in our thinking. In short, be prepared for everything, trust no one outside the family, and verify everything."

Apartment 3A was developing a viable business plan. The objectives were to keep the group in cash, stash, and school, without having to have low-level jobs that did not pay enough.

The group stopped for pizza and potato knishes.

Vash said, "Livingston's book shop, owned by my brother, is the perfect front. It is a respected bookseller of art, music, business, and law books. Customs, postal, and Border Patrol would not expect a London bookseller to be a drug distributer."

Marguerite said, "And graduate students do not fit the profile of drug dealers, so the law will never suspect us."

Howard added, "Hopefully."

Damian said, "It is an excellent plan."

Marguerite reasoned, "It is plausible for graduate students to order books and have them mailed to New York. The funds sent would be payments for the book invoices."

Vash explained, "These are expensive textbooks, law books, business books, and art books, so a large dollar amount would be normal. The books are large, thick, and heavy, and we could import a nice weight of product, maybe ten pounds of quality opium and hash. As long as we are careful, this method of distribution might work."

Damian replied, "Caution is our passion." He asked, "As our resident chemist, Roger, can you adjust the final product to be cost effective and consistent with the highest quality at the lowest price?"

Roger replied thoughtfully, "I will experiment with various formulas. The group will be the guinea pigs and rate the mixtures until we find our trademark product."

The group smoked, walked, and talked back to the apartment. Their collective brains were exhausted.

Lori joined the conversation at Apartment 3A after her shift.

Vash explained, "The top quality hashish costs in India about $200 per pound in U.S. dollars. A kilo is 2.2 pounds. Raw opium is priced the same. We want only the highest quality, and the purest product." He continued. "Our trademark must be organic quality. The raw product will cost us $440 per kilo. We will use less opium than hashish, depending on the exact formula Roger chooses. There are sixteen ounces in a pound, and 28.35 grams per ounce.

"The other expenses are distribution, transportation, security, couriers, bribes, and money laundering that must be factored, and thus will reduce our total profit margins."

Vash said, "Let's do some numbers. If we sold the product at $10 per gram, there are 28.35 grams per ounce, call it twenty-eight grams, equals $280, times sixteen ounces, equals $4,480 per pound, or $9,856 per kilo. Actually, we will round it out to an even $10,000 per kilo, which is an easier number to work with. The raw product costs $440 per kilo, plus transportation costs." He quipped, "This is a nice return on investment."

Damian's mind was racing. The potential profits were enormous. It was awesome, exhilarating, and frightening.

Lori said, "I think we need a reality check about greed. Greed makes you blind, and when you are blind, you believe you're invincible, and feeling invincible is when you are caught or killed."

Damian said, "There is an old saying I heard years ago: A greedy little pig soon becomes a fat slaughtered hog. It means greed kills."

Lori said, "I agree with Damian. We need to be very careful, and not get all caught up in the money. We need to think logically, not emotionally."

Vash started writing numbers. "My family controls the suppliers. The best hash and opium comes from northern India. The problems are that the trade export routes can be dangerous, and expensive, unless one has long-established relationships."

Vash was speaking volumes of wisdom. The family was framing an international importation business plan. The O/H plans and operational procedures must be scalable, flexible, profitable, and as safe as possible.

The wonderful irony was that as graduate students, the group was doing exactly what the professors had taught in classes, but they could not tell another human being outside of their family network.

Vash continued the lecture, like a preacher on fire.

"Listen up," he said. "If we double the price to $20 per gram, that works out to $560 per ounce, and $8,960 per pound, which is $19,712 per kilo. For easy numbers, make it $20,000 even. On the streets, O/H will sell for $30 per gram, if not more, and I predict we can raise the prices as word spreads. We allocated $10 per gram to our network of campus distributors.

"Larger campuses with more affluent students, we will retail the product for $50 to $60 per gram. I predict within twelve to eighteen months, when word gets around about the fabulous medicinal qualities, the average price on campus will be determined by supply and demand curves."

Vash added, "The higher the campus price, the more the distributors earn, the more the family will earn, and the less volume we must turn, which reduces exposure and increases desire. It is a precise dance."

George was listening intently, understanding that he would play a significant role in the future success of O/H.

Damian said, "The bigger the footprint, the more people know about us, and the more likely we get arrested by the law or killed by the real bad guys, for money and product. That is what scares the crap out of me!" He looked lovingly at George. "Who would take care of you, George?"

"Seriously," Lori said, "Damian is correct. We are talking about some dangerous shit that can make us huge money, or have us making license plates in prison, or dead. We have gone from intellectual curiosity to a major reality check."

Howard said, "However, we will soon cross that threshold. I will help on the logistics, and be available for consultations as needed, but I do not want to be involved in the daily operations. For me it is too dangerous, and I have too many family expectations. Is that okay with the group?"

It was agreed, everyone was invited to become as involved, or as uninvolved, as they wished, with no pressures. Roger, Marguerite, Vash, Damian, Lori, and George had their parts to play in the business venture.

Lori continued. "The marketing challenges we must solve are how we sell the product to our target audience of graduate student consumers."

Howard stated, "For me school is first, and all else follows. There are not enough hours in the day for all this."

Damian replied, "Then we will work harder and sleep less."

The cold winter was fading into a warm spring. On a Sunday afternoon, Lori, Damian, Vash, Marguerite, Roger, Howard, and George met for another board of directors meeting.

The water bong was clean, loaded with O/H, and filled with crushed ice and rum for flavor.

"Meeting assembled. All members are accounted for," declared Marguerite in a formal business tone. "We need to work through all the details, and look for all the flaws," she said directly.

Marguerite had a legal pad in front of her. She meticulously took notes. Analytical thinking and thorough research were her trademarks, which the group cherished. "Okay," she said, "hear me through and correct me when I miss something."

She picked up her legal pad and adjusted her glasses.

"First," Marguerite said, "the product is a combination of opium and hashish. We are calling it 'OH.' Excellent! I approve of the product and marketing name.

"Item number two: Roger will develop the correct product formulas, optimizing for the highest quality, best high possible, at the lowest unit costs possible."

Marguerite continued as if she were delivering a lecture. "Item number three: We will use college textbooks to ship the products to the U.S., and move money around the world as needed. Roger has the textbook and formulas part covered."

She turned to Roger.

All eyes turned to Roger.

George stared at Roger.

Roger nodded and said, "Yes. I have that covered. Do not worry."

Damian was thinking about a line from *The Godfather* and said, "This is the business we have chosen."

Lori said, "We have to think like highly intelligent business people, and not like stoned graduate students. This is real. If we are arrested, the law will not care that we are broke graduate students trying to support ourselves selling drugs. No. In the eyes of the legal system, we are nothing more than a band of international drug smugglers trying to make money and not do time."

Lori was right.

She said, "We need to think of every detail, and look for all potential problems. Because of the complexity of the business plan, we need to develop alternatives that can be deployed on a moment's notice. In other words, we definitely need a plan B and a plan C and a plan D."

Marguerite was not one to be outdone by another headstrong female. "May I continue with the review?" she said sarcastically,

"Yes, you may continue, Queen Nguyen," Lori replied in an obsequious tone.

It was getting frosty in Apartment 3A.

Marguerite adjusted her glasses and read from her notepad.

"Item four: We are selling to graduate students primarily, and only on large campuses that are politically liberal and who will welcome our products. It is easier to blend in on a large campus with many thousands, than on one with only a few hundred."

She paused to let this information sink in.

Damian packed another bong as the group processed the information.

George was studying his humans as they interacted.

Lori said, "I would like to expand our sales base to include medical students, ER doctors, and nursing staff. They are extremely overstressed and underpaid, and forced to work twelve-, twenty-four-, and thirty-six-hour shifts. We have to think on our feet and make the right diagnosis, or the patient dies. It is that simple and that stressful.

"Medical folks and medical students would greatly benefit from our products. We can work better, faster, and smarter smoking O/H than taking those damn pharmaceutical drugs we use all day and all night. Trust me, I know. I take all kinds of crap every day just to function and survive, and it truly sucks. I want to get off this stuff, but I cannot, because the pharmaceutical drugs are easier to get. I help myself out of the cabinets, as do the other Emergency Room folks. We are no better than the street addicts are, except it is our job to save their lives," Lori continued. "What a sorry irony that is!"

Not a dry eye was in the house.

George got up from his red beanbag bed, walked over to Lori, and put his head on her lap.

Damian had not been aware of the extent that Lori and her coworkers essentially were pharmaceutical drug addicts.

He gave Lori a big hug and kiss, and ran his hands over her body.

Lori smiled.

George approved.

Lori collected herself and said, "Ladies and gentlemen, may I have your undivided attention? Here is my business plan: I will test the market for O/H and ask my coworkers for feedback. They are very cool." She said, "Damian and Vash, let me ask you a question."

All eyes were on Lori.

"Can we set it up where I sell to someone else and they distribute to whomever? This way I do not have to do door-to-door type sales. I would rather be a small distributor. Residents and nurses are pretty much poor, and having them distribute O/H would supplement their incomes. This way, we all benefit."

"I like your business plan, Lori," Damian said.

Lori continued. "I would sell it as an alternative to all the pharmaceutical drugs we consume daily at work. It makes perfect sense. Many times we have talked amongst ourselves that we wished for an alternative, but knew of none. Trust me; this would have a huge positive financial impact on our enterprise, with little security issues. We all win."

The voice of logic and reason had just spoken.

Lori continued. "Hospitals are a captured market, and resident doctors, staff, and nurses are usually short of cash. I would use one or two trusted friends as distributors who would make money selling retail to their hospital coworkers and friends. The group's exposure would be minimal."

Howard said, "Are we all agreed that we market our products to large universities, and Lori is in charge of marketing to the medical world?"

All hands went up, and George raised his right paw to agree.

"So agreed," said Marguerite.

"Let's eat," Vash added.

After a simple but fabulous meal, and Greek pastries, Lori brought out the wine jug, followed by the bong.

The meeting was called back to order.

Howard started by saying, "I have been thinking about the business structure of this enterprise. We need to establish business operational parameters and an organizational chart. We must think about plans B, C, and D, just in case the unexpected happens.

"Expect the unexpected at all times, never let your guard down, and we just might all make some serious seed money for our separate futures and do real social good at the same time. It is absolutely imperative that we have escape hatches, so to speak, because prison and death are not on the agenda. I propose an investor-franchise business operation."

They looked at each other and someone said, "You mean like White Tower or A&P?"

"Actually," Howard said, "A&P stores are company-owned, but hamburger places like White Tower are typically franchises. In a franchise operation, the franchisee owns their store and services a protected market area. The local store buys all its products and service from the franchisor on credit and payment methods established in advance. The franchisor earns their living by selling franchise rights, and wholesales the products to the franchisees, who then sell to their customers. Everyone makes a nice living, and everyone has clear lines of responsibility."

Damian said, "Individual autonomy, yet working together for the common good is a Zen way of looking at life and fits with our values."

The group was silent as they furiously scribbled notes on legal pads.

"You mean," Vash said, "we can run the entire O/H operation as an investor-franchise business, Howard?"

Howard nodded and said, "Yes. In my opinion, that would be the best method to maintain control over many continents, cultures, and currencies. Here is how it works on paper.

"Vash has the master franchise, which includes Europe, Africa, and Asian markets. Vash has investor-franchisees in these markets. Damian has the North American market as a prime franchisor. He chooses the regional investor-franchisees based on geography and specializations. Each investor-franchisee has local distributors."

Howard continued. "Damian wholesales the products to his investor-franchisees. The investor-franchisee has distributors who move the product through their networks to the actual customers. The local distributer earns a percentage of sales in cash or product. As an example, Lori, as an investor-franchisee, has the medical community. She has local distributers who sell to the customers. Everyone makes money in the system.

"Damian is tasked with establishing reliable business contacts at major U.S. universities. This can be a dangerous flaw in the system that concerns Marguerite. One has to be very careful when trying to establish contacts. I say this for a few reasons. We do not want involvement with the legal system of any kind, and we do not want to alert the gangster element. Law enforcement looks for trends and spikes in drug activities, and the gangster element smells profits. It could become very ugly. For these reasons, O/H always stays in the shadows and always flies below the radar. No exceptions and no deviations. So we need to be extremely careful and only have relationships with people we absolutely trust and respect."

Damian added, "Remember, trust but always verify."

Vash interjected, "Unfortunately, the international drug importation business model has a large gangster element, from the Mafia to the Russian black market to local street gangs. Everybody wants in on the action because they think it is easy big money."

Howard stated, "Vash is the 'Mother Ship' in these endeavors. Without Vash, there is no O/H business model."

The group reached immediate unanimous consent on that.

George seconded the motion by raising his right paw.

Marguerite said, "We can add number five to the list: Investor-franchise business operations. I wonder how many international drug dealers have ever thought about franchising as a business model, and not killing each other. This is business, and dead bodies are bad for business. Probably none. Why? I asked myself. The answer is they do not think like intelligent, overeducated graduate students. We absolutely have a brain edge, and we can out-think most of humanity when we put our minds to it."

She was not a woman who came by modesty easily.

"We all agree completely," said Vash.

Damian mused, "I can't help thinking, if the only professors understood how well we have learned our lessons and the benefits of higher education, I think they would be amazed. This is PhD dissertation work we are doing. We graduated past the MBA thesis stuff a few weeks ago."

A bong break was requested by unanimous consent. George requested a walk by executive decree. The family required fresh air to clear their overworked brains.

Another week went by. The group actually had to go to classes, pass exams, and write esoteric papers about stuff. School and excellent grades were vital to career development. The group knew that in a few years they would be marching off in different directions to their chosen destinies.

Good grades were also a method to keep Damian's sorry ass out of the Vietnam War. For Damian, that was all the motivation he required.

Vash said, "Meeting is called to order. After a week to digest this stuff, are there any concerns?"

Marguerite said, "I am concerned about trust and information leaks. Just for argument's sake, let's say one of us is busted. What is to prevent that person from turning against the family? The Feds are good at offering a plea deal for a lesser sentence in exchange for information into the international workings of our drug enterprises. Most likely, if you hold citizenship from another country and are here on a student visa, you will be deported to your home country. The theory is that your home country will arrest and prosecute you. Some of us are U.S. citizens, and we will rot or die in a U.S. prison."

Marguerite raised an issue that was in the back of every person's mind.

"Obviously," she continued, "there is no perfect way to protect the group. The only way is for us all to trust each other completely. That is one of the many flaws in this arrangement. World history has taught us that trust can be bought and sold as a commodity, depending on circumstances."

Marguerite was correct as usual.

"How do we guard against this?" Marguerite asked rhetorically.

Lori replied, "We must establish loyalty and a trust system amongst each other. Otherwise, we could all be deeply screwed if something goes wrong. We have to declare a trust pact with each other, and give our word that we will practice the Mafia code of silence known as 'Omerta.'"

Lori paused for emphasis.

"Agreed," the group said almost as one voice.

Damian added, "We are all one family, 'la familia,' and as such owe our loyalty to the family. The family provides the protection. This is a family-business loyalty relationship with equal partnership. In unity we all prosper, and divided we all fail."

Damian looked at George and asked, "What do you think, Mr. George Carlin Dog?"

George responded with a deep bark, to second the motion.

Motion carried by unanimous consent.

"And," Vash said, "no one person should know the entire operation. We compartmentalize the information. Each knows specific details of their part, but not the entirety. That way if something happens, one person cannot be tortured, bribed with either a deal or their life, or forced to say what they do not know. Knowledge is power, and lack of knowledge is protection."

Damian bowed and said, "Yes, Godfather. We are our own family, Don Vash. We will love and respect each other and always work together for the common good. We will never lie, and we will always be straightforward with the family. We will always protect each other from harm, and will never do harm to each other." He smiled. "And this is the business model we have chosen."

"Are we all agreed?" Vash asked.

The group responded as one. "Yes, we are all agreed."

George barked.

Vash asked, "What routes and ports of entry should we use?"

Damian said, "All the Mexican weed, cocaine, and heroin are coming up from Mexico and South America. Drug Enforcement, Customs, Border Patrol, and the local cops are all working the southern border." He smiled. "Canada is a lovely country. In the rural areas one can literally walk across the border from the U.S. to Canada and back, and no one would care."

Lori said, "You are correct, Damian. A few summers ago, I stayed at a dude ranch that was on the Montana and Canadian border. I would horseback with the owner to a swimming hole in Canada, past a small town, and ride back to the ranch on the U.S. side. And no one noticed or cared.

"It would be a perfect place to bring stuff. Jason is about three years older than I am. It would have worked out, except I could not live in the isolation of the country, and he could not live in a big city. The sex was nice. We smoked excellent weed, and he would appreciate O/H. Maybe I should get to know him again."

Lori caught the pained look on Damian's face and quickly said, "Of course, this would be strictly business, and not personal. No really, guys, this is not personal. This is for real. If we can get the stuff from Canada and into the U.S., using Jason's place in Montana, then it would be harder for the Feds to track. The Feds are not looking for drugs entering the U.S. from rural Canada. They are concentrating on the Mexican border."

"She is correct," said Vash.

Lori continued. "We can ship the stuff to Vancouver, which is a mellow place, then drive the products through Canada using a family driving to see relatives, and bring it into Montana using Jason's as our port of entry."

Vash added, "From Montana we can transport it through the U.S."

Damian said, "I have been to Vancouver. It is a very friendly place. The people are open to the drug and alternative lifestyle culture. There are a number of very good schools and universities. University students always need books and always need money. We can ship books. Perhaps we could find a small bookstore as a front."

Vash, Damian, Lori, Howard, Marguerite, Roger, and George agreed Jason's was perfect. Another milestone was solved.

Apartment 3A had the tenacity and an absolute belief that as a family they would succeed, knowing they completely trusted in each other.

The O/H business models and operational plans were in the development stage, and the family had yet to sell a single gram of O/H.

A few days later, another staff meeting was called to order.

Howard said, "Ladies and gentlemen and Sir George. May I have your undivided attention, please? We must keep up the pace and work out the details, because lost time is lost revenue."

"Regarding routes," he said thoughtfully, "I feel we should always change our methods of operation, without routine patterns. That way it is harder for the Feds and international law enforcement to track our movements and set traps. Change our routes, change our couriers, and change our patterns randomly."

"Agreed," said Damian. "Vash, please explain how the product gets to the London bookstore your brother owns, and how it is transported to the U.S. and payments made to you. I need to map out the mechanics of the operation so I can connect the dots."

Vash stood by the large chalkboard and said, "I will share with you what you need to understand, and the rest must remain vague. This way, no one person knows everything about the complete operation. Each person knows what he or she needs to understand, and the rest is not his or her concern. This protects us all equally."

Vash said thoughtfully, "I probably have told this family more than I should have. We have absolute trust in each other, so all is good. In India, my family is protected because they are loved and respected. My family does business with the surrounding communities, helping the farmers in the hills of northern India. The love extends through blood relatives, marriages, friendships, and money. How do you say it in America? Family is very thick, and loyalty runs very deep."

Damian said, "Vash, we have our own family right here. We are family, and our loyalty runs very deep."

Vash replied, "I know." He continued. "The world's best hashish and opium is produced in northern India, on land that family members own or control. This control means the quality is outstanding, with reduced costs and security assured. Are we good so far?"

This information was more vital than any theoretical class lecture. It did not get any more real-world than importing opium and hashish to college campuses and medical facilities.

Vash was writing bullet point notes on the blackboard.

He said, "The separate opium and hash products will make their way to London and my brother's store. Let me just say that there are ancient smuggling routes that have been used for centuries, and that is how stuff moves around. Money comes back the way the products went out."

Vash continued. "The products will be shipped to Damian inside the hardcover of books, as we have talked about before. We can use music books, law books, or textbooks. It really does not matter. What matters is that the books have the same weight, look, and feel of the original books when clearing customs, x-ray machines, and dogs.

"The books will have invoices, including shipping and customs paperwork. Our payments for the product are made to the store as payment for book invoices. Unless customs gets lucky, or there is an organizational leak, there is virtually no way for them to find our books."

They never teach this stuff in business school.

Vash continued. "This works well for smaller orders, such as a few kilos or so. The problem is that customs and the other police agencies can track all packages leaving the store and addressed to the U.S. Sending stuff to Canada is excellent because it diverts attention and makes it look like the store has a large customer base of loyal buyers.

"Depending on the demand driving sales equation, it might be safer, and a more efficient business process, to have a large stockpile of product in the U.S. ready for faster distribution. Just a thought," Vash added quietly.

Lori said, "Vash, that is more than just a thought. That is the long view of solving supply chain disruptions."

Marguerite asked, "How are we going to show our money? We cannot just deposit money in the bank if we are supposed to be starving graduate students, without attracting attention."

Even on a smaller scale, one has to be careful not to deposit large sums of cash into personal savings or checking accounts. It would have been virtually impossible for Damian to justify a swollen bank account since he was officially a graduate student who drove a cab part time for extra money.

The rest of the family would have similar issues.

Damian said, "Inconsistencies can cause the Feds and IRS to start examining things too closely. The lesson learned is that one must be thorough in thinking and actions. Study all issues from a 360-degree perspective. When the bottom becomes the top, and the left side becomes the right side, metaphorically speaking, then there is a 360-degree view of the situation. Analyzing scenarios from all perspectives greatly reduces mistakes, and mistakes must be avoided."

Lori said, "We need to understand our risks appetite. How much money do we need, and how much risk are we willing to take?"

Howard replied, "When we solve this question, we can move forward. We need to be analytical and methodical. If not, we are nothing more than common drug dealers, which is not a vocation to put on your résumés."

A week later, Roger, the resident chemist, called a meeting.

Roger started the meeting by saying, "I have been working nights and weekends in the lab, trying to get the right formulation for OH. The hash we know is excellent, and the opium is a thick black paste, and superb."

The group smiled.

Roger continued the class lecture, saying, "Vash gave me samples: a raw, dark, thick liquid, a sticky black paste, and crystallized. The raw liquid opium has an acrid smell and taste. When heated the vapors give off a very strong odor, and strong odors in apartments are not good. And it tastes horrible.

"I can continue to experiment with the liquid, and over time, I probably can blend a product that has even consistency, potency, and costs control. Such things take time.

"The sticky paste opium we all know is superb. I am having problems blending the sticky opium equally and uniformly with the hash to form our quality O/H product. It is like blending thick taffy. I could not get a uniform blend unless I heated both substances. When you do that, you change the molecular structures and the compounds that affect taste and potency. Over time, I am sure I can find a system that will work. It is doable, but it will take time."

Roger said, "From a production viewpoint, I am worried franchisees are not interested in setting up a chemical lab to sell the product. They require prepackaged and consumer-ready products. The franchisor must control brand quality and product consistency.

"Finally, that leaves us with the crystallized opium product to blend in with the hash," he added. "It has the most potential and the least negative production issues. It is not as harsh or acrid as liquid opium, and does not smell or taste foul. I am having trouble sprinkling it evenly on the hash. It is in crystal chunks and does not stick to the hash. The crystals fall off the hash. I need to find some way to make it work."

Vash said, "I think we should set up a taste experiment. Damian, are the bongs cleaned and ready?"

"Yes, Godfather," Damian replied with a smile.

Vash continued. "Let us load equal amounts of each product in the three travel pipes we have. Most graduate students would be using smaller pipes rather than big bongs. Roger, could you do the honors of conducting our scientific product-tasting experiment?"

"My pleasure, Don Vash," Roger said in an overdramatic tone. "Pipe number one has the liquefied opium mixed with the hash. I have taken great care to keep everything in proportion. On a larger production scale, we would be smoking the same percentage mixture. The potency and taste would be the same, which is vital to protect brand quality and organizational reputation." He paused and looked at the group. "Who would like to volunteer to taste test pipe number one?"

Lori reached for the extended pipe.

"Good," said Roger.

Lori studied the pipe's contents. She smelled the bowl and said, "This smells like dog poop. Sorry, George. It smells like harsh chemicals, like butane and formaldehyde. This crap is nasty. You want me to actually smoke this stuff? Okay. Here goes."

Lori lit the wooden match and took a long puff. She started choking and coughing violently.

"Oh hell no," Lori finally was able to say, still trying to catch her breath and gasping for air. She grabbed a glass of wine from the table. "Screw you, assholes. I will take my clean pharmaceutical meds over this crap. You could not *give* me this shit. I would probably kill your sorry damn asses. You get my message?" she hissed loudly.

Lori was seriously pissed off.

This formulation was obviously dead on arrival.

Roger said, "I am sorry, Lori. I did not mean to hurt you. I can go back to the lab and work on this. It will take time, perhaps months. I am sure I can refine the process to a workable combination."

Vash said, "Roger, we do not have months. We need this product to market in weeks!"

Roger replied, "I got it. Let us move on with the taste test. It gets better. Trust me, Vash."

"Pipe number two," he continued, "contains the paste opium and hash. This is a scientific combination of 25% opium and 75% hash by weight. The problem is blending. I have two different samples. One is heated. The other is hand-rolled. You decide." With a big smile on his face, he said, "Who volunteers to be our next taste victim?"

Marguerite, not to be outdone by Lori, offered herself up as the next volunteer. She examined the contents, smelled the product, and lit the pipe with a wooden match, inhaling deeply. She started coughing as she exhaled the product, though not to the extent that Lori did.

Marguerite said, "The heated version tastes very thick and heavy, and my head feels fuzzy. I prefer each product separately. I would give the heated version a low 'C' grade. Let me try the hand-rolled version, and that way I can compare the difference."

Marguerite lit the pipe with a wooden match, inhaling deeply.

"I would give the hand-rolled a 'B plus' grade. It tastes better than the heated. You are making great progress, sir. The Maestro Chef is getting better at his craft," Marguerite said sweetly.

"Thank you for the encouragement." Roger smiled. "It can be difficult working in the lab and hoping no one sees the lights on or comes by to do their own lab work. It would be impossible to explain to the dean why I am cooking raw opium and hash in the universities lab."

"The hand-rolled and the crystal version have the best potentials for success given the time frame to go to production," Roger added. "The major problem is the crystals are chunky and do not spread evenly when I try to sprinkle the opium on the hash. I steamed the hash to get it moist, and sprinkled the crystallized opium. The opium does not spread evenly. That is my dilemma. Otherwise it smokes nicely, maybe a little harsh, but good."

Vash reached for pipe number three, examined it carefully, smelled the contents, and smiled. He lit the pipe, inhaled deeply, and gave a small thumbs-up.

"This is good. It is close, but not completely ready for prime time," Vash finally said after exhaling. "It tastes like burned coffee. I see what you mean about the crystals. They fall off the hash."

Vash started to cough a little.

"Perhaps, Roger, we can sweeten this up, add some flavor, and get the product to look pretty," Vash added. "How do you say, 'Sell the sizzle with the steak?'"

"If it tastes pretty, looks pretty, and gets you pretty stoned, then it is a pretty good product," Damian quipped.

The group laughed.

"I am happy you approve," said Roger. "Just help me solve the sprinkling and taste dilemma, and then we are good to go. My head is baked and I am out of ideas."

"I have the munchies. We need to get something sweet from Rosenthal Bakery a few blocks away," Damian said.

"They have some of the best handmade pastries and baked pies, great coffee, and teas from different continents," Lori added.

"Dessert is on Damian," Damian declared.

The group quickly mobilized. Food was the great motivator.

The sweet smells of the bakery brought them inside. It did not get any better than going to a 24-hour, always fresh bakery, where you could watch the baker making pies and pastries.

They were standing in line, placing orders, when Roger stopped in midsentence, mesmerized by the baker. He walked over like a spaced-out zombie, studying the baker, who was shaking crystallized sugar onto a flat cookie sheet.

"That is it," Roger stammered excitedly. "Look at how the baker sprinkles the sugar crystals onto the cookie sheet."

The group studied the baker intensely.

Roger said quietly, "If we can make a shaker with smaller holes, we could do the same thing. Then we can mix the crystal opium with sugar, add maybe vanilla or banana extract flavoring, sprinkle the stuff on a steam cookie sheet, and let cool."

Marguerite, the coy one, was not shy about using her sex appeal if it gained her what she wanted. She leaned over to talk with the baker, showing just enough cleavage.

Damian and Roger backed away and let her do her thing.

It was amusing to watch.

"Pardon me, sir," Marguerite said in a smoothly sexy voice.

Unable to resist, the baker came over to chat.

She smiled like a cat ready to pounce on her unsuspecting prey, and said, "I have been watching how you sprinkle the sugar powder on the cookie flat. What is your secret to get it to shine? It almost glitters."

She leaned over to expose more flesh for the baker to soften his loins.

"My secret is the cookie mixture," the baker said nervously. He smiled. "First, I lightly steam the baked cookie flat and let the steam absorb into the dough. I mist warm, distilled, flavored sugar water, and then I sprinkle the powdered sugar."

Marguerite had the baker wrapped around her finger as she bent forward, showing more cleavage.

"Immediately after that, I run the hair dryer. That locks the crystals in when it cools. That is my secret," the baker said with a proud smile.

"That is so marvelous," Marguerite cooed. "How would I get a smaller shaker? Perhaps one with smaller holes, so less comes out at once. Where would I get a mist sprayer, like the one you have? I want to do some baking, but I have a small apartment."

The baker was melting under Marguerite's sexy smile. "I will be happy to give you this misting sprayer and a smaller shaker. I can give you vanilla and banana flavors. Oh, one more thing, before I forget. My secret trick is to flash-freeze it. After I have sprayed and sprinkled, I place the tray into the freezer for three minutes, then take it out and let the dough sit at room temperature for ten minutes. This locks in the crystals, makes the sheet shine, and keeps it from being gooey or brittle." The baker added, "Good luck on your baking. Come back and tell me how it goes."

The baker's wife was watching warily from the front cash register.

Marguerite placed the small shaker and mist sprayer in front of Roger.

Roger's eyes lit up like a child who had seen the real Santa Claus for the first time.

Marguerite had unlocked the secret ingredient that would make O/H a top-selling product. Through trial and error and dedicated determination, the production issues were being resolved.

O/H was really happening.

Back at Apartment 3A, Roger and Marguerite went to work producing a prototype batch, following the baker's instructions exactly.

Roger used a quarter-pound sheet of fresh hash, which was sticky like taffy, as he calculated the correct mixtures of opium, sugar, and flavorings.

Roger said, "The opium effect is strongest when the product burns slowly and hot. Sugar burns slowly and gives a sweet flavor of vanilla or banana, or both if we wish."

After spraying and sprinkling the correct proportions of opium and crystal sugar, Roger placed the product in the freezer for three minutes.

When it was completed, the O/H cookie sheet looked beautiful. It was a work of art. The dark hashish shimmered in the light with the flecks of crystallized opium encased in sugar.

The O/H cookie sheet looked delicious.

Roger and Marguerite brought out their work of art for all to behold.

The group applauded and started to sing "Happy Birthday" to their newborn creation as it was ceremoniously placed on the special table.

Lori packed the water pipe with the first batch of the new O/H creation, and Roger took the first hit. He smiled like a cat that ate the canary, and exhaled happily.

The group waited in tense anticipation for a ruling.

"Oh my, that is excellent. So sweet! I can feel the hit taking effect now," Roger said, half stoned on one hit.

The bong was passed around and all agreed this was one of the most delicious highs ever experienced by humankind.

Roger said, "All good experiments must be retested to confirm accuracy, and therefore a second taste test is required for confirmation."

At the end of round two, the group decided that O/H was ready for prime time. The product tasted nice and sweet with a hint of flavors. The "medicinal" effects were marvelous, with a high that was clear thinking and intelligent. One could write papers smoking this stuff.

Lori said, "This is great. I could work all night, thinking clearly and making life-saving decisions. When my coworkers taste O/H, I guarantee demand will outpace production very quickly. Mark my words, ladies and gentlemen. The medical community is going to smoke this stuff up. O/H has the potential to go global."

Damian added, "It is that good!"

Lori and Damian were ecstatic.

Vash was elated.

Roger was very proud.

Howard and George were overjoyed.

Roger said to Vash, "How much hashish do we have on hand? I want to make up batches so I can experiment with the exact formulation, and get the look, texture, and taste just right."

Vash replied, "About four pounds, give or take."

Marguerite added, "You know we are going to need kilos of fresh, moist hashish, and kilos of crystallized opium. We must have a continuous and reliable supply chain of opium and hash products."

Vash replied with a slight edge in his voice, "I am working on it. I have a few kilos coming shortly. I need to finalize arrangements."

A few moments later, he said thoughtfully, "We should relax and enjoy the fruits of our labors. Our creation, from conception to birth, is a once-in-a-lifetime experience. We must savor the sweetness as a family."

After the euphoria wore off, Vash walked over to George and said, in an adult voice, "Let us go for a walk, George." He looked at Damian playfully and said in a tone reserved for dogs, "You coming, Damian? You want to go for a walk, Damian? Good, Damian. Sit, Damian."

Vash was rolling in laughter at his own jokes. He kept up the banter down the three flights of dark, stinky stairs to the street.

After a few blocks, Vash said pensively, "I have a loaded pipe. We should smoke, eat, and talk tonight. I have some things I need to share with you that I did not want the group at large to know. It is both bad and good."

Damian and Vash bought potato knishes with hot sauce, and pizza slices all around, with cups of ice cream and sherbet.

George favored pepperoni pizza with Italian sausage, Sicilian style.

The three amigos sat at a park bench, eating with dedication.

When they were satiated, Vash lit the glass travel pipe. "I have a few problems to work out," he said.

"Stop," Damian responded quickly. "*We* have a few problems to work out, not just *Vash* has a few problems to work out." He looked Vash in the eyes and said, "Capice?"

"Yes, I do understand completely," Vash replied thoughtfully. "I did not want to share what I have to say with the others because everyone must be on a need-to-know basis. It is safer that way.

"Here are my problems. Problem number one is that I do have about twenty kilos on order, to be delivered when I send money. Money I do not have, which is problem number two.

"Remember a few months ago when I casually said I got my stupid ass arrested by Customs in Detroit for carrying stash and cash across the border? It was supposed to be an easy deal. Arrangements were made and money paid to a certain 'friend' to check me through."

"Yes," Damian replied.

Vash continued. "Looking back, it may have been a setup, but at the time I was assured it was a solid arrangement. The 'friend' changed his schedule the night I crossed to the U.S. side of the border from Canada. Obviously, something went wrong.

"The third problem is I may be deported, or go to prison, or be forced to skip the country, depending on what magic Attorney Grain in Detroit can create, or not create." Vash's voice started to quiver. "I might be facing serious time in your U.S. maximum security prisons for drug smuggling and money laundering. If I am lucky, I will be voluntarily deported to India, where I am to be arrested by the local police and tried for drug smuggling. That is not a major problem, because officials can be bribed and convinced to forgive my indiscretions."

Vash continued. "Attorney Gershwin A. Grain is an odd fellow who has connections and solves problems. Or so he says. He cost me $12,000 for his fees, which was most of the money I was going to pay for the kilos I ordered. Now do you understand my problems?"

Damian corrected, "You mean OUR problems, Vash."

"Okay, OUR problems," Vash said. "I am in a corner, and I have no idea what to do. I have hit many brick walls at one time."

Vash put his head in his hands and started to cry, which was one of the few times Damian ever saw Vash lose total composure. It took Vash a few minutes to regain his self-control.

Vash said, "Problem number three is what the hell should I do about Marguerite when I get deported or imprisoned or escape? She is falling in love with me, and I am falling in love with her. I do not want that commitment! This is bad timing."

Damian, Vash, and George contemplated their shared dilemma.

Vash added, "And problem number four is continuing my American education, which is not possible from prison, escaping, or deported."

Obviously, the issues presented severe challenges that must be resolved. The family was approaching the crunch period in school, before final exams, which only added to the pressures and time constraints.

Damian and Vash lit the pipe as George patiently waited for his turn.

George was standing guard by the picnic table. A group of punks approached, thinking they were an easy mark for drugs or cash.

George stood up at attention, showing his teeth, and growled deeply. The punks backed off, and Damian and Vash continued thinking through their very serious problems.

Damian said, "Vash, there is an old saying that goes like this: When you are tasked with eating an elephant, it is best to chew it in small bits, and not swallow it whole."

Vash thought about this and started to chuckle. "You Americans have some funny sayings. Actually, so do the Brits. I understand how you think in New York. I like your style. Which part of the elephant do you want to start chewing?" he asked sarcastically.

Vash was back to his normal intuitive self.

"Let us start with the money issues," Damian said analytically. "We need money!" His brain was starting to gear up. "Who can we tap for that kind of money? As an investor, they would become part of the operation. O/H would have to guarantee a rate of return, in either cash or stash, or most likely both. Any ideas, Vash?" Damian asked with a hopeful look on his face.

Vash responded, "Actually I do. Attorney Grain is a possibility. The problem is he is also the attorney for some of Detroit's Mafia types."

Damian replied, "That could cause a huge potential problem or be a major benefit. Perhaps your attorney can make profitable arrangements."

"Either way, it could be dangerous or profitable," Vash concluded.

"Great," Damian said sarcastically.

Vash said, "It is an intriguing concept."

Vash packed another bowl, and George stood guard. The three amigos smoked in silence. George waited his turn.

Damian continued his thought process. "Follow me on what I am about to say, because it will take a while, and it is complicated. You know Boris's Laundromat and Dry Cleaners, where we go to do our laundry?"

Vash replied, "Yes, that crazy-looking Russian dude with those shoes and tight-ass pants. He looks like a short, fat, and balding pimp."

"Do not judge a book by its cover, my friend," Damian said. "Let me tell you briefly about Boris. He has a PhD in Russian Literature, writes poetry, teaches college class, and runs his cash businesses. The dude has more women in his bed than you and I will ever get. The Laundromat is a cash-generating machine, and it is difficult for the IRS to prove exactly how much money he actually makes.

"Boris says his father was a former KGB high-ranking official, and his family was smuggled to New York as part of some secret stuff. I know better than to ask stupid questions I do not need to know. In ignorance there can be safety, to quote an old saying."

Damian continued. "Anyway, the Boris family found the American dream in New York. The family pulled resources together, worked very hard, raising their families, and now they have Laundromats and dry-cleaning stores in Brooklyn, and they are expanding. They bought buildings in their neighborhoods and established territories.

"They are into all kinds of enterprises. Boris has told me that anything I may wish, just ask him, and he will accommodate. He is the second generation, and he has made good. The dude controls the black market in the neighborhood, which he runs through the Laundromat business. He is not into selling hard drugs, like the street gangs that are moving into the neighborhood. Our products may be something to his liking. He is a businessman, and understands market share and business investments."

Damian added, "O/H is a softer drug and therefore attracts a higher class and safer clientele. Boris Cooper and Attorney Grain could be offered the opportunity to become investor-franchisees. That way, Attorney Grain could handle Detroit, and Boris could move the product through the black market system into the Soviet bloc nations. They could make a fortune over time. Vash, O/H could easily go global!"

Vash said quietly, "That is heavy, man."

Vash was absorbing all the data, thinking through the various options and choices. Damian and Vash were doing a 360-degree analysis of the pros and cons. This was serious stuff and could have long-lasting consequences, hopefully very good, possibly very bad.

Damian said as an afterthought, "Boris could also be useful to wash money. The Laundromat is a cash business, with few traceable records."

Vash seized on the joke. "I get it, Damian, wash money through the Laundromat. That is cute."

Vash and Damian lit another bowl as they thought about the potential outcomes. George waited for his turn.

Vash looked at Damian in astonishment. After a long pause he said, "How do you say it in America? Holy shit, man, are you for real? If Boris is all that you say he is, then establishing connections with the black market and the Russian Mafia could be very interesting. It has potential. Not all potentials are bad, and not all potentials are good."

Damian said, "If the professors and our classmates only knew what real-world business experience the family was doing, they would be amazed. And we would be in prison."

Vash and Damian were determined to chew the elephant slowly in small bites, and work each challenge out from a 360-degree perspective. When the bottom looks up and the top looks sideways, then you can fully understand all the multiple parameters of the issues to be resolved. That is what analyzing everything thoroughly, and from all perspectives, using the 360-degree business model is all about.

The three amigos had covered enormous ground. The galaxies in Apartment 3A were changing quickly.

The following week, when Lori was working the night shift, Damian, George, and Vash borrowed her apartment. Lori maintained two homes: her former apartment pre Damian, and Apartment 3A. They needed a quiet, safe place to think, work, and not be disturbed. The bowls were loaded, the legal pads ready, for fast-track 360-degree thinking. This was crunch time.

Damian started. "Okay, easier stuff first. Yes, you will miss school. I am sure you can go to the finest universities in India or elsewhere that money and power can buy. That should not be a problem."

Vash thought about it. "Yes, I agree," he said thoughtfully. "I wanted a degree from an American university. I am not smart enough for MIT, Harvard, or Yale. There are great business opportunities in New York. It is growing rapidly. I will miss you guys in New York. This has been an educational experience for me, and I am sure for all of us. It could have been fun and interesting working in New York City, and becoming rich and successful together."

Damian said, "Vash, my brother and dearest and only real friend I have ever known, we can still become rich and successful together. We can help each other and be equal partners. We divide O/H equally, including all profits and all risks, and we shall always protect each other.

"Maybe there is a bright side that we have not looked at, and maybe we are not examining the situation from a full 360-degree perspective. We are only looking at one side, not the other multiple sides."

Vash looked confused.

George curled up on the big couch, deciding to sleep this one out.

Damian continued. "Vash is in India or wherever, and Damian is in New York or wherever. We are the only two people who can truly trust each other, and we live on opposite sides of the globe."

Vash started graphing out the organizational structure on his legal pad, writing cryptic notes.

Damian said, "Vash controls the sources from India and the products in terms of quality and quantity, and arranges shipments, security, couriers, and money. The London bookstore is the base of operations. From the bookstore, the books are sent to New York and various locations."

Damian stopped talking and lit a fresh bowl. Lori had a collection of prized hand-blown glass pipes in beautiful colors. The pipes had a small hole on one side, used as a carburetor to modulate the air intake.

Damian continued with his reasoning. "The bulk product is assembled to order, using Lori's apartment and Apartment 3A. Distribution is to investor-franchisees on a cash or credit basis. Security needs to be increased and vigilant. This is for real. The only way for O/H to succeed is to outsmart EVERYONE, all the time, and without fail. Or," he added, "we go to prison, or die unnaturally. Obviously, locations can change on a moment's notice. Damian worries about his organization in North America. Vash worries about the other side of the universe. It is that simple and that complicated.

"It can become dangerous and can get beyond our control. We have to know when to hold and know when to fold. And we must always watch out for each other. If we choose to get out, we will let the other know. Perhaps buy-out arrangements can be agreed to, whereby one partner acquires the other, to both parties' complete satisfaction."

Considering the negative outcomes from Vash's drug charges, they were reworking negative issues and creating positive outcomes.

It was munchies time, and Lori's apartment was well provisioned.

Vash said, "Americans have strange expressions. How do you say it? 'So be it. That is the way the cookie crumbles.' Well, I guess, it is, so be it, and that is the way the cookie crumbles." Vash was clearly enjoying himself. He said with a smirk, "What is the other one you Americans like to say? Oh yes. Don't cry over spilled milk." He repeated with a smirk, "Don't cry over spilled milk. How odd. Why would you cry over spilling milk? Yanks have very strange ways of saying things. Now I can understand why the British wanted to get rid of you pesky Americans."

Vash and Damian started laughing hysterically. Laughter is excellent stress relief, and they were extremely stressed.

Damian said with a warm smile, "I know you will miss Marguerite, and she will miss you, even when you both bitch about each other. Both of you are headstrong, lovable, and the nicest pain-in-the-ass people I have ever had the pleasure of sharing life with."

Vash replied, barely able to hold in his laughter, "I agree exactly. Yes, Damian, you can be a complete asshole occasionally."

"Thanks, dude."

"Seriously, I will miss Marguerite. She is a wonderful woman, with a giant brain and a body that is divine. And the sex," he added softly, "Damian, let me tell you, it is the best I have ever had."

Damian smiled. "I know. Actually, we all know. She shares."

Vash sighed. "So be it."

Damian said, "Perhaps you could send for her after everything settles down. After she graduates and gets her degrees and licenses, she might join you in India or England or wherever."

Vash replied, "The thought has crossed my mind. I am not sure that is what she wants."

"Marguerite will always succeed in her chosen fields, and you will always excel in your chosen fields, Vash my brother."

Damian understood that Vash and Marguerite's happiness was a vital part of the business continuity. "I believe that the four of us may actually make awesome international power couples, doing it our own way," he said.

Vash chuckled. "Maybe not exactly mainstream power couples, but awesome international power couples nonetheless."

Vash was happy with the thought of reconnecting with Marguerite sometime in the future. "We both need to see how our feelings and emotions are going. She may tell me to go shove it. Marguerite can be very volatile. The woman has a cranky temper, especially when you hit the wrong switch accidentally," he said with a smirk.

The elephant was becoming smaller.

Damian said, "I must confess I am feeling very connected to Lori. She is seriously smart, with an icy sense of humor and a very warm heart. She is a sharp-tongued woman who will speak her mind, and a damn great lay."

Vash smiled and said, "Sounds like you are perfect for each other."

"I just wish Lori would get off those damn pharmaceutical drugs," Damian said wistfully. "Maybe O/H is the alternative she needs."

Vash added, "Time will play this movie out."

The next items on the agenda were the deportation problems and related legal issues.

Damian quipped, "It looks like the elephant is back on the menu. Let's deal with the deportation issues. What are the options your Attorney Grain is working, and what are the probable results?"

"Grain is trying to get the Feds to agree to voluntary deportation. It means I agree to pay my own way to India, by a certain date, or they arrest my skinny brown ass, and I go to your lovely U.S. prison. How do the American rednecks say it? 'Ain't happening,'" Vash joked. "At first they wanted to send me to prison for twenty years or something. I freaked out. They plea bargained down to ten years. I freaked out worse. Attorney Gershwin Grain knows his way around town, and is working deals and greasing palms, helping various important people make the correct decisions in my favor. You understand, Damian?"

"I understand completely. You must do whatever is required to grease the wheels of justice, to gain your freedom. What can I do to help, brother Vash?"

"If it goes the way smart money has it, I will agree to voluntary deportation to India, and your government will allow me thirty to forty-five days to finish my affairs in America."

"What are the worst-cases scenarios, Vash?"

"I will go to federal prison as charged for transporting with the intent to sell hashish and opium. I was also carrying large sums of cash, so the Feds have added money laundering to their list." Vash said in a nervous voice, "I am facing real time in prison, Damian. I am way too skinny and way too cute to survive in prison."

"What will you do? They have your passport."

Vash replied without hesitation. "I have another passport. I will go to Canada and find my way to India. I can reach out to family, who will help. It will work, but I cannot travel with Marguerite, Damian. It is easier to make travel arrangements for one person."

"Damian, my brother by a different mother, do not worry. I will make it and be fine."

"I cannot do prison!" Vash confessed.

Damian replied, "I know. That is not an option. If Attorney Grain cannot pull off the voluntary deportation, I will help you get to Canada and then India. It will be my honor to get Vash home to India and safety."

Damian and George gave Vash a big hug of friendship as brothers.

The multiple scenarios had been thoroughly researched and vetted, using collaborative thinking and strategic, decision-oriented planning.

"They never teach this stuff in graduate schools," Damian stated.

That left only the front money for the drug purchase to resolve.

Damian finally said, "The questions before us are who to invite to our party? Attorney Grain or Laundromat Boris?"

"How about we invite both? They are in different states, different territories, and different markets. We can separate the enterprise, and they may never know about each other. Whichever way, I am sure the Detroit family will leave the mad Russian alone, and vice versa. It is a risk we must take, given our current financial state of affairs."

Vash was correct.

Damian said, "This is the business we have chosen."

And so it was decided that Attorney Grain and Laundromat Boris would become part of the O/H extended family enterprise.

Vash would talk to Grain, and Damian would talk to Boris.

Vash said, "I will call Grain. It would be nice to get ten thousand from Grain and another ten from Boris. That way we are well capitalized until the franchise system becomes operational."

A few days later, Damian, Vash, and George met at Lori's apartment to finalize the arrangements.

Damian said, "This is the plan. I will invite Boris to our casa Friday night. We will make him welcome, offer him vodka, and Vash will cook something Indian, which will please his taste buds. Boris enjoys good food. After we eat, we break out the bongs and let him try the O/H product. Once he is good and stoned, we talk business. I think the group, including Lori, should join us."

Vash said, "A new business partner does involve all of us."

Damian said, "This is business, and Boris has a sharp eye for making money. This should appeal to him."

Vash spoke with Attorney Grain, and reported his findings. "Grain is okay with fronting ten grand. He wants to keep it low key, and sell only to other stressed-out attorneys. We could never penetrate his market. Grain is interested in becoming an investor-franchisee for Detroit and the eastern Midwest and the legal profession. I told him it was a deal. The money is being wired."

Vash paused to let this information sink in, then continued. "Grain said he has good connections in Canada, should I need to leave the country quickly. This could become a reality, and given the circumstances, this may be the only reality I have," he said with a positive feeling in his voice. "From Canada, I can book passage as a paying passenger on an India freighter ship. Once in India, I can arrange transportation. I would blend in easily," he said jokingly.

Once again, more parts of the O/H building blocks were coming together and forming a solid structure.

Boris and the O/H family enjoyed a wonderful Friday evening, eating well, drinking well, and enjoying each other's company. It was time for the serious business to start

Boris said to the group, "Before we light up, I want to understand the financial aspects of my potential investment. This is a business franchise operation, and Boris would be an investor-franchisee. Boris does business as he wishes, with no direct involvement from Vash or Damian."

Vash said, "Correct. How you make money after buying our product is of no concern to anyone, as long as it does not jeopardize the group."

Boris said with emphasis, "Good."

The group nodded in the affirmative.

Boris continued. "Damian will charge Boris by the gram, packaged as ordered, and cash money paid prior to delivery. Maybe Boris would like to buy pounds, or kilos, or hundreds of kilos over time. How would that work out?"

Lori smiled sweetly and leaned over to Boris. "Then Boris gets the special wholesaler's rate. We will discount for volume and cash paid prior to delivery. Not to worry, Boris, Nurse Lori will take care of you," she cooed.

Boris said, "Let's light a bong or two and see what this magical product tastes like, smokes like, and gets you stoned like."

The group smoked a few bong hits from a multi-snaked water pipe.

Boris said with a large smile on his face, "This is good shit! Why did I not know of this stuff before, Damian? I thought we were friends."

Damian replied, "We are friends, and that is why we have invited you to become an investor-franchisee. We want to keep this exceptionally low key. O/H has the potential to become a very profitable global enterprise. We do not want any gangster stuff. We do not want Feds, police, and absolutely, positively, no prison and no dead." Damian said with a smile, "It can get a little dangerous, working with certain folks in this business. We must be careful at all times."

Boris responded, "I understand. I will sell to universities and hospitals in the Soviet bloc countries. I will test market it first. O/H will be a success. It is not very nice in Russia and the Soviet countries. It gets very dark and cold. They are in need of O/H to replace the excessive alcohol consumption. They do not know it yet, but Boris will change that. Boris is in. You can count on me! This stuff is excellent. Do you want cash?"

Lori said, "That would be nice, Boris."

Boris replied, "I will bring ten thousand in cash. It will be in tens, twenties, and fifties, used bills, non sequential numbers. It is in my safe, but it is too late to walk around the streets with that much cash. I will bring it tomorrow evening, about eight o'clock. Is that all right, folks?"

The group agreed with unanimous consent.

The pleasant evening continued. Boris crashed in the spare bedroom, and the family collapsed in their rooms, until the next day.

The following afternoon, Vash and Damian, over coffee, agreed that the money issues went very smoothly.

Damian said, "I have to admit, getting new partners was easier than I thought. These arrangements can work out well for all of us. The only problem is keeping supplies to meet demands."

Vash added, "We need more product than we have cash. That is going to be the challenge."

Vash was busy attacking a piece of toast, when Damian asked, "What is the story with Attorney Grain, Vash? Is he in or not?"

Vash looked up, toast in mouth, and coffee cup in hand. He placed the items on the plate and wiped his mouth with a napkin. "Let me tell you about Mr. Grain. He is trying to squeeze me. He wants half the product. If we split with Grain, then we will not have enough for our other investor-franchisees, like Lori, you, and Boris. If we cut others short for Grain and his Detroit gang, then we are hurting our family, and that cannot be allowed to happen.

"I told Grain it was not going to happen his way. I told him he would get a starter package, maybe three pounds ready to be distributed. We need operating cash. I told him this was a test market. If it worked, then more was on the way. We would balance the books once business was rolling. I told him it would take six months to a year to be in full operations. I also told Grain I wanted to know for sure what my deportation outcomes are so I can make arrangements accordingly. Grain said he is working on it, and not to worry."

Vash added, "When I am told to stop worrying about life-altering changes, then I get really worried. So now I am really worried. I told Grain that he better start pulling rabbits out of hats. Is that how you say it in America? And I am not a 'happy camper' as you Yankees like to say. I also told Grain I expect positive results with the voluntary deportation, and not prison."

Damian said, "What was Grain's response to all this?"

Vash, smiling from ear to ear, said proudly, "He said YES. In fact, he said YES to everything."

Damian was smiling, "Very cool, Vash. You are the man! That is excellent. We might actually get this ship afloat after all. I appreciate what you pulled off with Grain, brother Vash."

"Thank you, Brother Damian. I appreciate our friendship. It is very important." Vash continued. "I will send him three pounds for now, and more as business develops. You have to crawl before you can walk."

Damian replied knowingly, "True that, Brother Vash."

"Grain agreed to push for voluntary deportation to India at my expense. It means I can never come back to the U.S., but I can travel the rest of the world. We can always meet in Europe, where it is safer." Vash said with a broad smile, "No American prison for Vash!" He asked, "Damian, what am I going to do with Marguerite?" He paused and added, "I want to protect her career and freedom. However, I am falling in love with her, and she is with me. This is getting deep, and is confusing my head."

Damian thought about this happy dilemma. "I would wait to tell her, until it is closer to court in Detroit, and then tell her a few days before we tell the group. We need everybody on board and fully focused, with no distractions, during the maiden launch of the O/H business plan. Perhaps, after Marguerite graduates and gets her law degrees, she can join you in India." Damian added with a smile, "Keep in mind, she must be the queen of her environment. That is her personality. Would your family accept her as your wife?"

Vash replied, "Yes, my family would accept her. They are open in their thinking, and understand that love is blind."

Damian smiled. "Marguerite and Vash married, living a long and happy life, with family and children, is a wonderful concept for the future. Over time it will work out and become reality, Brother Vash."

Vash changed the subject and said, "I am thinking to do twenty kilos, which is forty-four pounds of hashish. Add six kilos of pure opium, which are another thirteen pounds and two ounces. That works out to fifty-seven pounds and two ounces of product. That is not going to be easy to get across the border undetected. The twenty kilos of hashish will cost ten grand, and the opium will cost another four grand. That is fourteen thousand, out of twenty thousand, which leaves us six thousand dollars for marketing costs."

Damian replied, "Once we get the product in house and Roger does his magic, we will divide it up to the various franchisees."

Vash sighed. "The cash problems are solved. Let me work on safe transportation, delivery, and moving money around. Are you and Lori ready for prime time?" he asked. "Welcome to the wonderful world of drug courier. You are going to see firsthand how this is done."

The seasons were changing, as late fall gave way to early winter 1972, with the semester ending shortly. It was crunch time for the group. Vash was working on finishing classes with the highest grade point average, reasoning it would make it easier to continue schooling abroad. The travel arrangements were slowly on working.

Vash decided an O/H business meeting, including Boris, was required to update the group on the operations and to resolve issues going forward. George positioned himself to be easily accessible to food, smoke, and affection sources. A fresh bowl of O/H was packed.

Vash started the meeting.

"Ladies and gentlemen and Sir George, I would like to officially call this meeting to order. Whatever we say in this room stays in this room. Do we all agree?"

Heads nodded, and George waged his tail.

Vash said, "The products are in London ready for shipment. The questions are where do we send them, how do we pay for them, and when does all this happen? We need to find easy ports of entries from Canada to the U.S., and near a university environment. Preferably, somewhere the Customs folks are not looking for drugs."

Lori said, "Remember, I know this guy Jason, who has a dude ranch on the border. I have told you the story, how we rode horses across the borders? Jason and I started in Montana, went swimming in Canada, and rode back for dinner in Montana, and nobody cared."

The group remembered, and agreed it was a definite possibility.

Marguerite said, "Winnipeg, Canada, is a university environment, and semester ends sooner than for us. End of semester means a lot of traffic crossing the borders. This is a perfect cover to blend in."

One cannot argue with the voice of reason.

Marguerite added, "School ends in two weeks. This is perfect."

Vash declared, "Damian and Lori can do the job, and be back before our final exams."

Howard smiled. "I love logistics. It is a precise dance, making sure everything fits perfectly and exactly as planned. It is a beautiful thing to behold," he noted philosophically.

"Canada is not known as a drug smuggling route. Customs and drug enforcement folks are busy with Mexico, South America, and Southeast Asia," Vash said with a smile. "That is very good for us."

Lori wanted details. "How do we get the stuff across the border to the U.S., Vash?"

Damian and the rest of the crew were also wondering.

Vash said, "Books, my friends. Books! Remember, we are graduate students."

Marguerite quipped, "I almost forgot."

Vash continued. "The cover story is that Damian and Lori are moving from Winnipeg to Chicago, to work, or school or something."

Lori said, "No, Vash. Here is the cover story and the act we follow." Acting as a general in charge of her troops, she declared, "Listen up! Damian and I are moving from Winnipeg to Chicago and getting married. It is perfect. Damian and I pretend we are in love and almost newlyweds. We become this cute couple as we cross the U.S. border with our belongings. College textbooks and papers are the normal items for us to be moving with."

Damian said quietly, "We *are* in love." He asked about transportation methods.

Vash said, "We can have Damian and Lori drive a car load full of personal stuff from Canada to Chicago, maybe a station wagon, with books, clothes, stereo, and stuff. Make it look authentic, and it will look normal. From Chicago, Damian and Lori can either drive to New York, or travel by train to New York. I would opt for splitting the loads and using different routes and times of arrivals."

Lori said, "One can never be too careful in this business."

"Welcome to the beginning of basic courier training," Vash replied. "The beauty of graduate students driving in a station wagon is that exact weight is not a concern. As long as everything looks normal, and the people play their parts, we can transport volume and weight. Remember, books, furniture, stereos, and records are heavy."

Marguerite interjected, saying, "This is a test run. We will analyze the results and refine the methods based on what we have learned."

Lori asked, "How do we get to Canada? Do we drive round trip or one way?"

Boris jumped into the conversation. "We use one of those 'drive-away' services in Winnipeg and drive to Chicago. The way it works is that the drive-away service arranges for people to drive someone's car for the owner and deliver it to a certain location on time."

Lori asked, "So we have a car, and we deliver it by a certain time and day, but we are free to do with it what we want?"

Boris said, "As long as you return the car clean, take care of it, and put in gas, you can use it within reason. They allow you a certain amount of mileage, so you have to stay on your route."

The group smiled.

"That is so cool." Vash chuckled.

Lori said, "I think I have the scheduling worked out in my head."

Damian said sarcastically, "What a surprise!"

Lori glared at Damian and ignored his comment. "I am thinking out loud, so work with me and add your ideas as we talk, please. Vash, where do we do the actual exchange of money for opium and hashish?"

Vash replied, "It would be at a house off campus, where we would blend into the crowd."

Damian told Vash in a very direct manner, "No gangster stuff, Vash. If it is not a clean deal, let Lori and me know now so we can be prepared."

Vash replied sadly, "Damian and Lori. I cannot guarantee anything. All I can do is try to make it work. Things go wrong, believe me, I know. 'This is the business we have chosen.' Isn't that from the *Godfather* movie, or book?"

Lori gave Vash a big hug and said in a warm tone, "Yes it is, my dear friend, Vash. You are so right. This is the business we have chosen. There are risks and rewards. We have to increase the rewards and cut the risks."

Marguerite said, "Lori, you said the logistics are worked out. Please share this with us."

Lori replied, "Damian and I travel by train from New York to Chicago. We change trains in Chicago. Maybe we lay over in Chicago, but hopefully we can change trains easily."

Vash said, "I like this so far. Keep on going, Lori."

"We travel on the same train, but not together. We travel separately. We do not acknowledge each other on the train. We pay cash, in small bills. We want to be completely invisible."

Marguerite interrupted. "When you change trains, or move from one car to another, you should have a signal to let the other know if it is clear, or if you are being followed, or tagged. Lori, you should carry your purse over your left shoulder if you have bad vibes, and over your right shoulder if all is good. Damian, you do the same with your briefcase."

Boris jumped into the conversation, saying, "Damn, you are good. That is perfect. I am impressed with the way you run your family business."

Lori continued. "From Chicago we go by train to Winnipeg. From the train station in Winnipeg, we call the phone number Vash provided for our contact. They pick us up, or we take a cab or something like that. We will be carrying books with cash and bringing back books with stash. We are very vulnerable to all sorts of potential problems, from the law to street gangs."

Vash said, "In Winnipeg you pick up the drive-away car. Of course, this is the sketchy part. Damian and Lori do not know whom they are meeting, but they know you."

"We are exposed," Lori said.

Vash said, "I will try to arrange the transfer point in a place that is secure. The products will be in the covers of various books. Place them on a scale to check weights and examine for evidence of tampering. Do not open the books. If all looks good, make the cash for stash exchange. Load the car with the books and the moving props like furniture and stuff, and begin your role as a student couple in love moving to Chicago." He added with a smile, "It is a long drive home."

Boris said, "It sounds easy, but it usually is never easy. Be flexible, Lori and Damian. If it looks bad, leave. If you are arrested, the punishment for carrying cash is less than for stash. Either way, I am sure they will lock up your skinny asses for years."

Marguerite added, "They like to make examples for political reasons so it looks like crime is being reduced."

Boris said, "You will never rid the world of crime, corruption, and smuggling, because these are extremely profitable business models."

Damian added quietly, "How sad is that?"

Marguerite asked Vash, "When are we going to do this?"

Vash responded casually, "In a few weeks. We have some time to make the final arrangements."

Howard said, "It is happening so fast. I worry that we may have forgotten the obvious. We must think with a 360-degree perspective, and somehow we are overlooking something small and important."

The group sat there in silence, thinking over all the details, conferring with each other and checking notes.

"Everything on paper checks out and I cannot see any major gaps," Roger said.

Marguerite, as if hit by a thunderbolt, said, "Look at us. We look like a bunch of dirty, unwashed hippies. Damian, your hair is in a ponytail, halfway down your back, and you have a gold earring." She was on a roll. "Lori, your hair is a frizzy mess, and you have a tight ass in those jeans. You are easy to spot, and people looking at you will think you are a pothead. We want to be invisible."

Lori replied, "Men like my tight ass, so don't be jealous, sister. It is not my problem if your skinny ass is all bones."

There is nothing like a little female rivalry to make life interesting.

After a long, cold silence, Damian said, "Marguerite, as usual, you are absolutely correct. We missed the obvious. In fact, I think we should all change our appearances and look clean cut and well scrubbed."

Vash added, "It will be best for business, and for all of us."

Boris said, "I agree. If you come to my store tomorrow evening, I will take you to Olga's Beauty Shop, where I get my hair and beard done. She will make us all look like corporate executives, and not stoned-out hippies."

Lori said, "After we clean up our appearances and clothing, we should have our passports and visas current, just in case we need them."

Vash said, "As of tomorrow evening we will look like executives and professionals. It will make it easier to blend into the crowd."

After Olga performed the amazing transformation on the group, they bought clothes from the street vendors. One must dress and look the part you wish the public to see.

A few days later, the group converged for a short final meeting. Boris had completely changed his looks and his body language. He transformed from peacock to professor, and the others became invisible in the crowds.

Marguerite said proudly, "Everyone looks so nice, professional, and straight. The authorities would not suspect we are a group of international drug smugglers, with a side of money laundering. This is excellent."

Vash announced, "Damian and Lori will be leaving the following weekend, so within two weeks we will officially be in business. When we have the products, we can start implementing the marketing plans."

The group passed a few bowls and relaxed. The enterprise was on the verge of take-off. The group collectively had developed a new product and a new business plan within a very short time frame.

Vash said to Lori and Damian, "Let's take George for a walk."

The look on Vash's face implied a private conference was required.

When the trio was on the street, Vash said, "Both of you will leave tonight on the train to Chicago, then catch the next train to Winnipeg. When you get there, ask the cab driver to take you to a hotel he likes. Pay the cab fare, and walk to a different motel, not hotel, register under a fake name, and pay cash. Change clothes and call me from a pay phone some blocks away, after you're comfortable in the Winnipeg motel."

Vash added, "I have a drive-away car ready for you. It is a large station wagon, which can hold all the stuff plus moving props."

Lori asked, "Why the change in plans and short notice, Vash?"

"It is very simple. It makes it difficult for a double cross, police stakeout, or other issues. There is greater security in invisibility, and changing plans makes one less visible and harder to track. Oh, one more thing," he added. "We are buying thirty kilos of hashish and ten kilos of raw opium. Lori and Damian, you will be carrying twenty thousand dollars cash total, or ten grand each in your book bags to Winnipeg. I just thought you might like to know."

Lori added sarcastically, "Are there any other last-minute changes or surprises you would like to share with us, Don Vash?"

Vash responded with a smile, saying, "If I tell you now, then it would not be a surprise, would it? Besides, you need to think on your own and act quickly in this business. I cannot tell you everything. This is on-the-job training, my dear friends."

Lori and Damian took the evening train to Chicago, paying cash separately and not acknowledging each other in any manner. Two train cars separated them, and they each had window seats on opposite sides of the train so they could observe any unusual activity.

Damian placed the book bag under the seat, and Lori did likewise.

Damian was an avid reader of Zane Grey historical western novels, and was happy reading *Riders of the Purple Sage* for the first leg of the business trip.

Lori enjoyed Agatha Christie mystery novels and was engrossed in a book for most of the trip. Periodically, they would walk past each other on the way to the bathrooms, carrying a bag or briefcase on their right shoulders. Everything appeared normal.

Damian and Lori changed trains. The passengers on the train did not look interested in them. They arrived in Winnipeg, confirmed the drive-away car, found a comfortable motel, and Damian called home.

Vash answered the phone. "I will call you back on this pay phone in ten minutes. Bring paper and a pen." He called back, saying, "Call this number and ask for Jim. When you talk with him, he will ask you, 'Do you have the movie tickets?' Your response will be: 'Yes, I have the movie tickets.' Jim will respond, 'Meet me at this place for dinner.' He will give you an address and time. If there is a problem, he will say that he cannot make it for dinner, and he will suggest another location or time."

Vash continued. "In the morning pick up your car from the drive-away place, have it ready, and park it at the motel. Follow the instructions Jim gives about where to meet and how to do the deals. The packages you will receive should be unopened and from the London bookstore. If the boxes are damaged, or resealed, be very careful. It may be a trap. Any questions so far?"

Hearing none, Vash continued. "Open the four boxes and examine the packages. The books are plastic-wrapped and labeled. There are twelve books per box, times four boxes, equals forty-eight books total. Each book has a thin yellow fiber running through various sides of the plastic wrap. If the threads are torn or missing, it means the books have been tampered with. If it does not look right, then get the hell out of Dodge City, like you Americans like to say, because it is a setup. If it looks good and you are comfortable, load the books in your car with the other moving items, and head out of town."

Vash paused and said with deep feelings, "Play your acting roles, and watch around you. Good luck and I love you guys."

Damian realized that he and Vash had talked for almost four minutes. Damian had forgotten to start his stopwatch, and he reprimanded himself for such careless behavior, vowing to learn from his mistakes.

Damian and Lori picked up the car and arranged dinner with Jim.

The exchange point was a group house near campus. After the introductions, Jim said, "I will need the twenty thousand you have first."

Lori replied in a straightforward business manner. "Then we will need the products first."

Jim backed down, saying, "Fine. I will bring the products here. Make yourself comfortable. It will take an hour."

Damian said, "Then we will be back in one hour and thirty minutes. At that time, we expect to conduct business quickly and efficiently. When we see what we like, we will pay you the full amount and be on our way."

Lori added, "Will there be any more questions?"

Damian and Lori returned two hours later, after driving around and surveying the area. Finding everything appearing normal, they entered the house to finish the business transaction.

The books and packaging were intact, and the yellow security threads appeared to be unharmed. Jim explained that the easiest way out of town, to avoid the construction, was to use a specific route, and he drew a map for them to follow.

The deal went smoothly.

Damian and Lori felt it went too smoothly.

In the car Lori said, "Why do I feel uncomfortable about this deal?"

Damian said, "I wonder why Jim went through the trouble to draw a map to help us avoid the construction?"

Lori replied, "Yes, that was very helpful."

They both turned to each other and their eyes got bigger. They realized the map was a setup route.

"Damn," Lori said. "They will pull us over at some point on this map, search the car, and then confiscate the stash and cash. Either the cops will be real cops or fake cops on Jim's payroll!"

Damian added, "Jim gets his products back and keeps our money."

Lori said in an angry voice, "Who is this Jim dude anyway? They think they are so slick. Watch out, bitch, you ain't met Lori Wilson!"

Damian, thinking quickly, said, "Okay, we ship the products back to the U.S. by train or bus as freight, and pick up the packages in New York. That way we drive a clean car and there is nothing they can do."

Lori replied, "We need to repackage these boxes to send to the U.S. Customs will clear the boxes as textbooks. It is perfect."

Lori and Damian placed the boxes on the New-York-bound train and watched as the train departed the station safely. Shipping packages by rail was reliable, and had a lower risk as long as the paperwork was in order.

The local police were nowhere to be seen, and this fact reaffirmed Damian and Lori's insight that most likely Jim had a roadblock set up for them. Apparently, Jim was confident they would follow his road map.

Lori called home and informed Marguerite of the change of plans. "The freight train arrives in New York in twenty-two hours. We will be the decoys. Pick up the packages, and have everyone carry separate packages, going in separate directions on the subway system. When everyone is comfortable, return to the house. It's show time!"

Lori and Damian walked back to the car and repacked the household items. They were ready for their cameo performances. The car was clean. They would pass any police or customs setup.

With coffee and food from a local diner, Damian and Lori headed out on the route Jim had mapped. Damian and Lori cross-referenced Jim's map with a state-issued road map and determined a possible police stakeout point, which was desolate. When they approached that location, a police officer pulled the car over.

The officer said, "Your rear taillights are not working correctly."

They knew this was not true, and prepared for the search.

Damian and Lori complied with requests for license and paperwork for the car. The officers asked if they could look in the rear. Lori opened the back doors and rear hatch.

One of the officers asked Damian and Lori to step back from the car, while the other officer examined the remaining books and household items. The officer reached into his pocket, pulled out a pocketknife, and cut deep gashes into the inside covers of the schoolbooks.

Finding nothing, he angrily rummaged around the car.

Frustrated, the law handed back their licenses and paperwork and told them to have a nice day.

The police drove off as Lori and Damian collected their thoughts.

Damian said, "Lori, honey, do you realize how close to death we were? If we had actually been carrying kilos, the cops would have shot us as drug runners or resisting arrest or something. The cops would be heroes, and we would be dead."

Lori said in a shaking voice, "Damian, my love, yes, I do."

They hugged and kissed, looking deeply into each other's eyes.

A few moments later Damian said, "The remaining questions are: were the cops real cops, or were they Jim's fake enforcers? That information tells us who our real enemies are. Knowing your enemy better than they know you gives you an edge."

Lori screamed, "You dumb motherfuckers! Do you really think we are as stupid as we look? Do not fuck with the godmother. I can be a complete bitch when I am seriously pissed off. And I am seriously pissed off."

Damian said with a smirk, "I can second the complete bitch part."

Lori gave Damian her famous "do not fuck with me" look and flipped the police the bird.

Damian and Lori continued the drive, replaying the events for clues.

Lori snuggled over to Damian and gave him a big kiss. "That was well done, Mr. Garcia."

"Why thank you, Ms. Wilson."

Lori said, "We think alike, you and me. That was good work, sir."

"Yes it was, ma'am," Damian agreed.

Damian and Lori popped some pills, drank coffee, and continued the drive without incident to Chicago.

The Customs folks at the border crossing were especially attentive of their vehicle. The personal contents were searched, and a dog was brought in to sniff the items. Finding nothing, the officers told Damian and Lori they were free to go. They were never sure if Jim had tentacles that reached across the border.

Back in Apartment 3A, the production team went into full action. The finest O/H had to be carefully processed to exceed all expectations. All operational procedures had to be in place. O/H was systems go.

The far back bedroom, which conveniently overlooked the side alley, became the de facto production room. It was furnished with a large platform table and a day bed. On the platform table was a triple beam scale, the most expensive and accurate scale available. The scale arrived courtesy of the chemistry lab. Two large fireproof safes were installed in the closet.

Vash called a Board of Directors meeting. "Let us do business first and work the numbers."

Vash and Marguerite stood up at the blackboard and whiteboard, and started working the volume of product and the money profit numbers.

Vash said, "We paid twenty grand for ten kilos of opium and thirty kilos of hash, all top quality. That is a total of eighty-eight pounds of raw product."

Roger said, "After production, we actually will have about ten percent, maybe more, by weight. The production will increase our net yield and therefore increase our profit. The spread is our bonus to enjoy."

Vash started writing numbers on the blackboard and said, "Forty kilos works out to 1,408 ounces and 39,424 grams. We sell the products to the investor-franchisees for $30 per gram; the total is $1,182,720, or about $1.2 million U.S. dollars. Not bad for twenty thousand dollars cash. Not all deals work out this profitably, but some do."

"Holy crap," Roger blurted out.

"That is a seriously nice return on investment," Howard stammered.

Vash added, "Investor-franchisees can easily double their money and sell for $60 per gram and more, depending on markets. Actually it would be more. If you add the ten-plus percent production bonus, it brings it close to 1.3 million dollars."

"Damn," Lori said slowly.

Professor Boris arrived with his entourage of two cousins to escort Boris and the products back to his nest.

"Boris, it is good to see you," said Damian.

Vash said, "Perhaps your security would like to wait at the corner deli. We need to talk business."

Boris said some words to his cousins, and they graciously departed.

Coffee and pastries were on the tables in the living room, and classical music was playing from the stereo system.

Boris enjoyed three very long bong hits of fresh O/H, while the group waited for his reaction.

After exhaling, Boris said, "This is excellent. Very sweet and has a nice taste. I am enjoying the feelings. Boris approves. This stuff is great." He exclaimed happily, "Holy shit, man, what the heck. Damn, boys and girls, you sure do know how to make some seriously good shit."

Lori looked at Damian, while Marguerite communicated silently with Vash, knowing that Professor Boris had just left the earth's orbit.

Boris turned to the group. "I will be able to sell this stuff for whatever prices I wish. I have no competition, and there is nothing like this available anywhere in the world. We have total control of the world's only known supply of premium grade O/H."

Damian said, "Yes we do, Boris."

Boris was like a child who had just received the toys of his dreams.

He asked, "How much supply can you get me on a steady basis?"

Vash responded, "It depends on what you want."

Boris said, "Okay, let's talk."

Vash said, "Prices vary, as will product mixtures, depending on market conditions, which may be determined by climatic, political, social, and/or supply and demand factors beyond our control, and all the rest of the blah, blah, blah, and blah that they teach us in school. You get my drift?"

"I got it," replied Boris. "What are the money numbers, unit numbers, and volume numbers, ladies and gentlemen, if you please?"

Vash walked over to the blackboard and erased it clean.

He looked Boris in the eyes. "My dear Boris." Vash smiled. "You bought eight pounds, eight ounces or four kilos. As an investor-franchisee, you will receive the finished product, which is of the highest quality and unavailable anywhere else in the world. It will be a major hit and very profitable for all, once we get past the initial start-up difficulties."

Boris replied, "I understand that, Don Vash. The numbers, please!"

Vash continued, saying, "There are twenty-eight grams to an ounce, sixteen ounces to a pound, and eight pounds, eight ounces of premium product equals to 140.8 ounces, or 3,942.4 grams of product."

Boris was uncharacteristically silent for many minutes.

Marguerite added, "Your money is well invested, my friend."

Marguerite was the lioness, and Boris was the prey.

Marguerite cooed, "Let's do the numbers at $60 per gram on the streets."

Boris's eyes beamed like a beacon.

Marguerite continued in her seductive fashion. "Boris, $60 per gram would equal $236,544 American dollars! O/H will become a multimillion-dollar-a-year business."

Vash continued. "We charge the investor-franchisee $30 per gram, or $118,272. After that, all the profits are yours to keep."

Lori said, "Boris, this is just the beginning. This is a prototype."

Damian added, "O/H will become the most profitable business no one will ever know about."

Marguerite stepped up to the blackboard. She was looking cute. Boris may have changed his looks on the outside, as they all had for business reasons, but he was still the same oversexed dude they all knew.

Marguerite said, looking Boris directly in the eyes, "It is a piece of cake, my dear Professor Boris. You will make a fortune."

"Or go to prison," Boris said stiffly.

Damian said, "This is about as easy a turnkey business operation as you could wish for. Keep it low key, and by invitation only. Keep the prices consistent with quality, and sell only to your comfort level."

Boris said thoughtfully, "The future potential is awesome."

Marguerite purred, "Yes it is. Yes it is."

Attorney Grain called a few days later to say thank you for the packages. Gershwin Grain was salivating like a hungry lion after Vash explained the financial aspects of the O/H business model. With Grain as an investor-franchisee, the enterprise would be assured of superb legal counsel, with Canadian connections and important friends everywhere.

It was time to take O/H on the road.

CHAPTER TWO

The Road Trip

THE following week, they departed chilly New York City for frozen Detroit. The crew consisted of Vash, Damian, and George, plus nice hardcover "school books" to help them study on the road.

The objectives were to develop a business prototype at a large Midwestern college campus and study the results. Lori and Marguerite were handling the distribution and marketing aspects from Apartment 3A.

The only form of transportation to Detroit and Iowa—and one should use that term loosely—was "Morgan." Morgan was a dilapidated car that was barely drivable, held together by willpower, bad tires, and broken parts.

Who could possibly question the sanity of two humans and one dog driving a vehicle that should never be allowed on any road in the free world?

Vash examined Morgan and said sarcastically, "Are we going to live or die in this incredible piece of shit you have the balls to call a car?"

Vash and Damian loaded the trunk. George climbed in the backseat.

Damian started the engine.

The trunk popped open.

Damian climbed out and tied the trunk lid with an old belt to secure it.

The engine backfired, smoked, choked, and sputtered as it warmed up.

Damian smirked and said to Vash and George, "You see, gentlemen, this is a fine automobile."

Vash replied jokingly, "I hope you like adventures, because this crap car is an adventure. I would not drive this car in India. And in India they drive anything!"

Damian smiled. "Vash, you asked me to drive you to Detroit, in case you might have forgotten that small detail."

"I need to have my brains rebuilt!"

"Most likely," Damian replied. "Considering you do not have a car, and Morgan is our only form of transportation, we should pray to whomever that this piece of crap vehicle makes it to Detroit and Iowa." He smiled. "And we stay out of prison and actually live to tell stories to our children and grandchildren about our adventures."

Vash thought about this for a moment. "This is going to be fun!" he added with a big happy smile.

Damian replied half jokingly, "Vash, please don't hurt Morgan's feelings. He is a very temperamental old man. He gets cranky easily. When he gets cranky, we break down in the middle of frozen nowhere with drugs. Trust me, that would be a bad situation, my brother. So please play nice with Uncle Morgan. It is damn cold in Detroit and Iowa. And I hate cold weather!"

Vash petted the dashboard. "Nice Morgan. Good Morgan. Please get us to our destination alive."

Damian said, smiling, "You will experience the real America, Vash."

"Only Damian could convince me to ride in this so-called car, in the middle of winter, to Detroit." A few miles later Vash said, "You are such a strange man, Damian Ogden Garcia!"

"Well, coming from you, sir, I shall take that as the highest form of a compliment! You are a little strange yourself, Mr. Gupta."

"I am going to miss the adventures in the U.S."

"I have the feeling, Vash my brother, the real adventures, as you call them, have yet to start."

Vash smiled. "You mean I ain't seen nothing yet, as they say in the movies?"

"Yep, pretty much."

It was very cold and Detroit was nowhere on the horizon.

Many miles and hours later, Vash said, "You must come to India."

Damian responded, "Very cool, Vash. I will visit one day."

"No, not a visit, but to stay, live, and raise a family. It is really beautiful and cool in the mountains," Vash said wistfully. "The villagers in the surrounding areas are part of our extended family, through marriage, blood, and money and provide protection. It is a business and family bond that has prospered for centuries.

"Sadly, India is very corrupt. The corruption works in our favor, as we buy protection. It is a known business expense and factored in to the operational costs equations. The corruption deprives the majority of the poor of basic human needs and dignity. Corruption destroys souls."

Damian said thoughtfully, "Vash, you will help correct the wrongs to the poor and restore their souls. And here is the really neat part, Vash. You will use the corrupt Indian system you despise, manipulate it to your benefit, and help the poor regain their dignity and prosper. That is how to use the system to your benefit."

More miles down the road, Damian said, "I would love to live in India and raise a family. Perhaps our grandchildren can take over the O/H enterprises when we have left for the spirit world." He turned to Vash with a big grin. "Now can we light the travel bowl, por favor, Señor Vash? Please share with Mr. Frozen George. Pass a few exhales into George's mouth and nose. He knows what to do. It is a long, hard, cold drive to Detroit."

Vash said, "I guess we need to be stoned because we are three fools driving into the frozen tundra of your northern Midwest in the winter."

Damian said, "Pass the pipe, dude."

Morgan had all sorts of mechanical issues. The brakes squealed when you tried to stop the car, but eventually it would stop, if you allowed enough time and distance. The heater only worked on low, when it worked at all.

The lights and electrical system were shorting, causing selected lights to stop working periodically. The muffler sounded like a racecar, not because it was fast, but because it had holes and rust, patched together with duct tape. Steam was hissing from the cracked radiator and bad water pump.

Morgan gave the world a plume of black and blue smoke belching out of the nonexistent tailpipe. The seats were terrible with missing padding and broken springs that poked one in the ass. The tires were of questionable quality, unmatched sizes, and lacked tread. The car listed to the driver's side because the suspension was cracked from hitting one too many potholes.

Morgan definitely had character.

Vash refilled the bowl, and the three stoned and frozen amigos drifted into their own orbits. The miles slowly clicked, rattled, and vibrated by.

The itinerary was to drive Vash to Detroit and deal with the deportation stuff. A few days later, Damian reasoned, Vash would fly back to New York, and then India. Damian would continue to Iowa, where his mother lived. She was doing her PhD in anthropology at the university.

More stoned miles down the road, Vash explained, "After the arrest, Attorney Grain and the government lawyers reached a settlement. The wheels of justice needed a little lubricating, and Grain greased the palms that were dry."

Damian looked at Vash, understanding how the justice system works.

Vash explained, "Attorney Gershwin A. Grain has a lucrative and very quiet legal practice specializing in helping clients with deportation issues, usually related to drug smuggling and money laundering. He does not take violent cases or gangster stuff.

"Grain puts on the persona of a humble and unassuming lawyer. This is a front. He is sharp, and not above bending a few rules in his client's favor. Grain has connections from the file clerks to the judges, and understands how to motivate the law for his clients."

George was curled up in the backseat, surrounded by sleeping bags for warmth. He was mellow and enjoying the adventure.

Vash said thoughtfully, "Obviously voluntary deportation sure beats doing hard time in the U.S. prison system. It is my first option. The second option, if all else fails, is to sneak across the Canadian border, make my way west to Vancouver. From there, I might be able to connect as a passenger on a freighter bound for India. Prison is NOT an option. No way! Ain't happening! I can't do small places with lots of ugly-ass men. With my luck, I would become the 'wife' of some 350-pound dude named Tiny. YUCK!"

Vash shivered at the thought as they drove on in silence.

A few miles later, Vash said sarcastically, "It would be sad to waste my education in the prison system. They would not appreciate my talents."

The three stoned frozen fools drove more miles in silence.

George was snoring in the backseat.

Many miles down the road, Vash picked up the conversation as if time and distance had not intervened.

"I agreed to the voluntary deportation plea deal, the judge agreed, and Grain said it was a done deal. So why does it not feel right, Damian?"

"Perhaps you are being overly paranoid."

Vash said thoughtfully, "Perhaps I am . . . Or perhaps I am not."

After twenty hours on the road, the frozen trio found a quiet motel near the Immigration Department in Detroit. The motley, stinky crew cleaned up, changed clothes, found a nearby diner, and ate their fill.

They walked to the local package goods store, bought a few six-packs of beer, and crashed until the next day.

Vash called Attorney Grain. "What are the arrangements? Is everything systems go, or are there potential problems? I want some assurances that I am not going to a federal prison for ten or twenty years."

Grain replied, "As your attorney I cannot guarantee anything, you know that, Vash. I *can* assure you that if the voluntary deportation deal falls apart, I will ask the court for time so you can wrap up your affairs. The courts may grant you thirty to forty-five days. I will say you have to finish classes and write a thesis, or some crap like that. Border Patrol has your passport and visa anyway, so I can tell them that you are not a flight risk.

"I can arrange for you to cross into Canada and then to India. Of course we have to talk about costs and risks, if it happens. So yes, Vash, that is what I can guarantee."

Vash said gratefully, "Thank you, Mr. Grain, I appreciate your help."

"You are welcome. I am just doing my job. I also have personal reasons to get you to India. Business is excellent, and the products are flying off the retail shelves, so to speak. In India, you will be able to control the supply chain, and I can invest more in the backend operations. Oh, one more thing," Grain said, almost as an afterthought. "You are expected at Immigration at nine sharp Monday morning. I will not be there. Contact me if you have problems. Good luck! See ya, dude."

Grain hung up the phone.

The conversation lasted 143 seconds.

Grain spoke quickly.

A phone company friend had told Damian that it normally takes the Feds and the phone company about 180 seconds to trace a complete call connection. The process, known as a pen register, records the incoming and outgoing phone numbers and does not require a warrant. A wire tap records the actual conversation and does require a warrant. Busy public telephone booths, such as at bus depots or train stations, may take longer.

Damian had a self-imposed rule that calls stay below the traceable 180 seconds. All calls of this nature were short and cryptic by design. Damian reasoned the world operates on precise time, and for these reasons, he always had a pocket watch like those carried by railroad conductors.

Monday morning Damian and Vash drove to the Immigration offices.

George chilled at the motel, watching TV and enjoying snacks.

Grain had told Vash it was a done deal, and to follow the formalities, and expect to be back at the motel around lunchtime, with no problem.

Immigration Inspector Jerry Patton was the intake officer assigned to Vash's case. Inspector Patton told Damian and Vash to go to a waiting room.

"You must wait for the Immigration judge to review the documents and give his consent to the agreements. The judge decides what happens next. This may take awhile. Relax and make yourself comfortable," he added with a smirk.

"No big deal," Damian said to Vash. "It appears that everything is happening according to the plans arranged by Grain. The legal system plods along slowly. Greasing the wheels can smooth the process. Justice wins in the end. We do not have any other choices. We can wait."

Damian and Vash sat in the waiting room, trying to understand what was really happening. Damian was sensing that something did not feel right.

Vash said, "Damian, you should continue the drive to Iowa. When this is over, I will fly to New York."

"No, Vash. I would rather hang around until all this is over. We can drive to Iowa later. What is another day or two?"

Vash smiled. "Thank you, Damian. You are a true friend, a true brother. I appreciate all your love, friendship, and help. This is very confusing. American laws are so different than the legal systems in India."

A few hours later, Officer Patton came over to the waiting room and said, "The judge went out to lunch and will be back in the late afternoon."

Damian remarked to Vash under his breath, "The judge is out to lunch in all ways possible."

Vash chuckled.

It was lunchtime and Vash and Damian were in dire need of good strong coffee and food.

There was a coffee shop across the street.

Damian said to Vash, "Coffee and a sandwich is an excellent lunch choice. There is a place across the street that looks good."

Vash and Damian rose from the chairs and put on their coats.

There was a deep, bellowing, forceful voice that yelled, "Where the fuck do you fellas think you're going?"

Vash turned around and said quietly, "To get some coffee and food, if you don't mind."

The voice belonged to a large man with a name badge that read, "Paul J. Christopher – Supervisor Immigration and Deportation."

Christopher yelled, "I do mind! Now get the fuck back in that room. You are both being deported."

"What the hell are you talking about deported," Damian exploded. His New York City attitude was rising to the surface. "This is the first mention of deportation." Damian was extremely angry at Christopher's degrading attitude. "I was not aware you can deport U.S. citizens," he said with a New York disrespectful, sneering tone in his voice. "I am a U.S. citizen, and therefore you have no right to hold me. This is a public building, and therefore my movements are none of your damn concern."

Christopher shut up.

Damian went out for coffee and sandwiches, returned, and sat down next to Vash in Deportation Holding Room #3. They ate ravenously, talked in low tones, and waited for His Honor to arrive.

Vash was called into court, and Damian followed.

The bailiff said, "Sit down, shut up, and wait."

The Immigration judge arrived some time later.

His Honor was old and cranky, and forgot to shave. The judge was half drunk and spoke about as fast and coherently as a tobacco auctioneer.

Before Vash and Damian realized what had happened, the judge said to Vash, "I have decided the original charges of international drug smuggling and money laundering will be upheld. Take him to prison."

He banged the gavel, missed, and hit the top of the desk. "The deal is dead," he slurred. "Bailiff, take Mr. Gupta to a holding cell. He is going to do ten years, and if he pisses you off, I will give him the maximum sentence of twenty years. Do I make myself clear, Mr. Gupta? The Department of Prisons will choose housing suitable for you for the next decade or two decades if I feel like it."

His Honor slammed the gavel down and missed again.

The bailiff said, "Next case."

Something had just gone terribly wrong.

Vash was held in a Border Patrol holding cell.

Damian spent the remainder of the afternoon talking with the officials involved. He had to piece together what was actually happening behind the scenes. He was playing the role of attorney and spokesperson on behalf of Mr. Vash Gupta. What to do next depended on accurate information.

Damian told the Immigration people, "My client, Mr. Gupta, should be well taken care of and separated from the other prisoners."

Damian was doing whatever he could to get Vash out of this situation.

Canada was looking like a viable option.

Damian determined that Agent Christopher, with his militaristic attitudes, would be a formidable obstacle and a very hard nut to crack.

"Fight fire with fire," Damian had heard.

Damian told Christopher that he was Mr. Gupta's assistant, with explicit instructions to report to his legal team everything that was going on.

"It is Mr. Gupta's legal counsel's opinion that the judge's decision was highly irregular, since a plea agreement had been reached and signed off by all parties concerned. The plea deal was binding."

Christopher was not impressed. "The judge withdrew the voluntary deportation, and therefore the sentence stands," he responded angrily, then added with a smile on his face, "Mr. Gupta will do a hard ten years, maybe twenty years. By the way, this is federal prison, not Club Fed! It is not pretty, and he ain't getting a parole. Accept this! Now get the fuck out of my office and stay the fuck away from this building."

Agent Christopher showed Damian the door.

Damian called Grain and reached an answering machine. Damian left a cryptic message for Grain, saying he needed to talk with him.

Three hours later, Damian reached Attorney Grain and told him the complete story.

Grain said, "Meet me at my office Wednesday morning at nine sharp. I will work on this tonight and all day Tuesday. That is why I want to see you Wednesday. Okay?"

Damian replied, "Yes sir. Wednesday at nine a.m. Thank you and good-bye." He thought to himself, *Dazzle them with your brilliance, or baffle them with your bullshit; either way it might work.*

You also have to know when to hold and when to fold.

Damian drove back to the motel.

George was happy for the company. They went for a walk in search of food, and found a comfortable greasy spoon diner. Damian bought various containers of hot food and cold beer, and they ambled back to their temporary home at the motel.

Damian and George sat on the floor with plates of the food piled high, and enjoyed a delicious meal. Damian opened a few beers and poured a can into George's bowl. Damian and George sat back with full stomachs, drinking cold beer.

Later that evening, George and Damian walked to the diner to call Marguerite.

Damian said, "Hello. Keep this short, please. We are in a jam, and the options are limited. Grain said he is working on things, and we are meeting Wednesday at nine a.m. The other option might be possible. It might just go that way. Things fell apart, and something went terribly wrong. The problem is we are not sure what really happened and why. The unknown is the issue."

Marguerite said in a concerned tone, "What is your advice, Damian?"

"For now, Marguerite, I am not sure. It depends on what happens Wednesday with Grain. Assemble the family and brainstorm for ideas. We need options we can use quickly, and we need cash to pay our way. I will contact you when I know more."

"I will wire $400 by Western Union to your motel."

"That would be great, Marguerite. Thank you."

The telephone call lasted 98 seconds.

I do not think the call could be traced to Detroit in that time, and certainly not to the pay phone, Damian thought.

Damian and George reached the motel parking lot. George became very alert. He sensed something was wrong. Damian watched him closely.

Apparently, the Detroit Police Department had become obsessed with Damian's role in this affair, most likely at the request of Immigration. An unmarked police car parked in the motel parking lot, and the police were watching Damian's movements.

Damian and George found it difficult to get stoned in the motel room with the law parked outside. It was damn annoying.

Tuesday morning at nine, Damian drove to the Immigration building. The secretaries must have thought Damian was an attorney, because he was buzzed into the inner offices without hesitation.

Damian strolled casually past the uniformed officers, raised his hat, and said good morning to Christopher, who was in his office.

Christopher did not look happy. Damian walked in and helped himself to some coffee. He attempted small talk, and opened Vash's file on Christopher's desk.

"Good morning, Agent Christopher. I would like a progress report on Mr. Gupta, please."

Christopher growled, "This case is an enormous pain in my ass because of the paperwork. I have other important cases, and they involve far less paperwork and aggravation." He leaned over and whispered gruffly, "I have no clue what is really behind this. It is very quiet upstairs, which is unusual."

Damian tried to get more information, but Mr. Ice Man was silent.

"I might be able to solve some of your issues if he would let me see Mr. Gupta," Damian said.

Christopher smiled. "He is downstairs in the Border Patrol holding."

"Thank you, Agent Christopher. Your assistance is greatly appreciated now, and will be appreciated more in the future."

Christopher looked at Damian, and he understood the message.

Damian Garcia walked downstairs and convincingly announced to the guard that he wished to see his client, Mr. Gupta. "Agent Christopher authorized the use of Conference Room A." This was a pure fabrication.

Damian leaned over to Vash and said in a low voice, "I have a meeting with Grain, Wednesday at nine a.m. Alternative options are being explored if the deportation agreement cannot be salvaged. Grain said to stay loose, as things are changing."

Vash responded, "Good, because I could not do a decade in prison."

"I know, my brother. Neither could I." Damian whispered into Vash's ear, "We are exploring the Canada option in case this does not work."

Wednesday at 9 a.m., Damian arrived at the Law Offices of Gershwin A. Grain, Esq. Attorney Grain's public areas were nicely decorated in conventional law office motifs, which is the image he wished to convey.

However, the private offices of Attorney Grain were decorated with signed Picasso prints and Day-Glo posters of Jimi Hendrix.

Damian was beginning to understand what Vash had said, that Grain was not entirely what he appeared to be.

Grain sat at his large and cluttered desk and listened in silence as Damian related the specific details of the Immigration events.

"A deal is a deal," Grain said. He was cranky. "I worked hard to put this deal together. The plea deal was agreed to by the court. Now some slow-brained, half-drunk Immigration judge will not go along with the program. Good money was paid, and I expect results for the money."

He pulled a mint from his desk drawer and contemplated the view from his office window in silence.

Damian watched Grain looking out the window.

After a long while, Grain said, "Why talk to the assistants when you can talk to the big bosses?" He grabbed the desk phone and placed a call to the district attorney and mumbled some choice words. Grain hung up, called the Regional Director of Immigration, and mumbled more choice words.

Grain was very angry. Nothing was going to stop him from making sure that the voluntary deportation agreements were honored.

"The Immigration judge did not follow procedures and went off the reservation. Maybe he was too drunk to remember the deal. If I remind the Regional Immigration Director of the judge's drinking problem, and what an embarrassment that would cause his agency if it became public, he might re-think the deal." Grain smiled at Damian and said, "What do you think, Mr. Garcia?"

Damian replied, "Fight fire with fire."

Grain smiled. "Absolutely!"

Another phone call later, Grain jumped up and grabbed his coat. "We are going to talk to a federal judge," he said excitedly. "I tried going up the normal chain of command, you know, follow protocol, but they want to play hardball with attorney Grain! Well, it ain't happening on my watch! It is time to go to the top and work our way down. You coming, Damian?"

Damian grabbed his coat and hat, pushed Vash's file under his arm, and they walked briskly to the courthouse a few blocks away.

Just before the courthouse, Mr. Grain leaned closer and said, "The new product Vash sent was superb. It is selling like hot cakes. The money is rolling in and the risks are small." Grain added with a large smile on his face, "When my wife and I say hello to O/H, the sex lasts forever. Damn, that is good shit."

Grain continued. "I have to keep Vash out of prison and get him out of the country soon. I can do business when Vash is in India, and not so much when Vash is rotting in prison for a decade or two."

Damian replied, "I completely understand, consigliore, and I will do whatever I need to help Vash and you."

Federal Criminal Court in Detroit was a large marble and glass structure. Damian sat in the judge's outer office, while Grain disappeared into the judge's private office.

Two hours later, Grain emerged, smiling like the cat that ate the canary. He strolled casually out of the office as Damian tagged along excitedly. When they had walked out of earshot of the judge's chambers, Grain jumped up and down, yelling and screaming for joy.

"We did it. We did it," Grain gasped. "Vash will be released by midnight. The federal judge was on the phone, chewing out everybody down the chain of command. He was barking orders into the phone like it was going out of style!"

Damian asked, "Why midnight?"

"Because they want to be complete pricks. Legally, they must release him before the next day, so they like to choose midnight, just to screw with our heads. It is a power trip, so I let them have their power trip."

"How do you know they will actually release Vash at midnight?"

"Trust me, they will. I pay them well. You have to meet Vash in the Border Patrol parking lot before midnight. Midnight is change of shift, so they want you gone."

"Let's get some coffee and food," Damian said as they walked back to Grain's office.

Grain escorted Damian to a small family-style Italian restaurant, and they ordered excellent meals, with nice wine and fine coffee and pastries.

After eating for a while, Grain reached for his wineglass. "I would like to propose a toast."

Damian put down his fork and reached for his wineglass.

Grain said, "To victory!"

Damian raised his glass. "And justice for all!"

Damian and Grain raised their glasses together. "To victory!"

They chuckled as they looked around the half-empty restaurant. The other patrons did not appear to notice.

After Damian and Grain had polished off the apple and cherry pie slices, with ice cream on top, Grain leaned over and said, "Damian, how are we going to get Vash out of the country?"

Damian looked at Grain over the rim of his coffee cup and said, "What do you mean? I thought the voluntary deportation deal was solid!"

Grain replied quietly, "Maybe or maybe not. Something still does not smell right. They could change their minds again."

Damian sat back in the booth. "Okay, what do you have in mind?"

Grain replied very quietly, "I have a 'cousin' type in Vancouver, and he works at the ports. Cargo ships leave weekly for India. My cousin can walk Vash past Customs, as a crewmember, and on to a ship. The captain must be paid, and he pays the crew. I will pay my cousin. I am sure product as payment would be appreciated. What I am telling you, you will tell Vash when you pick him up. Vash needs to understand the options. Okay?"

Damian replied, "Yes sir, consigliore."

Grain slid a card under Damian's hand. "This is my cousin's number. Have Vash contact him. My cousin will be waiting for the call. Vash can stay with my cousin until we can get him on a ship bound for India." Grain chuckled. "Vash will blend in with the Indian crew, and he will be as safe as possible. Let's walk back to my office. It is quitting time for Attorney Grain. Besides, you and Vash will have a long night ahead of you."

Grain paid the check at the front counter, and Damian went to the men's room.

Grain was flirting with the waitress. "Honey, you are so cute, I wish I could take you home with me and hug you real tight and all night."

The waitress replied seductively with a big grin, "And if you did that, your dear sweet wife and your three cute boys, all three years apart, would divorce your sorry ass, Gershwin. That big suburban house you live in, with the glass-enclosed indoor pool and the attached guesthouse, would be your ex-wife's house. Then you would be real broke, living in some rented room, and your law practice would go to shit." She smiled. "You know that, and I know that, honey bear."

The waitress leaned over and gave Gershwin Grain a big hug and a kiss on the lips. "Honey, a girl can dream if she wants to. I would love to live your suburban life. Maybe someday a knight in shining armor will come by and sweep me off my feet." The waitress added with a smile on her face, "My hunk of a husband would not be happy!"

"Oh well, he will get over it," Grain said jokingly. He gave her a large tip.

Damian tipped his hat and said, "Thank you, ma'am."

Grain and Damian walked back to Attorney Grain's office.

Grain said in a quiet voice, "I helped her husband out of a jam. He was caught carrying ten kilos of Vietnamese marijuana. When it came time for the trial, the police were not able to find the pot. Imagine that! Without physical evidence the government dropped the charges."

Damian asked, "What happened to the ten kilos?"

Grain replied sarcastically, "It disappeared." He waved his arms and fingers. "Poof! Gone, as if by magic!"

Damian smiled. "I believe in magic."

A block later, Grain said with a twinkle in his eye, "Excellent weed!"

They walked in thoughtful silence.

"Poor Agent Christopher," Damian said as they turned the corner towards Grain's office. "All that paperwork for nothing. Now Christopher will have to do new paperwork, to rescind the old paperwork he previously filed. What would Agent Christopher ever do if the world ran out of trees? To add insult to injury, he will have to work after five p.m., and Agent Christopher is a nine-to-five type of guy." Damian chuckled. "I guess I will not be on his Christmas list."

"You really do not like Christopher, do you?" Grain said.

"No, he is too straight for me."

"He survived three tours as a sniper in 'Nam. My opinion is he is wrapped way too tight."

"That explains his attitude," Damian said thoughtfully. "Grain, you are an incredible attorney, the best I have ever known. I am amazed that you managed to pull the proverbial rabbit out of an empty hat. You fought the law and won."

Grain smiled. "I was just doing my job."

"Vash and I are forever thankful and grateful for all that you have done on his behalf. Future generations are dependent on current decisions."

On Attorney Grain's overstuffed desk was a triple beam scale, and Damian said, "That is a nice scale. What do you tell your clients?"

Grain replied with a smile, "I tell my clients it represents the scales of justice. Then we weigh out some product and get high!"

Damian looked around Grain's private office and marveled at the Woodstock posters hanging on the walls. Grain had original signed posters, which were under glass, by all the greats of the times, from the Beatles to Hendrix. Day-Glo posters on black velvet of Elvis and wild animals hung on the bathroom walls and kitchen area. Given the personality of the occupant, it was a perfectly normal inner office decor.

Grain said, "Please get comfortable. Let me check my answering machine for messages. I also want to check on Vash's release progress."

Ten minutes later, Grain walked over and said, "It appears that we are good as far as Vash's release is concerned. Pick him up at the Border Patrol parking lot at 11:30 p.m. sharp. After that, get the hell out of Detroit, pronto. I can stall for thirty to forty-five days. One more thing," he added. "Stay in touch. Things change quickly, and you and Vash will need to know what is happening. I keep an apartment around the corner, where we can talk and adjust our attitudes while increasing our altitudes. It is my escape from reality, and allows me to stay in town when I have serious cases. Like Vash's."

Damian said, "I need to go back to the motel, pick up George and my stuff. I will return shortly, if that is okay?"

"Sure. Who is George?"

"George is my canine companion, and part of our family. He is our director of security and is in charge of all things human. George is the one who smelled Detroit's finest in the motel parking lot."

Grain replied, "Yes, I heard about your extra security detail."

Damian said, "It is hard to get stoned with the cops parked outside."

"You understand Detroit can be a rough city, and the police were just looking out for your welfare," Grain added sarcastically.

"Of course," Damian replied, smiling.

Grain's second-floor apartment was a comfortably furnished two bedroom, with an exceptional stereo system. Grain had an extensive record collection, including opera, classical, and all the great music of the times.

Damian knocked on the apartment door and Grain opened it.

"Attorney Grain, may I introduce Mr. George Carlin Dog. George Carlin Dog, this is Mr. Grain. Say hello."

Grain bent down, shook George's right paw, and chuckled. "Damian and George, welcome. I like that name, George Carlin Dog."

He dropped an album on the turntable and cranked up the sound. He loosened his tie, walked to a closet, and opened a safe. Grain brought a pipe and some of the O/H product Vash had shipped.

Grain, Damian and George smoked a few bowls as they let the stress of the last few days leave their souls.

George lay on his back on the floor, waiting for a good scratching. Grain obliged happily.

"I love dogs. Especially really smart dogs like George." Grain turned to Damian and said, "Let's do business. We have two major issues to solve. They are related. My motivations are personal and business. Issue one: Vash's safe return to India. Issue two: the O/H business. As I said, they are related."

Damian replied, "Are the arrangements on the Indian ship solid?"

"Yes. You have to trust me on this, as your attorney."

"How do we get Vash to Vancouver to meet up with your cousin?"

"There is a Canadian underground railroad system I use. It is popular with American draft dodgers and pot dealers. The underground transportation system is very good. They know their craft. They may become my Canadian distributors," Grain added.

Damian said thoughtfully, "Vash must cross the U.S. border to Canada quietly, which rules out border crossings. Then we have to connect him with your Canadian underground people."

"Do you have any other ideas, Damian?"

"I might. I just might."

Grain looked at Damian questioningly.

Damian added, "I need to call Lori. I will get back to you later."

Damian thought about Jason and the dude ranch Lori had mentioned.

Damian and Grain were mentally exhausted, and George was snoring happily in a comfortable chair.

Sometime later Grain said, "I am hungry. I know this cozy organic pastry shop on the next block. They have the best sweet pastries and great coffee. One can buy powdered mixes to take home. The shop has small barrels, like the old-time dry goods stores, where you can mix and match different types of organic flour and make your own flavors and textures."

Damian said, "That sounds wonderful. I have the munchies, and so does George."

The shop was cozy, and looked like an old western trading post and dry goods store. The décor included a soda counter, with a glass-enclosed pastry display case. Handmade ice cream topped the dessert of your choice, with exceptional coffees and teas from around the globe.

The store had a few tables and a booth on the far end.

Grain, Damian, and George chose the booth.

George decided on a pastry with vanilla ice cream and a bowl of water on the side. The humans indulged themselves.

After they were all satiated and caffeinated, Grain said, "Fifteen years ago, I ran for district attorney with the slogan 'Gershwin Will Win,' and I won the election. I learned how to play the system from the inside."

Damian was surprised. "I had no idea that you were a former DA. You have gone from putting people in prison, to keeping them out of prison. I like that. That is very cool!"

"After some years, I grew tired of the politics and the small salary. I decided to represent the accused. I pick my clients carefully. I have been known to help certain drug dealers and Mafia types with specific legal issues, such as money laundering and deportation problems, as long as it does not involve murder, kidnapping, or unnecessary violence." Grain smiled and said, "I also do not do gangster stuff, Damian."

Grain continued. "Then I met Vash. He found me through the word-of-mouth method. Vash opened my eyes to a brand-new business opportunity, with a scalable business model that can grow as large or as small as we wish. I am in the O/H enterprises for the long haul!" He added jokingly, "Sorry, buddy, but I am your partner for life."

Damian said, "Yes, so am I. Except prison cannot happen, and dead is not on the agenda."

"Completely understood." Grain said thoughtfully, "With my legal skills and my connections, and your New York brain trust that developed this product, combined with Vash's connections in India, London, and the world, we have developed a powerful business system. The beauty is we can earn many multiples of millions of dollars yearly, and only a few people will know we exist. The investor-franchisee business model is truly brilliant. Owners are more loyal to the organizational structure, and therefore have vested interest in protecting their long-term success.

"Damian, we can be as big or as small as we wish. We control all aspects of the market for the O/H product line, so there is no competition. We can make our money as we wish. We must keep the law out of our lives, and the real gangsters away." Grain said as an afterthought, "Here is a piece of trivia for you, Damian. Over time, O/H will develop into a multimillion-dollar business, and we will have absolutely no employees, ever! Not one single employee, so no payroll taxes and no withholding and none of that crap."

Grain chuckled at the irony of not paying payroll taxes.

Damian said, "That is very cool, when you actually think about it. We have created an awesome business model, developed it into an awesome business plan, created awesome operational procedures, and we will all make awesome money!"

Grain joked, "It is awesome!"

Grain, Damian, and George left the Wild West Organic Desserts store and walked back to Grain's apartment.

As they walked, Damian said to Grain, "A store like that would be perfect for Lori and me. What I found interesting were the various organic flours and grains that the customers bring home and bake into cakes and brownies. People like to buy organic flours from old wood barrels. We could grind up hashish and opium into various brownie mixes and baked goods. The imported organic flours could be moved around the world. It would be easy to transport and easy to taste. Think about it. A new product called O/H Brownies! We could call the products something like 'Happy Brownies and Cakes.'"

Grain stopped walking and stared at Damian. "O/H BROWNIES! Happy Brownies and Cakes! Absolutely brilliant! You are a very strange genius, Mr. Damian Garcia." He looked at George and said, "George, your dude is smarter than the average human."

George looked at Grain as if to say, "I know. That is why I found him on the streets long ago."

The trio walked in thoughtful silence.

Grain mumbled under his breath, "I could underwrite a nationwide chain of coffee shops selling organic O/H Brownie mixes, and we will make a fortune. Damian, you have the scariest mind. Damn, I like that!"

As they walked, Damian stopped at a pay phone and called Lori in New York. Damian briefed Lori and explained the issues.

"Lori, honey, would your friend who lives in the country be willing to transport a horse to Canada?"

Lori replied, "Where can I call you back after I make some calls?"

Grain gave Damian a back line number, and he told Lori.

The telephone call lasted 42 seconds.

Damian turned to Grain and said, "Lori will call us shortly at this number, and then we will know about transportation."

Grain stopped in the middle of the block, turned, and said quietly, "By the way, my associates call me Gershwin, and my friends call me Win." He paused and said with a smile, "Call me Win. When we are in public, I am Attorney Grain."

Damian quipped, "Certainly, counselor."

The three amigos made themselves comfortable at Win's apartment.

Grain brought out another fresh bowl of O/H to enjoy.

He said, "We have a few more hours to conclude business. We need to get to work. Explain the business operations, please."

Damian said, "Attorney Grain is an investor-franchisee, with a designated territory, and all business belongs to the franchisee. All product arrangements are made through the New York office. Manufacturing may be in New York, or by the I-F at their locations, using established production systems. Production quality is vital. The business and operational plans must be respected. The Gupta families have the rest of the universe.

"We must remember that a successful business requires happy customers at all times. Happy customers are solid repeat customers, and happy customers also will protect their sources and keep us safe. Therefore, happy customers are an absolute!"

Grain smiled. "I like what I am hearing. I do believe, Mr. Garcia, that another bowl might be in order."

The trio enjoyed the ascent to Earth's outer orbits.

Damian said, "Besides being my partner in crime and co-conspirator, Lori has the medical community as her territories. Our empirical research indicates that the professional communities are excellent markets for the O/H product line. Hospital folks like doctors and nurses, and lawyers and accountants are solid and reliable buyers, willing to pay nicely and accepting only the best quality products. Our Russian professor friend, Sir Boris, has the Russian black market network and the Eastern European countries."

Grain commented, "If the Russian black market is successful, then O/H might wish to consider other markets, like the Italian and Arab markets for example. Each market must be vetted before moving forward."

Damian explained, "Our business model is based on each unit serving specific markets. We keep our families close, and develop relations based on trust, respect, money, and self-preservation. Counselor Grain, I have a business axiom I try to live by: 'Trust but always verify.' To seek the real truths, one must verify vigilantly."

Grain said thoughtfully, "Wise man, Mr. Garcia."

The phone rang on Win's desk.

Grain answered, saying, "It's Lori."

Damian took the phone and wrote down directions, names, addresses, contact numbers, and code words. "Thank you very much, Lori. I will keep you posted."

The telephone call lasted 78 seconds.

Damian asked Win, "Is this phone secure? I have to call Jason and make arrangements."

"Yes. It is unlisted. I paid a telephone dude to hook it up. I use this number for all my off-the-books transactions."

"Good. Can I make the call?"

Grain nodded in the affirmative.

Damian placed the call, writing down details as he spoke with Jason.

He walked back to Win.

George went back to sleep on the couch.

Damian said, "Arrangements have been made for Vash to be at Jason's dude ranch in twenty-seven days from today. Jason will transport Vash, using back roads into Canada. Jason said that the Farmers' Almanac called for a sliver moon. The cowboys call this a rustler's moon, because there is just enough moonlight to rustle cattle and not be seen by others."

Grain nodded in agreement to the plans.

Damian continued, "I believe you have connections in the Canadian underground transportation system."

"I do, yes. I will make connecting travel arrangements. My cousin will arrange the ship transportation. If all the pieces of the jigsaw puzzle fit together, and stay together, we are good to go. If something goes wrong, we are in deep shit."

Damian said optimistically, "Nothing serious will go wrong. I will not allow it. Growing up, I never had much of a family, and Vash is family to me. Attorney Grain, please use your skills and make this work for all of us."

"Not to worry, my worried friend. Attorney Grain has it under control. Your newfound friend Jason is actually part of the Canadian underground. He was a conscientious objector and war resister who went back to living off the land and fighting the man from his ranch in northern Montana. Actually the ranch started out as a hippie commune in the sixties, and Jason developed it into a working horse ranch," Grain said with a big grin. "He found me the same way you did, by word of mouth. Jason was busted transporting the finest Thai sticks you have ever tasted. This stuff was sweet gold, and worth lots of cold cash."

Damian said, "Hmm, let me take a wild guess. The stuff never made it to court as evidence, and no evidence, therefore no crime."

Grain smiled and nodded. "We smoked some and sold the rest. Mr. Jason is now part of my expanding universe, which is a surprise to you."

"Actually, yes it is a surprise. I remember Lori saying something about him. Apparently, they had a relationship thing going."

Grain smiled and said, "Small world, isn't it, Damian?"

"Yes, it sure is a small world."

Grain refilled another bowl for the road.

The time was getting closer for Damian to pick up Vash and beat a hasty retreat out of Detroit. Next stop, Iowa.

Damian said, "I already called and you should be getting a large shipment of books for your professional services. Vash wanted to make sure you are well compensated for your legal services."

Grain said, "When Vash is free, he will need to increase the supply chain from India. I can foresee demand exceeding supply issues."

Damian said, "Not to worry, more is on the way."

Grain smiled approvingly.

Damian continued. "The rest of the itinerary is to drive to Iowa City, to visit my mother. She is finishing her PhD in Anthropology. We need a break from the big city stress."

Grain added, "We are all burned out."

"Besides, the graduate student population appears to meet our profiles, so it would be a good place to test market our O/H product line. My mother has like-minded friends who might be interested in becoming distributors."

Grain said, "I can stall the law for thirty, maybe forty-five days. Vash departs in twenty-seven days. Can you make this happen?"

Damian replied cheerfully, "Absolutely."

Grain said, "Follow me to the Border Patrol parking lot. I will park nearby where I can see you and make sure everything is copacetic. Good luck on your journey and in Iowa."

Damian said, "I want to thank you for all you have done, and will do in the future. You changed the direction of all our destinies."

Grain responded with a twinkle in his eye, "I was just doing my job. Mr. Garcia and Mr. Dog, it has been a pleasure doing business with you. Call me on the back line daily after seven p.m. so we can stay connected. Things change and you need to know what is happening."

Damian drove to the Border Patrol parking lot, as instructed. George curled up in the backseat. Damian was greeted with a very cold reception.

"Wait in your car," Agent Christopher commanded. "Your friend will be out soon. We have to process his exit papers."

Victory tasted sweet, if only for a short time.

Exactly at 11:30 p.m., Vash was released.

Damian greeted Vash with a hug, and George offered a paw shake.

They climbed back into the car, and Damian drove out of the Border Patrol parking lot, to freedom.

Grain watched from his car.

Damian kept an eye in the rearview mirror for company.

None was visible.

Vash leaned over and said, "How can I ever repay you?"

Damian replied dryly, "Buy me a cup of coffee."

Damian and Vash started laughing hysterically.

George made himself comfortable on the backseat.

A few blocks later, Damian pulled into the same coffee shop that had been their surrogate home for the last few days.

The trio ate and drank coffee, knowing they had a long, cold drive ahead. George had a large hamburger and fries with a side of fresh water.

At the end of the meal, as the trio was getting up to leave, an interesting woman leaned toward them. She smiled and said, "These are for you to enjoy."

She handed Vash four very fat, sweet-smelling joints.

Vash and Damian stared at each other, not exactly sure what to do or what had happened.

Damian ordered two large coffees to go, and paid the bill.

Outside of the diner, as the trio climbed into Morgan, Vash said, "What just happened?"

Damian replied, "I have no clue. Call it providence, or call it one of those weird things that happen for no reason. Life can be like that."

Vash said quietly, "Or maybe it was meant to be. Maybe it is a sign from the gods, and we mortals are too slow to understand."

Damian replied with a smile, "Okay, get your mortal ass into this piece-of-shit car. We need to get the hell out of Dodge City before the Feds get pissed off even more. Por favor, my dearest friend!"

Damian stopped at a large gas station many hours down the road. Morgan was in need of fuel, oil, and antifreeze. Damian bought six quarts of oil and two gallons of antifreeze and a few cans of dry gas for the colder weather ahead. He filled the engine with three quarts of heavy-duty oil, added antifreeze in the radiator, poured two cans of dry gas in the gas tank, and put much-needed air in the sorry-looking tires. The humans and canine bought mass quantities of munchies, coffees, and drinks for the road.

Some more miles and more bowls down the road, Damian said happily, "To Iowa, my brothers, Vash and George."

Vash added, "Tally ho, and away we go!"

A few miles later, Vash said with thoughtful emotion, "It feels good to be back on the road and taste freedom again, my brothers."

The cold, uncomfortable miles rattled by.

Damian and Vash downed Dexedrine to stay awake, and smoked half of the first joint.

After two hits, Vash said, "Damian, this shit is excellent. You and I smoked two tokes each, and I am seriously in another reality."

Damian said, "I am curious. Open the joint and see what is inside."

Vash studied the situation for a few minutes, and peeled back the 1.5 yellow banana papers. He sniffed the joint, studied the paper, and said, "This has hashish mixed with Thai sticks. No wonder we are ripped."

Vash's eyes got big as he studied the joint. "This is real stuff. Look how they fold over the tip and twist the second roll of paper underneath the top roll." He looked at Damian seriously. "This is jungle-made stuff. I mean this is straight off the boat or plane from the jungle in Thailand. This is real shit, Damian. The only logical way to get it into the U.S. is through the military. Are there military installations nearby?"

"What are you talking about? Jungle-made Thai sticks, in Detroit, in the WINTER? R-E-A-L-L-Y!"

Vash responded, "Yes, R-E-A-L-L-Y!"

"Okay," Damian said, "this could get interesting."

"Who was that woman and why us?"

Damian replied, "It could be coincidental, or it could be a message. What message?"

Vash said, "Okay, logically, it could be random, but if it was random, then why us, and why at that diner?"

Damian shook his head. "It was not random."

Vash continued. "If it was a message, then from whom and why, and what is the message?"

"Okay, brilliant one, what is the answer?"

Vash replied, "I have no idea. Worrying about it could make a crazy man go insane."

Damian said thoughtfully, "Not worrying does not solve issues, Vash. Thinking solves issues. We have to do a complete analysis and think 360 degrees again. Use our brains, not our brawn."

Vash added philosophically, "The answer may appear in the future."

"Yes, and I want to know all the answers before the future arrives, not after the future has passed."

They drove on in deep thought.

George was snoring in the backseat.

Damian broke the silence a few hours later, saying, "Vash, I must brief you on the instructions from Attorney Win Grain. There have been many changes in plans."

Vash smiled sarcastically. "Please tell me what others already know."

Damian explained, "For now, you are out on bail, and must report to the Bureau of Prisons in thirty to forty-five days. Grain convinced the courts to allow you to finish school. Besides, it takes the Bureau of Prisons that long to find you a bed and decide where they are going to lock up your skinny ass. Immigration has your passport and visa, to prevent you from becoming a flight risk."

Vash said angrily, "Well, screw them and the fucking horses they rode their sorry, fat, stinking asses on. How do you say it in American movies? I ain't doing any stinking hard time in the joint for anybody."

"Win and I know that. You are going to Canada in a pickup truck over the back roads. Jason has a dude ranch in Montana, near the border. In twenty-seven days from now, we meet at his place. From there, you will be the guest of the underground transportation system, used by draft dodgers and pot dealers to escape the U.S. law."

Vash looked elated and worried.

Damian continued. "In Vancouver, you will be connected with Grain's 'cousin,' who will escort you to an Indian-crewed and India-bound ship. Ship time is about six to eight weeks. You will be part of the crew and have uniforms and papers. In India, you are on your own."

Vash asked, surprised, "Who arranged all this?"

"The underground railroad and Indian ship was Grain's. The dude ranch was Lori's idea. We put the parts and pieces together to formulate Vash's Freedom Plan."

Vash said, "Grain has many interests, and he is the best unknown attorney in the business. As an immigration attorney, he also arranges quiet escapes out of the country. He knows his way around obstacles. Damian, listen to me on this: Never get on Grain's bad side. He is the godfather of the underground business world. He is very brilliant and very dangerous. You will understand.

"You will love his wife. She is cute and even more cunning. She will seduce you with her charms as she takes you to your grave if she wishes. Together, they are very sweet, loving, and extremely clever. They are the nicest, smartest, and most dangerous people on planet earth. Trust me on this, Brother Damian. Trust me. This is one family you always want as your friend. Smart people would never contemplate an alternative."

Damian said, "I agree he is smart and sly. No other attorney and business partner could have arranged your freedom, and secured our business interests, all at the same time."

"Yes, I am pretty lucky. I call it providence. Actually, we are all pretty lucky. Somehow things are managing to work out, even when we hit stone walls and large obstacles. We collectively search for ways around problems, and so far we are still free."

Damian turned on the radio as the weatherman announced a large snowstorm heading in their direction. The weatherman stated, "The roads may be closed depending on the wind directions and severity of the snow. The National Weather Service is predicting up to eleven-foot snowdrifts and fifty-miles-per-hour winds, and it is advised to take cover in a warm, secure building until the weather emergency passes."

"Great," Damian said sarcastically to Vash and George. "What a wonderful combination. We have no other choice than to trust this old bucket of rust to get us to Iowa City. Might as well accept reality and finish the first Thai stick."

The three amigos drove on in high silence.

George stretched out and continued his nap.

More miles down the road, Damian noticed a car following them. The vehicle stayed back far enough so Damian could not make out what type of car or their intentions. When he switched lanes, the other driver switched lanes. It was a message.

"Hey, Vash. Wake up, dude. We have a tail."

"Oh shit. Where is the stash, Damian?"

"The books are in the trunk. Put the travel stuff under George's blanket. The cops are not going to search a dog, especially a cranky dog that just woke up."

Vash said, "It could be the police. It could be Immigration. On the other hand, it could be a setup. You never know in this business."

About ten miles down the road, Damian looked up in the mirror and saw flashing lights. "Okay. Here we go. Let's see what this is about."

"Oh shit, Immigration changed their minds, and now we are fugitives. I hope we do not go to prison for drugs."

Damian pulled the car over and they sat in the car, trying to look as normal as possible.

The officer sat in the police car behind them for a long ten minutes.

Vash said nervously, "Why is he just sitting there and not getting out? I do not understand your American police and laws."

Damian replied, "This is scaring me too. I have no idea what is actually happening. Stay calm and play it cool. Show respect."

The officer cautiously approached the car. He pointed a large, powerful flashlight into Damian, Vash, and George's eyes. George sat up, growling and daring the officer to try any stuff.

Damian and Vash smiled, trying to look coherent.

The officer, in a very businesslike manner, said, "May I have your license and registration please?"

Damian replied politely, "Yes sir." He handed the requested documents to the police officer.

The officer walked around the car chuckling to himself. He walked back to Damian and said, "I pulled you over because the car has broken lights, bad tires, your exhaust is belching smoke, and you are missing a muffler. This car is a deathtrap waiting to happen."

Damian replied apologetically, "We are trying to make it to my mother's house in Iowa City, if this piece of junk makes it."

The officer smiled. "You should rest for the night, because your eyes are bloodshot and not dilating correctly."

I wonder why? Damian thought. "We are exhausted and have been on the road for a long time."

The officer smiled. "Yes, I know." He returned the license and registration to Damian. "Thank you, gentlemen. You are free to go."

The officer tipped his hat, returned to his cruiser, and drove away.

Damian said, "The officer said he knew we had been on the road for a long time. Just a thought, I wonder if the Feds have been tracking us."

Vash said, "Hmm. That is always possible."

"I am sure the cop knew we were stoned," Damian added.

"We were lucky, Damian and George. I will take this as a good omen for the future. The prophets are smiling upon us."

The trio traveled in silence for a few more hours, stopping only for fuel, food, and to relieve kidneys.

Damian broke the silence. "Vash, since we are getting closer to Iowa City, let me tell you about my mother and my early childhood. This might explain things, and deepen our bond and trust.

"My mother, Maya Katz Garcia, is a unique person. You can call her Maya, or Moms, whichever you please. We will be staying at her house, which is way out in the country, off a dirt road, near a cattle and horse auction sales place."

Vash said excitedly, "You mean I am going to see real American cowboys, like in the movies?"

Damian smiled. "Maybe. It depends on when they have livestock auctions. Remember, we have O/H business to do at the university, Vash."

"I know that. It is not often that an Indian dude sees an American cowboy ranch."

"You will in twenty-six days, when I drive you to Jason's dude ranch in northern Montana. Now that truly is in the country!" Damian continued. "My mother drove an old VW bus from New York City to Iowa City, to finish her doctorate in Anthropology. Mom wanted to live in a small town where she could breathe fresh air and not lock doors."

"Now I understand why we are driving from New York to Iowa in this broken-down contraption you actually call a car." Vash smiled. "The apple does not fall far from the tree, Mr. Garcia. You have an interesting family, Damian." Vash chuckled.

"Just wait. It gets more interesting." Damian paused and said, "Vash, do we have another fat Thai stick?"

Vash smiled and reached under the seat. They shared the slow-burning Thai stick, blowing smoke into George's mouth and nose.

George Carlin Dog was happy and stoned.

The humans were orbiting earth in parallel realities.

Morgan was not a happy vehicle and let the human world know of his discomforts. Damian tried to ignore the warning noises, because they had to make it to Iowa City. There simply were no other choices.

Damian continued. "My mother is German-Jewish and lived through Hitler, the anti-Jewish sentiment, and World War Two. As a child, she was smuggled from Germany to London during the Nazi occupation."

Vash listened attentively.

George snored happily.

Damian continued. "During the London bombings, the children were smuggled by ship to Canada. Eventually, Mom found her way to New York City, because that is where the jobs were. She went to art school and, decades later, chose Anthropology."

Vash said, "American families are complicated. Indian families are simple to understand."

Damian chuckled. "Just wait, Vash. It gets more complicated."

Vash said, "I need to stop and pee on the side of the road. That damn coffee is talking to me."

George woke up, saying, "Hello, humans, I got to pee also. Hurry up and pull this damn car off the road."

Vash said, "Sorry, Damian, I am not allowed to drive in your country. Immigration took my international driver's license when they took my passport and visa. Otherwise I would offer to drive. Except you Americans drive on the left-hand side of the road. The rest of the civilized world drives on the right side." Vash enjoyed chuckling at his own jokes.

The three amigos climbed back into dying Morgan.

Damian picked up the narrative. "Mom met my father, Enrique Garcia, at a Teamsters' labor union rally, where as she told it, he gave a fiery speech about workers' rights. He was a union shop steward and worked as a bus mechanic for the City of New York Transit Authority. They lived together, struggling to make ends meet.

"I hardly knew my father. The joke was that I was a product of a late Saturday night mistake. An oops baby, they called me. They forgot to get legally married, so I guess I am also a bastard child."

Damian continued. "My father moved the small dysfunctional family to Puerto Rico when I was a baby. I am told we lived in an old cottage, on a mountainside. We had well water and grew food or something like that. It was a very rural lifestyle with no medical care. My mother moved back to New York City when I was about four. My father stayed in Puerto Rico."

Vash said, "Would you prefer Thai sticks or O/H, Mr. Garcia?"

Damian replied in a mockingly formal tone, "Why, Mr. Gupta, I do believe some O/H might be in order."

"An excellent choice, Mr. Garcia. Should I consult with our director of security operations?"

"No," Damian said with a straight face. "Let sleeping dogs lie."

Damian and Vash started laughing hysterically.

George woke up scratching his neck.

The humans and the canine filled their lungs with the sweet, succulent flavor of the finest opium-hashish product unknown to most of the world.

The Midwest would soon discover O/H.

Damian drove on in silence, listening to the loud symphony of noise from Morgan and wondering if they would actually make it to Iowa City. The heater stopped working completely, more smoke was belching from the engine, and the front wheels were vibrating. Morgan was on life support.

Vash slowly crawled out of his altered reality, reached for the cold coffee and chips. The munchies had arrived. George woke up, smelling food.

More miles and more bowls down the road, Vash said, "Damian, if you are taking me to Montana, how are we getting there? This piece-of-crap car may not make it to Iowa, let alone Montana."

Damian turned to Vash with a deer-in-the-headlights look and said, "Until this moment, I had not thought about that."

"I guess we are going to buy a vehicle in Iowa." With all the excitement of a ten-year-old boy, Vash added, "Cool. I want to buy a pickup truck like the modern-day cowboys use. That would be so cool to drive in Iowa, and then drive to Montana in a pickup truck. At least it will have heat."

"If you are cold now, wait until we drive to Montana. That, my warm-blooded Indian friend, is REALLY COLD."

"Yes, my mixed breed spic friend, but I will buy proper clothing and boots for the weather. I will be prepared. I am not prepared now, and that is why you have a frozen Indian in this damn car."

Damian paused and finally said, "You know how ridiculous this is?"

Vash looked confused. "What is?"

"We are driving in this absolute crap car to my mother's house in Iowa, with a goofy dog, in the middle of the freaking Midwest winter, and in a blizzard. We are carrying enough cash and stash to have us all do life in prison. I just bailed your sorry ass out of jail in Detroit, and I really do not like cops or the law." Damian smiled. "And one more thing. Shortly, you will become an international fugitive outlaw. And I will be aiding a fugitive to escape." He chuckled. "Now you understand what is so funny? You, my good friend Vash, are an international drug dealer, who in twenty-six days will be smuggled over the Canadian border, and then on a ship to India. Vash, my friend, you are a criminal!"

Vash replied, "And you, my dear friend, are also a criminal. You are an international drug dealer and money launderer. Welcome to the wonderful world of international crime. We will both do a zillion years in prison if we are arrested. Alternatively, we will all make a zillion dollars and do lasting social good with our money. I prefer the latter alternative."

"True that."

The three friends drove on, each in their own outer orbits.

Vash said through chattering teeth, "Pray to your gods and ask them to make Morgan arrive in Mom's driveway in Iowa. Just please get us there. Then we can buy an American cowboy pickup truck."

Damian replied with a sigh. "Yes, Vash. We will buy your American cowboy pickup truck just like you want."

Vash smiled. "Cool. I am good with that. Damian, you now have the family you never had as a child growing up. It is our close O/H family business enterprise. If we are lucky, we will marry the loves of our lives, and raise families, and have grandchildren at our knees."

Damian added, "Or something like that."

"And we can call the global company O/H Inc."

And that is how O/H Incorporated was born.

The trio was heading directly into the fifty-mile-per-hour winds and blizzard conditions. Morgan was gasping. About 100 miles from Iowa City, the engine started making serious knocking noises and losing more power.

Damian pleaded, "Please, Morgan, not here, not now, and not at three a.m. in a freezing blizzard in the middle of frozen nowhere."

He drove into the only service station open and cautiously got out of the car to survey the scene. Morgan had a severe engine oil leak. Oil was dripping on the snow-covered ground, like Hansel and Gretel and the breadcrumbs.

Vash and George climbed out of the car to pee.

Damian said to Vash, "I need to pour more thick, heavy oil, like gear oil. Maybe we can make it. Of course, when we shut the engine off, the oil will freeze until next spring."

Vash said through chattering teeth, "We have no choice. We cannot stay here. The only option is to keep going, gentlemen."

The gas station had a coffee shop that sold pancakes and eggs all day. The three brothers were cold and hungry. Breakfast was an excellent idea.

Damian said, "Let me walk over to the coffee shop and check it out."

"Why, Damian? I am hungry and so is Sir George."

"True that. We are in the middle of frozen nowhere. We need to be careful, and not attract attention."

"What do you mean, not attract attention, Damian?"

"What I mean is we are in a part of the country that does not see too many half-frozen, dark-skinned Indians, with a half-baked spic and a goofy-looking hound dog. We do not need the cops, and we do not need to get shot. We are easy to spot and track. Now do you understand, my brother?"

Vash was not happy, and fell into his own thoughts. Finally he said, "America is a racist country, Damian. Why should it matter what we look like? We are not criminals."

"Technically and legally, we actually ARE major criminals. We are drug dealers, and we are carrying, which means prison. At least we are not murderers and we don't do gangster stuff. And yes, America is a racist country."

"Okay, Damian. I will get off my soapbox. This is business, not race relations."

Damian replied, "Please stay with the car and keep the engine running. I am going to check out the coffee shop."

He walked into the coffee shop casually. He looked around and ordered four large coffees and eight breakfast sandwiches to go. As Damian was waiting for the order, he noticed a group of people in the corner. They smelled like the law.

Damian paid for the order, smiled, and said, "Thank you ma'am."

As casually as he had walked into the coffee shop, he slipped out. He motioned to Vash and George to get in the car.

The group departed quietly and quickly.

After a few miles Damian said, "That joint had the law times four in there. We would have been busted if they saw you. I don't think they noticed me, which is really good." In his best butler imitation, he added, "Breakfast is served, gentlemen. We have coffee and breakfast sandwiches for all."

Damian looked in the mirrors, and Vash turned around.

Vash said, "I do not think they are following us. We are the only assholes driving on the road in this weather, and in this kind of car."

Damian replied, "True that, my brother."

The last stretch was frozen agony. Pouring vital fluids into Morgan did help delay the inevitable. The fastest Damian could get Morgan to go was thirty miles per hour, and that was decreasing.

Vash smiled and said jokingly, "How many more miles to Grandma's house, like in Little Red Riding Hood?"

"Why, Mr. Fox, I do not know, because I have no clue where we got gas. I would guess less than a hundred miles, maybe sixty miles."

"Is it time for a re-light, gentlemen?"

"Speaking for myself and Sir George, I would say that is an excellent suggestion, Don Vash."

"May I recommend Thai sticks?"

Damian replied, smiling, "An outstanding choice, sir."

The trio drifted off into three separate time and space environments. George went back to sleep and had dog dreams. The furious winds and high snowdrifts made visibility difficult. Morgan was struggling, and the mammals were freezing.

In the morning, Damian pulled into Mom's driveway. They were hungry, stoned, exhausted, dirty, and thankful to be alive and not in jail.

Welcome to Iowa

Morgan expired in a series of small explosions in the rear driveway of Maya Garcia's house in rural Iowa. The group had made it, and Morgan had fulfilled his promise to deliver the crew to Mom's house alive.

George bounded out of the car and frolicked in the snow like a puppy. He needed room to run and stretch his legs. George and Damian had been living in small motel rooms and in a stinky car for too many days.

Vash had been living in jail.

Damian and Vash slept like logs until early afternoon, and when they woke up, the fireplace was blazing. Over French toast, honey, fruit, and strong Jamaican coffee, Maya asked about their adventures.

Damian introduced Vash and George to Maya.

Vash said, "Can I call you Moms?"

Maya replied, "Yes, of course. I like that name, Moms."

Damian said, "This is George Carlin Dog. He found me one day in front of the apartment building we share. George is our director of security, and in charge of most things human."

Maya said, "You all must drink real milk, straight from the goats. It tastes better than anything you will ever buy in the store in New York."

Vash tasted the creamy milk and exclaimed, "Wow. This is great. I love it. Thank you, Moms."

Vash, Damian, and George ate heartily and drank fresh goat milk.

Maya sat back and watched. "When was the last time you men had a real meal?"

Vash said between mouthfuls, "It feels like years ago." He added, sipping coffee, "Prison food sucks. I have no idea how one eats that crap. I am a vegetarian and all they served was fat, salt, and grease. It was horrible!"

Maya smiled. "I have a water pipe if you have the stuff, gentlemen."

Vash replied, "Coming right up, Moms."

The four amigos were orbiting earth's mid orbits.

Maya chuckled. "You mean that car that blew up in my driveway brought you from New York? And you guys actually lived to tell about it? That is amazing."

Vash said to Maya, "Your son has issues. He is also pretty much of an asshole."

Maya laughed. "Tell me about. Try raising this kid yourself."

Vash said, "He is the most complete asshole you will ever meet, but he is a nice asshole, and has been a really good friend and loyal brother. For these gifts I am very grateful. Otherwise, he is totally insane and probably should be institutionalized."

Maya chuckled and rolled her eyes. She said, "Damian is way too crazy to be institutionalized!"

Damian laughed. "You found me out again, Vash. I am crazy like a fox, and you are an even crazier fox than me."

Maya laughed. "Okay, you are both completely nuts. Make that all three of you are completely nuts. Sorry, George, but I think the humans under your control need some canine intervention."

George lifted his sleepy head as if to say, "That's easy for you to say. Try living with these guys!"

Maya finally said, "Let me get this straight. Damian is going to drive you to Montana. From Montana, Vash will connect with the underground in Canada, and go to Vancouver. From Vancouver, Vash will travel by Indian ship, as a crew member, and then home to the mountains of northern India."

Damian said, "And all these connections were stitched together by Attorney Grain, with help from Lori."

Maya continued. "And the Montana rancher is an old lover of Lori's? Do I have this correct?"

"Yes," said Damian.

Maya said quietly, "Oh good. I was just checking." She smiled. "Really! I am proud of you guys. You have the true entrepreneurial spirit, attitude, and fortitude that make a mom proud. Welcome to the slightly dysfunctional Garcia family."

Vash replied with tears in his eyes, "Thank you very much, Moms. You have no idea what that means to me. We are all family. And yes, we are all slightly dysfunctional, completely nuts, and a little brilliant." He said quietly, "I cannot do prison, Moms. The Feds want me to do ten to twenty years in prison, and prison is not an option. Look at me. I am a skinny, dark-skinned Indian man. The boys in the hood would love my tight ass. So you see, escape IS my only option!"

Maya replied, "Vash, I totally understand. How can we help you?"

"Wish me well crossing the border and arriving in India."

Damian said, "We also have business to do in Iowa before Vash leaves. Time is short and we have to cram in a lot of stuff before Montana. Iowa will be a prototype. The results of the prototype will be incorporated into the Operational Procedures, as part of the investor-franchisee agreements."

Maya said calmly, "Okay, I am good with your decisions. I can help. You will need to buy a good vehicle to get to Montana and back home. That piece of shit is dead. I will have someone tow it away."

Vash said gleefully, "I want a white pickup truck, like the cowboys have in the movies."

Maya laughed. "Okay, cowboy Vash, I just happen to know where such a truck might be. I can talk to her and see if she wants to sell it."

Vash said, "Did you say 'her'?"

Maya smiled. "I did. The Spencer sisters, Susan and Sky. Professor Steven Spencer owns 320 acres of fertile farmland a few miles outside of town. The property sits on a hill. They can watch the roads in the valley. Oh, by the way, we are going to their party on New Year's Eve, and you will meet the women."

Damian and Vash looked at each other and smiled broadly.

Vash said, smiling, "That sounds like fun. I would like a nice woman to keep me warm until I leave."

Damian replied, "I agree, my brother."

Maya said thoughtfully, "This smuggling and running from the law can be a little dangerous. Trusting people is the hardest part. Be very careful, and trust no one completely.

"Tell me about your business plans. Maybe I can help you meet new friends. Sometimes having a third party, who has not been directly involved, might help you to see things from a different angle."

Vash turned to Damian and said, "It sounds like Damian's 360-degree perspectives. Damian always says to look at something from all 360 degrees, and you will better understand all viewpoints."

"Hmm, that does make sense, Damian," Maya said.

"Okay, I can tell my side and Damian can tell the rest," Vash said. "I have a large family back home in northern India. We have farms and grow crops, including some of the finest marijuana and opium. Most of the world does not know of our exquisite cannabis. Opium, hashish, and cannabis are part of our culture and have been used as commodities for centuries. India has always been a nation of merchants and traders.

"The raw materials are relatively cheap. What are not cheap and a little dangerous are the transportation systems. In modern times, moving goods is more dangerous and more expensive. Bribes and strong willpower are the currencies used to smooth the wheels. It can get tricky, and very complicated.

"We only transport quantities of the highest grades of opium and hash. This is exquisite stuff. Ours is clean and the finest. I have a brother who has a bookshop in London, and they ship heavy textbooks to colleges worldwide. It makes perfect sense to have textbooks mailed to graduate students. The products are compressed into the covers of the textbooks, and delivered by the post office to an address near you!"

Vash paused, sipping his coffee.

George went back to sleep.

Maya smiled. "I love the idea that the government is cooperating with your venture. There is something sinister and sweet in that. The system will work for smaller orders, such as a few pounds, maybe a couple of kilos. Your exposure increases, the more you use the post office. I would use couriers myself. You will need multiple systems to transport quantities. Quantity and quality are what people want, and that is where the money is."

Vash replied, "Yes, I am aware of these supply chain issues. So far it is working. We have couriers posing as college students traveling from India to the U.S., with acceptance letters. They carry boxes of heavy college texts through customs with no problems. The cash money goes back to India the same way. College students returning home to India on holiday are just as useful as those going to America, Canada, and worldwide. If you think about it, the system is sweet."

He continued. "Let me ask you a question, please. Think about this: How many thousands of college students travel worldwide? We plan our shipments and money returns coinciding with the semesters at the various universities. Customs are inundated with students carrying books, so it is virtually impossible for them to check everything. Our couriers can play their parts perfectly as most good actors should.

"Moms, let me explain what your son and I have developed. We could not have achieved any of this without the loyalty and brains of Marguerite, Howard, Roger, Lori, and of course George. The group developed a new product previously unknown. The product is a combination of 25% opium to 75% hashish. The hashish is top grade, and varies from deep rich purple to dark green. The opium varies from large crystals to a moist, sticky paste like warm taffy. The group named the product O/H, which tells the world what it is and creates brand identity. The family created a new product, and created a market for the new product. Pretty neat?"

Maya said in awe, "Yes, gentlemen, I would have to agree."

Vash continued. "We also created the manufacturing and packaging processes for each product variation, using unique methods our resident chemist, Roger, invented."

Damian added, "We are enjoying our O/H product now."

Maya said with a big smile, "I am sold."

Damian said, "Let me explain the business part, because this is cool. Howard created the investor-franchisee system. Each I-F has invested as a franchisee with a designated territory. They enjoy control of all market segments within their franchise area. And the funny thing is, we are doing all this without having one single employee. No one works for us. We work for the investors, and we are investors too."

Vash said, "Believe me, there are no drug dealers who operate the way we do. The Feds are looking for brawn and muscle. We have brains."

Maya said jokingly, "There are no international drug smugglers who are also PhD graduate students, either."

Vash, Damian, and Maya laughed at this realization. George opened his eyes to see what was happening, and went back to his nap.

Maya said, "And who are Marguerite and Lori?"

Vash said, "Marguerite is with me, and Lori is with Damian."

Maya said to Damian, in her best fake Yiddish accent, "So this Lori woman, do you like her?"

Damian replied reluctantly, "Yes, Mom, I do like her very much, but we will see. There are things that have to be worked out before it can be a forever relationship. It may work; it may not work. Time will tell."

"Like maybe grandchildren? It would be nice for you to have what you never had growing up, and that is a stable family."

Damian smiled. "It would be nice to have a family. Well, actually, we do have a family, Mom. The O/H family is about personal relationships and business relationships."

Maya said in her best theatrical New York Yiddish accent, "And the grandchildren, so when am I going to get grandkids? You know I am not getting any younger, and neither are you! Oy vey, what am I going to do with you?"

Damian looked exasperated. "Mom, I will keep you posted."

Vash smiled and wisely kept his mouth shut.

A few moments later, the mother-son-grandchildren friction abated.

Vash said, "I have had similar discussions with my mother about marriage and grandchildren and family name, and all that pressure. I smile and do whatever I choose to do. It will happen, or it will not happen. Forcing something to happen is not going to make it happen. So let things just move along their chosen paths."

Damian said directly, "We have a business to run, Vash!"

Maya said, "It is New Year's Eve, and the first day of 1973 is only a few hours away. The Spencer party will be fun and good for business. I told Professor Steven Spencer about your business enterprise. Steve is impressed, and the sisters are lovely. You'll understand. Unless, of course, Lori would mind." Maya smiled sarcastically.

Damian smirked. "You have always been very subtle."

Maya continued. "I think your products are ready for distribution, and I believe the Spencer family can help. Large extended farm families have traditions of loyalty."

Vash said, "Yes, I understand the extended family and loyalty thing. It is the same in my country also."

Maya said, "When the sun goes down, the party starts at the professor's house. The farmhouse is on top of a hill overlooking a pasture. It is beautiful, quiet, and private. No police will bother the festivities. Bring a few books to show the folks the products."

Damian said, "I need to make a phone call to Attorney Grain to check in and see what is happening."

Damian gave Grain Maya's number just in case.

Grain ended the conversation, saying, "Did you enjoy the surprise?"

The conversation lasted 47 seconds.

Damian said, "Grain said everything is good, no problems yet, and we are systems go for Montana. He wants us to check back tomorrow. And he asked about the Thai sticks."

Vash replied, "Really! That explains it. Grain was letting us know he was watching us. Cool move on his part."

Maya, Damian, Vash, and George climbed into Maya's VW bus and drove to the farmhouse party. On the way, Maya said, "The party is at the house of the dean of the Anthropology Department. His students call him Professor Spencer, and his friends call him Steven. I call him Steve. He calls me Maya." Maya smiled. "If you get my meaning."

The Spencer farm was a large working farm that commanded an excellent view of the valley below.

Daughters Susan and Sky were delicious, as Damian and Vash would soon discover.

Maya explained how things worked. "Different rooms are for different events. Drugs are available in various rooms depending on what you wish. Sex is where it happens."

Maya quietly disappeared. Damian and Vash looked at each other and decided they might as well enjoy the party. Before the month ended, they would be in Montana, and Vash would be sailing to India.

George was the life of the party.

A few hours later Vash and Damian stepped outside on a back porch.

Vash said, giggling, "Man, this party is a blast. I am having so much fun. They don't party like this in India."

Damian said, "This is better than the wild parties I used to go to in my younger days. There is everything here and anybody you want, with no questions asked." He stopped and looked straight ahead. "Damn, they are sweet."

Vash turned around and smiled.

Two beautiful women walked up to Damian and Vash. They smiled kindly and introduced themselves. "We are the Spencer sisters. I am Susan, and the cute one is Sky, in case you were not sure."

Vash smiled. "And this goofy-looking fellow is Damian, and I am Vash, in case you were not sure."

The sisters smiled.

Sky said to Vash, "It is my pleasure to meet both of you gentlemen. George is the life of the party. We have heard about your travels from New York to Detroit and then Iowa."

Susan said, "Maya said that car you drove was a piece of crap."

Vash said, "True, but Morgan did get us to Mom's house. It blew up in her driveway, but at least it got our sorry frozen asses to Iowa."

Vash, Damian, Susan, and Sky talked and laughed for a while.

Susan said, "It is cold. I suggest we go the guesthouse. We can have our own party."

Vash smiled broadly. "Absolutely." He turned to Damian. "I love it when women come right out and say what is on their minds. In India, women are much more repressed."

Damian smiled. "How can a man resist the temptations of two beautiful women?"

The guesthouse featured two bedrooms, an open kitchen, and a living room with a warm fireplace and comfortable seating.

After everyone was seated in the guesthouse, Susan brought out hot cocoa and pastries on a tray. Sky offered the ceremonial four-stemmed, double-chambered bong. Susan poured four ounces of bourbon and filled the rest of the chamber with crushed ice.

Sky said, "When you smoke the herb of your choice, the bourbon evaporates and adds flavor, while the crushed ice cools it down. This way you do not choke because you are inhaling iced bourbon-flavored product."

Susan said, "Our dad has heard about your O/H business and feels it would be a wise Spencer family investment."

Sky smiled at Vash and said, "We would like to study the product."

Vash brought out a sample from one side of a book.

Sky examined the product, using a small magnifying glass to study the fibers and blending. "Interesting. I can see the swirl of the two products. The O/H is marbled, moist, and fresh. The marbling is the combination of the opium and hashish."

She passed the sample to Susan.

Susan added, "It smells sweet."

Vash cut small slivers of O/H with a razor blade and placed the slices in the bowl. He repeated the process, but altered the angle of each cut. This method distributed the product evenly, allowed air circulation, and added to the taste and medicinal effects.

Damian lit a wooden match until the wood burned evenly. He lightly singed the top of the sliced O/H pyramid in the bowl. All four participants inhaled deeply and slowly. The smoke was cool and soothing.

One by one, each person slowly exhaled into George's nose and mouth. George would lap up the extra smoke in the air.

Sky finally broke the silence and said, "Wow! This is great. It tastes sweet, goes down smooth, and takes off nicely."

Vash said, "You sound like a beer commercial jingle."

Susan said, "Excellent, and very tasty. This is going to be a huge hit."

The five amigos drifted just within earth's outer gravitational pull. It would take awhile for the slow descent into earth's mid-range orbits.

George found his way to whoever would give him a good belly rub.

The next hours were enjoyed having exquisite sex and smoking more O/H. Happy overindulgence might be an appropriate term.

Late the next afternoon, the bodies slowly started to stir out of their cocoons. Damian and Susan were at the kitchen table ingesting coffee.

Damian said, "That was some serious herbal product. The sex was delicious, ma'am. You farm girls sure know how to please a man."

Susan smiled. "Yes, we do . . . "

Vash and Sky stumbled in, looking dazed and confused.

Susan said, "Good afternoon, my lady and lord."

Sky gazed at Susan and said in a foggy voice, "Good something."

She ingested half a cup of coffee. Vash looked bewildered.

Susan turned to Vash and said in a cheerful tone, "It is the first day of 1973. How did you guys sleep last night?"

Sky smiled. "What sleep? We fucked our brains out. Is that okay with you, sis?" she added mockingly.

"I am so glad we are well laid," Susan said with a smirk.

"I will second that, sis. These New Yorkers are so much better than the local farm boys," Sky said with a smile of satisfaction.

George came into the kitchen to see what was happening.

A few minutes later Maya and Professor Spencer came downstairs and joined the group.

Susan and Sky both said, "Good afternoon, Dad and Maya."

Vash said cheerfully, "It is the first day of 1973. This is the first day of a new life for all of us, in whatever direction life directs or we choose."

Maya said, "Steve and I keep our relationship quiet. I did tell you, in my own way, but maybe you were not listening, Damian. I would have told you earlier, but how was I supposed to know you and Vash would shack up with Steve's daughters?"

"And how were we supposed to know that you were shacked up with their father?"

"We try to keep our private life, well, private. This is a large university town with a small-town mentality. It is bad politics for the chairman of the department to have an affair with a PhD student."

"Maybe this will work out to be a very good thing for all of us," Damian said.

Damian, Susan, Vash, Sky, George, Maya, and Steve sat at the table drinking coffee and munching food. George was enjoying his afternoon breakfast.

Professor Steven Spencer said, "I would like to talk about the future direction of the O/H business. I intend to have a vested interest, and my family as investors must understand the details of the operations before an investment can be made. I am interested in the financial aspects from an investor-franchisee position. I have a large family, as you understand, and they are interested in specific markets within a territory.

"My daughters tell me the product is excellent and the profit potentials are extremely excellent. I like excellent," he added with a smile.

Susan said, "Father, I believe a wake and bake is in order."

Professor Spencer replied, "Excellent idea."

Vash looked confused.

Sky said, "What wake and bake means is smoking really great stuff and having strong Turkish coffee and pastries. So as you wake up from the Turkish coffee, you are baking from the Indian opium-hashish product."

Vash chuckled. "Wake and bake. I like that." He directed the conversation back to business. "Essentially it goes like this. The investor-franchisee pays a unit price fee for the product delivered, be it pounds or kilos. We can also ship opium and hashish separately in bulk quantities. In that scenario, the I-F is responsible for the manufacturing and packaging, adhering to strict operational procedures and standards. This is the lowest cost, highest profit margin method to operate, and gives the greatest flexibility to control your markets.

"The product will be in demand, and the profit margins will soar. Most likely, there will never be any serious competition. We own the product category completely. My family controls the supply chain, and Damian operates in the United States and Canada."

Damian added, "We would like to use Iowa as a test market prototype, and apply what we learn as the basis for future marketing development and distribution systems. Our current price is $30 per gram wholesale. The startup cost is reasonable. The street prices will soar, but currently, we are not hearing of any push back at $60 and more per gram."

Professor Spencer said, "Excellent. I will make arrangements on my end, and Vash and Damian will take care of the rest."

Vash said randomly, "You know what we really need is an American pickup truck. Like the cowboys drive in the movies."

Sky smiled sweetly. "I have a cowboy pickup truck for you, Vash. It will get you and Damian to Montana and back to Iowa."

Vash smiled, excited. "Really. Can we check it out?"

"It is in the barn," Sky replied.

Damian studied the vehicle carefully. "We are talking cowboy pickup truck, Vash. Here is your dream vehicle, sir." He walked around the vehicle, studying it thoroughly.

Vash walked around the vehicle, admiring it thoroughly.

Damian said, thinking aloud, "White truck blends with the snow, making it harder to outline from a distance. Excellent tires, heavy suspension, hard springs are good for weight distribution, an AM radio, and vinyl green seats. It has a solid engine, with no visible leaks. The truck has low mileage and is very nice."

Vash burst out, "SOLD. We will take it. Okay. Damian will pay Sky for the truck, and I will ride around as a passenger." He smiled.

Damian said, "I will buy it, Sky. Can we keep your license plates and registration on the vehicle until after Montana? I do not want my name to pop up on some government form."

"Sure, no problem. I understand completely."

Vash was ecstatic over his American cowboy pickup truck.

A prototype business model had to be developed, and time was short.

Damian checked in with Grain on a regular basis, and it appeared that things were quiet.

After a few days of camping out, Maya said, "Gentlemen, I love you all, but this house is too small for everyone."

Damian replied, "Yes, we know, Mom. Vash is leaving in less than two weeks. Do you have any ideas?"

"Funny you should ask. I have a friend who wants to leave as soon as he can sell his mobile home."

Vash laughed hysterically. "You are going to be trailer trash, like rednecks and hillbillies. Oh, that is too funny." He was having a great time.

Maya was not amused. "Seriously, it is nice. It has two bedrooms, a nice kitchen, and a comfortable living room, with a carport for parking. It is really close to school. It sits on a hill, which means you can see who is coming up the driveway. Security is a consideration in your line of work, Damian."

They climbed into Maya's VW bus and visited the property. It was better than she described. It was perfect.

The housing issue was resolved. Damian and George were the proud owners of their first piece of physical real estate. They actually owned their own home!

Damian said, "George, old man, we actually own a home. Well, okay, a two-bedroom mobile home; some people may call it a trailer. For the first time in my life, ladies, and gentlemen, Damian Garcia actually owns a home!"

Vash smiled and said, "Wow. That is so cool."

Damian owned the mobile home in Hillside Park. It measured 14 x 60. The lot included a driveway with a carport and a screened-in side porch, perfect for watching the world. Damian paid $35 per month lot rent to Hillside Park, plus about $60 per month for all the utilities.

Time had moved at warp speed, considering that a few weeks ago they were doing the Immigration escape dance.

Damian smiled to himself. *I will paint, read, work, smoke hash, and make cash. Life will be good.*

Vash order 20 kilos or 44 pounds from Apartment 3A, and the books arrived five days later by U.S. mail.

Damian and Vash would need enough product and cash to pay for events, those anticipated and those that just happen. It was a long way from Montana to northern India.

Over the next weeks, business increased substantially. The Spencer Group proved instrumental in making things happen, and the profit potentials were becoming obvious to all involved. PhD doctoral candidates Susan and Sky Spencer directed the daily operations of their network, and things were going well. O/H was a definite hit and had unlimited potential.

A few days later, Damian said, "Vash, my brother from a different mother, it is time to mobilize for Montana to India, and freedom for you."

"I know, Damian. Let me spend some quality time with Sky and screw my brains out. I am going to be sitting in the middle of the ocean for eight weeks, in a large piece of rusted metal before I get home to India."

Damian smiled. "Brother, screw until your dick falls off. We leave at midnight. I have it all mapped out. I will call Grain before we leave, to make sure we are systems go. Grain will contact Jason so he knows when to expect us. The rest is a tight dance."

"Is my pickup truck ready for the trip?"

Damian saluted as he reported in a drill sergeant's voice, "Sir, yes sir! Don Vash, the pickup is fully serviced, and the gas tanks are full. Sir!" He laughed. "We have an extra gas tank just in case. George will stay at Mom's house. He will love racing around in the snow. Midnight departure, my friend."

"Betsy" was the name Damian christened Vash's white cowboy pickup truck. It had a low-roofed camper top over the truck bed, and Damian placed the knapsacks and sleeping bags in the back. Under the center panel of the seat was a small locked box, which Sky had installed. Damian placed the travel O/H product inside the armrest and locked it.

Damian and Vash had purchased the needed cold weather items, and Vash had extra ship survival clothing. They were as prepared as possible for the frozen elements this time. Dying of frostbite was not on the agenda.

Vash had extra duffle bags containing books of stash and cash. In this business, money talked, and money bought security and access. Cash and stash lubricated transactions. They were prepared.

Vash was traveling as a graduate student, with false papers.

Vash and Damian departed at midnight. Damian leaned over to Vash when they had been on the road for an hour or so and said, "You look worn out, dude. Sky screwed you well, I can see."

Vash looked over and just smiled.

Damian said, "This is the plan, dude, so pay attention please. We are systems go, according to Grain. Jason has us on a clock. It is a three-day trip, but sooner is better, like maybe two and a half days. Your departure on an Indian ship has been arranged, and you are listed as a crew member. Grain is stalling the Immigration folks in Detroit. It is best if you are on that boat before the thirty days so they cannot find you. When your sorry ass is sailing the ocean blue, my sorry ass will be stuck on land and easier to find."

As the sun was rising, Damian pulled into a busy truck stop. Betsy needed gas, and the humans needed food, to pee, and to clean up for the long road trip ahead.

Feeling well fed and well caffeinated, Damian and Vash climbed back into their proud white cowboy pickup truck and continued the journey.

They consumed Dexedrine to stay awake. To calm the nerves, they smoked more bowls. This was going to be a very long trip, and they might as well be comfortable.

Vash said proudly, "Betsy is a great pickup truck, Damian. I am enjoying this trip. It is much more comfortable than Morgan." He chuckled. "This is a story to tell the grandchildren, when I am old and retired."

Damian smirked. "Maybe I will write a book about our adventures."

Damian continued the drive with the intensity of a truck driver on a tight schedule. This was a business trip, not a pleasure trip. "The more miles we cover now, the less we do tomorrow."

Vash said, "Good, because I have been doing a lot of thinking during this adventure. I would like to chill out in a comfortable motel and talk." He leaned over and said in his best Italian with a British-Indian accent, "Capice, paisano?"

As the sun was setting, Damian pulled into a medium-size town and checked into a comfortable motel across the street from a diner.

Vash and Damian cleaned up and ate well.

At the motel room, they unpacked and arranged things for Vash's ocean voyage journey to follow.

Damian said sadly, "Don Vash, my friend, this is a bittersweet time. We beat the law, at least so far. We are building a very profitable enterprise, with untold potential. Money like this can do a lot of social good. We will use our extra profits to help people and save lives, and we should be thankful for that opportunity."

Vash said, "We have every right to be proud for what we have created. It is too bad they will never do a case study in graduate schools about our business and humanitarian successes."

Damian added sadly, "I will miss you."

Vash said with tears in his eyes, "I will miss you too, my brother."

The two brothers embraced as men do.

A few moments later, they stepped back and looked at each other.

Damian said thoughtfully, "Who knows when we will ever see each other in person again. Maybe never! Maybe in forty years when we are all old and gray, with grandchildren at our knees."

"We have no choice. I am lucky, I could be doing ten to twenty years in your American prison, and you are still a free man, Damian. Count our blessings and count our sorrows. Perhaps you could come to India in a few years, when this blows over."

"*If* this blows over. I have a feeling the Feds will be following me for decades."

Vash said after a long pause, "We sure as hell had some fun, dude."

Damian smiled and replied, "Yes, we did."

Vash said, "Sky is hot. Man, can that girl screw! She has a big brain. She is doing her dissertation on something esoteric about microorganisms. I got lost when she explained it to me."

"Obviously you do not have a very big brain, Vash."

Vash replied, "Clearly not."

Damian said, "Susan is hot. I understand how one keeps warm in Iowa. Find a really hot woman, and spend the winter in bed."

Vash laughed. "True that, my brother. True that."

Damian was thinking about how life had changed in a short time. As they both slowly drifted into earth's near orbit, he said, "You know, Vash, I have been thinking about our adventures, and the short but intense history we have developed."

"Yes, it has been intense and very crazy. It will take me some time to sort this in my brain. Maybe I will take notes when I am on the ship about life in New York as a PhD graduate student, and then as a fugitive from your American justice. That might be remarkable to share with my family and grandchildren."

"Vash, since we all met a year ago, the group has gone from starving graduate students to the business developers of an international O/H enterprise."

Vash said, "Remember, my dear friend, the old adage that soft drugs lead to hard time. You are too pretty to survive in prison for very long."

Damian filled the bowl with the choicest black marbled O/H. He smiled and said in his best wine taster imitation, "It tastes great. Very sweet, with a wonderful bouquet of wild sweet rose. It has the fragrance for the nose, and a wonderful clear buzz for the brain. I highly recommend this new edition of O/H. Would you agree, Mr. Gupta?"

Vash turned to Damian and with a straight face replied, "Why, yes, Mr. Garcia. I do concur that it is of the finest quality and highest grade to arrive on your American shores since the pilgrims."

Damian and Vash burst out laughing.

When they composed themselves, Vash said, "You know, Damian, the Spencer sisters are fabulous. There is no doubt about that! They are smart, educated, and damn fine company to spend those long winter nights with. But, there is something missing."

Damian listened.

"No matter how cute and educated Sky is, I would not want to spend the rest of my life with her."

"Funny you should mention that. I was thinking the same thing about Susan when you were zoning out. I think we belong with our women back east, young man," Damian said with a twinkle in his eyes and a smile on his face.

Vash said sadly, "I agree, except I am being deported to India, and traveling there is not so easy."

"We will find a way for you and Marguerite to connect, have a family, and have those grandchildren when you retire."

Vash said, "You and Lori will make it and be happy. She needs to get off those narcotic pharmaceutical drugs and change her lifestyle."

Damian said, "I know. She knows. We will make it happen, because we feel a love for each other. At least I think we do."

Vash said finally, "Be careful, my brother. America is a rough place to be in the soft drug business. I am afraid that hard drugs will take over, and then your country will not be about peace and love anymore."

Damian said very sadly, "I believe we are rapidly slipping from the happy times to the ugly times. We are going from peace and love, to hard drugs, hard crime, and hard times."

"Maybe I can make my own small changes, and help those in need in northern India. I am just thinking out loud, Damian."

"I like your style of thinking, Vash. I agree. Maybe our futures are predestined to follow different, but similar paths, and to connect periodically in life's journeys."

Vash replied with a big happy smile on his face, "You are becoming very mystical, my American brother. I think the Indian in me is rubbing off on the New York-German-Jewish-Puerto Rican in you."

"And quite possibly the New York-German-Jewish-Puerto Rican thinking is rubbing off on the Indian in you, and then we will both prosper."

Vash lifted the pipe and said, "I'll toast to that!"

"We should call home and talk with our real women."

"You are one smart Nuevo Rican."

Damian looked puzzled.

"You know, a New York Puerto Rican! Americans are so slow! I just don't know what to do with you, Brother Damian." Vash smiled jokingly.

Vash and Damian walked to the diner and went directly to the bank of telephone booths at the far end of the restaurant. They climbed into separate booths, closed the doors, and called their women.

Damian spoke with Lori. He explained the situation, what was happening, where they were going, and things like that. Lori briefed Damian on sales and marketing figures.

"Damian, we are going to need more products. Vash being out of pocket for eight to ten weeks is going to mess with the supply chain. There are major negative developments that will result from delays."

"I got it. I will make arrangements. Lori, I am hanging up and switching phones."

Lori knew the drill.

Damian hung up. He walked over to Vash and said, "Hang up and switch phones. NOW! We are almost at three minutes."

Vash hung up instantly.

Damian said, "Sorry, Vash. You know that a phone trace would place us in Montana. It would not take a rocket scientist to assume we are trying to make a run for the border. We cannot afford to take chances. Always assume they are tracing the calls, and always assume they are listening into conversation. Do not say anything that gives locations or details that the Feds can use to trace us or bust us."

"You are absolutely correct, Damian. My bad! I forgot."

Damian smiled. "Call your honey bunny back, but talk less than three minutes, por favor."

Vash spoke with Marguerite on a different phone.

Damian called Grain to get last-minute reports or changes.

Grain said, "Be careful. I have smoothed the wheels as best I could, but there may be rough spots that you will have to handle."

Damian replied, "I understand. We have extras just in case."

"All the arrangements and precautions have been made. He leaves in five days, at midnight." For the next 42 seconds, Grain asked about the supply issues.

Damian said, "Expect supplies shortly, instructions to follow."

Grain said, "I understand. All is good. Take care."

The total conversation lasted 97 seconds.

Damian's objectives were to keep Grain happy, alert, and on the job at all times. It was Damian's duty and loyalty as brothers and business partners that Vash arrived safely home in India.

Obviously, the long-term supply chain issues must be resolved.

Damian went to another booth and called Lori back.

Lori said, "The cooking business is excellent, and the clients are happy. They want more. Your friend is also a happy camper and wants more cooking supplies."

Damian added, "And our friend here is a happy man. All is good. I love you. I will call you when I get back. Peace." He said to Vash, "The first phone call time was 176 seconds. That is much too close for comfort. The second phone call was 156 seconds, which was still cutting it close."

Vash said, "We have to be more careful in the future, and not leave tracks that can be traced."

"I spoke with Grain for ninety-seven seconds," Damian added. "He said business is good in the legal community. Grain is making quiet money. He smells the huge potential, and expects to cash in on the big bucks in the years ahead. I think Mr. Grain will be our attorney and banker for life."

"I would not expect anything less. That is his game plan. We fit into his game plan, and he fits into our game plan. Everyone is making money. That is what makes it all work smoothly." Vash added thoughtfully, "You know what makes Grain so effective is that this is business and personal."

Damian and Vash sat at the counter drinking coffee, and ordered food to take back to the motel room. Breakfast was not that many hours away.

At the motel room, Damian asked, "How did it go with Marguerite?"

Vash swooned like a lovesick child. "She loves me, and I love her. I think we love each other. She will finish school, get her law degrees and stuff, and eventually start an international practice with Vash Gupta as her special client."

Damian looked puzzled.

Vash sighed and smiled happily. "We may get married sometime in the future. HELLO! Grandchildren!" He smirked. "For a very smart man, you are a very slow man."

Damian laughed. "Very cool, dude. I am happy for the both of you. I hope it works out. Sometimes things do work out happily ever after."

Vash was enjoying the afterglow. "When things get settled in India with business and family, Marguerite and I can meet in London, or someplace where we are safe." He smiled like a happy schoolchild and said, "All is good with the world. It will work out."

Damian said, "Okay, Vash, let me report on business issues."

Vash looked surprised. "Issues? What do you mean issues?"

"Lori, Boris, Grain, and the Spencer sisters ALL need products, pronto. They are yelling about supply chain disruptions and financial targets missed, and all that. We have a growing organization that we must feed a steady and healthy diet, without interruptions. Sales are excellent, and going through the roof. We have a major money hit on our hands, dude. Except for the supply issues!"

Vash smiled. "I am not as dumb and as stoned an Indian as you may think. I have thirty kilos of raw on order, going to Apartment 3A, and ten kilos going to Hillside Park. Expect delivery within ten days."

Damian smiled at Vash in surprised appreciation. "Really! Cool! I should have known better. I will let Lori know so she will not trip out on me. You know that chick is amazing, but high maintenance."

Vash smiled. "You mean, just high. She needs to get off the junk."

Damian sighed. "I know. She knows. It will happen."

They crashed for the remainder of the night.

Dawn in the northern plains states comes cold and early. They had a long day's drive ahead, and Vash had longer weeks to follow.

Damian was showered, dressed, and eager to go by 6 a.m.

Vash was fast asleep and having a deep conversation with his pillow.

Damian acted like an army drill sergeant and said in a loud voice, "Soldier, wake your sorry ass up. NOW! That is an order!"

Vash rolled over and shoved his middle finger in the air and said, "Fuck you, man. Let me sleep."

Damian continued in his best imitation Army voice. "Get your sorry butt out of bed, soldier! Shower and shave so we can roll. You need to look good. Now you look like some stoned-out dude, and that is unacceptable."

Vash looked at Damian and hissed, "All right, all right. Damn, you make a lot of noise."

He grumbled as he stumbled into the bathroom and emerged fifteen minutes later, a new man. "It is amazing what a hot shower and a shave does. I am ready to fight the law and win."

Damian said, "I hope we can avoid the law or sneak around and escape. Confronting the law is not a good thing for people in our position."

"Good point, Don Damian."

"Thank you, Don Vash. Shall we load up and slink out of town? We need to check the room for tells."

"What do you mean by tells?"

"Tells are small pieces of evidence that will tell the Feds we were here. Like a cigarette butt or a piece of paper you dropped with a phone number, or something that gives them more information. Capice, paisano?"

"Si, señor."

Betsy was ready to go.

As they were heading out of town, Vash asked, "Hey, Damian, why are we heading south when we need to go north by northwest?"

Damian smiled. "Observant, my friend. I want to see if we have company, and I want the motel clerk to see us heading south. I had a short conversation with the desk clerk this morning. I asked him for directions and the best roads for us to take. I told him we were heading to Dallas, Texas, for a wedding."

"So if the Feds ask about us, the story the desk clerk will know is we are heading to Dallas for a wedding, and he saw us driving south. That is very smooth, Mr. Garcia."

"Why thank you, Mr. Gupta."

Vash smiled. "My pleasure, sir."

As Damian was driving, Vash was checking the mirrors for signs of company. After 20 miles, Damian and Vash felt comfortable that they were not being followed.

They headed north by northwest.

Damian said, "I think we are cool, Vash. I have not noticed any signs of company. Jason said to call him around noon so we can arrange a connection location. Apparently he likes to keep things fluid."

Vash said, "Apparently Grain is the best in the business, too. None of this would be possible without his connections. The man is blessed."

"And we are lucky to be his friend and partner," Damian said.

"I do believe, Don Damian, that another bowl is in order. Would you agree, sir?"

"Why yes, that is an excellent suggestion, Don Vash. I thought you might never ask."

Damian and Vash enjoyed the sweet smoke of the finest O/H product on planet earth. They gently zoned out into separate worlds.

Vash returned to low earth's orbit. "I have been doing a lot of thinking. O/H has helped put life in perspective."

Damian quipped, "O/H does have that tendency."

Vash continued. "I think I want to go to medical school in India, and become a doctor."

Damian said in admiration, "Doctor Vash Gupta. I like that."

"I would like to start a medical clinic system in India for the poor. The government does not provide any medical help for the poor. The rich pay their way and get excellent care. The poor die. The needs are there, but the money to meet those needs is not there."

"Doctor Gupta, there is always a solution to a problem if you think in a 360-degree mode."

"I would need a source of income to develop the clinic systems. After that, perhaps a non-profit entity might raise funds."

"Doctor Gupta must retain full authority and control, and the funds must be used to directly help the poor, with low operational overhead. Those would be my requirements."

"So you think this is a good cause, Damian?"

"Yes, absolutely. You must do it. It is your destiny. You have the business skills, which is very obvious with the O/H enterprise. With your medical skills as a doctor, the medical clinic you envision will become reality. You will make it happen! I will invest some of my profits in the clinics."

Vash smiled. "Thank you, Damian. I was hoping I was not too crazy."

"The income from O/H Inc. would be very helpful in supporting the clinic. It would also be a nice way to wash money." Damian smiled. "This is almost too perfect."

Vash looked at Damian questioningly. "What do you mean?"

"Follow me on this, my brother. Income from O/H goes via various methods, such as foundations, trusts, and corporate entities, to help support the clinics, and the clean profits are returned. Here is the best part. Dr. Gupta will own the land and the physical hospital properties through various legal entities, and O/H Inc. will quietly become an international landholder and investor."

Vash smiled. "As you say in America, this is nice work when you can get it. How do you say it in America—when you do well, you must help those in need by doing good?"

"I completely agree, my brother. That is wonderful. I know you can make it happen."

Vash added, "You know, if we ever get out of this business, you and I will need something else as income sources."

"I do not want to do this business for the rest of my life." Damian paused, thinking. "If I was involved in a method where no links could be established, then perhaps I might just stay longer. Actually, I might stay forever, if the situations were correct, and it was safe. I value freedom and safety above all else."

"Possibly I could establish legal businesses in India, where the profit margins are large enough to support the non-profit clinics."

Damian said with a jolt, "I have an idea; how about for-profit medical clinics that specialize in certain high-volume medical procedures? Follow me on this, please. Hospital prices are very expensive in Europe and the United States. In India, you have excellent doctors who are highly educated and from the world's best schools, very well trained, and multilingual."

Vash said quietly, "Establish a medical-tourism type business plan."

"Say that again Vash, please."

"Establish a medical-tourism type business plan."

"That is brilliant! You are a genius, Brother Vash."

Vash looked surprised, but recovered quickly. "Here is the business plan. It has been cooking in my head, so work with me please, Damian. We offer high-margin and high-volume surgeries, and medical procedures found in the best hospitals worldwide. The patient enjoys a vacation while recovering in a nice seaside resort, or the mountains, or whatever. The objective is to have the patient fly home and tell all their friends and neighbors about their great experience and how much money they saved on their medical procedures and how they also enjoyed a relaxing vacation."

Damian said, "A medical procedure plus a nice vacation to recover that costs less than the medical procedure alone would cost in Europe or the United States. The quality will be better and the costs lower. More for less!"

"A satisfied patient is our best customer."

"Wow, Vash. That is an excellent slogan to use for your for-profit clinics. *A satisfied patient is our best customer.*"

Vash added, "Word of mouth is the best advertising because it adds credibility and validity. Friends do not lie to friends."

Vash's brain was processing information at the speed of light.

Damian's brain was trying to keep up.

Vash smiled. "Here is the best part. Because we can do the medical procedures for less than in the patient's home country and still enjoy a huge mark-up, we will provide a much-needed public good. The profits go to support medical clinics for the poor. The profit margins in India are huge because the expenses are less. I will buy the land and own the hospitals, using O/H as quiet investors."

Damian smiled in admiration and approval.

Vash went on. "The profits, beyond those needed for business growth, will be used to fund the non-profit hospitals. The for-profit hospitals will support the non-profit hospitals."

Damian said thoughtfully, "Basically, the well-off would support the needs of the poor. Vash, I do believe you have just had an epiphany. I think you will go to heaven."

Vash smiled. "But first grandchildren."

Damian Garcia and the future Doctor Gupta continued the long drive in thoughtful contemplation. Before the future could happen, they had to deal with the present.

Vash said, "Man, look at that snow. It is coming down thick."

"Betsy is a very good truck. Your cowboy pickup truck was a good choice."

Vash smiled and said, "It sure beats that sorry-ass car, Morgan."

Damian made the sign of the cross. "May Morgan's soul rest in peace."

Vash joked, "Amen."

Damian and Vash pulled into a truck stop, and Damian checked in with Jason and Grain for instructions.

Damian said, "We need gas and food."

Vash said jokingly, "I can do the truck thing, like gas and oil. It is my truck. I am just letting you chauffeur me around the United States."

Damian smiled. "Sure, whatever you say. Dr. Gupta."

Damian called Grain from a large bank of phone booths used by the long-distance truck drivers.

Grain said, "The wedding reception in Dallas is at seven p.m., and the groom is waiting for your call. Five days at midnight, he will be dressed as needed and have papers. Bring school supplies. Destination transportation arranged. No worries, all is good."

The conversation lasted 62 seconds.

Damian translated Grain's conversation for Vash, saying, "Jason is waiting for my call. The connection time for departure to Canada is seven p.m. The ship leaves in five days at midnight, boarding will be earlier, and you will have papers and be dressed like a seaman to blend in. Bring books of product as payments. Arrival protections and land transportation arrangements have been made when you arrive in India. Understand? Capice, paisano?"

Vash replied, "Yes, I got it. Things move fast."

"I think they will move even faster shortly."

Damian walked to another bank of telephone booths. He randomly picked a booth and called Jason, scribbling the information on a notepad.

"I understand, Jason. Mom's Diner, seven p.m., east end past the sawmill; park in the rear left side in the back of the diner. Fill up the truck first. Walk inside and sit in the far rear booth. The waitress will bring Vash water and coffee. Tell her you wish Mom a happy seventy-third birthday."

Jason said, "Be careful. The state police are more aggressive. It is an election year, and the politicians want to be hard on crime. It happens every election year. They like to set up roadblocks to see what they can catch in their big fishing net. They are after the transportation system."

Damian said sarcastically, "That pretty much describes us."

Jason continued. "Come in to Independence Junction from the west, then head east. Roads are passable if you drive carefully. Drop him off quickly, in the back, and continue east, then head southeast for Iowa. Say good-bye before. This is a quick drop-and-go scenario. I want the police to keep their eyes on your vehicle while we quietly move him and some friends to Canada overnight. You are the decoy, Damian. Are we good?"

"Understood. Vash has books."

"Good."

Damian replied, "Thank you."

That telephone conversation last 142 seconds.

Damian repeated the conversation and instructions to Vash, who asked, "What happens when I am in the coffee shop?"

"I guess you drink coffee and order food. I am sure they will take it from there. That is the confirmation number assigned to you by Grain and his underground transportation connection system. Names are unimportant. You are number seventy-three until you set sail for India."

Vash said, "Let me clean up and change clothes for the trip. I want to look like a college student on holiday, carrying my books. If I am going to play the part, I must look the part. You should change clothes too, Damian."

"You are absolutely correct, Dr. Gupta."

Vash smiled and said, "I like that title, Dr. Gupta."

With Betsy fueled and Damian and Vash fully caffeinated and stoned, they resumed the journey to Independence Junction.

Damian said, "I believe Mom of Mom's Diner may actually be Jason's real mom. It is just a feeling. It is a very small world after all."

Vash said, "You said I would be traveling with two or three fugitives to Vancouver. I wonder who my travel mates will be."

The snow was intensifying, which made driving more challenging.

Damian and Vash crested a hill at 30 miles per hour. At the bottom of the mile-long hill before a bridge crossing was a large roadblock.

Damian looked at Vash and said, "Oh shit. We are deeply screwed!"

Vash said, "Can we turn back?"

"No, they have us spotted. If we turn back, they will chase us, and then we *are* deeply screwed! We have no choice than to play it through. Put your best acting face on, my brother. We have done this movie before; maybe we can do it again."

Vash said with a panic in his voice, "I am going to change my accent to more American. Maybe they will not think I am a fugitive Indian with no passport, license, or papers."

"Yes, you have papers. Use your student ID card. Say you packed the other identification in your knapsack. I am driving, so they will not ask for your driver's license."

"Where is the stash?"

"The travel stuff is in the armrest lock box, and the books are in the knapsack. Vash, when you were arrested, did they take photographs and fingerprints?"

"Why yes, of course."

Damian said, "When they took pictures, did you have your glasses on or off?"

Vash looked puzzled and said, "I think I had my glasses on. I usually have my glasses on. Why are you asking at a time like this?"

Damian said quickly, "Take off your glasses. They are looking for drug dealer fugitives wearing glasses."

"But I cannot see shit without my glasses."

"Neither can I. I am pretty much blind too."

Vash said extremely sarcastically, "The blind leading the blind at a police roadblock. God almighty, now that is a true metaphor! Is there anything else than can happen today?

Damian smiled and said, "The day ain't over yet."

Vash stashed his and Damian's glasses under the seats.

Damian said, "I am nearsighted. What are you?"

Vash replied, "I am farsighted."

They both looked at each other, and realized their visual deficiencies could be turned into advantages.

Damian joked, "This is truly the blind helping the blind."

"Okay, Mr. Garcia, I am ready for my close-up shot."

Damian replied, "Lights, camera, sound."

"Roadblock. Scene one, take one." Vash said with a final theatrical flourish, "Action!"

Damian and Vash approached the roadblock cautiously.

They were the only car, and the police were bored.

Damian rolled down the driver's window and said respectfully, "Good afternoon, officers."

The sergeant pulled out a large powerful flashlight and pointed the light into Damian's eyes.

Vash opened his window and greeted the deputy. "Well, howdy, sir. How are you today, gentlemen? Nice weather we are having." He leaned out the window at the falling snow.

The deputy pointed a large powerful flashlight into Vash's eyes. It was afternoon, and sun was reflecting brightly off the snow.

The sergeant on Damian's side said, "The driver is not high. His eyes dilated correctly."

The deputy on Vash's side replied, "Yes, Sergeant. The passenger is okay too."

Damian and Vash looked at each other and mentally communicated the message that if these cops thought they were straight, then these were some dumb-ass cops, or they were being played and needed to be very careful.

The sergeant said to Damian, "Your license and vehicle registration, please. And I would like to see ID from your friend."

Damian handed the paperwork and replied, "Yes, sir."

The sergeant studied the driver's license and registration carefully. He said to Damian in an authoritarian voice, "Explain to me why you have a New York State driver's license, driving a vehicle registered in Iowa in a chick's name, in the very cold winter in Montana?" The sergeant smiled. "Now do you understand why I am slightly confused, gentlemen?"

Damian's brain was thinking at warp speed.

Vash's brain was in hyperactive drive.

The sergeant glared at Damian and with a sarcastic smile said, "This better be good!"

Damian thought, *We better put on a great performance, or Officer Pain-in-the-Ass is going to bust us, and everything we have worked for, and hoped for, will be lost forever. Our futures, our family's futures, and our lives depend on an outstanding performance from both of us right now, with no rehearsal. It is show time for Garcia and Gupta!* He smiled outwardly and thought, *This is method acting at its finest, driven by absolute fear.*

Damian said cheerfully, "Certainly, sir. My friend and I are graduate students in New York. Here is my friend's college ID card. This is my girlfriend's pickup truck, and she asked us to pick up some furniture and stuff that her sister left in her dorm room at the university. You understand. When my girlfriend is happy, the sex is great. My friend's girlfriend is her sister. We have to keep both women happy, which ain't easy. So you see why we are driving in the middle of the cold and snow in Montana."

The sergeant was surprised by the quick and straightforward reply. He said with a smirk, "What we have to do to keep our women happy."

"It is amazing, isn't it? So there you have it, sir." Damian smiled.

The sergeant was only 95% convinced. "Okay, sounds reasonable."

Damian asked, "What is going on, sir, if I may ask."

The deputy said, "We are looking for an escaped convict who may be heading for the Canadian border. We think he might have help from a friend."

"Really! I did not know there was a prison nearby."

The deputy said, "No, this has something to do with drug smugglers escaping from Detroit last month. They have been on the run, and a citizen thought he might have recognized one of them in a truck stop coffee shop. Sergeant, the sketch we have of the fugitives shows two guys with glasses. The description says the men are stockily built. These guys look like they could use a good meal. And these guys don't have glasses."

The sergeant asked Damian and Vash, "Do you boys wear glasses?"

Damian and Vash both responded, "No, sir."

Vash said, "My vision is perfect."

Damian replied, "Yes, my vision is very good too."

Damian and Vash lied. Neither one of them could see the broad side of a barn without their glasses.

The sergeant responded thoughtfully, "Good point. Okay."

The deputy said to Vash, "You have a lot of books with you."

"Yes sir, this is a semester break, and I have some heavy classes next semester, so I thought I would get ahead of my reading."

The deputy examined the books suspiciously; he opened a few books to inspect the pages closely. "What is this book about? It is not written in English."

Vash recovered quickly, saying, "It is written in German, and it is about the chemical compositions of planetary matter."

The deputy looked both impressed and confused, which is exactly the position Vash was directing.

Vash said in an intellectual and professorial manner, "In fact this is one of the finest research works on the gaseous and molecular composition of matter and anti-matter, when encountering the reverse gravitational pull of asteroids. In this context it is theoretically possible to form another gas. Would you like me read from the text and explain?" Before the deputy could answer, Vash grabbed the book and said, "Here on page 221 is a graph explaining the relationship." He opened the book to page 221 and showed the good deputy a multicolored graph of something.

The officer said, "It sounds like a bunch of mumble-jumble to me."

Vash mumbled quietly, "That it is, for sure." Louder, he said, "Oh no, it is very interesting stuff."

The deputy said to the sergeant, "They are not the fugitives. They are just some college kids." He said to Damian in a stern voice, "One more thing, college boys."

Vash turned his head to listen.

Damian thought, *Oh shit. This copper figured out it was the college boys he was talking about when he said that stuff about the Detroit fugitives. We are deeply screwed!*

Instead, Damian smiled politely and said, "Yes sir."

The sergeant said, "I like these fishing and hunting stickers you have on the side of the camper. I see you like to fly fish. You know, I make my own. I have this special technique where I twist the fly just so."

The sergeant demonstrated by twisting his hands.

Damian looked fascinated. In reality, he had no clue what the sergeant was talking about and couldn't have cared less. Instinct told him to learn quickly and act interested.

The deputy said, "Hey, Sergeant, these guys like to hunt bear and elk. They have stickers from a hunting club in Iowa." He leaned through the open pickup truck window and asked Vash, "What is your one-shot kill ratio, and from how many yards away?"

Vash smiled as he went into extreme internal panic, because he had no idea what the question meant.

Damian stepped in. "What the gentleman is asking, is what your percentage of one-shot kills is, compared to misses and wound shots, and at how many yards."

Vash said modestly, "Well, I don't like to brag, but I am very good."

The deputy smiled.

The sergeant went on. "Anyway, you should try fly fishing on these lakes and rivers in the spring. The fishing is excellent."

The deputy said, "And the fish are really fat and tasty. We have fish dinners at the church once a month."

The sergeant looked at his watch and said, "It is close to quitting time, and I need some coffee. Okay, college boys. You can go, and do not pick up hitchhikers. Remember, keep your girlfriends happy."

Damian smiled and said, "Yes sir. Thank you very much. We will not pick up hitchhikers. Happy girlfriends are a good thing. Have a good day."

The sergeant watched as they crossed the bridge at a slow speed.

The deputy said to the sergeant, "Nice college boys, helping their girlfriends move."

The sergeant scratched his head and said thoughtfully, "Maybe. I am not sure, it is just a feeling I have."

The deputy said, "Let's pack this up and get coffee and clock out. I checked the schedule, and we are both off for the next three days."

"We should go ice fishing on the lake tomorrow."

"Good. I'll tell the wife."

Damian said to Vash, "Please find my damn glasses. I would like to see the road before I hit a tree or an elephant or something."

About ten miles later, Damian and Vash started to breathe.

"Damn, that was close," Damian said.

"I just about pooped in my britches when the deputy started talking about kill ratios. That was smart thinking to put decals on the camper."

154

"Like I always say, blend in with the environment. I call it hiding in plain sight." Damian added, "Make your opponent think you are somebody else."

Vash said in disgust, "I am a vegetarian, and I do not kill anything unless it is going to eat me. I have never eaten meat, and never intend to."

"Vash, do you have any idea how close we came to losing everything? If these dumb-ass cops knew who we were, our lives would be over. They were looking for us and did not know it. Damn, we were lucky."

"I need another bowl to steady my nerves."

"I will second that motion, Dr. Gupta."

Vash loaded up the travel bowl. They inhaled deeply, allowing the rich, sweet smoke to fill their lungs, release stress, and clear their minds.

Damian said, "We came so close to going to prison for life."

Damian and Vash were driving through hilly countryside as the snow was falling steadily, covering their tire tracks.

Vash said, "I need some coffee and food. I see lights up ahead, which maybe is a town."

"No. Absolutely not! The cops said they were going to warm up and get coffee before they clocked out." Damian added apologetically, "Sorry, Vash. I did not mean to snap. The last people on planet earth we need to see are the two dumb-ass cops."

"Damn, you're right. Most likely they would stop in the next town and get their coffee and stuff."

Damian said, "We need to keep going and get closer to Independence Junction as scheduled. We wasted time at the roadblock that we needed."

A few miles later he said, "Hey, Vash, we are going up a long hill. I am going to bypass this town. Check behind us for company, please."

Vash turned around on his seat. "Damn, two police cars about five miles back."

"Can they see us?"

"Maybe. I don't think so. The snow is falling heavily and covering our tire tracks. The snow is also obscuring their visibility when they look up the hill into the falling snow. The afternoon sun makes visibility over distances difficult. I think we are good."

Damian said, "Okay, I am taking this county road to the left. The map tells me it reconnects about ten miles up, and is a straight shot to Mom's."

Vash looked behind and said, "We are clear, Mr. Garcia. It appears the law is going to feed itself."

"As they should, Dr. Gupta. As they should."

Damian and Vash continued the slow drive over quiet backcountry roads. They smoked a few bowls and drifted off into separate mental orbits.

"Tell me something, Dr. Gupta," Damian said, "what was that crap about asteroids and chemical compounds and anti-matter?"

Vash replied with a big smile, "Pure cow poop, my good brother! The stupid cop thought the book was written in German. It was not German. The book was written in Hebrew, and it is an historical account of Jewish persecution in Germany. The cop was actually fondling a pound of the highest quality pure opium. So yes, dude, I babbled on. The cop was studying the covers, and the seams started separating when he turned the book over and shook the pages. That is why I offered to show him some nice pretty graph. He was impressed when I quoted from page 221.

"By the way, I opened page 221 by accident. I saw the pretty graph of something and showed it to the cop. It is lucky for us the cops were brain challenged. If they were smart, we would be dead in the snow, or in prison."

Damian said, "Actually, most likely dead, when they figured out we are carrying more stash and cash than they will see in their lives. And the cops would say that we tried to escape or overpower them or some bullshit, and they had to shoot us in self-defense. The poor beefcake cops had to protect themselves against two unarmed, skinny assholes in the snow."

Vash said, "Good point. It is better for us to have stupid cops."

"I am not sure the sergeant bought our bullshit completely. I was watching his eyes."

"You know what they say about eyes being the window to the soul, and eyes never lie."

"I do believe, Dr. Gupta, that the fates have blessed our enterprise, and our futures. At least we have passed each test so far. At this moment, we are still alive and free."

"Perhaps the gods know that we will find our personal outlets to do good from our O/H earnings, and that is why we are still free."

A few miles further Damian said, "Vash, you are one fine good actor, sir. I was thinking about how you fooled the deputy cop. That should be an Academy Award performance."

Vash smiled proudly. "Thank you. Like I said, I have to look and act the part I am playing. I do believe, Sir Damian, that you gave one of your best performances ever. My compliments, sir! I wish to thank the Academy for honoring me with this award, and I wish to thank the Academy for their kindness."

Damian theatrically added, "I also wish to thank my agents, producers, and publishers at Vash Enterprises, and my mother, for giving me this opportunity to better serve my country and to provide my fellow citizens with the finest opiate/hashish products available worldwide. Please contact your local campus representative or retailer."

Vash and Damian looked at each other and burst out laughing.

Damian pulled the pickup off the road and parked between two trees. He positioned the vehicle so they could see both sides of the road, without being observed from the road below.

Damian had to allow for a quick escape route, if it came to that.

They sat in the vehicle laughing hysterically, realizing that laughter was excellent stress relief medicine.

Damian and Vash chose this place to say good-bye to each other. Independence Junction was an hour away, and the Canadian border and freedom was another hour north.

They both knew that in a few hours, their individual challenges would continue, but for now, they needed a break.

Vash said, chuckling, "Sir Damian, I have a fresh bowl of the finest, sweet-tasting and aromatic O/H, if you wish to partake."

Damian replied with a big grin, "Why yes, Sir Vash. I think that is an excellent suggestion."

Vash ceremoniously leaned over to light the bowl for Damian.

Damian returned the favor, and dramatically leaned over to light the bowl for Vash.

They both laughed at the silliness as they each left earth's low orbit.

They leaned back, with the windows open, the engine running, and the heat on full. Betsy was an excellent vehicle and had served them well.

Damian said, "When we get close to Mom's, I would like to fuel up, get some food and coffee, and call Grain and Jason. The sergeant may have a larger brain than we gave him credit for. I hope we are wrong."

Vash said, "You are making me worried."

"I promise you I will get you to Jason's, and you will get to Canada, and on a boat for India. We will continue our business enterprise, to pay for the good we will do in the near and far futures. Vash, I am your brother for life. Never forget that. Never, please."

Vash replied sincerely, "Brother Damian, I am your brother for life. Never forget that either. Please never forget that!"

"I promise you safe passage. You have my word, and my soul as collateral."

Vash smiled. "Thank you, Brother Damian. You are a man of honor with a good heart."

Damian replied with deep respect, "Vash, *you* are a man of honor with a great heart."

They hugged as brothers do.

Damian continued. "I also know deep in my heart and head, we will advance our relationships, both business and personal, and vastly exceed our personal goals. Our long-distance relationship is based on respect, honor, love, and mutual admiration."

Vash said with a smile, "And money, and the good money can buy." He smiled at Damian with brotherly love in his eyes.

Damian went on. "And I promise Doctor Gupta and Attorney Marguerite will unite. I will make it my mission to place Marguerite on an airplane to London, Paris, or Athens, or to a destination of your choosing, where it is safe for you to move about freely. And you will have grandchildren."

"And why would you promise all this, when we are freezing our collective asses off in northern Montana, in the fucking winter, high on the finest Indian O/H, and I am about to have the journey of my life, across a very angry ocean, in a rust bucket freighter ship?"

"Because, I want my grandchildren to be close with your grandchildren. That's why. Any more questions, sir?"

"Why yes, Don Garcia. What are you, a guru or some kind of soothsayer who can see into the future and divine the meaning of things?"

Damian smiled and quietly replied, "Yes."

Damian and Vash sat in silence watching the road for signs of company. All was quiet, maybe too quiet.

Vash and Damian were nervous, as well they should be. This was for real. Lives, futures, and generations were at stake.

Damian said in a warm, yet business-like tone, "Vash my friend, when I drop you off at Mom's, I am instructed to casually drive out of town, to act as a decoy. You will be in the diner, and whisked away in a vehicle that will go over the backwoods to Canada."

Vash listened intently, taking mental notes of the details.

Damian continued. "You will cross into Canada and be transported to Vancouver, where Grain's cousin will escort you on the ship. Grain will provide uniforms and all the required papers. The objectives are to become invisible. Hiding in plain sight is the best place to hide.

"Grain tells me the accommodations are basic, but comfortable. You have a small room, and share a bathroom and shower with the crew. You eat in the mess hall with the crew and the other paying passengers. Be careful of what you say, and to whom. The captain knows about this, but not all the crew or your fellow passengers. The captain has a nice side business, transporting freight and passengers."

Vash quipped, "Sounds like my bony ass will get very sore."

Damian smiled and said, "Most likely, your whole body, not only your bony butt, will be very sore by the time you get home. I am sorry, Dr. Gupta, but given such short notice, I was not able to book your first-class accommodations, accompanied by your mistresses, on the Queen Elizabeth."

Vash joked, "Next time, perhaps?"

Damian replied with a straight face, "Certainly, your majesty!"

They were enjoying the relaxation before the excitement.

Damian packed another bowl of the sweet deliciousness as they drifted high above earth's outer orbit.

After some time, Damian said, "I should call Grain and Jason before we go to Mom's. Just in case. It pays to be cautious."

Vash rolled his head towards Damian. "Makes sense."

The two amigos were leaving earth's orbit.

Vash said casually, "I was doing some thinking. In the time it will take Marguerite to finish law school and the bar exams, get a job in law, and all that stuff, I will have my medical degree and licenses in India. However, I can set the groundwork first, and open the clinics when I am licensed.

"It is different than medical school in the West. I have family members who can help in these matters. In India, such things are very helpful."

Damian understood completely. "Meaning accommodations can be made."

"Exactly. That will speed the processes."

"Will your family become involved?"

"Yes. I am sure they will. It makes good business sense, and they believe in using the rich to help the poor, as I do."

Damian added, "The investor-franchisee business model is flexible and adjustable to accommodate almost any product or service."

Vash replied, "That is what makes it so brilliant. Howard is a genius for developing this entire concept."

The two amigos sat in silence, enjoying the peace and tranquility.

Damian said, "We need to get our act together slowly. We should split the Dexedrines in half, and the stash, because we will both need them."

They separated the travel stash and each had a pipe, and the knapsacks and book packs were ready to grab.

Vash was ready to run.

"And you, Brother Damian. What are your plans?"

"For now to stay warm and free."

"And after that?"

Damian looked at Vash thoughtfully and said, "Maybe Lori and I will work out, and we will live happily ever after. Your grandchildren and our grandchildren will carry on the traditions. Or maybe . . . who knows? I will continue school and get my PhD in Art History. That was my primary objective in life, until our paths crossed. Then I will earn a living doing art restorations, painting, writing, and teaching."

Damian added playfully, "Or maybe Lori will open up a hippie-dippie coffee shop and bakery on the ground floor of an old brownstone, like the place Grain took me to in Detroit when you were enjoying the hospitalities of the Immigration system. In my fantasy, my lovely wife Lori and I will have three adorable daughters, and a white picket fence, with large flower pots that will surround the patio. We will have a suburban garden in the urban jungle."

"A suburban garden in the urban jungle. I like that metaphor, Damian." Vash added, "And a dog."

"Absolutely, must have a smart dog, or two dogs."

Vash said jokingly, "I see it now, my brother. You will have two smart dogs, and a patio surrounded with a white picket fence in the city, with a cute wife and three adorable daughters and a PhD in Art History, making a nice living doing private art restorations, painting, writing, and teaching. And earning multiples of millions over time operating O/H Inc. and various businesses and our humanitarian ventures."

Damian said, "O/H will be the funds that drive the other enterprises. We will invest in legitimate businesses which have growth potential and our professional development. We will run our chosen non-profits helping those in need, and make a nice living, as long as we stay below the radar."

"Pretty much, that should cover it."

"That sounds like a nice, comfortable, intellectual life."

Vash added, "I wonder what paths Roger and Howard will follow?"

Damian said, "They will enjoy extreme happiness and great success."

Vash replied, "Yes, I agree. We will all go far. If we stay alive and out of prison."

Damian turned sharply. "Unless we get caught first. I saw a reflection off the snow, about five miles on the left, down the hill. We have company. Let's roll."

Damian pulled Betsy slowly out of the trees, trying to minimize the tire tracks and the snow cloud made from a moving vehicle.

Damian said, "Betsy is white, the snow is white. Camouflage works well for animals; pray to your gods that it works for two hunted humans."

"Maybe this is nothing, and we are being unduly paranoid, besides being overly stoned."

"Or maybe this is for real, in which case we have a serious problem."

Vash looked back and said, "It appears our company is unhurried."

"This may be a trap, and we are the rabbits."

Vash and Damian were not happy campers with that thought.

Damian said, "The map tells me there is a small town a few miles up the road. We will find a gas station, and I will call Grain and Jason while you fill up Betsy and check her vital fluids, please."

A few miles later, they pulled in to the only place open. Vash fueled Betsy while Damian walked to an outdoor pay phone.

Grain said, "My cousin is expecting you. All is good with the trip. Departure is on schedule, and you will be with more friends. All arrangements made on arrival."

Damian asked, "Where are we with the legal issues?"

"The thirty-day window is fast approaching, and I can hear loud noises. The sooner the better is best. I will do my part, and delay as much as possible."

"Thank you. Expect the packages within ten days. More will follow, as needed."

"Music to my ears! That is much appreciated. Business is outstanding and growing exponentially. It is quite amazing, actually." Grain added, "We are family. All of us together as one unit are stronger than any army."

Damian replied, "Yes, sir. I agree. The future is all ours to make."

"Keep me posted."

"Likewise. Gracias."

That telephone call lasted 96 seconds.

Damian hung up and walked over to another outdoor pay phone.

Jason said, "I heard about the roadblock. Listen, we have problems. At six p.m., go to a farm driveway three miles east of town. The mailbox on the right says 'Wagner.' Drive up the hill and into the barn in the back. We wait until dark to connect for the rest of the trip. You will head east as a decoy while the guests head north by northwest."

Damian said, "I am not sure, but maybe we were tagged. It is just a feeling."

Jason replied, "It may not be 'just a feeling.' There is more police activity, and I hear more chatter on their radios than usual. Be careful."

"Thank you."

That telephone call lasted 105 seconds.

Damian and Vash left the gas station as quietly as they had arrived.

On the road, Damian related the conversations with Grain and Jason to Vash. "Grain said all is good on schedule and arrangements made for safe passage. Cousin Grain is waiting for you."

Vash smiled. "That is good to hear."

"I told Grain the books are on the way within ten days, with more to follow. He was as happy as a kid in a candy store. A happy Grain is a happy family. Grain is part of our family. He said that together we derive the strength to fight any army because we are united as one family, for our common good."

"That, Brother Damian, is a very good thing. We will either prosper or perish as a family. How do they say it in American movies? 'Watch your back.'"

Damian replied, "Trust most things, but verify everything."

"Precisely."

Damian was following the directions to the Wagner farm. "Do we have company?" he asked.

"I am not sure."

"Let me relate Jason's conversation. It is not so pretty."

"Oh, please do share the bad news."

Damian smiled and said, "Mom's is out, and a farmhouse is in."

Vash looked exasperated. "Speak English, man. You are confusing me. Damn Yankees, can't speak English and make sense."

"It is very simple," Damian said. "Are you ready?"

Vash replied, somewhat frustrated, "Yes, damn it! Just tell me! Why am I always the last one to know anything?"

Damian chuckled and continued. "Mom's is too hot. Jason switched plans. We drive a few miles, to a mailbox that says 'Wagner' on the right side. We drive up the hill and into the barn and close the doors."

Vash said, "This is sounding spooky."

"This is for real, dude. This is not a game. Lives and futures depend on things working as planned and people thinking quickly. After dark, Jason has arranged vehicles that can go over the back roads across the border. You will be traveling with three other people in similar circumstances, and will be driven to a safe house in the backcountry in Canada. From there, you and the group will be transported to Vancouver. You are a high-value guest and will have extra care. In Vancouver, Cousin Grain made arrangements for your safe passage on the boat, along with the other traveling companions."

"Wow! I got it. I am very good."

"In India, I understand arrangements have been made to get you off the boat quietly, and then home."

"I have family, and friends of family, and such like, so that should not be a problem. I will keep a journal of the events and turn it into a screenplay."

Damian replied, "That would be interesting."

"One more toke, Don Damian?"

"Yes. I would enjoy that very much, Don Gupta, or should I say Don Doctor Gupta?"

Vash chuckled. "How about you call me Vash."

Damian replied with a big smile, "Yes, Don Vash."

A few minutes later, Vash turned around and said, "It appears we have company."

Damian said, "Put the stuff away. Damn, we are in very deep shit. The law figured it out."

Vash said with fear in his voice, "His friend has a roadblock up ahead. We are boxed in."

"Okay, we need to think and talk our way out of this."

"How?"

"Somehow, that's how!"

Damian stopped Betsy about ten feet from the roadblock and opened the driver's side window. "Hello, sir. How may we help you?"

The sergeant stepped forward and said, "Well hello, gentlemen. And how are we doing on this fine cold evening?"

Damian and Vash were inwardly terrified but outwardly smooth and cool. The only options were to play it through to the maximum. They mentally analyzed the situation. The choices were bleak. The cops could shoot their sorry asses in the woods, say they escaped, and plant a gun on them. They were carrying stash and cash. The other option was the police arresting them, and they would do maximum time in prison. The final option was the cops wanted a bribe. They needed to work on the bribe option.

The sergeant leaned into the pickup truck window on Damian's side. He placed his left foot on the running board, placed his left hand on the door handle, and casually placed his right hand on his gun.

Damian smiled and said, "Sergeant, sir. There is no need for that." Damian was looking at the gun. "We are graduate students and do not have any guns or weapons."

The sergeant smiled and said, "I know that."

The deputy leaned on Vash's side and said with a smile, "Why lookee here. The college boys are wearing glasses."

The sergeant said with a smirk, "Ain't that simply amazing."

Damian and Vash were petrified because they had no idea where this was going. It was not looking good at all.

The sergeant and deputy glared at Damian and Vash for a long time. No one said a word.

The sergeant broke the silence and said, "What are we going to do with these college boys, Deputy?"

"I think we should do what we said we will do." The deputy smiled and said, "The ice fishing is good this time of the year. The fish are large and very hungry."

Damian and Vash looked at each other in fear, assuming the deputy was referring to a method to dispose of their bodies in the ice.

The sergeant and the deputy looked seriously at the two rabbits in their net. No one said a word for a few more moments.

The sergeant nodded to the deputy and said in a serious tone, "Let's do this compassionately."

Vash and Damian froze in their seats, barely able to breathe.

Damian finally regained his composure and, as casually as possible, asked, "So, now what do we do, gentlemen?"

Vash echoed, "What do we do?"

The deputy said, "Nothing. Shut up and listen to the sergeant."

Damian and Vash had no idea what to expect next and were trying to prepare for the various possible outcomes, including death.

The sergeant said, "We know who you are and your stories. You never hurt anybody or stole from anybody, so you guys are not bad people, just people with really bad luck. The only thing is, Gupta, you were stupid and trusting, and you were set up at the border. What you may not have known is that Customs often switches employees' schedules with little or no notice, for exactly those reasons. They want to catch inside deals."

The deputy said to Vash, "And they caught you. The system works."

The sergeant continued. "I know you were promised a deal and they lied. Something went wrong, and I know who and why."

Vash and Damian stared in amazement, barely breathing.

It was clear the sergeant and the deputy were enjoying the mental anguish they were inflicting on the two hapless human rabbits.

The law fell silent again, and no one said a word.

Finally, the sergeant said, "Agent Christopher."

Vash and Damian looked like they had seen a ghost.

The deputy said, "Long story short is that the sergeant and I worked in Detroit under Christopher. We had a good money tree working before Christopher became our boss, and he killed the golden goose."

The sergeant said, "We had a long and prosperous history of helping other people with their deportation and immigration issues, sent by Grain, and making a nice living. That is until Christopher took over the division. Over the years I bought a new truck and the home for my wife and children, plus some land and a cabin in the woods."

The deputy added, "Yeah, we did okay for ourselves, if you know what I mean."

The sergeant said, "We offered Christopher a nice percentage of the action, but he refused and said that was un-American and unethical."

The deputy said, "He reported us and we were lucky to get a job in law enforcement anywhere. We were blacklisted. At least it is quiet around here. Detroit was too busy, dangerous, and expensive. I save money because the living is easier."

The sergeant went on. "So I have no love lost for Christopher. Letting you nice college boys go would be payback."

The deputy said in a venomous tone, "As far as I am concerned, may Christopher get eaten by a mountain lion or fall from a cliff."

Damian smiled and said quietly, "He could drown in a frozen lake."

The sergeant and the deputy looked at Damian and Vash and smiled.

The sergeant said casually, "Mom's is a really good place to eat. You should try their Blue Plate Special. It changes every day. When your friend leaves for Canada, you are the decoy; we will follow you out of the county. You can relax now."

The deputy said, "Go up the road and follow the driveway."

Damian said politely, "Yes, I know."

The sergeant said, "Of course, you do."

The deputy said, "Your drivers know the back trails to Canada."

The sergeant said, "One more thing. A cash payment of a grand each would be appreciated. For two grand you buy freedom, and we have never seen you men before in our lives."

The deputy smiled. "Unless of course, you would like to hang out in our wonderful prison system, for let's say, two decades!"

The sergeant smirked. "Catch our drift, college boys?"

The deputy said to Vash, "Small bills, unmarked and non sequential. I believe you have some German books with cash." The deputy looked directly into Vash's eyes and said, "By the way, the book was written in Hebrew, not German. German is read left to right and Hebrew is read right to left. Your eyes were looking right to left."

The deputy stared hard at Vash and said nothing further.

Vash and Damian felt the silence and the heat.

The deputy finally said, "It is always the smallest of details that gives one away. I watch the small details that others ignore. They are called 'tells,' because they tell on you, and the small 'tells' that people exhibit can say more than words or controlled body language. That is a lesson learned, college boys."

Damian and Vash looked at each other.

Damian replied, "Thank you. It is good to remember."

The sergeant interrupted, saying, "I hate to break up this love fest, but it is damn cold outside. Your cash contributions would help warm us up and help our poor, cold memories to forget we ever saw you guys." He sergeant smiled. "Catch my drift? Good. I thought so."

Vash happily obliged and handed the law the $2,000 cash gift.

Damian reached into his wallet and pulled out a fat wad of bills. "Gentlemen, may I have the pleasure of giving you each an extra $500 as a bonus for your outstanding law enforcement work?"

Damian handed each a $500 wad of bills.

The sergeant said, as he placed the money in his pocket, "Thank you very much. It is appreciated and will be enjoyed! And now you understand the Christopher issue. Somehow, I expect to see you again, Mr. Garcia."

The deputy said to Vash, "I really do wish you the best of luck. I do not envy your next three months traveling. It will be rough, but exciting."

The sergeant said with a smirk, "That is if you survive."

The deputy added, "By the way, your hiding place in the trees is one of my favorite spots to catch speeding tourists in season. They love to speed up and down the hills and are always surprised when I stop them."

Damian said, "Meaning you knew where we were all the time."

The sergeant smiled. "Never judge a book by its cover. That is another lesson you college boys need to learn, if you plan to survive in your chosen business."

The deputy said cheerfully to the sergeant, "Let's go ice fishing. We have cash money, beer to drink, and three days off."

The sergeant replied, "I have my gear packed in the trunk of the car. You nice college boys are free to go. Again!"

The deputy smiled. "Have a nice day, gentlemen."

The sergeant put his hand up in the air and said, "Oh, by the way, say hello to Grain, will you?" He saluted smartly.

The deputy saluted smartly.

Damian and Vash drove slowly away for the next mile.

As they turned right into the driveway, Damian and Vash exhaled.

Vash said, "What the hell else can happen?"

Damian replied, "Be careful what you wish for." He added, "I believe the sergeant about Christopher."

"Yes, I do also. I was watching their eyes and body language, and they spoke the truth."

Damian pulled into the barn exactly on time and as instructed.

They got out of the white pickup truck and stretched their legs. They walked around to the back of the pickup, and Vash picked up his duffle bags with cash, stash, clothing, and survival gear.

"You know, Damian, I have been thinking about how to describe our friendship. We are brothers from different mothers."

Damian stopped for a moment and said, "Wow, that is so true. We *are* brothers, but with different mothers!"

Vash smiled. "Damian, those are my parting words, and they have very deep meaning. Be safe and be happy, my brother, and we shall connect when it is safe to do so for both of us."

He leaned over, gave Damian a brotherly hug, and whispered into his ear, "Be careful who you trust. Grain is very evil, but necessary. We need him, he needs us, but his wife Ayesha is seriously more dangerous. She is smooth and cunning. Stay flexible and light-footed for the next ten years until we build a very stable operation. Then you can move upstairs and broker the international operations without getting your nails dirty." He looked Damian straight in the eyes and said, "Capice, paisano?"

Damian smiled. "I understand completely, my brother."

Vash grabbed his gear. They hugged, knowing the future was theirs to make, but they would always be lifelong brothers from different mothers.

As the skies darkened, the fugitive passengers boarded the vehicles. Vash and his companions departed north by northwest through the snow- covered woods.

Damian waited ten minutes, drove out of the barn, and headed east by southeast, and to the relative safety of Iowa.

The weather was cold, the roads were snow covered, and Damian was emotionally and physically exhausted. His body and mind ached.

Damian had breakfast at a truck stop, fueled Betsy, and called Grain.

"They left on schedule. The same cops stopped us again. They don't like Christopher."

Grain said, "I know, they told me."

"You mean the sergeant and the deputy?"

"Yes, they are part of the Grain transportation system. They are on my payroll, so to speak. Nobody likes Christopher. He is a hard man to do business with, and he is making things very difficult."

"So the sergeant and the deputy are freelancing, and on your payroll? We gave them three grand for our freedom."

Grain replied dryly, "You got to love the free enterprise system!"

The call lasted 149 seconds.

Damian crashed at Maya's house. The drive back to Iowa had given Damian time to process all the information and formulate long-term plans.

The next day, Damian and George drove to the Spencer place to talk business with the professor. It was also time to have some great sex with his lovely daughter, Susan.

They met in the living room around the fireplace. Turkish coffee, small sandwiches, and pastries were on the sideboard table.

When everyone was comfortably seated, well fed, and caffeinated, Damian said, "As you understand we are in the middle of a transition period, and we ask that everyone work with us during these times. I understand business is good and getting better. That is excellent news for all of us because we all thrive or starve together. We are all growing on the same grape vine, so to speak.

"This is just the beginning, and when we get past the rocky roads, things will be more reliable. We will be stable within three years and will grow exponentially every year forward, as much or as little as each investor-franchisee wishes."

Professor Spencer replied, "I am a long-term investor, and I know that over time we will be well established and making very serious money."

Damian replied, "The future is ours to control, and we can all prosper beyond imagination."

Damian understood the strategic importance of establishing strong family and business relationships. The relationships with the Spencer Group, Attorney Grain, and Apartment 3A were becoming stronger and would last for generations. This was the basis of success for O/H Incorporated.

Damian also understood the need to be invisible. To this end, he required a cover job, and he found one driving a bus route through the university's sprawling campuses. The hours were flexible, which allowed for those occasional long business trips.

As far as the neighbors knew, Damian was a bus driver who was taking classes part time.

Damian's weekly take-home pay was $198.50, and he was happy for the paycheck. It made him appear legal to the IRS and the Feds. On paper, Damian could afford the mobile home, lot rent, utilities, and truck and food expenses for himself and George. It was the perfect cover job, and Hillside Park was the perfect cover place to live.

Damian presented himself to the world as the antithesis of an international drug smuggler. He was clean cut, polite, and dressed the part. He referred to this as "hiding in plain sight, by blending into your surroundings." Operate very quietly, stay invisible, and fly below the radar.

The Iowa business model was integrated into the Operations and Procedures Manual as part of the investor-franchisee packages. O/H Inc. required all associates to be clean cut and behave normally. Blending into the environment by looking and acting the image you wish to convey was a safety and security measure that was the hallmark of the organization.

Damian called Grain for an update.

Grain said, "They should arrive as scheduled. Packages enjoyed."

"The prototype will be finished, and we will be ready. We need to meet and talk in person about establishing a long-term relationship."

"When you are established in the east, and he is established in the west, then we meet and talk details."

"Thank you for everything. It is appreciated," Damian replied,

"It is my pleasure. I am just doing my job."

The call lasted 89 seconds.

Damian received the products from New York as scheduled. The postal service is a very reliable transportation system.

Damian established the second bedroom of the mobile home as a manufacturing and production facility. The workbench area consisted of a large solid piece of plywood resting on two file cabinets. Opium and hashish have strong aromas, and Damian installed a fresh-air intake and exhaust ventilation system. The crawl space beneath the mobile home was used to slowly exhaust the product aromas.

Damian placed the triple beam scale on the workbench and calibrated the scale to zero. He assembled the tin foil and waxed paper used to package the final products. The butcher block and sharp razor knives he used to cut the pliable opium-hashish substances into one-gram temple logs were on one end of the workbench. The far end of the workbench held the various baking trays used to roll the products into thin sheets.

Damian cut open the inside book covers of the opium-coded books, and the hashish-coded books. He weighed each book and checked the products for color, aroma, quality, and density, with a magnifying glass and using a black light to see through each product.

Two special-titled books held cash dividend payments to Damian, part of his returns on investments. The dividends fluctuated depending on the market factors, but the returns on investment always exceeded expectations.

The other books were decoys, which contained nothing.

This shipment of hashish was deep purple in color and very sticky. It smelled rich with a rose fragrance. The opium shipped was black specked, heavy with resin, with the consistency of soft taffy. The crystallized opium was not available. One must adjust to changes. Damian sampled small pieces to determine the freshness, quality, and taste. As expected, it was top quality.

The dilemma was to combine two sticky substances in such a way that the final product had an evenly marbled look and texture. The objectives were that each gram must have the same proportions of purple hashish and black opium. O/H was a product known for excellent consistency and top quality, and only the very best was acceptable.

Damian had learned from Roger that direct heat would alter the chemical properties of the hashish and opium, which would affect the taste, potency, and quality. Damian needed another way to blend the two substances evenly and consistently without harming the chemical properties that would make O/H the most sought-after designer drug.

He discussed the blending issues with Susan and George as they were running errands.

Susan said, "So direct heat is bad. What about indirect heat?"

Damian said, "Not so bad. It can actually be good. Wet heat will open up the resin contents and make the product more intense and improve taste."

"Let me duck into the dry cleaners, and get my father's shirts steam cleaned and pressed."

Damian absentmindedly followed her into the store.

He stopped in his tracks.

Susan stared at Damian.

George stared at Damian.

The clerk behind the counter stared at Damian.

Damian had an epiphany moment and stammered, "Steam."

He regained his composure.

When Damian and Susan were out of the store and on the street, Damian said in an analytical voice, clearing his throat, "Steaming the two sticky products together would make them more pliable. I think. Maybe." He lowered his voice. "The more pliable and soft, the better the marbling. The steam increases the moisture content of the product, increasing the weight and ultimately the yield, and higher profits.

"In New York, Roger discovered that steam worked for the crystallized opium and helped it stick to the moist hash. It should work to combine this new batch of sticky opium with the purple hash."

Susan responded purposefully, "We need to buy two commercial high-quality steam irons from Sears or Wards and experiment."

"If Roger's numbers are correct, then steaming should yield us between thirty and thirty-two grams per ounce, when normally it is twenty-eight grams. So we have increased our profit margins just by using steam."

"And when you multiply that by the volume we will be doing, you are talking about millions. I like that," Susan added.

After buying the two commercial high-volume steam irons, Damian, George, and Susan drove home to Damian and George's mobile home.

Susan and Damian sat around the kitchen table.

Damian said, "Let's do the numbers."

Susan added with a smirk, "And then let's do sex!"

Damian brought out a pad of paper and a pen and started writing.

"Twenty-eight grams per ounce, times $30 per gram, equals $840 per ounce." He continued to write as he talked and Susan listened.

"Okay, $840 times sixteen ounces equals $13,440 per pound. Times ten pounds equals a grand total of $134,400." Damian chuckled. "Of course, that is plus tax and licensing fees."

Susan gave him a look.

Damian continued. "Add in the two or more extra grams by weight, plus the discounts for cash payments. That would be $130,000 cash please, ma'am."

Susan reached into her knapsack and counted out a large wad of bills. "That should cover it, Mr. Garcia."

Damian went to the back bedroom and opened the closet door. He had a fireproof safe installed, bolted to the floor, with a double locking system. The first lock was a combination lock that Damian could change. The safe door would not open without the key placed in the second lock and turned at the same time as the handle. Damian had the key.

The safe, which was disguised as a dresser, blended into the bedroom furniture. Damian had also installed two similar fireproof safes in Apartment 3A. One safe held cash and documents, the other safe held products.

Susan smiled, knowing she had made a very lucrative deal. "I speak for my father and the Spencer family. The profits have been nice so far, and the potential is better than excellent. We have happy customers at $60 per gram, and we have happy distributors. Over time, the prices will probably be $100 per gram, and worth more."

Damian said, "So if you continue the scenario, at $60 per gram, you will gross $268,800. The product costs $130,000. That leaves the Spencer Group with a nice net of $138,800, less operating expenses."

Susan smiled. "That ain't too shabby, Mr. Garcia."

"And of course, the expenses are tax deductible."

"Why of course, Mr. Garcia. My family members are law-abiding and upstanding American citizens."

Damian and Susan laughed at the absurdity of that statement.

Damian said, "I would like the Spencer Group to control all aspects of your territory. Within your geographic area, you can market to the universities, hospitals, and professionals. What is Sky's involvement?"

"She works with me and my father."

"What other market segments could O/H service?"

"Hmm, let me think," Susan said. "Well, my brother is doing his medical residency at the university hospital. My stepbrother passed the bar exams and finished his law degree."

"Sky and your brother sell the product to the hospital people, and your stepbrother sells to lawyers and law students."

"With Sky and my brother selling to the doctors and staff, and our stepbrother selling to the legal types, my dad selling to the professors and administrators, and myself selling to the grad students and staff, we have the university and professional markets wrapped up into a neat profitable package."

Damian smiled. "My point exactly."

"I like the way you think, Mr. Garcia. You have a scary mind for details."

"I am just doing my job, ma'am."

Susan purred, "Then just do your job on me, NOW! We will be up working through tomorrow making this stuff."

Damian seductively smiled. "I will be happy to oblige, ma'am."

Susan and Damian emerged hours later, energized and ready for a long night until the next day of O/H production. George was on guard duty, protecting the interior and perimeter of their home from intruders.

The neighbors were oblivious.

Damian and Susan spread one pound of purple hashish and a quarter pound of black opium on separate cookie sheets, each lined with wax paper. They rolled the separate products one-quarter inch thick.

Susan loaded the steam irons with pure distilled water. When the steam irons were hot, Damian and Susan moved each iron back and forth at full steam, four inches above each cookie sheet. The objective was for the steam to penetrate the products slowly. When the opium and hash were equally soft, pliable, and moist, Susan blended the opium and hash, kneading the two together, much like kneading bread dough.

The blended opium and hashish product was spread on a larger cookie sheet and compressed flat to half an inch thickness. Damian lightly misted the finished product with vanilla flavor, which added taste when smoked. Damian sliced the cookie sheet, weighing each temple log to one gram. The finished O/H product smelled sweet with a hint of vanilla, was moist and sparkled, and looked gorgeous.

Susan said, "I would like to try our new product, Mr. Garcia."

Damian said, "I believe George also needs a good buzz."

Damian placed a small nugget of O/H into a clean hash pipe. He passed the pipe to Susan, offering her the first ceremonial hit. Damian singed the O/H and Susan inhaled deeply. The smoke was delicious.

Susan exhaled the smoke directly into George's nose and mouth.

George happily lapped the air to capture the extra smoke.

Susan passed the pipe in the same ceremonial fashion to Damian. She singed the O/H and Damian inhaled deeply, held it, and he exhaled slowly into George's nose and mouth.

Damian said, "I do believe, my lady, that we should reload Mr. Pipe and do this over again. Do I hear a second to that motion? Oh, Mr. Dog seconds the motion. Good choice, Sir Dog."

Damian, Susan, and George sat back on the couch, smiling and giggling. George rolled on his back, looking lovingly at Damian, with his paws up in the air. He had a big goofy smile on his face.

George was stoned and in his own canine orbit.

Susan and Damian were well on their way to earth's very high orbit.

Sometime later, when they slowly returned to earth's mid-range orbit, Susan said, "It took us two hours per pound from start to finish, and we have nine pounds left. We need to develop a faster product system."

Damian said, "I agree we need to improve production speed, but not at the sacrifice of quality. Quality is our primary goal. A quality product will always sell itself, and value will always command higher prices."

Twenty hours later, the last batch came off the assembly line. Through each stage of production, Damian and Susan were obsessed with consistently maintaining the highest quality. It was a lengthy process, which produced exquisite results.

Damian said bleary-eyed, "Well done, Susan. I could not have done this without you."

"Yes, you could have. But it would have taken you twice as long, and you would have missed all that great sex."

"Good point."

Susan smiled as she groped Damian casually. "It would be a nice way to end the work week and crash."

"I will ask staff to put it on my agenda."

"You do that, Mr. Garcia. I will be waiting."

"Can we talk business first, ma'am?"

"If we must. I am ready for some servicing, dude."

"I would like to arrange a big sit-down meeting with the Spencer family," said Damian.

"Done! Sunday afternoon at four at Dad's house. The family will be there for Sunday dinner, and the brothers will be there. I will let Dad know that you would like a meeting after dinner."

Damian and Susan closed the production facility, locked the cash and stash in the fireproof safe, and had wonderful O/H sex.

They crashed for the next ten hours.

The following Sunday around four, Damian and George arrived at the Spencer house. Susan and Sky greeted them at the door. George made himself at home, and trotted off to the food tables.

Sky said, "Does this bring back memories of the New Year's Eve party?"

Damian said, "Vaguely. That was one hell of a party. I am not sure I remember much, which probably proves I was there."

Susan added, "George is having a great time. He has new best friends around the food tables, and he is doing very well for himself."

Damian responded like a proud dad. "That's my boy!"

Damian and George mingled with the crowd.

Professor Spencer walked over and said heartily, "How are you two men doing?" He leaned down and said, "Mr. George, it is a pleasure to see you again. I see you are making yourself comfortable and eating well, my friend."

George looked at Professor Spencer and offered his right paw to shake. The professor smiled and shook George's paw. He gave George a belly rub. George was happy and the professor was smiling.

Professor Spencer turned to Damian. "George is a special dog. He is very cool."

Damian smiled and said, "Thank you. Yes, he is a very cool dog. He is more like a human than a canine. George is smarter than me."

Susan jumped into the conversation and said sarcastically, "That is not saying much. Of course George is smarter than you!" She added with a big smile, "And he is way cuter than you also."

Professor Spencer was obviously enjoying the banter.

Sky walked over to see what was happening.

Professor Spencer said, "Following dinner and after the guests have left, we will go to my study and do business." He asked his daughters, "Where are your brothers?"

Sky replied, "They just called and said they cannot make it. One has car trouble and the other must work a double shift."

Susan smiled. "Even if they are not here, I will talk with them. They usually do what big sister tells them, especially if Dad encourages it."

Sky quipped, "Susan trained the boys well."

Professor Spencer turned to Damian. "My daughters tell me you have plans and I should listen to your ideas. We will talk business later. For now, enjoy yourself, kids. I have a party to enjoy."

The party was enjoyable; the conversations fun and free flowing. Damian did not participate in the extracurricular activities. He was there on a social and business call, with a mission to build the O/H business.

After the guests had left, Professor Spencer invited Damian, George, Susan, and Sky to his study. Maya was already comfortably seated. The study was a large room lined with books, and included a ladder on wheels to reach the upper bookshelves. There was spacious seating around the fireplace. Facing a picture window was the professor's desk, piled high with books, files and folders, and shelves lined with more books.

Professor Spencer opened the ample liquor cabinet and said, "Brandy, everyone?" He looked around, and everyone nodded. "Then brandy it is."

Sky and Professor Spencer poured large shots of the finest quality aged brandy into beautiful glasses.

Sky placed the glasses on a silver tray and walked around the room, offering each guest a glass.

Professor Spencer clanked his brandy glass with a spoon.

"I would like to propose a toast," he said, "to life, liberty, and the pursuit of happiness."

"And wealth," Sky piped up from the corner.

Susan shook her head, looking perturbed, and mumbled to Damian, "My sister does not know when to keep her flaps shut."

Professor Spencer heard the comments and smiled, as a benevolent father should. "Enjoy the brandy, relax, and smoke a few bowls of O/H. My daughters, who know such things, tell me it is excellent. We do business when we are happy."

Susan and Sky brought out the ceremonial water pipe. The pipe was about three feet tall and had six flexible smoking tubes attached to a glass bowl in the middle. Professor Spencer poured six ounces of brandy into the glass bowl, and shaved ice. "Using brandy gives the opium and hashish a rich flavor, and helps vaporize the smoke. The shaved ice cools the smoke."

The mood was perfect for the business Damian had to discuss. He placed a pad of paper and a pen in front of each guest and stood up to address the audience.

"I would like to conduct a formal-style business meeting, and explain the business advantages of investing what will become a multimillion-dollar enterprise, exceeding all expectations."

Allowing time for the information to resonate, Damian continued. "This is an open meeting, meaning I welcome questions, ideas, and suggestions. We all can learn from each other. We all hold all the keys to our knowledge and success."

Damian had the undivided attention from the audience.

"We are in this together. Together we will prosper. If the family trust is broken, then we will all suffer together. It is basically that simple and that complicated."

Professor Spencer said, "Damian Garcia, you are well referred. Maya has told us about your adventures in Detroit with Vash. She told us about your trip to Montanan to get Vash across the border to Canada and on a boat to India. She has shared with us the business enterprise that Vash and you and your New York friends and family have developed." He sat back and scratched his chin thoughtfully. "I am very impressed. And I do not get impressed easily. Just ask Maya, my daughters and sons. They will be happy to tell you."

Susan, Sky, and Maya all nodded in agreement.

Professor Spencer added, "I would like to become a major investor, along with my family. We are in this for the long haul. I am sure we can come to mutually beneficial and agreeable terms and conditions."

Damian said, "I am absolutely confident that if we all work together, we will all prosper together."

Professor Spencer said with a slight smile, "This business can become a little dangerous."

Damian immediately replied, "We do not do any gangster stuff. That is our rule. We are collectively and individually too smart to have to resort to violence, ripping people off, or hurting people and dogs. We are *honest* drug smugglers and money launderers. We are the nice bad guys!"

Sky chuckled. "I love the oxymoron of 'honest lawbreakers.'"

Damian added, "We happen to have larger brains than your average drug dealer, and hopefully we can out think most law enforcement issues."

Professor Spencer smiled. "Let's talk serious business, please."

Damian said, "I am the cautious type, and do not like to take chances. Planned and managed risk, yes. Taking unnecessary chances, no. What is said in this room stays in this room. Nothing said in this room, from now until the end of time, will be discussed with anyone, except the people in this room, and then only as needed. If this is not to your liking, or if you are not comfortable in any way, please feel free to excuse yourself from the room. No hard feelings at all, and we will all stay friends."

No one moved. The room was still, except for the crackle of the fireplace. A few moments passed.

"Good," Damian said with a smile.

Professor Spencer said, "We can relax now. We are amongst friends and family. We can trust each other."

Damian sat down in a comfortable armchair, thinking, *This is going to be a very long night.*

He continued. "Trust is the backbone of the operation. Without trust, we have nothing. Without trust, we could all go to prison for pretty much life, or be killed, or both, or who knows what."

Susan said, "That does not sound very comforting."

"That is why we must all be very methodical," Damian replied. "I call it the 4T solution. Think Things Through Thoroughly."

Susan added, "Intelligent minds usually win."

Damian continued. "Let me explain the business model, business plan, and operational procedures. I would like everybody to be on the same page. We are all equals, and can only stay equals if we earn each other's trust."

Susan loaded another bong of the premium O/H product.

"This enterprise is based on always flying below the radar and staying off the grid, as much as possible. Low profiles or no profiles are the methods we use to survive. The objective is to become as invisible as possible. There is security in invisibility."

Damian paused for a moment. He swirled the fresh brandy in his glass, sniffed the aroma, and placed the glass to his mouth, allowing his lips to savor the flavor. He smiled as the brandy slowly flowed past his throat, warming its way into the stomach.

George was full and happy and curled up by the fireplace.

Damian said, "It is important that we look and carry ourselves as normal people. We want to be the kind of neighbor, or coworker, or professor, or whatever, that could never be involved in the opium and hashish drug importation business. We are always good citizens.

"The O/H business model is based on the investor-franchise system, with defined territories. Investment expansions are encouraged as business grows. Sharing the wealth within the family units and limiting outside investors reduces risk and is the basis of O/H Inc."

Professor Spencer nodded his approval, and the audience was in complete agreement.

Damian smiled. "This is also a cash flow business, which has definite advantages and a few challenges. The excess cash must be invested in long-term tangible assets, like income-producing real estate, farms, and legitimate businesses, including professional career development. O/H will provide the cash to build asset wealth, which is long-term wealth."

Professor Spencer said, "I like what I am hearing. This is good stuff."

"As a franchisee for the Midwest, you control the distribution within your territory. I will go into the mechanics when we work the details and numbers. O/H is a thinking person's enterprise. It is like a chess game of life. The logistics coordinating the international supply chain are remarkable when you think about it. It all has to flow perfectly to work smoothly.

"This is a dangerous business," Damian said seriously, "and the risk factors can be high. There are thousands of moving parts, and a disruption in one can affect the whole system."

Professor Spencer and the audience nodded in understanding.

Damian asked, "Do you have any questions so far, Professor Spencer?"

Damian said quietly, "Good."

George was asleep by the fireplace.

Sky said, "Perhaps some really good Turkish espresso to go with the pastries would be a good thing."

A few moments later, the group was happily consuming the delicious desserts and drinking eye-opening Turkish coffee. George woke up to the smell of food and came over to investigate.

Damian said, "I like your farm. It is a nice location on a hill. One can see the surrounding areas, and they cannot see you."

Professor Spencer smiled. "I bought the place twenty-five years ago because of the views and privacy. We have been happy living here and raising the family. The farm has served us well, and will serve us well in the future."

Damian said, "This farm would make an excellent facility. The entire operation could fit comfortably into a small building, as long as there is electricity, water, and heat. Just a thought."

"That is actually a very good thought. I think using a secure outbuilding, and installing all the equipment and supplies, is an excellent idea." Professor Spencer asked the group, "What are your opinions?"

The group agreed.

Damian said, "So it has been decided that we move O/H from the mobile home to the Spencer farm."

Professor Spencer nodded. "It is so agreed."

Damian said to Professor Spencer, "With your indulgence, I would like to use the blackboard to talk about market expansions and the financial aspects of the business operations."

Professor Spencer responded, "The floor is yours."

Damian said with a smile, "This is serious information all investors should know and completely understand if you are going to prosper in this industry and enjoy your freedom as well. I would like to explain two more items before we finalize specific details.

"I call this thinking in 360 degrees. What I mean is, to analyze issues from a 360-degree perspective, you must thoroughly understand everything from all sides and all angles. The objective is to look for flaws and determine the success versus failure possibilities. Planned risk is acceptable; avoidable risk is not acceptable.

"Okay, folks, this is the fun part. I am sure you will be pleasantly surprised to understand the return on investment potentials from the O/H business plans. Bear in mind the system is completely scalable, and this is a business that can be transported in a suitcase.

"First of all, I think Susan and I learned many lessons about production efficiencies and inefficiencies. It took us two hours per pound to process this batch of O/H. We were striving for quality."

George snored by the fireplace.

Professor Spencer said, "I believe that is where a facility on the farm would improve production efficiencies and increase security. We can use commercial bakery equipment for the production process. O/H is much like soft taffy. This will increase quality and reduce manufacturing times."

Damian replied, "With an established production facility, we would reduce the production time to thirty minutes per pound. The goal is always to strive for the highest quality."

Susan, Sky, and Professor Spencer nodded in agreement.

Damian said, "This is how the numbers work: O/H is 25% opium and 75% hashish. There are twenty-eight grams per ounce, sixteen ounces per pound, and 2.2 pounds per kilo. This translates to $840 per ounce, $13,440 per pound, and $29,568 per kilo, based on $30 per gram. Street prices are now $60 per gram with no push back. I foresee street prices easily increasing to $100 per gram as word spreads and demand increases. Prices may increase as required, but each I-F will always enjoy a large spread and excellent returns on investment. This means your profit margins will increase also. Wholesale volume prices based on kilos are $26,400 per kilo. This works out to $26.79 per gram. O/H will only be sold wholesale to investor-franchisees at the multiple kilo rates. Each I-F will have their own production labs, following strict quality requirements. Expect variations depending on farming condition, transportation, politics, and market functions."

Damian smiled. "Which leaves everyone a very profitable margin at street prices of $60 per gram. Wholesale prices will increase proportionate to retail price increases, and your profit margins will increase also.

"The goal of O/H is NOT to flood the markets. O/H is a designer product, and making it exclusive increases demand; flooding the market will alert the Feds, who track such things, because they will notice spikes on the street level, and flooding the market reduces our profit margins and increases our risks."

Damian reached for a cup of excellent Turkish coffee with cream. He sipped at the coffee slowly, savoring the full aromas and flavors. He placed the coffee on the saucer and reached for a dessert.

Professor Spencer said, "That is a very nice return on investment. This could become a multimillion-dollar industry over time."

Susan was writing numbers and said, "Actually, Dad, O/H has the long-term potential to become a billion-dollar industry in two decades."

The room was completely silent, except for the crackle of the fireplace and George's snoring.

Sky said, "Wow, Dad. That is amazing."

Susan added, "And we can buy surrounding farms and expand our farm production while we expand our O/H production."

Sky interjected, "And we must be able to donate excess food supplies to food banks to feed the poor, homeless, and hungry. O/H must help those in need so they may progress in society."

Professor Spencer said, "I like the humanitarian concept of feeding the hungry. That is very loving and caring, Sky. You were always the sweet child."

Damian smiled approvingly. "The corporate social goal of O/H Inc. is to give back to the communities they serve. O/H must have a definite social conscience; otherwise, we are nothing but lowlife drug dealers. O/H is a designer drug with a social conscience. O/H is about using excess profits to help those in need."

Professor Spencer stated, "I completely approve of the social goals."

Damian smiled happily. "Now, does everyone appreciate the awesome financial and social potentials of O/H? Each family chooses how to give back to their community. Vash will start a group of non-profit hospitals in India serving those in need, with hospitals funded by for-profit hospitals specializing in medical vacations catering to the wealthy. All of this will be funded by O/H Inc. investments. Are there any questions or concerns?"

Professor Spencer smiled. "I think we have developed a very unique family, business, and social responsibility relationship that will prosper for generations. O/H is truly a business with a social conscience."

It had been a very productive meeting for all.

Damian and George said, "Good morning," as the sun was rising over the frozen farmland.

It was the start of a new day, and Damian had to go to work.

On the drive home to Hillside Park, Damian let his thoughts travel. "This meeting went very well, Sir George, even though you snored through most of it. Vash would be proud of us."

George looked approvingly at Damian.

Damian drove a few miles and said to George, "I like my job driving a bus. I get to interact with interesting people, from students to professors. It keeps my social skills tuned. I will miss this job when we leave Iowa. Don't worry, George, we ain't moving until the weather breaks."

Damian and George arrived home. Damian showered, put on his bus driver's uniform, and drove to work. The neighbors would look at Damian as a hardworking bus driver, not an international drug dealer.

After work, Damian had telephone calls to make, which meant driving to various truck stops outside of town to use the pay phones.

George stayed home happily curled up on the couch watching TV.

Damian placed a call to Lori. "All is very good. He is safe, and business is very solid and getting stronger. I would like to do the same thing again, except double, as soon as possible, please."

Lori replied, "I think separate events are best. I will make the usual arrangements and let you know."

"Thank you very much, honey, for everything you are doing at home. I appreciate it very much."

"I am just trying to keep the kids happy, you know."

"How are the kids doing with their projects?" Damian asked.

"Well, let me see if I can explain their projects. Sonny's (Boris) project is doing very well. The other kids are also doing very well. I already have ordered the usual food for the party, and I may increase the amount."

"I would double the food order, Lori. I expect the party will get bigger and we will have to feed more kids."

"I understand completely, honey."

The phone call lasted 127 seconds.

To anyone listening in, it sounded like a husband calling his wife and asking about the kids' school projects and party arrangements. There was nothing in the conversation that would provide any information in court.

In reality, the conversation was full of useful information for Damian.

Damian was experiencing a potential supply shortage. He asked Lori to send twice the normal amount in two separate shipments. Damian could expect the first ten pounds of product, in the normal opium to hashish ratios, in ten days or less, under the "usual arrangements." The next shipment would follow ten days later or less.

The kids Lori sweetly referred to were actually Boris and his folks. Things were going smoothly, and Boris had shipped product out of the U.S. The "other kids" included Grain, and seeing to his needs. As a major investor and formidable ally, Attorney Grain was an important element to keep satisfied. Grain came first.

Lori had her connections in the hospital world, and her franchise was growing. The overstressed medical types enjoyed the medicinal values offered by O/H and were happy to transition from the pharmaceutical drugs.

"Ordering more food" for the party meant double the product order.

"Prove that conversation in court," Damian said silently in his head.

He thought about the stresses supply chain shortages can bring to the markets. Businesses operate best when they have stable environments.

The problem had a solution. When Damian returned to New York and business was stable, he would allocate a percentage of each shipment to be stockpiled, like a squirrel stores nuts. In this manner, the reserve product would be used to minimize supply chain interruptions, and their investors would be assured of a continuous supply. How many other drug dealers could provide that level of business continuity?

Damian drove to another location, a mall with indoor pay phones. *Warmth is a good thing*, he thought as he called Attorney Grain on his secure line.

Damian and Grain could express things more freely, though caution was still advisable. In this business it was better to be cautious than sorry.

Grain said, "I have direct word that our friend has arrived safely, and the trip was rough but manageable. He is on land and transportation might take two weeks, depending on conditions."

Damian said, "That is a relief to know. I have been worrying about the trip and safety. I am happy he is on his way home. He will be with family, and business will move forward as planned."

Grain said, "On a personal note, I believe our friend misses his lovely lady back east. I have the feeling they may come together in the future." Damian said, "That would be a very good thing indeed. Our grandchildren will need to know each other."

"Grandchildren?"

"Sorry, it is an inside joke. The children will run the enterprise when we are alive. The grandchildren will be running everything when we are gone."

"O-k-a-y, Damian, if you say so."

"I do say so. It will happen, if they get married and she becomes the queen in charge of all things, as she is meant to be."

Grain changed the subject. "Apparently this event has created some excitement in law enforcement circles. I hear that heads may roll, and Christopher is one of those heads."

"Is this a problem for us?"

"Getting rid of Christopher would be very good, but it depends on who they replace him with. I have to wait and see. I have to protect my business interests. There are many mouths to feed. I am very busy these days, which is good."

Grain explained his immigration transportation business.

"I usually charge $10 to $15k depending on who and what is involved. After expenses, I netted about $30k for making a bunch of phone calls, paying off whomever, and dancing for the judges. By the way, Jason does well for himself. I keep him very busy traveling in the winter. He is excellent at his craft. Lori chooses her men wisely, and

Jason is well connected. I have another run next week. I am sure you understand why I need to protect my interests."

"Completely," Damian replied. "How hot am I with the law?"

"Well, kid, you ain't exactly ice cubes."

"I think it is time to move east, as soon as the weather breaks."

Grain said, "I could not agree more. Stop by my place on your way east. It is important we have that talk. I would be careful when you leave Iowa. I do not think the law knows you are in Iowa yet, but it won't take them long to start watching Maya for clues of your whereabouts."

"That is good to know. I will be more cautious," Damian said. "I understand that you are concerned about supply disruptions, so double the usual amount, in two events, is on the way to you. Normal procedures apply."

"Thank you. That makes me very happy, and makes my people even happier. Business interruptions are bad for business."

"I will contact you when I am leaving, as soon as the weather breaks. There is a major blizzard heading from Canada by the weekend. I will leave when the roads clear up, so in about a week or so."

"I am looking forward to the meeting. We can hang out for a few days, eat, relax, talk, and get to know each other. We can spend time at my suburban home, and you can meet my lovely wife." Grain added, "I have an indoor pool."

"Wow. I will feel like the rich and famous, swimming in an indoor pool, in the winter in Detroit, and drinking mint juleps. George would love the pool. That sounds wonderful. I am looking forward to a relaxing change of pace and a quieter lifestyle."

Grain said, "Keep me posted. Good-bye."

The phone call lasted 162 seconds.

Attorney Grain was proving to be a useful and resourceful person.

Damian thought, *To understand Attorney Gershwin Grain is to realize that whenever you peel back an onion, you reveal another previously unknown layer, and you never really find the core.*

Damian walked out of the mall into the freezing cold, and drove to another pay phone location to call Marguerite.

"Hello," Damian said to Marguerite. "We need to keep this short." He listened to the dead phone line sounds between words. He heard crackling noises, which could be poor connections or listening devices attached to the incoming phone number. He was not sure. *It is better to be extremely cautious*, he thought.

Marguerite was obviously happy and waiting for news.

Damian said, "I have been told he has arrived and is safely on his way home. All is good. No major problems."

Marguerite said, "Oh good, I have been worried. I am so happy to know he is home."

"Marguerite, he loves you. Do you know that?"

"He never really said that to me."

"That is not his nature. He keeps it inside. Trust me, the man loves you. He wants to be together with you, to live at his home."

Marguerite was silent except for the sound of joyful tears streaming down her face. She composed herself and said, "Wow! I had no idea. I just thought I had to keep it inside me, and he was not that interested in me."

Damian said, "He loves you, and is working in the direction of being together forever. It will take time. You need to finish school and get established professionally, and he needs to work on his goals. I will explain everything. Be strong and be happy."

That telephone call lasted 142 seconds.

Damian reprimanded himself for being sloppy, talking too much, and taking chances.

The telephone line noise concerned him.

As he drove home, he said aloud, "Note to myself: Close off future investors. By keeping the family smaller, we keep it secure. Allow the current investors to expand into new territories and markets and get rich. I see positive futures. Lori was ahead of the game. She solved the supply chain issues before they became issues. It was very good that Vash had given her a contact name and phone number to call and place orders."

Damian was thinking, *Fluidity is a basis for security, because the law cannot be everywhere. By changing situations on a dime, it makes it more difficult for the law to set us up. Lady Luck is a major factor.*

Supply chain disruptions are bad for business. By stockpiling extra products, we are self-insuring against market fluctuations that are difficult to control and harder to predict. This is a prudent business decision and must be incorporated into procedures.

O/H has targeted densely populated parts of the country serving our markets. All appears to be running smoothly and meeting projections.

As he drove into Hillside Park, Damian continued the conversation in his head. *Dr. Gupta can start the hospitals for the poor in a few years, funded by O/H Inc. and sustained by the boutique hospitals for the rich.*

Damian prepared a spaghetti dinner, with an extra side of meatballs for George, and red wine for them both to enjoy. George and Damian ate well and slept well.

The packages arrived as scheduled. Damian was always amazed at the efficiency of the post office. "Through sleet, snow, and hail, they deliver the mail" was more than a slogan. The books and packages always arrived on time, undamaged and unopened.

The Spencer Group installed the commercial bakery equipment to process the opium and hashish into temple logs. The facility was running smoothly. It was efficient, scalable, and adjustable to production changes.

On the marketing side, Sky, Susan, and associates were getting the word out selectively and quietly. Business was expanding at a controlled pace. Invisibility provides its own form of security.

One afternoon, Damian asked Susan and Sky, "What should I do with Casa de Damian and George?"

Susan, the more logical of the sisters, said, "Damian, you should keep it. It is the first home you and George owned. It has sentimental value."

Sky said, "We could use it for business, and I could stay there when the weather is too bad, or my schedule is too tight."

Susan added wishfully, "That way you and George have a home in Iowa when the New York big city life gets too stressful."

Damian said, "What do you think, Sir George? Should we keep our little trailer house in the Iowa prairie?"

George responded by barking and wagging his tail happily.

Damian replied, smiling, "I will take that as a yes, George. That was easy. George and I keep our mobile home and have a second home in Iowa. The Spencer family enjoys our house when we are not in Iowa."

It was a bittersweet moment for Susan and Damian. They had traveled many miles together metaphorically, and it was time to depart. Both knew this moment in time would arrive.

Susan and Damian spent the next 16 hours having passionate and steamy sex to last them a lifetime, knowing they would always remain close friends and business partners, but not lovers.

George entertained himself on the couch watching TV, munching on snack foods, and drinking beer and water. Damian had a built a doggy door so George could come and go as he wished, without human intervention.

Damian and George drove to Maya's house to spend time and say good-bye. The boys had another long, cold trip ahead of them.

Damian left a fat envelope for Maya, with more than enough to keep her comfortable in Iowa. "Your main concentration, Mom, must be writing your PhD dissertation. I do not want you distracted by financial pressures. It is all because of you that O/H is becoming a viable business enterprise. The Spencers are your friends, and I would like to say thank you for setting this up."

Maya replied, "Oh sure. It has been fun having you and George. Steve is a nice man, a good friend, and a great lover. His kids are very interesting people, as you know. I like my freedom and independence, at least for a while, but who knows what my future holds."

With Betsy loaded and fueled, and Damian caffeinated, Damian and George drove east from Iowa towards Detroit for the meeting with Grain. The drive was cold and uneventful. Betsy performed flawlessly.

Damian called Attorney Grain from a truck stop outside of Detroit.

"Remember the place we went for the sweet candy?" Grain said, then quickly added, "No names."

Damian answered slowly, "Yes."

"Next block over is a parking garage. Park in space thirty-two and have some coffee at the candy place."

"Instead of coffee, I will have two Number Nine teas if that is okay?"

Grain said, "Okay, bye."

That phone call lasted 48 seconds.

Damian translated the cryptic message to mean: On Thursday evening at nine, Damian was to park in space 32 and walk over to the Wild West Organic Desserts and have some coffee. One "T" meant Tuesday, and the second "T," for tea, meant Thursday. It made perfect sense to Damian.

What did not make sense was Attorney Grain directing the dialogue in such a manner, since they were talking on his private, secure phone, and Damian was a client. Client-attorney privileges applied. Damian would follow instructions, perhaps deviate enough to check for friends following and other events.

Damian and George arrived in Detroit at 7:30 p.m. with no adverse events. Damian parked in another pay parking lot three blocks away in the opposite direction from Grain's instructions. *Something does not feel right. One can never be too cautious. Think for yourself and always have an exit plan in place, just in case.*

Damian and George walked casually around town, looking into store windows, and George was having a great time checking out the neighborhood. Damian had learned a long time ago that store windows make excellent mirrors. He could study the street by pretending to admire the merchandise in the store displays.

Damian and George strolled into the Wild West Organic Desserts at 9:30 p.m. and ordered a double espresso, dessert for himself, and a nice dessert and a bowl of fresh water for George.

They relaxed and enjoyed their meals. When they were finished, the waitress came over and asked, "Was everything okay, sir?"

Damian replied, "Oh yes, ma'am. Everything was great."

The waitress smiled. "Mr. Grain is in his office and waiting for you. Have a good night, sir." She added, "I like your dog."

"Thank you. His name is George."

She replied, "Yes, I know."

Damian understood that Attorney Grain had eyes everywhere. He paid the bill and left a nice tip.

Grain opened the door and welcomed Damian and George. "Welcome, gentlemen. Please make yourself comfortable. You are my honored guests and good friends." He bent forward and put out his hand for George.

George lifted a paw and they shook hands.

Grain stood up and shook Damian's hand.

Damian smiled. "I see that I am second behind Mr. George."

Grain said with twinkle in his eye, "As it should be. George is first and you are second." He said to George, "Dogs have humans for a reason."

George barked and wagged his tail.

Damian and Grain laughed as George danced around the office.

Grain brought out a water pipe and fresh O/H. "What would you two gentlemen like to drink?"

"Mr. George would like a nice cold bowl of fresh water, and I would be happy with a soft drink."

Grain placed the water for George on the floor and handed Damian his beverage. He lit the water pipe, and the three enjoyed a sweet ride into earth's mid-orbit.

Some minutes later, Grain broke the silence. "I like that you parked in the public parking lot three blocks over instead of number thirty-two like we talked about on the phone. You backed the vehicle in and parked in such a way for an easy escape."

Damian smiled and nodded his head at the acknowledgment.

"That was good thinking, Mr. Garcia."

"One can never be too careful these days."

"Agreed, but still sharp thinking. I like that."

Grain and Damian sat in silence for a few moments.

Damian said, "Tell me something, Win. What would have happened if I had followed your directions, arrived at nine p.m., and parked in number thirty-two?"

"That would tell me I have total control of you, and you will follow directions exactly, without using intuitive reasoning. The second scenario was to park another vehicle in number thirty-two, which I did. My guess, you would have driven carefully in the garage and parked in number twenty-three, the opposite of thirty-two." Grain smiled. "Does that make sense to you, Damian, my friend?"

"I am impressed. What information have you learned?"

Grain sat back and sipped his drink.

George stretched out on the couch.

Grain said finally, "Okay, here goes. If you parked in number thirty-two at exactly nine p.m. as instructed, without deviating from the instructions, I would know that I have a very good and obedient soldier. It is good to have obedient soldiers in this business, do not get me wrong. But I can get soldiers. What I need are brains that can think independently, without directions from me. That is harder to find."

Damian listened intently, realizing he was getting an education in forecasting human nature. They did not teach this stuff at any university.

Grain continued. "The other scenario, you would arrive at the garage at nine p.m. and, finding space thirty-two occupied, park in space twenty-three—this would have told me that you follow directions, but are able to think quickly and independently, when needed. That is a very good thing and better than a soldier. I like people who can follow directions and do some thinking for themselves when faced with an event not on the schedule."

Damian realized that he had been out thought by Attorney Grain.

"I learned from you, Mr. Garcia, and did a complete 360-degree analysis by anticipating your probable actions. Based on your known habits, I reasoned you would choose the parking garage furthest away because it was the least obvious and provided the best escape routes. I also reasoned you would back in, to facilitate a fast escape if needed."

"Damn, Grain, you are very good!"

Grain smiled cheerfully and said, "You will understand in time. So, you arrived at seven-thirty instead of nine and parked in the public garage without driving by the garage that I told you to use. This told me that you follow directions and modify as needed, and you think and act independently, using your own judgments.

"Arriving at seven-thirty and parking in the garage three blocks in the opposite direction was brilliant. If the setup were for nine, the law would be mobilized by eight-thirty. You were safely parked an hour earlier, three blocks in the opposite direction. If it had been a real police setup, you would be watching the cops who would be looking for you." Grain laughed. "Now wouldn't that be hysterical! The city hates to pay for overtime, and the police are not paid well, which is why the criminals do so well in Detroit, and cops can be bought."

Damian asked, "So how did I perform in your stress test?"

"Let me answer your question this way, Damian. Remember, Vash said you should get to know Attorney Grain?"

Damian thought about it and said, "Yes."

"Damian, there was a reason Vash wanted me to check you out. He wanted me to see how fast your brain works and how fast you react to changes."

"You mean Vash arranged this for a reason?"

Grain smiled. "Yes. He wanted me to know the Damian Garcia that Vash Gupta knows. Damian, you have the street smarts and the school smarts. You are cautious and you are not a greedy person. These are all rare combinations indeed."

Damian said sarcastically, "So, teacher, what is my grade?"

Grain replied in a false professorial tone, "Well, let's see. Mr. Garcia, I do believe, after careful and thorough evaluation, the committee and I have come to the conclusion that you have graduated with a grade point average of four point zero! In other words, you get an A plus. Does that answer your questions, sir?"

"Thank you very much for the honor that has been bestowed upon me by my esteemed mentors. It is with great privilege and deep humbleness that I accept the duties and responsibilities that come with this honor. Blah, blah, and blah . . . "

Grain smiled and said, "Welcome to the Grain Group family, Mr. Garcia and Mr. George Carlin Dog."

Grain, Damian, and George embraced as men do.

"Whenever you guys are ready, we can mobilize to the real Gershwin A. Grain home." Grain grinned. "I have my car in the garage, in number thirty-two."

Damian understood the meaning.

Grain drove Damian and George to the lush suburbs in his brand-new, large and luxurious 1973 Cadillac. As they drove out of the parking garage, Grain said, "This was a gift from a client who showed extra appreciation for the services I provide."

Damian replied, "It is a very nice gift, and nicer-looking car than the pickup truck that Vash is so fond off."

"Vash told me about your adventures in Morgan. That is funny. I would never drive such a wreck. It was also a little risky to be driving to Iowa in a broken-down car with stash and cash."

"No, not really. We are college kids on a semester break. How many drug dealers are driving a piece of crap car from New York to Iowa, carrying kilos and cash?"

"Hmm. I see what you mean. People will see what you show them."

"Exactly. That is how I live."

"I like that."

Damian sat in thoughtful silence as Grain navigated his luxurious land yacht through the neighborhoods. Finally he said, "I think Vash has matured, and I know I have. We both started out as naïve graduate students. We created this product to stay high, pay bills, and put food on the table. We had no idea that the O/H business would transform our futures."

Grain drove a few more miles, as the neighborhoods morphed from gritty to beautiful upscale luxury. After a few turns, he stopped in front of a large gate and pushed a button on the car's sun visor. Grain said proudly, "This button is to open the gate automatically. This other button opens the garage doors."

The gate opened automatically.

"There is a radio transmitter set to a frequency that communicates with the gate to open it. I push the button again, and the gate closes automatically."

Damian said, "Pretty neat."

Damian and George were impressed by the circular driveway leading to the front entrance of the home of Gershwin A. Grain and family.

Damian said respectfully, "Apparently the legal profession has been good to you, Win."

"That it has, Damian. That it has."

The trio walked to the front door, and Grain opened a small box in a sidewall. "I have an intrusion alarm system that a friend installed. I set it for high security at night, and in the day at normal security."

Damian mused to himself that Gershwin A. Grain's initials spelled "GAG" as in a "gag" order. The irony made perfect sense. Grain had the ability to change legal directions to benefit his clients' needs. This irony was usually not lost on witnesses.

An exquisitely elegant and sophisticated woman opened the door.

"Hello, honey," she said to Grain.

They embraced in a lover's kiss.

She composed herself, standing in the foyer, bathed in soft lighting, and turned to Damian and George. Graciously extending her hand, she said, "Mr. Garcia and Mr. George, welcome to our home." She looked at Damian with a warm smile and bent down to shake George's paw. "Hello, my name is Dr. Ayesha Grain. It is a pleasure to meet you, Mr. George Carlin Dog."

George wagged his tail and handed Ayesha his right paw.

Ayesha smiled broadly, saying, "I love smart dogs." She stood up and firmly grasped Damian's hand. "Hello, Mr. Garcia."

Damian smiled sincerely and said, "Thank you for the invitation to stay in your lovely house and swim in an indoor pool. I am looking forward to relaxing."

Ayesha said, "And talking, Damian. We will need to talk."

Damian thought to himself, *You sly devil, Win. You never mentioned your wife is Indian. I am beginning to understand the complete picture.*

Ayesha turned to her husband and said, "The kids are at the ski lodge along with the staff for three days. The inside cameras are disabled, just normal intrusion security measures. We are invisible."

Win explained, "We have three boys, all three years apart."

Ayesha said, "They are a handful, believe me."

Win said, "They are fine boys and will grow up to be fine men."

Ayesha said, "Yes, we are so proud." She turned to Damian and George and said, "Gentlemen, a light supper is served."

"Food" was one of the primary words in George's vocabulary.

Ayesha turned to Damian and said, "The look on your face tells me you are beginning to understand the larger picture." She smiled. "Am I correct, Damian?"

Damian smiled and said, "Yes ma'am. I am a little slow, but there is slow glow of realization happening."

Ayesha said sweetly, "It will come to you, and you will understand."

She led the group to a glass-enclosed room with comfortable seating. There was a large table with assorted Indian dishes for all to enjoy.

George was the first to the table, and he chose his foods wisely.

After all had eaten, Ayesha said, "I will show you to your room, which is a cottage by the pool."

The cottage that Ayesha modestly referred to was a separate building attached to the glass-enclosed pool area. The cottage consisted of a living room with a killer stereo system, a small, fully stocked kitchen, and a nice bathroom. The bedroom had all the comforts of a fine home.

Damian said to Ayesha, "Wow, I am impressed. George and I could be very happy living here."

Ayesha quipped back, "I will keep that in mind, boys."

Damian commented to Ayesha and Win, "Going swimming in the winter in an indoor pool! Now that is what I call living well."

Ayesha said, "We work hard for the money and what we own. It has not been an easy ride, and it can get bumpy occasionally."

Win said, "When we met we were broke college students, similar to you and Vash."

Ayesha added, "We come from modest families."

Win said, "I grew up on the other side of Chicago, and Ayesha grew up under similar circumstances in Bombay. My dad was a prison guard at the county prison, and Ayesha's family had small shops in Bombay."

Ayesha said, "Yes, that is all true. I have relatives who sent for me to live in America and go to school. My family wanted me to become a doctor. They understood that being a doctor is very prestigious, you will not be poor, and you can help others."

Win said, "Ayesha is a mental health doctor. She cures sick minds."

Ayesha quipped, "I cannot fix this man's mind to save my life. I have spent years trying, and believe me, it is beyond repair. Which is why I love you so much, Mr. Grain."

Grain replied, "You can keep on trying to fix my mind, Ayesha."

"I will," said Ayesha smiling lovingly at Win. She said to Damian, "Now that things are financially solid, we give more money to charities so we can help more disadvantaged peoples."

Win said, "It is our social responsibility to help those in need. So you see, I do legal good."

Damian said to Ayesha, "Your husband is an excellent attorney. Without Win's skills, none of this would have been possible. Vash would be rotting in prison for a decade or two, O/H would be a pipe dream, and our futures would not be the same."

Ayesha replied, "Thank you. I know he has the most Machiavellian mind in the legal profession."

Ayesha and Win sat closely together snuggling on the couch.

Ayesha turned to Damian, smiled, looked him deeply in the eyes, and said, "How did you like that little parking test? It was my idea."

Damian smiled. "It was very clever, and well thought out."

"Thank you. I am a psychiatrist or 'mental doctor' as my dear husband likes to call me. I enjoy studying human behavior patterns and understanding how to manipulate those patterns. If we are to do serious business together, we must understand your inner brain and how you think."

Damian replied, "It raises my level of respect for you, Dr. Ayesha. It is good to know that I have been well vetted and passed the tests. I assume that I have passed the tests!"

Ayesha and Win chuckled and nodded their heads affirmatively.

"Yes," Ayesha said, "you have definitely passed all the tests."

"Out of curiosity, what would have happened if I had failed your various tests?"

Ayesha smiled and said very sweetly, "Why, Damian, we would not be having this lovely conversation because you would most likely be resting very comfortably someplace for eternity."

Damian smiled politely. "Message received and understood."

Win broke the silence. "Ayesha also writes children's books."

Ayesha added, "Yes, I have four popular children's books published, and there is some talk about making a TV series for kids. My books are very popular in India and England. The books are for fun, and keep me thinking young."

Win said, "Let's go for a swim and talk business tomorrow."

Ayesha turned to Damian and said, "I placed a bathing suit in your size and a large bath towel on your bed. I will join you gentlemen in the pool shortly."

Damian went to the cottage, changed into the bathing suit, and jumped in the pool. George paced nervously around the pool, thoroughly studying the water, before he decided to jump in with a big belly flop. He dog-paddled to Damian, and they swam around laughing and playing in the pool.

The four amigos swam, laughed, and splashed around like children enjoying each other's company.

After a while, they climbed out of the pool, drying their bodies. George shook his body to get the excess water off, and Damian finished drying him with a bath towel.

Ayesha said, "I am going to turn in. It has been a very long day, and it is almost dawn. We can talk tomorrow." She smiled warmly. "Good night."

Damian and George went to their cottage and fell into a deep sleep together on the comfortable bed.

They woke the next day around mid morning. George went outside and discreetly took care of his business around the bushes. Damian showered and dressed.

They joined Ayesha and Win for a late breakfast. The smell of rich coffee attracted Damian's attention. George enjoyed his breakfast choices.

Ayesha asked, "How did you gentlemen sleep last night, or was it earlier this morning?"

Damian said, "Excellently. We snored like two babies in a crib. Thank you very much. It has been relaxing, and your hospitality has been so kind."

Win said, "It is our pleasure. A friend of Vash is a friend of ours."

Ayesha said, "What you did to help Vash was above and beyond the call of duty and way above normal college friendships. You started as poor graduate students sharing an apartment, and have grown as brothers."

Win added, "His family very much appreciates your kindness. I just thought you should know that."

Damian said, "Thank you. That is good to know."

Ayesha added, "Vash wanted to go to grad school in New York and work in America because of the career opportunities. He wanted to do it on his own terms, and in his own way, of course."

Grain smiled. "Does that sound familiar, Damian? Living life on your own terms. Hmm . . . "

Ayesha said, "And you taught Vash how to live in New York, how to read the streets, as the locals do, and how to think on your feet. From what I understand, Apartment 3A is not exactly the Waldorf Astoria."

Damian responded, "True that, but it still is a home we share with our housemates. It is the best apartment I have ever lived in. It is sad that Vash was deported and could not fully experience New York."

Ayesha added quietly, "Marguerite is very sad also."

Win said philosophically, "Sometimes bad things have good outcomes in the long term."

Ayesha turned to her husband. "Honey, that boat captain . . . I think he is someone we should cultivate further and keep on our Christmas list."

"You are right, honey. I will reach out to him and develop a deeper personal and business relationship. We could both make a lot of real money, with little risk and low exposure. I could then offer a full package deal to our very special clients, and be able to control all aspects of the transportation system. O/H Inc. and the Grain Group would have control of a vessel large enough to carry our special cargos, both ways, when needed." Win sat back and said, "I like that!" He looked Ayesha deeply in her eyes. "You are a brilliant woman, Dr. Ayesha Grain." He gave Ayesha a loving kiss. "Ayesha, my dear. I married you for your beauty and your brains."

Ayesha smiled sweetly. "Also, Win, in case it may have slipped your simple mind, we were pregnant with our first son before we were married."

"Technical details, Ayesha."

Ayesha rolled her eyes with a warm smile. "I am told directly that Vash arrived at the ports with no drama. Vash is healthy, stronger, and ten pounds lighter. I am sure the women will fall all over themselves chasing after him. After he gets adjusted, Vash will increase production. The supply chain will fluctuate with the growing seasons, product demand, including legal and not-so-legal elements, and logistics. One must control the logistics as much as possible. There are always the unknowns."

Damian said, "A smooth supply chain must be the backbone of the O/H business operations. We have agreements with our franchisees. This is a business problem we must solve. I do have some ideas how to help smooth the peaks and valleys, and to achieve more control."

Ayesha and Win said almost in unison, "Please share with us."

Damian sipped his coffee and nibbled on breakfast food.

George ambled over to his plate.

Damian said, "I suggest we set aside a certain percentage of each shipment, for example 10 or 20 percent. This set-aside will be used only to smooth dry spells, or for specific emergency business reasons. Think of it as saving for the future and reinvesting in the product for the long term. We will be storing our products in our own physical bank."

Ayesha said, "This sounds interesting. Please continue."

"We release quantities only when needed, to supply our investor-franchisees during product shortages. We always replenish the bank and keep it full. Hopefully, we may never have to do this, or only release small quantities. Well packaged and with humidity and temperature controls, the products should have a shelf life of many years."

Ayesha and Win turned to each other and smiled.

Win said, "Damn, I like that!"

Ayesha smiled. She turned to George and said, "George, you happen to have a pretty smart human with you."

George looked at Ayesha, wagged his tail, and gave her a lick.

Damian said to Ayesha, "George will be your friend for life if you give him a really good belly rub."

Ayesha sat down on the floor, and George enjoyed his belly rub.

Damian thought, *George, you are a smooth dude. You can play people so well. I am impressed.* He said, "This captain, can he bring stuff into the U.S. and take stuff and people out of the U.S.? Larger shipments from India belong on cargo ships, wouldn't you agree? That way you have total control of the incoming product to Vancouver. It is easier to travel through Canada and then drop down to the U.S. from various locations, like Jason's.

"Actually, Jason's place is perfect for many reasons. It is a large wilderness area, and remote, with many farm buildings that can be used to hide vehicles and produce O/H, serving the Canadian and

U.S. markets. We could establish a production facility and distribution point."

Ayesha exclaimed, "Win, Damian is brilliant!"

Win said, "Jason's place is already a safe house for fugitives, so it is a lateral business expansion for him. I am sure he will jump on the opportunities in a micro second, when we explain the potential rewards."

Damian continued. "I believe you now understand what I mean about analyzing all options from a 360-degree perspective. That way you have 360-degree control of all sides of the trade, so to speak. Controlling the shipping methods, and having a distribution and production facility in the wilderness of northern Montana, serving the Canadian and U.S. markets, is a business operation other drug smugglers and the law do not understand."

Grain added, "Yet."

Ayesha had a happy smile on her face and said, "Win, honey. I love this man. He thinks like we do."

Win smiled. "I will make it happen."

Damian said, "The only thing that really scares me is getting too loud with our business. Our objectives must be to stay quiet and below the radar. Speaking for me, I can't do the time."

Win said, "Damian, I understand your obsession with flying below the radar and keeping things low key and in the family. Nobody is going to do time, if Gershwin A. Grain has anything to say about it!"

Damian stated, "I will let a shipment go if I feel things are not right. I do not take chances, and I need escape options. That is how I operate. When it gets too dangerous or it is not fun anymore, then Damian and George will retire from the business. When we retire, you are free to do as you wish, in exchange for allowing us to live quietly and peacefully, on a very comfortable lifetime pension, of course."

Grain replied, "Of course, a very comfortable lifetime pension."

Damian said, "Agreed?"

Win replied, "Agreed."

Ayesha replied, "Agreed."

George replied by lifting his paw to shake. Agreed.

Damian said, "Done. So it is agreed, if or when Damian and George retire, the business is yours, and peace and tranquility are ours."

Ayesha said, "Definitely. Greed blinds you into believing you are invincible. Greed alters your perception of reality! Trust me, Damian. No one is invincible. We will all die one day. That is a fact. What counts in the next world is what you accomplish when you are in this life. What kind of a human being you are in this world is very important.

"Vash, for example, wants to develop his hospitals serving the poor, paid for by hospitals serving the rich. He wants to expand the medical-tourism business model. It is unique and has incredible financial possibilities. O/H Inc. will provide the funding, and we will all become major investors. The sustained funding will be provided by the for-profit hospitals, which are intended to be self-sufficient."

Damian added, "And it is also an excellent method to launder money. O/H will need to keep money in various parts of the world. Having investments worldwide allows greater freedom and mobility."

Attorney Grain smiled in agreement.

Ayesha said, "The hospitals will attract the best medical minds in the world by offering a chance to do real and important medicine. We only want doctors who care about people, not money or power. The needs are there on both sides. The well-off deserve excellent medical care, as do the poor. The wealthy classes can pay, and the poorer classes cannot pay."

Grain added, "This is altruism with a profit motive."

Damian said, "I believe that medical tourism is a unique business model. It is a new concept that over time will become extremely profitable. This is an example of entrepreneurism at its finest."

Ayesha said emotionally, "The medical conditions in urban and rural areas of India are so absolutely sad. Poverty and disease are everywhere. It is so sad, so very sad."

Win said, "The model of using the O/H profits to fund the hospitals is actually a brilliant business strategy, when you stop to think about it. We are also quiet investors in the hospitals. This is a long-term investments that will benefit future generations."

Damian smiled slyly. "Including all the grandchildren."

Win said, "In fact, health care and related fields will become the growth engines of the future. Think about it, Damian, as people get older, they need better doctors and specialists, and better hospitals."

Ayesha said to Win, "But first Vash has to finish school and obtain his medical degree from the university before he can become a doctor. However, the ground work will take some years to develop, and the timing should coincide. I believe there are family members who will become involved in the hospitals."

Damian said, "Helping others is a deed we should do every day. You never know what good may happen and what may be returned one day."

Win said, "Vash has his hospitals, and Damian will find his calling."

Damian replied, "I have my thoughts, and ideas are developing."

Ayesha said, "The O/H business, when fully operational, will employ many families worldwide and help the farmers in India prosper. Vash pays higher prices for top quality products. We sell high quality for less money. It is that simple."

Win said, "When Vash pays for products in a local currency, he gets lower quality product. When he pays in U.S. dollars, he gets higher quality for less money. U.S. dollars buy more and are more valuable in India."

Damian said, "So, if we ship U.S. currency and do not have to convert money, it is actually easier, less risky, cheaper, and better for Vash."

Ayesha said, "We fly below the radar once again, gentlemen. If we do not have to convert money, we avoid the banking system, which also means that government agencies worldwide will not know we are alive."

Win said, "We can ship money to Vash by courier. That is not very complicated." With a wink, he added, "It is tax free, of course."

Win packed the ceremonial water pipe with fresh O/H.

George stretched and sat up, ready to enjoy the sweet smoke with his human companions.

For the next few hours, the four amigos talked business, splashed in the pool, and enjoyed the shared friendship and companionship.

George was the center of attention. He loved to jump in the pool after a tennis ball, chase the ball in the water, climb out, and do it over again.

The group changed clothes and feasted on a small buffet of food.

Ayesha said, "I am glad my guests are enjoying themselves. Please spend the night and leave whenever you feel like it. I would like you both to get plenty of rest and relaxation. You have a long drive to New York. You also have a lot of information to process in your mind."

"Thank you very much, Dr. Ayesha." Damian asked, "Tell me something to satisfy my curiosity. If I am a patient of yours, does that mean that whatever we say together is protected by doctor-patient privileges, similar to attorney-client privileges?"

Ayesha replied, "Why yes, it does."

Win said, "Doctor-patient and attorney-client are protected by law."

Damian smiled and said, "Good. So everything we have talked about is protected by law."

Ayesha and Win both nodded and smiled. "Yes."

Damian smiled. "I like that a lot. I feel like I am wrapped in a blanket of medical and legal protection."

Win smirked, "Except for the small fact that the drug business, smuggling people out of the country, and money laundering are not really appreciated by all things law enforcement."

"True, but you are the best attorney a graduate student drug smuggler could have. If it can be done, you can get it done. It is that simple and that complicated."

Win and Ayesha both smiled proudly.

Ayesha said, "Thank you for recognizing Win's legal talents."

Win added, "Yes, thank you, Damian. You are becoming one of the best drug smugglers, and over time and training, you will become the best in the business. And O/H Inc. will become the largest company no one will ever know about."

Ayesha and Win at the same time started talking, saying, "What are your plans for the future?"

Damian said at exactly the same time, "I would like to tell you my plans for the future."

Win, Ayesha, and Damian stopped talking and started laughing, realizing they had all began talking at exactly the same time.

Win said, "That was interesting. I guess great minds think alike."

Damian added, "What would you call that, Dr. Ayesha?"

Ayesha replied, "Very amusing. We all had the same ideas at the same time and started talking at the same time. I will get back to you."

Damian said, "My goals are to finish school and fast track to a PhD in art or art history related. From there I will do art restorations for galleries, plus paint, teach, and write. And have children, maybe. I do not have the big brain for medical stuff that Vash has. I have a simple mind, and I hate blood, especially my own blood!"

Ayesha said, "I understand completely. I went to medical school, but I hate surgery and smelly patients. I like things neat and clean. That is why I chose psychiatry. I fix the mind, and I do not break my nails."

Win took out a private stash of black opium. He placed the opium into a vaporizer and said, "Take a toke of this. Maybe we talk more, or maybe we just watch the world go by in our heads."

The three humans enjoyed the sweet, smoky mists, and they exhaled into George's nose and mouth. George lapped the air with his tongue, catching the escaping vapors. He lay on his back, legs stretched out, looking at the world upside down. He was smiling and happy.

Ayesha said, "What about on a female level?"

Damian smiled and said, "I miss Lori, but I will see her soon. I think Lori and I and George could become a strong and happy family together."

Ayesha said, "Except for her pharmaceutical dependencies."

Damian said, "We are working on that. Hopefully it will be history."

Ayesha said softly, "Yes, it must become history!"

Damian understood that Ayesha knew more about his personal life, past and present, than he had realized. Ayesha was very cunning and the brains behind the Grain operations. Her controls and influences were deep. This woman was more devious than sweet, and she was very sweet.

Ayesha said kindly, "I think you would make a lovely couple. I also think that Vash and Marguerite would make a lovely couple."

Win said, "It is important to have a solid family and home life, with a loving spouse and smart children. It gives me strength and a reason to fight the dragons every day."

Damian said, "I agree. I am also ready to settle down and change gears, so to speak. It is time for Damian Garcia to grow up, sort of."

Win said, "Damian, tell me about the business structures you have set up in New York, please."

"Certainly. The products come to Apartment 3A usually by U.S. Mail. I love the postal system. The packages are marked as books and sent from a London bookstore, operated by a relative of Vash's."

Ayesha quietly said, "Yes, Livingston's is a lovely bookshop."

Damian thought to himself, *Message received.*

Ayesha said, "How do you distribute the finished products?"

Damian speculated why Ayesha was asking questions when she knew the answers. Perhaps it was another truth test, he thought. "Lori distributes to the medical world."

Ayesha said, "And this Russian fellow, Boris?"

Damian smiled and said, "We go back a long way. I have known him for years. He has connections through the Russian black market system. It is a market that we could not exploit ourselves."

Ayesha smiled. "Very logical thinking, Damian."

"It is very lucrative for the O/H business."

"And the other housemates?"

"Howard and Roger are close and reliable friends who are paid well for their expertise. Howard has an excellent business operations mind. He developed the investor-franchisee business model."

Damian continued. "Roger is our resident chemist, and he developed the chemical formulas and production procedures. It was a learning process to get the finished product to taste sweet, smoke clean, and produce the desired cerebral effects that make O/H the natural designer drug of choice.

"Marguerite is our legal expert. Her talents have created the legal frameworks we operate under. Based out of Iowa, and serving the Midwest region as another investor-franchisee, is the Spencer Group. My mother introduced us, and it has proved to be profitable. I used Iowa as a prototype and learning facility. The Spencers are developing a large network of universities, hospitals, and professionals. Their territories will expand west, and as far as they are able to service. We will all prosper."

Damian said seriously, "My theory is the fewer people involved, the less opportunities for security issues. We will thrive when we keep it tightly controlled within the families. And there you have it in a nutshell."

Ayesha smiled sweetly and said, "Very good. Thank you."

Win said, "It all checks out."

Ayesha said, "Yes it does, honey."

Damian had passed all their tests.

CHAPTER THREE

Apartment 3A

As dusk was setting on New York City, Damian and George turned the corner on West 123rd Street. Damian parked Vash's mud-splattered cowboy pickup truck near the apartment building. He took out the knapsacks from the back. The bigger one had books, and the smaller bag had old clothes.

Damian and George stopped in their tracks as they stood in admiration at the front entrance to their apartment building. Somebody had changed the building from filthy and ugly to clean and beautiful.

The front of the building had been sandblasted down to the original stone blocks, removing decades of grime. The front steps had been cleaned and repaired, as were the railings and gates.

Damian and George decided it was either a miracle or a mirage.

They looked around them. The street was still the same grime-infested street, in the same crime-infested neighborhood, but the building looked new and beautiful.

Damian and George gazed in amazement like two stoned country bumpkins from another time zone, as they walked slowly into the building. The formerly broken front door that never locked had been replaced with a door that had an electric buzzer and intercom to the apartments. The door was new and strong, and the locks worked.

The front lights that never worked had been replaced with attractive bright lighting. It is widely accepted that bright lighting deters crime, and the added security was appreciated.

The building was safer and pretty.

Tentatively, Damian and George walked up the stairs. Gone was the one light bulb hanging by wires. Gone were the old urine and food smells. The single light bulb was replaced with bright lighting, the walls painted light colors, and the halls were clean and smelled nice and sweet.

Damian and George heard piano music. As they climbed the stairs to Apartment 3A, the music became louder and the singing happier. Damian unlocked the door to see Boris, a female whom Damian did not know, Marguerite, Roger, and Howard gathered around a beautiful upright piano, singing ragtime and old blues songs. They were drinking wine, laughing, and having fun as friends and family should.

The good times continued as Damian and George watched. When the singing stopped, Damian dropped his bags loudly on the floor. The group turned in surprise, and collective shrieks of joy erupted.

Marguerite ran over and bent down to say hello to George first. George responded by handing her his right paw and wagging his tail.

George was happy to be home.

Roger and Howard followed Marguerite's lead and said hello to George. Damian pretended to look shocked and surprised.

Boris walked over casually, saying, "Well, well, look what the cold wind blew in from the Midwest. The boys have returned!" Boris gave Damian a bear hug and smiled happily. "It is really good to see you."

Damian smiled happily and said, "It's great to be home, Boris."

"I heard about your adventures."

"I might call them more like life-altering experiences. We learned to think and act quickly. In other words, we learned the fine art of survival by instincts, adjusting to change, and dumb luck. They do not teach this stuff in graduate school, my good friend Boris." Damian smiled.

Boris replied, "Perhaps they should."

Marguerite and friends stood up and warmly hugged Damian.

Damian said, "I guess George is number one, and I am his person."

He petted George. "I am good with being your person, George."

Damian and George studied the interior of Apartment 3A, and Damian was amazed how the place had changed. He decided the interior was either another miracle or mirage. It was beautiful.

The dark walls, with holes and gray peeling paint, and the ripped carpets were gone. Gone were the milk crates. The rooms were beautifully painted with bright colors, impressive crown molding, and color-coordinated accent walls. The walls held paintings, and real bookshelves.

The fireplace actually worked. The windows were clean and locked. The two kitchens had been upgraded, with new cabinets, sinks, and countertops. The bathrooms had been completely renovated, and it would be a pleasure taking hot showers.

The former slum apartment had been transformed into a palace. The neighborhood was the same, but the building and apartment were awesome.

Howard said, "We are bug and rodent free. We had to move out when they renovated and exterminated the place. So there are no creepy crawlies or furry things running around. That is a miracle considering we still live in the same shit neighborhood in New York."

Damian replied, "This is like a dream, or trip. It is hard to believe."

He noted that Apartment 3A had also undergone heavy security upgrades. In the business the family had chosen, security was a major concern. To this end, the front apartment door was actually a double door. It looked like a normal apartment door. Behind the front door was another door made from high-grade solid steel, and fireproof, with crossbar locking systems, and hard to break down.

An intrusion alarm system, using motion and light activated sensors, had been installed throughout the apartment. The windows had sensors that would set off a loud alarm to warn of a break-in, and the sensitivities could be adjusted to accommodate the security levels needed.

The production workroom had been completely fortified with another steel door and motion, light, and window sensors. A six-digit combination lock was installed to open the door, which also required a special key to release the tumbler. Lori had a key that she carried around her neck, and Damian always carried a key around his neck, as he always carried a pocket watch in his pocket.

Inside the workroom closet were two bank-quality fireproof safes; one held cash, the other held products. Roger had installed a ventilation system that worked well during the manufacturing process. The table had been set up and leveled, so the triple beam scale was accurate.

Apartment 3A was ready for full-scale O/H production and secure.

The special conference table had been repainted, and the blackboards were new. One wall held shelves and a china cabinet with real dishes, cups, and silverware. The conference room was gorgeous. The group was beginning to enjoy the fruits of the O/H business, as they were maturing and bonding even tighter as a lifelong family and business unit.

After the tour of their beautifully modernized home, Damian and George were trying to understand if this was reality or a very interesting hallucinogenic trip. It was one of the few times in Damian's life when words completely escaped him.

Damian regained his composure a few moments later as he turned to the group for a long-needed group hug. George was happy to join in. It was an emotional moment. The family was together, except for the future Dr. Vash Gupta, who was always with them in spirit and soul.

Damian walked back into the living room.

Quietly standing in the corner near the fireplace was a lovely woman, whom Damian and George had not met.

They walked over. "Hello, this is my handsome friend, Mr. George Carlin Dog, and my name is Damian Ogden Garcia. His friends call him George, and my friends call me Damian."

George offered this beautiful woman his right paw. She bent down and graciously accepted. George kissed her hand with a lick and wagged his tail in approval.

After socializing, a nap was on George's agenda, and he ambled to his red beanbag chair nearest the kitchen.

George was home with his family.

Damian smiled. "Apparently, Boris Cooper is keeping you a secret and not introducing us." He understood this woman was with Boris. What he did not understand was their relationship, and specifically how much she knew or how much she did not know about the O/H business.

She replied with a very sweet Tunisian accent, "Hello, my name is Aleta Church." She smiled warmly. "It is a pleasure to meet you, Damian Ogden Garcia. Boris and your friends have spoken lovingly of you."

Marguerite, sensing Damian's curiosity and discomfort, jumped in. "Aleta and I are practicing on the piano, which you heard at the front door. We are trying to do duets, but I am afraid I cannot carry a note. Aleta can really sing," she said with appreciation. She sighed. "This bony broad sings like a sick bullfrog!"

Boris said, "How do you like the building and apartment so far?"

Damian replied, "I am still in shock and awe."

Boris smiled. "As you should be, my good friend. As you should be."

Howard said, "That was our intention. We wanted to surprise you."

Roger said, "Let's go to the conference room and have some of the best Tunisian coffee in the world. Trust me, it is excellent."

Aleta said cheerfully, "I have a large fresh pot ready, and fresh cream, with some of the best pastries from Rosenthal's Bakery. Then we can get to know each other better. Conversation is better on happy stomachs."

The family wanted to know what really happened. Damian had not told the family, which now included Boris, and maybe Aleta, about the sequence of events. Damian needed answers about the lovely Aleta

Church before he felt completely comfortable discussing all but the vaguest details.

Women can be more dangerous than guns.

Sensing this, Aleta said, "Damian, I am sorry, you look distressed. I know all about everything. I am married into the family, so to speak, with Boris Cooper. Well, we are not actually married, yet."

Damian looked at Boris.

Boris nodded. "Yes, it is true. Aleta is a CPA accountant and has her PhD in Forensic Accounting. She also writes the best poetry. I love this woman," he said proudly.

Aleta responded passionately, "And I love this man."

Boris smirked. "Does that answer your questions, Mr. Garcia?"

Damian replied cautiously, "Maybe." He turned to Aleta and said sincerely, "I am sorry if I offended you, but I was not sure. I like to be as sure as possible. I hope you understand."

Aleta replied warmly, "I would have expected nothing less, Damian Garcia. You are known and respected for being very cautious. I completely understand."

The group sat at the conference table, enjoying coffee and pastries.

After some pleasant conversations, Damian asked, "Aleta, tell me what kind of accounting work you do."

Aleta said proudly, "I am very good at creative accounting techniques that make the Internal Revenue Service happy. And we always want to keep the IRS happy! Remember, Al Capone was brought down for tax evasion, and not for killing people or bootlegging whiskey."

"Possibly O/H Inc. and its future business entities may be interested in your services as the exclusive accounting firm, at favorable terms and conditions acceptable to all parties." Damian added, "That is, if you are willing to hire O/H as a client."

"Yes, most definitely! I would be honored to represent O/H Inc., including future legal entities and not-so-legal entities and the various business enterprises that will follow. That should just about cover it, I think."

Damian said, "Boris, my friend, adding Aleta Church to the family business completes the circle of specialized talents. Now, here is how the corporate structures of O/H Inc. will work. Follow me on this, family: Aleta Church does our accounting and financial management services. Vash is the source of the raw products. He provides the international transportation systems, the London bookstore, and all the rest. Vash is the mother ship, because none of this is possible without Vash Gupta. Attorney Grain provides O/H Inc. with exceptional legal and immigration work, and has the amazing ability to grease the gears of the legal system. Roger is our resident chemist. He created the manufacturing processes and production facilities, plus the packaging techniques. Roger will also supervise the construction of additional production facilities as needed. Marguerite provides the legal expertise and legal frameworks by which O/H and all the legal and not-so-legal entities operate. Marguerite will also develop the future legal frameworks, such as international foundations, corporations, and trusts that will shield O/H from various preying government agencies. Damian holds the North American Master Franchise. He and Lori control all aspects of O/H Inc. and the other business entities. Damian is responsible for all aspects of internal transportation and investor-franchise networks. Lori also has exclusive control of the medical community as an investor-franchisee. Actually, Lori and I share in all these responsibilities.

"Howard is our consultant on all things financial and business methods. By his request, Howard is not directly involved in the actual day-to-day operations. Howard developed the investor-franchisee operating systems that govern the methods of doing business, and is available as a fee-based consultant. And George Carlin Dog is chief of security and director of all things human."

Boris said, "That should cover it."

Howard stated, "All the parts fit together precisely, making O/H Inc. an interlocking business structure that is impenetrable."

The group listened intently.

Marguerite said, "Ladies and gentlemen and Sir Dog, I do believe that sums up the upper management levels and administrative functions of our business enterprises. Our combined talents are awesome. Would you not agree?"

The family nodded in agreement, each understanding that the group collectively had created an amazing business structure that would remain completely unknown to all but a few, and they would never tell.

Howard smiled. "We have another surprise for you, Damian. Aleta Church is related to Mario Anacapri by marriage." Sensing that Damian had not made the connection, he said, "As in Mario's Garage, where you buy gas for Morgan and snacks for George."

Damian made the connection slowly.

Aleta said smoothly, "I am Mario's sister-in-law. I have two younger sisters. Celina Anacapri is Mario's wife and our older sister. Her maiden name is Celina Church. There are four sisters in the Church family, and Mario Anacapri is the oldest of four brothers." She smiled. "I find that interesting."

Damian and George had been home for a few hours, and things were changing quickly. Intelligent people adjust quickly, and Damian did.

He had known Mario and his brothers only as a casual customer, having Morgan repaired there when it was necessary, which was not often.

"It is a very small world," he replied quietly.

Howard said, "Mario bought the building we are living in, and that is why it looks beautiful. I helped put the deal together, and it went smoothly. Mario owns the garage and now this building, and he is thinking about buying other smaller run-down buildings. He also owns a tire warehouse in New Jersey. He sells tires and stuff to service stations in the tri-state area."

Aleta said, "Yes, the tire business is very profitable. You would be amazed at the markup. Here is the interesting thing. Most of the tires and batteries and things are made in India, and are shipped by cargo ships to New York, California, or Vancouver. American companies manufacture where it is cheap, stamp their trademark, and Americans are willing to pay more thinking it is made in America."

Damian smiled. "I love the free enterprise system. It is so creative."

Howard added, "Mario always pays in cash for the properties and buys the building in as-is condition. Usually the apartments have long-standing housing code violations, and he can make those issues disappear. Mario knows people, and he knows how to take care of those people. Mario and his brothers have a real estate development business, Anacapri Development, which buys and renovates old properties."

Aleta added, "He has the New York City building department in his pocket. They do pretty much what he pays them to do."

Damian said, "I had no idea the car repair business was so profitable, and Mario had so many other business interests. You would never know that as a casual customer."

Marguerite smiled. "Isn't that what you have always called 'hiding in plain sight,' Damian Garcia?"

Damian smiled, understanding that perhaps Mario was not all that he appeared to be and Damian may have completely misread him. "Mario has done an excellent job of doing exactly that. I never saw that side of him, until now. He is very good!" He turned to Aleta. "Convey my compliments to Mario Anacapri."

Aleta nodded and said, "It is true there are many sides to Mario, the Anacapri and Church families you do not yet know. But you will soon." She smiled. "There are more parts to your welcome home that we have not talked about yet."

"You mean there are more surprises?"

Aleta smiled sweetly. "Yes, Damian, there are more surprises. Mario would like to join the extended family as an investor-franchisee. He would only handle the markets that O/H could not, and the businesses would never interfere. Mario wants me to convey to you that the businesses would only complement each other. He feels we will all prosper as a family, beyond imagination. He is asking your permission to become a loyal member of the O/H extended family."

"And what markets would he handle that we do not?"

Aleta said in a lower voice, as Roger turned up the stereo, "Mario, as you know, is Sicilian and his wife is Tunisian. There is a strong connection."

The group gathered closer.

Aleta said very seriously, "He is a real-life godfather, not like those portrayed in books and movies. You will understand over time and as we get to know each other. He is the godfather of New York no one has heard about, and no one will ever hear about. That is why he wants to be part of the O/H families, because discretion is the O/H trademark. He has studied our methods of operations and likes what he sees.

"Don Mario Anacapri sees great potential in O/H. Perhaps he sees further into the future than we do. He wants in on the ground floor, before it becomes too expensive. Mario would be a very valuable and welcome friend and a very unwelcome foe." Aleta said quietly, "Trust me on this."

She looked the family individually in the eyes, to be certain they completely understood the significance of the message.

Roger said, "Message received and understood. It is in our interests that Damian and Aleta should make the arrangements with Don Mario. I am but the humble chemist in the family, and know little of business and finance matters."

The group laughed.

Damian listened carefully as he absorbed the dynamics of the Arab and Sicilian relationships as they would pertain to O/H Inc. He looked around the group to determine the other's opinions.

"Boris, how do you feel about another investor-franchisee based out of New York, but operating in foreign markets? You have your Russian underground. Are you okay with a Sicilian-Arab cartel?"

Boris replied thoughtfully, "As long as we all do not compete, but complement and appreciate each other, then I welcome the addition. Mario would be good for business. Besides, he owns the building we are living in and doing business. It would be very awkward to say no."

Howard said, "Phrased that way, I would agree. I have been doing the real estate transactions for Mario Anacapri, and they go smoothly, and all parties benefits. Mario has the resources to help convince reluctant sellers it would be to their advantage to sell their run-down crap property without unnecessary discussions. His development company pays all cash and buys in as-is condition. Sellers understand the wisdom of graciously accepting his most generous offer." He smiled. "If you catch my meaning."

The group understood completely that Mario would be a positive asset to O/H Incorporated, and a very dangerous enemy.

Damian said, "Now that you mention it, I have noticed on the wall behind the counter at Mario's Garage three flags; the American flag is in the center, on the left side is the Tunisia flag, and on the right is the Italian flag. I never really paid it any mind before. I guess I am slipping in my old age and need to be more attentive to details. What are his interests in O/H?"

Aleta replied, "He wants to market O/H in Tunisia. There is a large market for a designer drug of this quality. The fact that it is unavailable anywhere in the world adds to the appeal and price. Mario would fulfill the market needs, and we would all prosper."

Damian said, "I thought the Western preconceived concepts are that Arab nations reject most things western, especially drugs, gambling, prostitution, and alcohol."

Aleta said, "Exactly, but also not exactly true. A large, wealthy subculture enjoys all the western drugs, the clubs, and the available women. The Sicilians have been providing the Arab nations with their pleasures for centuries, and the Arabs pay well. Money is not their issue when it comes to paying for their pleasures."

"Really! I had no idea there is a market for our products in the Arab nations. Damian smiled sarcastically. "I should get out more and see the world. However, I have been a little busy this year. I hope you understand."

Aleta smiled. "That is how it works if you are connected, and the Anacapri and Church families are well connected. The Church families are Christian Arabs. Christian Arabs are a small minority, but they are a very tight group and protect each other to survive. Now do you get the larger picture, Damian?"

"Yes, I think I do."

"Nothing really happens in the Arab nations without directly involving the ruling families, tribal chiefs, and corrupt government officials. The money tree starts at the top of the food chain and trickles down slowly. They must approve of the business and share in the financial gains."

Aleta continued. "High-quality opium and hashish in the Arab world fetch high prices. Our combination of O/H would be very popular amongst the wealthy and elite, because it is unavailable and therefore exclusive. They will profit and we will prosper supplying their pleasures.

"Mario would like to test the market in Tunis. Like Damian, Mario believes in developing a prototype and learning from this before beginning full marketing and production. This is a market O/H could never penetrate. So you understand the businesses complement each other and do not compete."

Another wise woman had spoken.

Boris said, "Damian, I am the one who started the conversation with Mario. He can be trusted. No gangster stuff, you have my word. He truly is a Mafia Don, but a nice Mafia Don. He is the unknown Don to the world."

Aleta smiled. "Unless you really piss him off; then he is not so nice."

Boris continued. "At first Mario was one of my reliable distributors. He was ordering small amounts on a regular basis. We became friends. Over time, we talked about the future possibilities. It makes good business sense to have investor-franchisees expanding into different markets that we could not penetrate, and clientele we could not reach. Mario would be doing for the Italian-Arab world what I am doing in the Soviet world. Mario likes it hot, and Boris likes it cold."

The family chuckled at Boris' joke.

Damian replied thoughtfully, "I agree. It makes O/H an international designer drug of choice for the educated, professionals, and élites of the world. This is a safer clientele to do business with."

Marguerite said apologetically, "Damian, with all that you had going on, there was no way we could consult with you and Vash. We wanted to consult with you and Vash about expanding the O/H family, but we had no safe way to contact you. You men were busy trying to stay warm and ahead of the law. We could not talk on the phone. That would have been too dangerous. So you see, we decided, as a group, that for all the best reasons we have talked about, we really did not have any other choices. Boris guaranteed that Mario and Aleta would be a positive asset as an investor-franchisee, and we accepted them as family. It is good business."

Another voice of reason and logic had spoken.

Damian said to Aleta, "We should arrange a meeting with Mario Anacapri in a few weeks, to work out the details. We need to get to know each other, and develop a family bond, before we do serious business."

Aleta smiled. "I will make the arrangements and get back to you."

"This has been a busy homecoming," Damian added. "Just out of curiosity," he asked Marguerite, "where is Lori? I called her phone, but it went to an answering machine."

"Lori is on a retreat for a few more days. It is part of her medical training. You will be surprised when she comes home."

Damian said, "There are more surprises?"

Marguerite smiled.

The family circle had grown. Boris Cooper and Aleta Church were correct; Mario Anacapri would be an excellent partner in the family. Each family member had their individual specialties, and as a group, they complemented each other. This concept fit well with the family's social responsibilities and their Zen beliefs and philosophies of life.

O/H was quietly going global in a big way.

A few days later, Damian, George, Marguerite, Boris, Aleta, Roger, and Howard were seated around the special table. Aleta had prepared a true Italian meal, unlike anything offered in a restaurant. A large jug of homemade mead wine was on the table. Fine Tunisian coffee was brewing.

The table had a beautiful tablecloth covering it, and Aleta had set out the fancy place settings, with real china and silverware. The napkins were cloth, and each setting had a water glass and wineglass. There were flowers in the vases as centerpieces. It was stunning.

The meal was delicious. The wine was superb, and the desserts and coffee were divine. Damian felt truly home. He had the love of a family, which he never had as a child.

After dinner, Damian recounted the adventures they had. The family was amused about the sergeant and deputy, angry with Agent Christopher and the immigration dance, and pleased about Attorney Grain and the miracles he created, and his lovely and cunning wife, Dr. Ayesha Grain.

In retelling the stories, Damian realized the humor, the challenges they conquered by thinking fast and acting quickly, and the complete terror they had experienced. The O/H family had an unbreakable bond.

The door opened, and a woman walked in.

Damian and George hardly recognized her.

"Lori," exclaimed Marguerite, "you are home at last."

George greeted Lori, wagging his tail and very excited to see her. He offered his right paw.

Damian gazed in amazement at the changes. Lori had lost weight; she still had the cutest tight ass. Her hair was shorter, and her face looked rested and less stressed. She looked delicious, radiant, and gorgeous.

Lori's eyes had changed. Gone was the dull look. Her eyes sparkled like fine diamonds. Lori had happiness and love in her eyes.

Damian's eyes locked on Lori.

Lori's eyes locked on Damian.

The love thunderbolt had hit. At that instant, they both had a flash realization that they would always equally share their lives together forever.

The group gathered around Lori, hugging and kissing her. When the commotion had calmed, Lori walked over to Damian, and they hugged, cried, and kissed in a deep and loving, passionate embrace.

It was so good to be home.

Aleta said, "I have a place set for you next to your man."

The family sat together, talking, laughing, hugging, and feasting on fine food, fine wine, and enjoying the finest of lasting family friendships.

When the meal was completed, the group shared in cleaning up and doing the dishes. They lived as a communal group house, and household chores were shared equally. Apartment 3A would always stay clean and neat. They were still graduate students, but they did not live like freshmen in a college frat house.

Lori said, "Damian, my love, I really wanted to surprise you with the new me. I have changed. I hope you will still want me."

Lori was teasing Damian, knowing he always wanted her, and she always wanted him. Damian had lust and love in his eyes. Passionate sex was on his mind.

"I had time to think, when you guys were freezing your asses off running around the country," Lori said to Damian and George. "You know I hated the hospital drugs, but I was hooked, as were my friends and coworkers."

Damian smiled. "Yes, we all know."

The group cried, and said they understood her pain.

Lori exclaimed proudly, "Well, I went to a drug rehabilitation clinic and am completely pharmaceutical free! No hospital drugs for the last three months or longer. I only toke a small amount of O/H occasionally."

Damian smiled warmly. "The drug-free look is really good on you."

"I have more energy, drive, and ambition." Lori winked. "You will have to see what it does to my sex drive."

Damian smiled in delicious anticipation.

"Oh, Damian, I almost forgot to tell you," Lori said casually. "I am changing jobs."

"More surprises," said Damian with a twinkle in his eyes.

"I will be head nurse for the doctor group that operates the rehab clinic that helped me become drug free. Part of my therapy program is to help others get rid of their addictions. I will teach them how to be free. As a nurse and former pharmaceutical addict and patient, I am the best equipped person to help others who are suffering through their personal drug and emotional addictions.

"This means normal hours, less stress, a lot more money, and a pension when I retire. We can live nicely off my salary alone. The salary is that good. They really want me."

Damian gave Lori a loving hug and warm kiss, and whispered in her ear, "I love you, Lori Wilson."

Lori smiled lovingly and said, "I have always known, since I picked your sorry ass off the emergency room floor, that I loved you. I love you, Damian Garcia, and George C. Dog."

Lori turned to the group and said, "I began to realize how the emergency room of a city hospital was not helping my mental or physical health. The job was killing me. It was like death from a thousand needles. It was time to change. And I have changed! So there you have it, ladies and gentlemen."

Lori turned to Damian. "That is my gift for you, Damian Garcia. I present you with the new Lori Wilson."

Damian quipped, "Never let it be said that Lori is a humble woman."

She smiled. "I know. That is why you love me. I am a strong woman who speaks her mind and does not hold back. And Damian Garcia is attracted to strong women, like a moth is to a flame."

Damian said lovingly, "I love the new you even more."

The following week, Damian registered late for his final classes. He pleaded with his professors and the dean, saying that he had to go to Wisconsin to help his sick father. Damian thanked them for their kindness, promised he would be the best student, and would be happy to be a teaching assistant.

A few days later, Aleta and Boris dropped by to hang out.

Aleta said, "Mario would love to make a weekend retreat thing with the family. He wants everyone to hang out with him, develop friendships, do business, and bond together. George will have a good time on the water. My father-in-law is old school. Families do business with each other, with few outsiders. This protects everyone."

Damian said, "That is fine with me. Where is this retreat you are talking about, and when is this happening?"

"The retreat is the Anacapri home in Great Neck, on the north shore of Long Island. The house is on ten acres overlooking the water on the bay. It is very private, and beautiful." Aleta added with a happy smile, "We would all be his guests for a long weekend on the bay."

Damian said, "Let's talk to the family and arrange schedules."

It was decided that the group would meet at Mario's Garage at 2 p.m. on the following Friday and return late Monday evening. It was going to be a relaxing three-day social and business trip on the water.

Damian thought, *How many times do humble graduate students get to hang out at a real godfather's estate in Long Island?*

As agreed at 2 p.m. on the following Friday, Mario greeted the Garcia Group at Mario's Garage. Aleta gave Mario a big hug. Mario shook hands with the group and gave Damian a brotherly hug. Mario bent down to say hello to George, and he responded by giving Mario his right paw, barking and wagging his tail happily. George approved.

Mario smiled. "I see George is happy." To Damian he said, "I checked, and your next class is on Tuesday at 11:45. The others do not have classes until Tuesday afternoon, and Lori is off work until Tuesday at nine a.m. So, having Monday off fits perfectly into your schedules."

Damian smiled. "Message received, sir."

Mario explained the transportation arrangements. "We will be traveling in four cars. We have four gray cars, dirty on the outside, clean on the inside. The cars are police cruisers, so they are fast and heavy duty. Lori, Damian, and George will travel with me, and the rest can choose how they wish. Trust me, everybody will be comfortable."

Aleta said, "It is about a two-hour drive, no stops. If you need the bathroom, I would do it before we leave."

The group followed Mario and his sons through the parts room and into the back alley. Four dirty gray cars were parked in a row. Mario sat in the front passenger seat, and his brother was driving. Damian, Lori, and George occupied the backseats, with Damian sitting directly behind Mario.

Mario was a cautious man and did not like people sitting behind him.

Damian explained to Mario, "The cause of my hearing loss is from a severe street beating. That is how Lori and I met; she was the nurse on duty who patched up my sorry ass when I stumbled into the hospital."

Lori said, "Then I took him to my home, and we have been together ever since."

Mario said, "So bad things sometimes have silver linings." He graciously accommodated the breach in protocol.

The four vehicles pulled slowly out of the alley, through the avenues and on to the highways that would take them to Great Neck.

Damian observed a very interesting driving technique. The cars always maintained the exact legal speed limits, and the drivers obeyed all traffic laws. On the highway, the vehicles would casually shift positions, with the front car dropping back and the third car moving forward. The choreographed dance of the vehicles continued, with the vehicles switching positions.

Mario smiled. "You have been watching the driving. I learned this technique in the Arab countries. When the wealthy travel around the country, it is harder for the bad people to figure out which car has high-value passengers. For example, we are only in three cars, but there are four cars traveling. We have a decoy and safety car if needed."

Lori said, "One can never be too cautious in this world."

Mario said, "While we are driving and alone, I want to explain a little about the Anacapri and Church families. As you know, the Anacapri family is the New York family no one has ever heard of. We do not get our names in the newspapers like the other families. They make too much noise. We do not even whisper. It is stupid to advertise what you do. It is best to stay very quiet and below the radar, as you say. I cannot understand why anyone would call attention to themselves in this business. It is nothing more than stupid egos. Egos destroy. Logic prevails. And, it is also very bad for business."

Mario smiled at Lori and Damian while his drivers continued their tactical driving maneuvers. "I know all about your passion for flying low and your understanding of passive security. The way you present yourself to the world will protect you, because who would suspect a hardworking and ever so humble Italian garage mechanic of being the unknown Don and importing O/H to Tunisia and the Arab nations?"

"Exactly," said Lori.

Damian added, "And who would suspect a group of starving graduate students of being major drug importers and money launderers?"

Mario smiled. "Exactly."

Mario was more cunning than Attorney Grain, and equally gracious.

Damian said, "Can I assume, Mario, that you have researched me, Lori, and O/H, and you know everything you want to know?"

Mario nodded. "I know how you two lovebirds met. What is exciting about the Arab countries, and completely unknown to westerners, is their huge appetite for all decadent things American. The profits are enormous, and you will share in the profits, Damian, as will Dr. Vash Gupta in India." Mario added casually, "I will also invest in his health care systems."

He paused for the various layers of information to be processed by Lori and Damian, and their brains were working in hyperactive drive.

Mario said with a twinkle in his eyes, "Let me explain briefly how this works, in theory of course."

George was stretched out on the seat.

"The products arrive in Tunis by fishing boats from Sicily. I am confident the Tunis subculture would be very receptive to a new designer drug. O/H has mystical and deep-thinking properties, and it is unavailable anywhere else in the world. Exclusive means expensive in a culture where, for some, money is no object. I predict it will be a hit, word will spread throughout the Arab subcultures, and we will all prosper." Mario chuckled. "Being exclusive increases the price, and money is not an issue when it comes to selling the pleasures that are officially forbidden by their society."

Mario was scratching numbers on a small note pad he always carried.

"I would not be surprised if we could move twenty kilos per month, maybe more when word spreads down the Arab peninsula. And the beauty is we can always raise prices as the popularity increase. This could be really huge, Damian. As the demand grows, the profit margins will exceed all expectations. This I promise you."

Mario smiled at Lori. "Is twenty kilos a month doable, Lori?"

Lori responded sweetly, "Twenty kilos. Done!"

"All you have to do is call that contact phone number Vash gave you, place the orders, and arrange the transfers."

Lori and Damian understood the message and smiled.

Damian said, "What are the risk factors and economics, if I might politely inquire?"

Mario replied, "I will offer the product to certain royal family members, tribal chiefs, and high-ranking government officials. After I explain the enormous cash potentials, they will enjoy O/H even more. I would not be surprised if prices exceeded $300 per gram, which is ten times your wholesale price in the U.S. Prices for their vices in the Arab world are of no consequence to an Arab sheik sitting on a 300-year supply of oil. Now do you understand the huge profit potentials?"

"Yes, I am beginning to understand, Don Anacapri."

Lori replied, "I had no idea the Arab markets are so profitable."

Damian added, "It defies conventional thinking."

Mario turned back in his seat and looked Lori in the eyes. "Defying conventional thinking is how I have been able to prosper. Think outside the box, my wife always tells me. So I do. That is why the Anacapri and Church families will become major investors in O/H, starting from today forward."

He sat back and observed the road ahead. He looked in the mirrors, confident the motorcade was not being followed. Sometime later, he continued. "I sell to the chosen leaders, who sell within their distribution networks. They profit and we prosper. They are business people, and O/H makes perfect business sense. The Arab leaders gain respect among their chosen friends."

Damian chuckled. "And get high."

Mario added, "That is how business of this nature is done. The ruling families must approve of all business and enjoy the benefits. Security and profits are guaranteed when a ruler or chosen leader is in on the action. If you play by their rules, no one ever gets hurt. Arabs may kill each other, but not foreign investors. It is all about profit margins."

The motorcade arrived at the ivy-covered stone wall and iron-gated compound. The gate swung open, and two well-dressed men looked into each vehicle, checked off the occupants, and allowed them to pass. The fourth decoy vehicle drove slowly around the neighborhood to check for unknown parked vehicles and suspicious activities.

Celina Anacapri greeted her husband with a big hug and kiss. She welcomed the group to their home. George was the star attraction. She announced, "Cocktails at six, and dinner will be at seven-thirty. Bring your thirst and appetites. Aleta, be a dear and show our guests to their cottages. I would like to be sure everyone is comfortable." Celina turned to Damian and Lori. "We take pride in our hospitality. If you need anything, staff is available."

Aleta responded, "Yes, big sister."

The cottages were large and comfortable. Aleta showed Marguerite, Howard, and Roger to their larger cottage. By doing this, Mario accepted their mutual sexual sharing relationships.

Mario had done his homework, with help from Aleta and Boris. Information inside the family unit was shared only when needed and then carefully and selectively. Secrecy and invisibility were maintained from the outside world vigilantly.

Lori, George, and Damian had a beautiful cottage overlooking the bay from the west. Aleta and Boris had an equally exquisite cottage overlooking the bay from the east.

Don Anacapri's ten-acre compound was well manicured and beautiful. Damian could imagine him and Lori living this lifestyle in a few decades. The property had a fishing dock and boat launch with a nice cabin cruiser. The grounds had a tennis court, indoor pool, and outdoor basketball court. There was a small putting green. Security was discreet but always present, and staff was attentive. The compound was well protected.

Drinks and dinner were held in the large banquet-sized dining room. George made himself available. Sharing in the festivities at the table were the four Anacapri brothers, the four Church sisters, the Garcia Group, and Mr. and Mrs. Anacapri. It was a large, happy, extended family gathering.

The food was superb, the homemade mead wine was excellent, the conversations were boisterous and free-flowing, and the friendships were warm and genuine.

After coffee and desserts, Aleta brought out the ceremonial multi-stem water pipe. She filled the bowl with brandy and crushed ice, and loaded the bowl with a fresh pinch of O/H.

After a few delicious and sweet, succulent bowls, separately and collectively their minds wandered into deep space orbit. George observed his humans from his favorite position, on his back looking at the world upside down. The family units were bonding in a Zen spiritual manner.

The days and evenings were enjoyed with swimming, playing tennis, eating, and drinking. Damian discovered that he was not the tennis type. He would stick to business, family, and quiet walks.

Sunday afternoon, Mario invited Damian, Lori, George, and Aleta on his 36-foot cabin cruiser. The other family members stayed at the compound or were escorted into town to go shopping and catch a show.

When the boat slowed and was comfortably in the bay, Mario said, "This is the place where I find true relaxation: on the open water, with no one around and no prying eyes. It is also the best place to do business. I do my best thinking here."

George was enjoying himself on the boat. It was a new experience and he was adjusting quickly.

Mario said, "My roles are as banker and deal maker. I rarely touch the products, but I always know the details of all transactions. Opiate-hash in the Arab world will be like a river of gold for us, with no competition.

"I am different from your Attorney Grain as a banker. I do not keep your money for safe storage. I lend money with interest and control the economic futures of the businesses I invest in. In short, I am the ultimate banker and investor. I have complete control of the businesses from arm's length, without my name attached. I secure the collateral, earn excellent points as return on investments, and control legitimate and not-so-legit companies. One point equals one percent. I am a reasonable man.

"I can foresee O/H Inc. and all the various entities blossoming into full butterflies. The profits will have to be invested and washed through solid and tangible long-term investments. I am thinking mortgage banker. In the old country, they are called moneylenders. I lend money on real estate and other transactions and collect points for carrying the note. If the clients are stuck, Anacapri Incorporated forecloses. No gangster stuff. Gangster stuff is for fools, and fools get caught. This is business, and violence is bad for business."

Damian said, "As long as we stay below the radar and do not attract attention, it will work. The moment we make noise, we will have problems. I work very hard to anticipate and avoid problems."

Mario said, "Yes, I know you do. That is why I am your new investor-franchisee. I have watched your habits, and you are a cautious one. I would like you to share in the wealth, and I will offer your group $50 per gram. This is more than the current $30 per gram you are charging your other investor-franchisees." He smiled at Damian and Lori. "Am I correct?"

Lori nodded in the affirmative.

Mario said, "For this price, I would expect a completely reliable and unlimited, smooth supply chain, with no interruptions."

Lori replied, "Mario, this is not a fail-safe business. There will always be supply chain issues. It is the nature of the beast. Too many moving parts and something will get stuck. But we will do our best to minimize and reduce the issues, and offer you as close to perfect as possible."

Lori and Damian looked into each other's eyes, and they both realized the solution to the supply chain issues. The answer was to stockpile extra raw products of opium and hashish, and only release the products as needed to insure smooth deliveries. This would require fronting large shipments and storing it in the "bank" as a hedge against interruptions.

Attorney Grain was on the agenda to be contacted next week.

Mario said, "Of course, I would like your help to set up a production facility in Sicily. My family has some land near the sea, which would be perfect to service the Arab needs. Having production facilities around the world benefits us all. It is good business to be near your clientele, and provides flexibility if a facility is compromised. One cannot always predict weather and politics . . . if you understand my meaning.

"You have production facilities in New York, Iowa, at the London bookstore, and of course India. India is the largest, followed by Iowa and New York. The London bookstore is best for repackaging, because it is short on space and privacy." Mario added cheerfully, "Now we will add Sicily to the list."

Damian said, "I will ask Roger to draw up blueprints and explain the processes. Then your people can build the facility to exceed O/H standards."

Mario smiled. "Good. Now we should eat. You must try this amazing mead wine. It is the best, so fragrant and with a lovely bouquet."

The nucleus of the extended O/H family enjoyed the next few hours cruising the bay, fishing, eating, and drinking superb mead.

A deep family bond was developing, with vested business interests that would last for generations.

Mario started the conversation during the Monday evening drive back to the city, using the familiar vehicle choreography methods.

"Damian and Lori, you know your group created a very special thing with O/H. It will become the global designer drug of choice, favored among the educated, professionals, and elite of the world. These folks do not do gangster stuff and do not call the law. It is about as close to perfect as perfect can be. Damn, it is brilliant."

Damian and Lori smiled proudly at the group's accomplishments. O/H had developed from concept to global at the speed of light.

Lori said, "We are the five families in the United States who control the worldwide O/H markets. The Garcia Group in New York controls the North American markets using the investor-franchisee business model. The Grain Group in Detroit controls the central states, and Canada. They provide legal and immigration services, and shipping methods from India to Vancouver. The Spencer Group in Iowa controls the Midwest to the Rocky Mountains. The Cooper Group in New York does business with the Russian underground and the eastern bloc countries. The Anacapri-Church Group, from New York, does business with Italy and the Arab nations. And we have the Gupta Group in India, without whom none of this would be possible. We must never forget that. The Gupta Group is our reason for being. We must always protect each family. United we prosper and divided we fail."

Damian said, "And failure is not an option!"

Loris said proudly, "We are six families that exclusively control the worldwide supply of opiate-hashish. That is an accomplishment."

Mario smiled. "We are the five New York families, and one Indian family, that no one has ever heard of."

Damian stated, "We are the six quietest families no one will EVER hear of in the future! We operate below the radar. That is how we prosper."

Mario and drivers escorted the group to Apartment 3A.

On the way up the steps, Mario said, "How do you like what I have done to the place? When I bought the building, it looked like a septic tank. Now it looks beautiful. You and Lori should think about buying real estate with your cash profits. It is a tangible asset that pays monthly dividends, called rent." Mario smiled. "Give it some thought. Maybe we can buy real estate together. We will talk very soon and work out the details."

For the next few months, Damian concentrated on school and business. Damian was obsessed with earning the highest grades, preferably with "cum laude" after the PhD. He was determined to finish school as soon as possible, and to this end, Damian devoted his energies.

Orders of books arrived periodically to Apartment 3A, and then were distributed to Detroit and Iowa. Damian and Lori would make quiet trips, using combinations of bus, train, and car, to deliver books and return funds. Damian's investor-franchise organizations and Lori's medical markets were growing and prospering.

Business was brisk. Sleep was optional.

Attorney Grain was the de facto U.S. banker for O/H. Grain kept the cash funds locked in extremely secure safes, buried in the cellar of his suburban home. Damian could not provide that level of security in Apartment 3A.

Vash's earnings were sent to London and then transferred to India. The student courier system was used, which worked well for larger volumes.

Damian kept his own set of books, not being one to trust completely. He preferred to handle his affairs directly, and withdrew his earnings periodically, while leaving a nice balance. Damian paid the family members generously, appreciating their services and expertise. The family shared well in the gains, proportionate to involvement. That is what families do.

As summer gave way to fall, Grain suggested that Lori and Damian meet in Detroit. The topic of conversation was importing hundreds of kilos of raw products to be banked and distributed as needed.

The five families decided that business required a large U.S. bank to withdraw products. It is good business to have warehouses closer to service geographic areas more efficiently.

Also on the agenda was the need to send one million U.S. dollars, in mixed bills, to the Gupta Group in India. Damian and Lori were making their first personal investment in the Gupta health care system.

Lori and Damian were invited to spend the Thanksgiving holidays with Gershwin and Ayesha Grain. George chose to stay in New York and hang out with the family. The busiest travel time of the year was the perfect time to travel because it was easier to blend into massive crowds.

Attorney Grain picked up Lori and Damian from the Detroit train station. Damian and Lori traveled on the same train, but in separate cars, using the shoulder bag and briefcase signals they had developed on previous travels. The trip was uneventful and crowded, which was perfect.

On the way to Grain's house, Grain suggested they stop for coffee and pastries at the Wild West Organic Desserts shop.

Lori was mesmerized. "Damian, I love this place," she gasped breathlessly. "It feels like an old-time country store and bakery in the middle of a big city. Look at the oak barrels with various organic oats and flours to bake your own pies, pancakes, and pastries at home."

Lori was amazed at the old soda fountain style and countertop.

Grain smiled. "This is the only place I know where you can get a real egg cream soda with egg. Just like in the old days when I was a kid!"

Lori said, "It looks like we are in a movie set and the director should yell, 'CUT!'"

Lori and Damian locked eyes.

Damian smiled. "Lori, we should find a store in New York, and you can open an old-time sweet shop."

Lori's mind was working at a zillion miles per hour. "And we can call it 'Rosie's Sweet Shoppes.' The logo will be from the old posters of Rosie the Riveter. You know the ones, from World War II, showing this woman in a red bandana, working in a factory. Only *my* Rosie will have a red rose in her mouth. Rosie will be a symbol for strength and beauty."

And so the concept for Rosie's Sweet Shoppes was created.

Grain smiled over his Turkish coffee and fabulous pastry. "I can see a national chain of Rosie's Sweet Shoppes in less than ten years."

Damian said, "The beauty is we could modify the O/H investor-franchisee business model for the chain of Rosie's Sweet Shoppes."

Lori was deep into her thoughts as Grain drove to the front gates and pushed the button. The gate swung open and then closed behind as they parked in the circular driveway.

Ayesha, elegant as usual, bathed in soft lighting, warmly greeted her guests. She gave Win a passionate kiss. Turning to Lori, she said, "What! Where is the only man I really wanted to see?"

Grain looked confused.

"Of course I mean George," she said. "Where is Mr. George Carlin Dog?"

Damian smiled. "He is spending the holidays with the family. He enjoys being a couch potato once in a while."

Ayesha replied, "Smart dog." She said sweetly to Lori, "Damian can show you around, and the guesthouse. I have two bathing suits on the bed, both in your sizes and styles. We will meet in the pool." Ayesha smiled lovingly at Win. "I am going to grope my husband for a few minutes, and then put out a light supper." She winked. "So take your time getting changed, kids."

Damian showed Lori the enclosed pool and the guesthouse. On the bed were two bathing suits. As they were changing, Lori and Damian groped each other lovingly.

Damian said lustfully, "Lori, you look hot in that bathing suit, and you look hotter naked."

Lori smiled lovingly. "Behave yourself, Damian Garcia. You will get yours tonight."

Damian's eyes twinkled as he licked his lips in anticipation.

Win and Ayesha joined Lori and Damian in the pool. Damian noted to himself that in a few decades, he, Lori, and kids could enjoy having a quiet house with an indoor pool.

Ayesha looked as beautiful and elegant in a sari as she did in a bikini. Grain had chosen wisely.

Around noon the next day, the group met for a business lunch.

Ayesha said, "There are many things on our agenda we must resolve before we can move forward and take the next steps."

The elephant is back on the menu, Damian thought.

Ayesha continued. "O/H is going global big-time, yet in a very quiet way. We need to be very smart and very careful; otherwise, we will be very dead or very in prison for life. In order to do this professionally, we must, and we will, resolve the supply chain issues. As we all know, this is not a business without issues, and sometimes the issues cannot be controlled. The solution is to resolve the problems first so they do not become issues. Therefore we must import a large quantity, say 500, maybe 1,000 kilos, and distribute from our bank to our investor-franchisees, as needed."

Grain said, "We are at the point that the old system cannot keep up with demand."

Damian asked, "And what are the risks?"

Grain said, "The risks are always present. The rewards are greater and the exposure is shorter with larger orders."

Lori added, "How do we physically store the products and arrange distribution as needed?"

Grain smiled. "If you appreciate the general concepts, the details will work out. We have our ideas. So, do you like the concepts, Damian and Lori?"

Damian and Lori nodded affirmatively.

Ayesha said, "Good. A few months ago, Win and I took a vacation to Vancouver to do business and pleasure. We met with the boat captain and arranged to have products brought over from India and passengers brought back to India."

Grain said, "Remember Vash was to meet my 'cousin,' and he would escort Vash to the boat? Well, my cousin is actually my older brother, Andre Grain, by five years, and he and the captain have known each other for ten years. Their relationship has been cemented and is solid."

Ayesha said, "Here is the neat thing. When we were in Vancouver, Andre heard of this large old farm for sale, about twenty-five miles away. It is in the country, up on a beautiful hill, overlooking the valley below. You can see everything from the farm below, but they cannot see you from above."

Grain said, "So we bought it. We paid cash of course. It is 350 acres of woods, streams, small lakes, and open pastures. The property has a large farmhouse, and extra guest cottages, three barns, and many outbuildings."

Ayesha smiled. "It is the perfect safe house for our guests who will be leaving the country by boat, and the perfect place to bank quantities of O/H. We can build an underground bunker to maintain the optimum storage temperatures for the O/H products, and store thousands of kilos, which we distribute to smaller facilities, as supply and demand requires. Andre will live there and run the farm. He will oversee the guests departing via ship and the manufacturing and distribution operations."

Lori said, "It is perfect. I like that."

Grain smiled. "It is also the nicest place on planet earth to retire, when that time comes."

Lori and Damian realized they were in the company of the smartest people in the world, and the world would never know.

Lori, being the practical one, asked, "How do we work out the money? I am not sure we can afford to front a thousand kilos of product."

Grain said, "Then we will need a bank to lend us credit."

Damian and Lori locked eyes.

Lori said, "Maybe we could invite Mr. Anacapri."

Damian said, "That has possibilities. We may wish to keep Don Mario doing what he does best, and that would be the Arab-Italian markets."

Ayesha said, "The other alternative is to pay for the actual costs, about twenty percent, and pay the profits off as we sell the products over time. Obviously, we pay the Gupta Group interest on the loan balance."

Lori added, "That way the Gupta Group has costs covered and earns interest on their investments. It is a solid business plan, with above average rates of return and collateralized security."

Grain said, "I like the concept of in-house financing. Keep the money in the family, and the family grows stronger and prospers."

Damian said, "If this was an open-market debt-financing deal, I would have to say absolutely no. It would be too risky with collateral that would be difficult to collect and people that could be difficult to control. However, we are not the open market. We are a strictly closed market, consisting of six families. In this regard, I would be happy to explore establishing the financing arm of O/H Inc."

Lori interjected, "As an example, let's say we charge ten points on the unpaid balance, compounded and paid monthly. We allocate enough per I-F to satisfy their clientele, and retain the balance of product as collateral. The loan should be paid in full within a year, assuming normalcy."

Damian added, "We can offer our franchisees revolving credit, which helps with their cash flow concerns and increases the O/H revenue stream."

Ayesha and Grain smiled broadly, obviously pleased with the birth of the internal financing division of O/H Inc.

Grain added, "I think it is best to have Don Anacapri concentrate on his Arab-Italian market while we concentrate on banking and financing."

Lori smiled. "We control the distribution systems and also provide the in-house financing, so we control all aspects of the worldwide market."

Damian said, "Except Vash still has to buy products on the open farm markets in India. There is only a limited quantity of raw materials. O/H only buys the highest quality, and that is a very finite amount. It depends on politics, climate, and farming techniques, not always within Vash's direct control. His cooperative farms also sell to the other importers, which can create complications, not the least of which is competition from other less friendly drug cartels."

Grain added, "This means we still do not control ALL the aspects of production and distribution."

Lori said, "Unless we own the farms that produce exclusively for O/H, in which case we will own ALL aspects of the supply chain." She and Damian locked eyes, thinking as one unit. "So all we need to do is own a large, remote, and well-protected fertile farm in northern India to produce the highest quality opium and grow the best marijuana to produce the highest quality hashish, exclusively for O/H Inc. Then we will own ALL aspects of the business."

Ayesha said, "That is brilliant, Lori. Absolutely brilliant!"

Grain smiled. "Mr. Garcia, you have chosen well. Lori is a genius."

Damian added, "That way we do not disrupt the other opium, pot, and hash cartels that also rely on northern Indian products. Those boys do not play very nicely, and I do not want to attract their attention or their anger."

Lori said, "From farm to pipe, and all aspects in between."

Grain said, "I really like your mind, Lori Wilson."

Damian said proudly, "So do I. I love this woman beyond words."

Ayesha said, "See I told you, honey, Damian and Lori are brilliant, with Machiavellian minds."

Grain said, "That is absolutely brilliant. Buy a farm in a remote area of northern India, and O/H Inc. controls E-V-E-R-Y-T-H-I-N-G!"

Ayesha said, "Yes, then we will own and control the complete supply chain. And as you said, Lori, from farm to pipe."

Grain said, "I will send word to Vash and ask for his help. His families know people, and things appear for a reason. Trust me on this."

Lori added quietly, "That way we really DO control all aspects of the O/H trade. If we wish, we can expand to include the marijuana trade. As you know, Ayesha, opium has legitimate medical value also. It is the basis for pharmaceutical drugs like morphine."

Ayesha added, "We could expand into the legal drug world by selling the highest grade pure opium to make into morphine, used by hospitals."

Grain scratched his chin thoughtfully. "Legal pharmaceutical-grade opium-based derivatives, plus the not-so-legal O/H business could become a multibillion-dollar industry over time."

Ayesha said, "We will have to research the legitimate markets for pharmaceutical-grade opium and develop business methods. It is very doable, and has tremendous potential."

Damian said, "I think we need to concentrate on the O/H markets. The pharmaceutical-grade opium markets will require extensive analysis first. It is a phenomenal concept for the future, especially if Lori and I wish to exit the less-than-legal trades. I do not want to get ahead of ourselves."

Lori added, "So far everything sounds logical and very doable on the surface. My question is how do we transport the O/H products from India to your farm in Vancouver, Consigliore Grain?"

Grain replied with a smile, "Funny you should ask. Most of the heavy industrial goods, like tires and machine parts, are made in India and shipped to the U.S. and Canada. The manufacturing costs in India are lower compared to American union wages, and the quality is equal. So companies go where they get the best values.

"The U.S. companies stamp their name on the product, and the public is happy to pay more, thinking they are getting U.S. made quality. In reality, Americans are buying cheaper Indian-made goods made for American companies who sell to American consumers. And that is how you make money in international manufacturing, Mr. Garcia and Ms. Wilson."

Grain continued. "These goods come by freighter from India, China, and Japan to the ports in California and Vancouver. From Vancouver, trucks transport goods to warehouses and then distribute throughout Canada. It is easy to drop down into the U.S. and deliver goods to a store, say in New Jersey, that sells tires wholesale to local repair shops in New York, as an example."

Damian replied, "I will let Don Mario Anacapri know, and I am sure he will appreciate your suggestions. Transporting products inside of tires and industrial equipment is brilliant."

Lori said, "It will x-ray the same, and is harder for dogs to smell. The stuff is heavy, bulky, and not easy to inspect."

Ayesha said, "I like it, Gershwin. It is an excellent plan. We need to smooth out the details."

Damian added, "From the New Jersey warehouse, the products can be distributed to the Garcia, Cooper, and Anacapri groups."

Lori smiled. "Very smooth indeed!"

Ayesha smiled politely and said, "Exactly, my dear."

Lori said, "I do believe the profits are enormous, as are the risks."

Grain replied, "Not really. True, the risks are there, but properly handled, the profits far outweigh the risks exponentially."

Lori said, "Mario Anacapri has offered O/H Inc. $50 per gram based on the knowledge that he can sell O/H for $300 per gram to the Arab nations. Given the new business model, and the risk-benefit factors with the increased demand, I believe we could raise the wholesale U.S. price from $30 to $50 per gram. O/H will sell for $100 per gram in the U.S."

Grain, Ayesha and Damian listened intently.

The mind of a great woman was working.

Lori said, "Work with me. O/H is becoming very popular and going global. Limited Indian farm production factors indicate we must control the supply and demand curves. O/H must be a value-driven product. To do this, we raise the U.S. wholesale prices to $50 per gram. The distributors would be increasing their profit margins. Instead of a spread of $30 per gram, the price increase would yield a $50 per gram margin, which means more money all around.

"The finished product weighs more because of the steam infusion production process, and this bonus can be used as the I-Fs wish. O/H must control supplies by eliminating supply chain disruptions, and by cornering the market for top-grade opium and hashish, which we will be able to accomplish when O/H owns the farm directly."

Damian added, "Our Zen philosophy says that all franchisees must be treated equally and given the same opportunities. Therefore, the prices and service must be equitable."

Grain said, "It makes sense and is a logical solution."

Ayesha said, "I agree. We are good with the decisions."

Damian said, "Lori and I will visit the Spencer Group and the other families, and let them know of the organizational improvements."

Lori added sweetly, "Are we all agreed? Hearing none, motion carried. Done!"

The elephant was slowly being chewed, again.

Damian said, "On another subject, Lori and I would like to make a cash investment of one million U.S. dollars to the Gupta Health Service Foundation, to start the first hospital. This is our personal money and our gift of lifelong friendship and love."

Ayesha replied, "Damian, that is so kind. But Vash has not finished school yet."

"Yes, I know that. This is for the groundwork. He can begin buying the land and building a hospital, plus equipping the hospitals and mobile units before he gets his medical licenses. I believe I have more than that in the Grain Bank."

Ayesha smiled and nodded.

Grain reached into his pocket and pulled out a black leather book. He flipped a few pages and said, "Why yes, Mr. Garcia. It does appear that you have exactly, $2,576,696. You have also withdrawn more than that. Your account grows quickly with each transaction."

Damian smiled. "Exactly, Mr. Grain." He acknowledged the books were correct, and Grain and Ayesha understood that Damian kept his own set of books for accuracy. "Trust but always verify" was Damian Garcia's business model.

Grain said, "The one million in cash will go through the London bookstore, and from there it will find its way safely to the Vash Gupta Foundation, to be invested, as you wish, to start the first hospital system."

Damian and Lori smiled and thanked Grain for his services.

Attorney Grain's word was his bond, and that was all the guarantees required. The six families operated strictly under the principle of integrity, and one's word was the only guarantee ever needed.

Lori said, "I like the concept of heavy tires and machinery going to the Anacapri warehouse in New Jersey. It is perfectly routine."

Damian asked, "Then the deals are done?"

Ayesha said sweetly, "Damian and Lori, I assume you will talk with Don Anacapri and the other families, so everyone is equally pleased."

Damian and Lori borrowed a vehicle from the Grain fleet, and drove to visit the Spencer family in Iowa. They stayed at Damian and George's home in Hillside Park.

A dinner meeting was arranged for the following evening.

Maya had been there all day, as were Susan and Sky.

After a fantastic meal, Turkish coffee and pastries were offered.

Lori and Damian explained the supply chain issues and resolutions.

Lori started the conversation. "We have a method to resolve supply chain issues. O/H will be stockpiled in North America, where distribution will be easier and more secure. Instead of waiting for books to arrive by mail or couriers, we will control the distribution directly."

Damian explained, "The products will be stored in several locations, and shipped 'Just in Time' with no service interruptions. To do this over the long term, we will need to bankroll hundreds of kilos of product, in the 25% opium and 75% hashish ratios."

Professor Spencer smiled.

Lori added, "The other factor is that we are raising prices, to partially pay for the added warehousing and distribution facilities."

Professor Spencer raised his eyebrow. "Oh really, and why would you do that, if I may ask?"

Lori replied, "Because O/H is worth $100 on the street. In fact, in Tunisia, the going price is $300 per gram, and the Russian underground is easily getting $250 per gram. The North American prices are cheap. Prices can increase, as business dictates, with U.S. street prices of $150 gram, or more, very feasible. So your margins and profits are even better.

"The higher the street price, the more money investor-franchisees earn, and the more your distributors earn. The public is receiving a valuable product at a cost-effective price. We control exposure by controlling supplies using the supply side of the demand curve. We produce only the finest products on planet earth. That is why, Professor Spencer, we are raising the prices and adjusting the business methods."

Professor Spencer agreed, as did Susan, Sky, and Maya.

Lori continued. "Here is how the money breaks down. The wholesale prices are $50 per gram; $1,400 per ounce; $22,500 per pound; and $50,000 per kilo. Terms cash unless financing terms have been arranged. We are also offering in-house financing and revolving credit, which will help with your cash flow issues. What I need to know is how many kilos the Spencer Group would like to stockpile?"

Damian added, "We will provide financing at 10% on the unpaid balance, compounded monthly, with the unused product as collateral."

Lori smiled. "Then the deal is done."

Professor Spencer said thoughtfully, "I like the concept of in-house financing. This will free up cash and increase market penetration."

Susan said, "Can we get back to you? We have to do some cost analysis, you understand."

Sky added, "I like the concepts. We should invest the money now, while things are smooth. One never knows what the future may bring."

Damian said, "Oh, one more thing. I believe your farm tractors and trucks need tires, lots of tires, and heavy machinery. Tell us what type of tires and machinery, and they will be delivered by truck. The products will be inside the tires between the rubber and the inside lining. Carefully remove the lining. The products will be dehydrated and compressed into kilo slabs. This reduces the weight and decreases the possibilities of exposure. You will need to rehydrate the products before manufacturing. Our chemist will explain the details."

Lori added, "O/H moves to the next level. Are there any questions?"

Once again, the voice of logic and reasoning had spoken.

Hearing and seeing nothing but smiles and praise, the group smoked from the ceremonial water pipe and sipped Turkish coffee into the late hours.

Damian and Lori returned Grain's car a few days later. Damian said to Win and Ayesha, "Let me brief you about the Spencer visit. The Spencer Group is on board with the new business plans. They like the higher prices and lower traffic count. I am sure the other families will enjoy the benefits also."

Win and Ayesha smiled.

Grain said, "I like that."

Ayesha smiled sweetly. "This is working out well as a multi-national company. The future looks bright."

Grain asked, "How many kilos are we talking about?"

Damian said, "I am working on an exact number. We will always keep the bank full, at all times, and for all emergencies."

Grain said, "We only want top quality, and that is a limited supply. Depending on conditions in India, it might take time to assemble."

Damian said, "I have been thinking about this, and I think I would like to test the waters before I fill the pool. So let us begin with maybe a hundred kilos and use it as a prototype. That works out to twenty kilos per family. Each family gets ten kilos, either cash or financed, and we keep fifty kilos in the bank."

Grain said, "You are the cautious type, Damian. It does make sense."

Damian continued. "We do not want to flood the markets and attract attention. Allow O/H to filter slowly into the drug culture ecosystem. If we make a splash, then we make too much noise. If we flood the markets too quickly, the Feds will notice the spikes, and we will attract attention. In addition, the basics of supply and demand take effect. More supply can reduce the prices. This is going to cost each family one million dollars in cash and/or financing."

Lori said quietly, "That is a reality check!"

Grain said, "It will take some time to arrange all the details. The ship's captain needs to be involved. I would like to coordinate the arrivals of products with scheduled departures of guests to India. It is a more cost-efficient business operation. The captain makes money round trip, and he will be happy."

Riding the train back to New York, Damian and Lori followed their normal protocols. Everything appeared to be normal. When they arrived in New York, they exited separately, using different subway and bus routes.

Safely back in Apartment 3A, Lori and Damian relaxed. George was happy to see them.

Damian said thoughtfully, "This has been an interesting trip, Lori. We accomplished a lot in a short time."

"Yes, Damian, I agree we have accomplished an amazing amount in a short period of time. My brain is stuck on Rosie's Sweet Shoppes and the way Grain said he would invest in a nationwide chain. Do you think that is possible?"

"Absolutely YES! I think it is a very viable business plan. In fact, we could adopt the investor-franchisee business model to Rosie's Sweet Shoppes. We sell the complete business package to each owner operator, and they enjoy an exclusive territory."

Lori said, "Rosie's will be located in trendy neighborhoods, where the clientele appreciates the atmosphere that Rosie's will provide."

Damian added, "Lori, my love, Howard invented something amazing with the investor-franchisee business model because it can be modified to fit virtually any business."

"I see Rosie's as a place that serves only the finest coffees and teas from around the world, and the most delicious home-baked organic pastries. The organic flour and other ingredients will be displayed in old-fashioned wood barrels. The clientele scoops out whatever they wish, and we sell it by the ounce or pound."

Damian quipped, "Just like we sell O/H."

Lori said, "It will also be a place to hang out. We will offer book readings, or invite local musicians to play, or comedians to perform. I want it to be a homey, comfortable atmosphere."

Damian smiled, knowing he was falling deeply in love with Lori. "Obviously you have given this a little thought?"

Lori replied with a twinkle, "Rosie's has been on my mind."

"Then we will take Rosie's from your mind and build the first Rosie's Sweet Shoppe chain in New York. Rosie's Sweet Shoppes will be the first legal U.S. business entity that O/H Incorporated invests in as a silent partner." Damian continued. "It would also be a good way to show legal income, something we need to do. We are closing in on the end of the education world, and soon will be entering the career world.

The tax man likes to see students graduating and making money. We always want the tax man happy."

Lori added, "And we are way too smart to get caught on tax issues."

Damian said, "You realize that O/H has grown to the point that the group must think as a multi-national corporate entity, and not as a bunch of poor, hungry, and stoned-out graduate students."

"Yes, honey, but we were those stoned-out graduate students less than two years ago. Things are moving very quickly."

On Valentine's Day 1974, the tires arrived in Vancouver. Each family had pledged one million dollars and received a total allocation of 20 kilos, with 10 kilos held in the bank, of raw product in the normal 25% opium and 75% hashish ratios.

Distribution to the Spencer Group in Iowa and Attorney Grain went as planned. Two weeks later a truck arrived at the Anacapri New Jersey tire warehouse.

The New York families were happy and well supplied. Damian assured the families that this was a test, and depending on supply and demand curves, more products would be forthcoming as requested.

Everyone was pleased, and business was good.

A few weeks later, Damian, Lori, and George decided to take a long walk. They headed into a neighborhood that Damian and Lori had not noticed. On the corner was a decrepit building in obvious need of serious repair.

It was for sale, and it looked like a dump.

Lori looked at the building and said, "What an ugly piece of shit. This is a rat hole of the first degree."

George seconded the motion by taking a long pee on the front steps.

Damian had been hit by a thunderbolt. "This is the most beautifully ugly building in all of New York City. You are correct; it is an amazing crap hole, and an absolute piece of shit. But ugly things can be made to look beautiful. However, it is in an up-and-coming part of town that will become a trendy neighborhood and has tremendous potential. The storefront faces the avenue, which means heavy foot traffic to the store. It is a perfect place for Rosie's Sweet Shoppes."

Lori looked at Damian as if he was smoking way too much of their O/H product. "Help me here, Damian. All I see is a filthy shit hole."

Damian grinned. "Yes. And I hope it is cheap."

He walked the side street side, and was even happier.

"Lori," he blurted out like a kid in a candy store, "it is attached to an apartment building on the street side. Judging by the mailboxes, there are twenty units, plus the store facing the avenue and a large apartment above the store. This dump can be made into diamonds with money and effort. Follow me on this, and try to see through the ugly." He pointed as he spoke, explaining in detail how this was the beginning of Rosie's Sweet Shoppes.

Lori was skeptical, but open-minded.

Damian said, "The store is about fifteen hundred square feet, with a large front patio. We put slate on the patio, have large potted plants between the tables for privacy, and we hand paint roses on the umbrellas." He grinned. "We have a white picket fence around the patio."

"I have always wanted a white picket fence surrounding my patio in New York."

"Then your dream will come true, Lori Wilson."

Lori and Damian peered through the plate glass windows, looking through the gates. They were studying the inside conditions and layout.

Damian observed, "The ceilings have pressed tin inlaid, and the walls appear solid. We will need to install lighting and upgrade the electric and water service. It has good bones. I do not see any major issues."

Lori said excitedly, "I can see how to arrange things. The soda fountain goes along that wall, the tables and chairs are in the other area, the barrels with flour and ingredients are in that alcove, and we can put a small stage in the corner over there, facing the tables."

Damian noted, "Above the store there is a large three-bedroom apartment. This was the custom decades ago, when the shopkeepers would live above their store. We could live above your store."

Lori's eyes were shining like diamonds with excitement.

Rosie's Sweet Shoppes was developing from concept to reality.

Lori exclaimed, "It is perfect, Damian. It is exactly what my head said it should be. Can we afford it?"

Damian smiled. "I hope so, Lori. We need Howard to put this deal together, and Marguerite to work the legality so we are completely invisible owners, but with complete control of all our enterprises. Our problem is that we can legally own in our names assets that we can financially justify. This way our friends at the IRS and the other nice law enforcement agencies do not have reasons to investigate us.

"We must establish legal entities that cannot be pierced to own assets and operate investments. And we need methods to move large amounts of cash and launder money. We can only operate with clean money. Clean money investments will justify our financial abilities, and keep us below the radar."

Lori smiled. "Marguerite has her legal work cut out for her. She has to build the legal systems to provide the veils, barriers, and protections to shield the assets and people from inquisitive law enforcement eyes."

Damian added, "I like as many firewalls as possible, and as much control, direct or indirect, as feasible. This is a major undertaking, and I think Don Anacapri should be invited to do the renovations. His construction companies have relationships with the building inspector and government agencies. And I do not want my face around this place. Mario should handle the details, without our direct involvement." He added thoughtfully, "It is good business, to stay invisible."

Lori said, "We must always be invisible, but always in control."

The three amigos walked back to Apartment 3A.

Lori called a house meeting.

"Damian and I have found a piece of crap building which will become the first Rosie's Sweet Shoppes. The store faces the avenue and has a large patio. Damian wants to put a white picket fence around the patio, have tables with a red rose hand painted on each umbrella, and plants for privacy."

Damian said, "Lori and I would move into the apartment above the store like the old-time shopkeepers. Facing the street is a twenty-unit apartment building. The apartment building is a long-term rental income producer whose assets will increase over time. Lori and I will still maintain Apartment 3A for O/H. Howard, we need you to put together this deal without Lori and I having direct or visible involvement, but having all the control. We want to pay cash and buy the property as-is.

"I will contact Don Anacapri and talk with him about renovations and dealing with the city bureaucracies." He added, shaking his head, "I hate bureaucrats."

Lori said, "Marguerite, we need to establish legal structures whereby we can operate the various business enterprises away from the prying eyes of the U.S. government. We need to be legally invisible, but in total control of all aspects of the enterprises. Is that doable?"

Marguerite's legal mind was processing the information as quickly as Lori was explaining the requirements. She nodded in the affirmative. "Perhaps if we establish legal entities, such as non-profit organizations or a foundation or maybe multiple foundations."

Damian said, "O/H Inc. would invest in the non-profit foundations. The foundations would own assets and earn income from the for-profit businesses. The foundations would invest those profits helping communities in need. It would be a method of giving back to the community."

Marguerite replied, "The business model of creating wealth using foundations could be the vehicle to accomplish our numerous goals. It is also an excellent way to launder large sums of money worldwide. And the foundations could be legally based in Geneva, Switzerland."

The room fell completely silent as everyone listened carefully.

Marguerite continued. "This has numerous advantages, not the least of which is the Swiss secret banking laws. O/H Inc. is an international business entity, and as such, we have to be careful about the money trails. The beauty of the Swiss banking system is that you do not have names, only numbers, and no one asks questions. This is a fee-for-service banking industry, and their integrity and accuracy are legendary. Obviously, an international foundation must have offices in New York to be able to do business. Therefore, we establish a New York business affairs office.

"There are legal mechanisms and procedures that will establish the various foundations frameworks. I will work on the specifics. Those are the broad brush conceptual details."

Lori asked, "So I can have the Wilson Foundation, as an example, and decide what investments and assets to pursue? And, Damian can have the Garcia Foundation, and make his separate investment decisions?"

Marguerite replied, "Exactly."

Howard asked, "Therefore the foundations are buying and owning real estate and other significant assets?"

Marguerite smiled. "Yes. Exactly."

Damian said, "It makes perfect sense for O/H to act globally."

Marguerite said, "Vash and I discussed this before he left. We had planned for O/H to go to the next level. The Swiss banking system is the logical step. In fact it is favored by most of the legal and not-so-legal money transactions in the world."

A week later, Damian, Lori, George, Mario, and Aleta met to discuss the renovation expenses and government bureaucracy issues.

Mario said, "Damian, it just so happens that Anacapri Development has very friendly arrangements with the various government agencies." He smiled. "In other words, they are on our payroll. This is how business is really done in New York. So I do not think we have too much to worry about. Of course we build to code, and they will not bother the construction process."

Howard made the owner of the property an all-cash offer far below the listing price. The seller pretended that he owned the crown jewel in New York and was holding out. Mario convinced the reluctant seller that the offer was more than generous, given the building's condition and housing code violations. Mario also suggested that the seller would enjoy a healthier retirement in Miami if he took the cash offer. The seller agreed.

A month later, the Garcia Foundation became the proud owner of a slum piece-of-crap property. Mario Anacapri's construction crew had to turn this dump in to a diamond in record time.

The 20-unit apartment building facing the street was structurally solid, but needed repairs. The exterior facades were sandblasted to remove decades of grime and dirt. The halls and stairs were painted in bright colors, and bright lighting was installed, providing for better security. A front door intercom security system was installed to each apartment for added security.

Three months later, the building looked beautiful. Mario's crew had performed miracles, as they had with Apartment 3A. Damian and Lori visited the property with Mario to offer suggestions. The total costs for the 20-unit apartment building, the build-out of Rosie's Sweet Shoppes, and the three-bedroom apartment above the store, including purchase price, complete renovations, bribes, and Anacapri profits came to $862,656. The Garcia Foundation's increased equity exceeded those costs.

Damian decided not to rent the 20 units to the public, even though rental rates were increasing rapidly. Lori and Damian renamed the building "Rosie's House" and provided apartments to homeless and abused women with children. Lori had contacts in the medical community that provided integrated social services assistance.

Damian had found his method of giving back to the community.

O/H Inc., through the Geneva-based Garcia Foundation and the Wilson Foundation, provided the housing assistance, fulfilling their social mandate. It would be virtually impossible to suspect, let alone prove, that O/H drug money was the financial basis for the foundations. O/H became silent partners in various business enterprises, including Rosie's Sweet Shoppes. The foundations reached out to those in need while enjoying exceptional returns on investments.

Rosie's Sweet Shoppes opened on the first day of the first quarter of 1975. The neighborhood vastly improved after it opened and the apartment building renovations were completed. The gods of goodwill were smiling on Lori Wilson and Rosie's Sweet Shoppes.

Lori said one evening, as they were snuggling on the couch in their spacious apartment, "I wish we could provide housing and help to more than the twenty families we have now."

Damian replied, "I did not realize how great the needs are, and how little those desperate needs are met."

"It is probably similar for Vash. The needs in India are everywhere, and those needs are not met." Lori smiled. "Perhaps we can change that. The income from our enterprises can go into buying more buildings and help meet those needs."

"I like that concept, Ms. Wilson. I think I will talk about developing real estate partnerships with Mario Anacapri. Combining our assets and skills increases our legitimate enterprises. This gives us legal income and assets, and provides a method to wash our O/H profits."

Lori was happy, and completely energized.

In the late spring of 1975, a local food critic discovered Rosie's Sweet Shoppes, and business expanded exponentially. Rosie's became the centerpiece of the local neighborhood. New York City is a large city made up of local neighborhoods.

Marguerite and Aleta helped Lori in the store. Lori and Aleta loved to bake, and they created delicious pastries. Marguerite was excellent with the customers and cheerfully explained the ingredients and the desserts. She offered baking tips and discussed the various blends of imported coffees. Having live entertainment, book readings, musicians, and comedians was a stroke of genius. Rosie's became the focal point of the neighborhood.

By the late fall of 1975, Rosie's was proving to be a successful business model. The per square foot earnings from Rosie's Sweet Shoppes exceeded expectations. Rosie's was building a cult-like following, and sales were brisk. Lori was ecstatic, and Damian was completely in love.

Lori Wilson determined that Rosie's Sweet Shoppes would be a business that directly performed social good. The Wilson Foundation invested in Rosie's House apartments in various neighborhoods where the Garcia Foundation and Anacapri Development could find properties that met their business model criteria.

The Garcia Foundation's method of doing business was to purchase run-down buildings—paying cash and accepting properties in as-is condition—and offered distressed owners fast closings. The positive cash flow from the for-profit rental properties funded the non-profit Rosie's House. The Garcia and Wilson foundations, using a complex web of corporate and investment methods, purchased, renovated, and operated buildings. The business model allowed for flexibility and provided layers, while creating charitable tax advantages. The appreciation values always exceeded the cash investments.

The Rosie's Sweet Shoppes business model of returning to the community while earning exceptional per square foot store profits proved the basis for nationwide store operation. Returning to the community appealed to Rosie's target demographics. It was adaptable to various markets.

Lori decided that after two years, she would approach Attorney Grain about taking Rosie's to the next level.

By the beginning of 1976, Damian had finished his PhD dissertation, and he graduated with a PhD with "cum laude" attached.
MISSION ACCOMPLISHED!

It was the first Sunday of the second quarter of 1976, and a quarterly Board of Directors meeting was scheduled at Apartment 3A. O/H family members were required to attend. A lovely buffet was offered for all to relax, enjoy, and do business. Excellent O/H was preloaded into various bongs, bowls, and water pipes to enjoy as they wished.

Every quarter, the group met to discuss concerns and direct the O/H operations going forward. Attending the meetings were the usual suspects: Mario, Celina, Aleta, Boris, Roger, Howard, Marguerite, Lori, Damian, and George. Each family operated independently and yet in concert with each other as cohesive units.

Damian opened the meeting.

He said, "O/H is in the process of establishing banks to store the products and cash. The goal is to arrange 1,000 kilos, which is 2,200 pounds of products, in the usual 25% opium to 75% hashish ratio. The central warehouse will be outside of Vancouver, operated by Attorney Grain's older brother Andre, with high security and in deep underground vaults that are climate-controlled to preserve freshness."

Lori said, "They are using it as a safe house for their guests escaping by ocean. Grain said it overlooks the countryside. We are outside of U.S. laws and jurisdiction. Canada is a quieter and safer place to do business."

Damian said, "From Vancouver, products will be distributed on a just-in-time basis throughout the O/H network. Franchisees service their domestic and foreign markets independently, following O/H protocols. This reduces the market fluctuations and supply chain issues, which have been a thorn in the operations. This process is ongoing and will take time to develop fully, with all possible safety methods incorporated into every aspect of these operations."

Lori added sarcastically, "It is not exactly easy to move a thousand kilos of product around the world without attracting some sort of attention. Done correctly, the banks will be a remarkable event. Done badly, we are either dead or rotting in some prison."

The families looked at each other, completely understanding the huge technical logistics involved in such an operation.

Lori added, "I just want to make sure the New York families are all on the same page."

All the family members nodded in the affirmative.

Damian said, "I believe Don Anacapri wishes to say a few words."

Mario said, "As the newest member, I would like to say thank you for the opportunity to join the family. Let me report about O/H in the Arab world. I have arrangements made with certain Tunisian ruling families who are in on the action to market O/H.

"The prices the Arab elite are happy to pay to enjoy their forbidden pleasures are outstanding. O/H sells for $300 per gram, and the demand exceeds supply by at least ten times. It is a river of gold. Word is traveling down the Arab peninsula, and I am moving twenty kilos a month, and then it will increase as demand increases. Remember, everyone in the kingdom is in on the action."

Boris said, "Let me tell you that I cannot keep up with the demands from my local vendors. My prices in the frozen Soviet world are $250 per sweet gram and will go up as soon as the local economy improves. I bribe the captain of the police, and they leave me alone. A little grease on the wheels, and everyone is happy. As word spreads and the economy ebbs and flows, I expect within two years to have a very steady market in this designer drug."

The families understood that O/H was exploding into a money machine exceeding the incomes of most major corporations.

Lori reported, "The medical community and professionals are quietly enjoying O/H, with total satisfaction and no complaints. The only complaints I keep hearing are supply chain issues, which will be addressed whenever Vancouver is operational. Business is brisk with no complications. Who could ask for more in this business?"

She continued. "Rosie's Sweet Shoppes is growing steadily. The concept is superb, and Rosie's has a loyal following that is growing, mostly through word of mouth. Attorney Grain and Mario Anacapri both want to take Rosie's national and then global. Imagine Rosie's as a national coffee shop chain, and then a global coffee shop chain. It will be operated under the brilliant investor-franchisee business model developed by Mr. Howard Pavel. Wow. That is an amazing concept! Rosie's worldwide!"

Lori regained her composure and said, "The basis for Rosie's Sweet Shoppes is to have a social conscience and invest our money towards those goals. Rosie's is a family business that provides real social needs, helping homeless women and children while providing integrated social services."

Damian said with pride, "Rosie's is the first U.S. legitimate business funded by O/H Inc., through various legal entities, of course." He smiled at Lori. "Rosie's is a prototype, and you know how I like prototypes, Lori."

Lori smiled. "Yes, honey, I do. You are *my* prototype, Damian."

Mario said, "If I may interrupt you two lovebirds, I have one more item on the agenda. The subject is lending money and laundering money so it is clean. I lend money at rates that make me comfortable. Terms depend on the person, purpose, collateral, and risk-benefit factors. It is business, but it also is very personal. There are legitimate business opportunities that may require stronger negotiation skills, if you understand my meaning."

Lori said, "Don Anacapri, your services will be used graciously and with appreciation, this we can assure you."

Mario bowed slightly. "It is always a pleasure doing business with you, Lori Ann Wilson."

Lori smiled. She whispered to Damian, "When I was in grade school, I was called Lori Ann. I have not used that name since."

"Lori honey," he whispered, "knowledge is his business."

Lori asked, "Are there any unfinished items on or off the agenda that we would like to talk about?"

Damian said, "Excellent. Meeting is adjourned."

The families chilled in Apartment 3A until the wee hours of the next morning. They crashed until past noon.

The first Sunday of the final quarter of 1976, and Damian suggested they walk through the park to Apartment 3A, stopping along the way to pick up munchies. It was a lovely brisk afternoon to take a stroll as a family.

As they walked, talked, and nibbled, Damian and Lori thought about the changes that had occurred in their lives. The group met by providence, fate, or bad luck, about four years ago. From hungry graduate students, they had matured to prosperous executives of their chosen domains.

Howard opened the door.

George trotted straight to the buffet table.

"That's my boy." Damian chuckled.

Howard smiled. "We miss Sir George, except we are so busy with our new lives and still working in the old lives." Sometime later he said, "I accepted a position on Wall Street, negotiating venture capital funding for business mergers and acquisitions. Profit is the prime motivating factor, and the firm is open to funding unique ventures, if the returns are justified."

Damian said, "Perhaps these venture capitalists would like to do some quiet side deals in the future. We can re-package O/H Inc.

as a legitimate multinational enterprise using the foundations and investment trusts as vehicles."

Howard said thoughtfully, "Perhaps they just might be interested. They like quiet money, especially cash money. Let me explore the possibilities over time."

Over his career, Howard would negotiate exquisitely sophisticated deals, which became the gold standard in deal making and venture funding.

Howard added, "They may become very useful when O/H is putting together international transactions requiring extensive debt financing. They are the heavy money boys, but they charge heavy money for their services."

Lori said, "So they may do the deals that others will not?"

Howard nodded. "Yes."

"That is always good to know."

Howard said to Lori and Damian proudly, "Let me tell you the survey results for Rosie's Sweet Shoppes. I believe that these concepts will apply to all units nationally and can be adapted for international franchises. The objective was to determine the most profitable business hours for Rosie's Sweet Shoppes."

Lori, Damian, and the group listened intently. Business expertise of Howard's caliber was rare and must be appreciated.

Howard continued. "Based on projected demographics, I suggest the hours between seven a.m. to eleven p.m. and extending to midnight on the weekends. This would produce the most paying traffic, and should become the store hours for all Rosie's Sweet Shoppes franchises nationwide and worldwide, if it gets to that."

Lori interrupted. "Trust me, ladies and gentlemen, it will get to that and beyond even what I can conceive. Just wait a few decades."

Howard said, "You could staff Rosie's with college students working part-time shifts. This allows for staffing flexibility. Hiring predominately part-time and college students eliminates the possibility of unionization when Rosie's goes national. That is a consideration for the future."

Celina and Mario Anacapri arrived.

Damian warmly greeted them. George handed Mario his right paw, and they shook hands. Celina gave George a hug.

The group congregated around the buffet table, and George supervised. Mead wine, coffee, and desserts were on a side table, as were lovely salads. After all the creatures had been fed and caffeinated, the meeting was called to order in the conference room. Two blackboards were in the front.

Damian stood up from the table and said, "Ladies and gentlemen and Sir George, the quarterly meeting of O/H is officially open. Secrecy and tight information control are the basis of operations. Agreed?"

Mario asked the first open question. "I understand that Rosie's is doing well. When you expand the hours to serve your customers' needs, then it will become a successful franchise business. I would like to invest in Rosie's Sweet Shoppes as a franchisee before it becomes famous and expensive. I am impressed with Rosie's, Lori Ann Wilson. This is a concept that it is in tune with the times. Neighborhood coffee shops in major cities that sell delicious homemade pastries and organic flour for home baking in a cozy setting will become very popular. This could be an extremely profitable legitimate business, and an excellent way to wash money. Washing money is going to become a major concern, ladies and gentlemen and Mr. George. Rosie's will become a hit, and I want in early." Mario smiled. "Capice, paisano?"

Lori smiled sweetly and said in a seductive voice, "We can talk about this later."

Mario smiled slyly. "Yes, Lori, you purr cat, we can talk about this later. But the answer will be the same. I would like to buy into the Rosie's Sweet Shoppes franchise. Understand, Lori Ann Wilson, my dear? Any questions?"

Lori understood Don Anacapri had out flanked her. "I would be honored to have Don Mario Anacapri and the Church family as long-term investor-franchisees. Can I assume you will be providing ongoing financial and operational assistance as part of your investment strategies?"

Mario chuckled. "Yes ma'am. I will be an active investor, interested in national expansion. I am a man who puts his money where his mouth is, so to speak. My word is my bond. The concept might actually work in other countries. Rosie's International. Let me work on this."

Lori said, "You need to know, Attorney Grain expressed an interest in taking Rosie's national when the business was ready. I promised him first."

Mario said, "Attorney Grain takes Rosie's North America and Mario Anacapri takes Rosie's International." He understood Lori Wilson had out flanked him. "Lori, you are a handful. I will do whatever you wish."

"I do believe we have solved the Rosie's growth dilemma."

Mario smiled. "Agreed. You drive a hard bargain, Lori Ann Wilson."

Lori smiled like a cat and said sweetly, "I usually do drive a hard bargain, Mario, and you know that."

George greeted Boris Cooper and Aleta Church at the front door. The group hugged warmly.

The O/H quarterly meetings were social and business. Individual families were conducting their own affairs and understood the technical details of the overall operations.

Mario and Boris had quiet security parked outside and discreetly walking the neighborhood. Sharon, on the Church side of the family, was a former Israeli military specialist who protected high-value families. She had become Lori and Damian's "housekeeper" and security companion.

When you have three of New York's unknown high-value families doing business and meeting in the same location, security issues must be taken seriously, but discreetly. O/H Inc. was a powerful enterprise unknown to all but a few.

Boris asked Damian, "I hear business is good with your real estate. Buying old crap buildings, for cheap, that have potential is strategic long-term planning, Mr. Garcia. One man's garbage is another man's gold. I like the humanitarian aspect, offering a safe place to live for homeless women with children and integrating social services."

Roger and Marguerite came out to the living room from the back bedroom. They were smiling and relaxed.

Roger said, "I had an epiphany one Saturday night turned Sunday morning, with the assistance of O/H. I concluded I am not ready for the corporate world of chemical engineering. I have little interest in creating household consumer products like glass cleaners. I need to control my destiny. I want to do fun stuff and have challenges every day. So I must work for me, and not for some large and impersonal giant company. I am developing a chemical testing laboratory in an old warehouse by the river, owned by Anacapri Construction."

Mario said, "We did not need the warehouse space. It was too small. We moved across the river to Jersey. So we worked out an agreement that benefits us both."

Roger said, "I am investing heavily in building a laboratory and testing facility that will be the finest in the world, using the best equipment and attracting the best chemists and engineers. Mario is a quiet investor. I am fascinated by a new concept of a special type of glass that responds to the touch. Instead of pushing a physical button or switch, you touch a screen button and it responds. They call it something like a capacitive touch screen. I want in on this cutting-edge technology. The startup will be expensive to develop and build into practical use, but over the long term, the returns will exceed investments, beyond infinity. I foresee this stuff getting smaller and better."

Mario said, "The world is changing very fast for this Sicilian auto mechanic. Who knows, my grandchildren may be repairing flying cars."

Celina said, "No Mario, our grandchildren will own the land and the businesses. They will not get their hands dirty."

"As usual, Celina, you are correct. There is a future in owning and no future working with your hands."

Roger said, "I want to personally thank Don Mario Anacapri and brothers for the warehouse. I can walk to work. I love it."

Mario replied, "It is my pleasure to do family business with you. We will prosper as united families."

Damian said, "Yes, that we will."

Roger said, "Private industry will hire Roger Labs to experiment with special purpose chemical compounds or to test for specific substances." He chuckled. "You guys will love this. I have an opportunity to bid on a government contract."

Damian said, "That sounds interesting."

Lori asked, "What would you be testing?"

"I would be looking for certain substances or the absence of certain substances or compounds." Roger grinned. "Are you ready for this? The government agency is Customs, and the substances are marijuana, cocaine, opium, LSD, and hashish."

The silence was deafening. No one breathed.

All eyes were on Roger in disbelief.

Damian smiled slowly with the realization.

Lori's eyes sparkled at the possibilities.

Boris broke the silence. "R-E-A-L-L-Y! How interesting. Our O/H resident chemist now works for the Feds busting drug smugglers."

Lori burst out laughing. "God, I love the irony."

Damian was analyzing the situation and examining the options from a 360-degree perspective to determine the probable outcomes.

Roger smiled and said, "Yes, I also love the irony. Here is the neat part. I will have an inside track on drug smuggling operations across U.S. borders. I will be testing the suspected shipments, and therefore I will know the smugglers' details and what got them busted."

Mario interjected, "So Roger will be our spy and counter spy."

Celina chuckled. "Roger, are you sure you are not Arab or Italian? You must have some of our blood in you."

Roger laughed. "Indians can be very devious also."

Damian said, "Roger, my friend, that is completely awesome."

Aleta said, "For the first time in history, drug smugglers will have an inside into the drug smuggling business from the Customs viewpoint. That is so perfect!"

Damian added, "That is truly using 360-degree perspectives."

Lori said, "That is excellent, Roger. It is incredible. We will be able to learn so much and make sure we do not fall into the same traps."

Celina said, "That is truly awesome."

Damian said, "If we think about the organizational structure that built O/H Inc. and will direct the future, it is amazing. Roger will have inside connections into Customs and learn about the smuggling operations from the Fed's perspectives. That inside knowledge is priceless."

Boris said, "Roger, that is awesome. Let me share with you about business in the cold Soviet world. It is excellent. Demand is very high, prices are very high, and profits are very high. I have raised prices equal to $300 U.S. It is selling well to the elite, which is safer because they do not like drama. There is not enough supply to satisfy demand. I raise prices until the lines bisect, and that is my optimal price point break."

Damian said, "We all know about the supply issues, and I will talk about the international long-term solutions that are in the planning stages. Grain is building underground storage vaults on the Vancouver property that have ventilation systems, where thousands of kilos of product can be securely stored. This will become the North American storage bank for O/H Inc. From Vancouver, quantities can be moved to regional positions within Canada and the U.S., which allows the risk to be spread, making it faster to get the products to the local markets."

Lori added, "There are separate climate-controlled vaults for the bulk quantities of cash which will need to be stored before being transferred to London, India, and Switzerland. Also the Garcia-Wilson Foundations will be banking large volumes of personal cash for safekeeping."

Mario chuckled. "One must save for retirement."

Damian said, "Grain is our O/H defense attorney and banker. He can provide a higher level of product and cash security than Apartment 3A. Having a powerful attorney provides a level of protection that is useful in this trade. He transfers the cash for a very reasonable fee and self-insures the risk. I am comfortable with the arrangements.

"The Spencer Group in Iowa is expanding in the Midwest, controlling the education, medical, and professional markets. They have a state-of-the-art production facility, able to produce O/H products at speeds consistent with top quality. O/H Inc. is establishing production facilities in various locations worldwide."

Celina said, "In fact, we are building a facility in Sicily. This facility is used to service the Mediterranean, Tunisian, and Arab markets, and it also is state of the art."

Marguerite said proudly, "Roger only does things first class and top quality. The finest facilities, using the finest raw materials, produce the finest quality products, which sell for the highest prices, earning the highest profit margins. And the best products get everyone really high."

Boris added, "It is a simple equation, often overlooked."

Damian asked the group, "Do we have any unfinished business we need to discuss?" Hearing none, he declared the quarterly meeting of O/H was officially concluded.

The families needed a brain break and George needed to pee.

Roger said, "Is it all right if I let George outside and come back in a few minutes to let him in? Besides, we have security outside."

Damian said, "George is a big boy. He knows how to get attention when he needs something from his humans."

Roger opened the door to let George do his thing. He asked one of Boris's men to keep an eye out for George.

The close-knit family enjoyed coffee, pastries, wine, and fresh bongs. The group collectively went into their own orbits, understanding that they were a family for life. The group relaxed and enjoyed each other's friendship, love, respect, and company.

About an hour later, Roger said, "I have gone downstairs twice, asked Boris's men, and there is no sign of George. Do you think something happened to him?"

Lori said, "Send someone to walk the neighborhood, please. Have them ask around."

Another hour or so passed, and no sign of Mr. George Carlin Dog.

Lori said, "Damian, we need to get home before it gets too late. I have payroll to do, and inventory to order for Rosie's."

Damian said, "I have O/H business to attend to, which is what pays for all this in the first place. Let us never forget that the roots of all this is the O/H drug business."

The group hugged and kissed, wished each other well, and made future social plans and business arrangements.

They walked down the outdoor steps and stopped in their tracks.

The group watched from the front door.

George was peeing on the yellow line, oblivious to the traffic. Next to George, also peeing on the yellow line, was a female companion.

Damian said, "George, you sly devil. You have a girlfriend."

Lori observed, "Somehow Damian, I think George has a wife for life. They are in love, and in lust, just like us."

George walked over very proudly and introduced his new wife to the group. Like her husband George, she was of many undetermined breeds.

Lori announced, "I am naming George's wife 'Jennifer Carlin Dog.'"

George and Jennifer showed their approval by barking, sharing many kisses, and wagging tails.

Lori bent down into the carriage to give their young daughter, Rebecca Garcia, her Sippy cup with organic homemade fruit juice.

George and Jennifer looked in the carriage and licked Rebecca's face.

Lori said, "Let's go home, please."

Damian said, "Yes, it has been a busy and productive day."

Lori thanked Sharon for taking care of Rebecca during the Board of Directors meeting. Sharon was wonderful with Rebecca, loved the family, and was a trusted member of the O/H family. She was also highly trained and deadly, providing the family with quiet security.

Damian reasoned in his head, *Who would expect an attractive Israeli housekeeper to be lethal security?*

Damian and Lori slowly pushed the stroller down the street with Rebecca; George and Jennifer were in the lead, and Sharon stayed back five feet, reading the streets. The expanded family walked down the street and turned left on the avenue, towards home.

Lori said casually, "Damian, I have been thinking."

Damian looked skeptical.

Lori said, "When I get Rosie's operating smoothly, I am going back to school and get my PhD in Clinical Psychology. Hell, I know more about brilliant, cunning, lovable, and strange minds than any woman on earth, so I might as well get a PhD in what I already understand."

Damian said thoughtfully, "That actually makes sense, honey."

Sharon added, "Yes, it does, Lori. I think that is an excellent idea. In fact, I would like to finish my PhD with you. I need to keep my skills sharp."

Damian was deeply in love with Lori and their expanding family.

Lori said, "George and Jennifer. Welcome home to the Garcia and Wilson family. Your journey has just begun."

Damian smiled. "George will explain."

Lightning Source UK Ltd.
Milton Keynes UK
UKOW04f2256011015

259666UK00001B/93/P